GHOST COUNTRY

Also by Sara Paretsky

WINDY CITY BLUES

TUNNEL VISION

GUARDIAN ANGEL

BURN MARKS

BLOOD SHOT

BITTER MEDICINE

KILLING ORDERS

DEADLOCK

INDEMNITY ONLY

Sara Paretsky

GHOST
COUNTRY

Delacorte Press

Published by
DELACORTE PRESS
Bantam Doubleday Dell Publishing Group, Inc.
1540 Broadway
New York, New York 10036

Library of Congress Cataloging in Publication Data

Paretsky, Sara.
Ghost country / Sara Paretsky.
p.   cm.
ISBN 0-385-29933-8
I. Title.
PS3566.A647G47   1998
813′.54—dc21   98-12294
CIP

Manufactured in the United States of America
Published simultaneously in Canada
June 1998
10 9 8 7 6 5 4 3 2 1
BVG

For Enheduanna, and All Poets Missing in Action

Thanks

The Ragdale Foundation in Lake Forest, Illinois, provided privacy and time to work on portions of this book.

Dr. Jeremy Black, Assyriologist at Wolfson College, Oxford, and Dr. P.R.S. Moorey, director of the Ashmolean Museum, Oxford, shared their knowledge of ancient Sumer, including a private tour of the Ashmolean's Sumerian artifacts.

Lorian Stein-Schwaber taught me fundamentals of vocal technique and allowed me to sit in on her own master class with diva Judith Hadden.

The Rev. Walter Green and his staff at Thresholds, who provide mobile assistance to the mentally ill homeless, took me to visit clients in parks, shelters, and encampments on the streets below Chicago's Loop. The Rev. Gail Russell and her staff at Sarah's Circle, a drop-in shelter for women, allowed me to spend time there as a volunteer. Cathy St. Clair, of the Community Emergency Shelter Organization, gave me information on Chicago's homeless. Alice Cottingham made all those connections.

Isabel Thompson helped me understand current diagnoses and medications for psychotic disorders. Beth Blacksin explained how managed care is affecting the treatment of mental illness.

Cass Sunstein, Karl N. Llewellyn Professor of Law at the University of Chicago, advised me on free speech issues.

Dr. Don Hogue provided essential help at a difficult point in the manuscript. R.D. Zimmerman made that connection.

Jo Anne Willis assisted with research on various topics.

An early version of this novel involved a composer who didn't survive the final cut. For help with that version, Chicago composer Gerald Rizzer worked with me on music theory. Thea Musgrave, composer in residence at the Virginia Opera, allowed me to sit in on rehearsals of *Simon Bolívar* and to attend the opera's world premiere. Ardis Kranik, whose passing I mourn, introduced me to Ms. Musgrave, and shared some of her own great experience of the opera world.

As is always the case, any errors of fact or fancy are due to my own shortcomings, not the words of the illustrious band who advised me.

Ann, Eve, Joanna, and especially SCW supported me on the difficult journey to the end of this novel.

For those worried about V.I. Warshawski, the detective has been on strike, but we are currently in mediation and should resume work together soon.

Contents

1

The Diva Warms Up

SOMEWHERE IN THE DISTANCE a bass viol vibrated. She struggled to remember what it meant: an angry person coming who wanted to hurt her. She tried to get to her feet but the floor was so heavy it pulled her down. Or maybe someone had attached weights to her legs while she was kneeling in front of the Madonna. The bass sounded more loudly and she panicked. She wrestled with her nightdress, which bunched above her waist as she thrashed about. Then saw the man leaning over her, his face red-black with fury.

"No, don't kill me! I didn't do it, it was someone else, they put weights on my legs!" She could hear herself laughing as she exposed herself to him, her voice bouncing from ceiling and walls and echoing over and over. "Look: I'm not hiding anything!"

"You goddamned bitch!" he hissed. "I wish I *could* kill you!"

He grabbed a pillow and pushed it toward her face. Someone else wrapped her flailing arms and legs in sheets and tied them tight around her body. She was coughing, gagging, praying for air, and then she was awake.

She fingered her throat. The muscles were so tense that it hurt to touch them. She couldn't remember the dream now, or even the events of the previous night, but the shadow of the ominous hovered below the surface of her mind. She stretched an arm out for her robe and snatched at empty air. Fear choked her: she was in a twin bed, not her own canopied throne, and she'd gone to bed—been put to bed?—in her clothes. Her silk skirt had bunched up as she slept, making an uncomfortable knot against her lower back.

She flung the covers away and jumped up, much too fast: the room rocked around her and her pantyhose-clad feet slid on the floorboards. Her stomach heaved. She looked about and found a waste can just in time. She hadn't eaten much recently; all that came up was a sour mouthful of green fluid.

Shuffling along on her knees, she scrounged on the bedside table for a Kleenex. A clock radio caught her eye. One o'clock. Could that be right? The blinds were pulled but sunshine seeped around their edges: it couldn't be one in the morning, but what was she doing in a strange bed in the middle of the day? Unless the clock was wrong.

She had been going to *La Bohème*. It might be amusing to see what a community company could do with it, that was why she was wearing her black shantung skirt. She remembered dressing, and even, if she concentrated hard, having a drink with her escort before they set out. That had been around six. She had a vague recollection of the restaurant, of a waiter being rude to her, but none whatsoever of the performance. Maybe they'd skipped it. What had her escort's name been? An admirer, there were too many to remember them all. This man had even opened his home to her for the last six weeks, but he often drank so much at dinner that he couldn't stay awake through the theater.

Next to the clock radio was a family photo: Becca dressed as Queen Esther for a Sunday school pageant, dark curls springing in wiry corkscrews around her head, Harry gazing at her with mushy fondness. Becca was a ringer for Harry, the same round face, dimpled cheeks, but pretty—on Harry those features looked like a frog's. She herself had always preferred Queen Vashti, the beauty standing up to the king's pointless commands, over the bleating, vapid Esther.

So she was in Harry and Karen's guest room—silly of her not to recognize it straight away when she'd lived there after Harry forced her to leave Italy, yammering as he always did about her extravagance. If only she were home—her real home in New York, not the apartment where she'd been staying the last few weeks—she could send someone for tea and a masseuse.

At least she could take a shower. She pulled off her pantyhose and dropped them on the floor. The guest bathroom was at the other end of the hall, so she couldn't undress in here, but she could take off her bra: it had slipped up on her in the night and was digging into her breasts. No wonder she felt as though she were being choked.

There was a large stain down the front of the blouse. Had that been there when she put it on? She hoped she hadn't embarrassed herself by wearing dirty clothes to a restaurant.

She draped the blouse around her shoulders, the silk cool against her nipples. Maybe it was long enough to use as a dressing gown. As she measured the ends against her thighs Harry's bellow sounded.

"Is she going to sleep all day? Where does she think she is? Goddam New York in the goddam Plaza Hotel?"

A female murmuring, too soft for her to tell if it was Karen or Becca, and then Harry's bellow again. "Go in there and get her up. She's been asleep since four, which God knows is longer than I have, and I want to talk to her royal highness."

A diffident knock followed by Becca's head poking around the door. "Oh! You're awake. Daddy wants to talk to you."

She pointed to her throat and shook her head.

"You've lost your voice?" Becca asked, coming all the way into the room. She was fourteen now, her teeth white behind the barricade of braces, but her hair still a wiry cloud. Instead of Queen Esther's blue flowing robe she wore layered tank tops over shorts and combat boots.

"Janice? Are you up? We need to talk!" Harry's blare made her wince.

"She's lost her voice!" Becca called back, enjoying the drama.

"Then she can goddam find it."

Harry stomped into the room, but seeing her breasts exposed beneath the draped silk blouse he blushed and looked away. He grabbed Becca and tried to frog-march her from the room.

Becca wriggled free. "Oh, Daddy, you act like nobody I know has breasts. We see each other naked all the time after soccer. I look at my own, for pity's sake."

"And don't talk to me like that: I'm not one of your classmates." It was an automatic plea, lacking conviction. "Janice, button up your damned shirt and come into the kitchen. We're going to talk."

Someone had dumped her jacket and purse on the floor by the dresser. She picked up the jacket and made a great show of arranging it neatly on the back of the chair, pulling on the sleeves to straighten them while Harry snapped futilely behind her. Another show of fussing in her purse for a pen. HOT TEA, she wrote in block capitals on the back of an envelope that she found on the dresser. SHOWER. She gave Becca the envelope and went down the hall to the bathroom, drowning Harry's protests by turning on the taps full blast.

When the room was filled with steam she stepped under the shower and started kneading the muscles in her shoulders. She let the spray bathe the back of her throat, gargling slightly, then turned her back to the water and gently trilled her tongue along the edge of her front teeth. Using the trill, she moved up and down a half scale in the middle of her range, barely making a sound. When her neck muscles started to relax, she began a series of vowel exercises, still staying in the middle of her range but letting the sound increase a little.

After perhaps twenty minutes of vocalizing someone hammered on the bathroom door, but there wasn't any point in responding: it was undoubtedly Harry. Not only did she know what he had to say, she'd only get a chill and have to start over again if she stopped now. For another ten minutes she eased her voice into shape within the protective steam, until she deemed it safe to get out of the shower and finish exercising in the music room.

She carefully wrapped her throat in a towel before leaving the tub, keeping her neck covered as she dried herself, then kicking the used towels into a pile in the direction of the clothes hamper.

A cotton dressing gown hung on the back of the door. Karen's, no doubt, judging by the vivid magenta flowers and tiers of lacy sleeves, but no one she cared about would see her in it and it was better than putting on that soiled blouse again.

The gown had a complicated set of ribbons; she tried to tie it up high enough to protect her chest from the air conditioner's drafts. To be on the safe side she took another clean towel from the shelf and draped it across her neck. She held her silk blouse over the heap of damp towels: surely Karen would have enough sense to dry-clean it instead of throwing it into the washing machine? She'd remind her as soon as she finished her workout.

Of course, Harry didn't have a real music room, but the family room held a badly tuned piano, the one from her parents' house she'd used when she first started singing. As she walked back past the bedroom and down the half flight of stairs she hummed, letting the sound fill her head with the tickling that told her her breath was flowing well. Becca ran up behind her and handed her a mug of tepid tea. She didn't break stride or stop humming, but did nod a regal thanks.

In front of the piano she let the humming turn back into vowels, and then into trills. At the end of half an hour she was sweating freely but feeling pleased with her flexibility. Partway through she had gulped down the tea and held the cup out for a refill. When Becca didn't respond she turned, surprised, to find the room empty. The child used to like to listen to her practice. Still humming, she walked back to the bathroom and filled the cup with hot water from the tap.

Karen popped out of the kitchen as she passed. "Oh! When you're done will you put the towels in the hamper? I'm not doing a wash until Tuesday. Do you want some lunch? Harry had to—"

She turned her back on the nagging voice, not interested in anything Harry might have to do, and returned—still humming—to the family room to finish her workout. In the past she always concluded with "Vissi d'arte" from *Tosca*. Her own voice, soaring to that final high D, exhilarated her with its freedom and power. But today she knew at some unacknowledged reach of her mind that she would never manage the aria, and that failure to do so would crack her self-control in front of

Karen and Becca. She contented herself with a couple of German art songs that did not place great demands on the voice.

Drying face and chest with the towel in which she'd swathed her throat, she left it on the floor by the piano. The mug she took with her to the kitchen, even placing it in the dishwasher. Harry would not be able to say she showed absolutely no consideration for his wife.

Karen had moved to the backyard, bending over in faded shorts and shirt to do something with the garden. A dull vibration overhead meant Becca was upstairs listening to a pounding bass that passed for music with today's teenagers. The child had actually preferred that to her own workout? She snorted like a high-bred racehorse.

Mercifully, Harry had disappeared altogether. Maybe the mounds of scrap iron called to him even on Sundays. She could eat lunch in peace. Not that there was much in Karen's refrigerator to tempt her: the remains of the family's Sunday bagel breakfast, with bright-colored squares of lox that looked like linoleum scraps; leftover roast lamb; cheese—which would produce phlegm in her throat—and iceberg lettuce. Wrinkling her nose she took out a bagel and a grapefruit and put on water for coffee.

Becca thudded down the back stairs into the kitchen. "Did you get your voice back?"

"Well enough to vibrate the glasses."

Without raising her voice, simply by using perfect airflow, she threw out a sound that returned a high-pitched whine from Karen's crystal. It was a trick that had delighted Becca as a toddler, and even now made her grin.

"Daddy's furious, but he decided not to give up his golf date for you."

"Harry's prone to furies. Any special reason?"

Becca hugged her knees. "Because Piero Benedetti called him at two this morning to get you out of jail."

She felt a jolt behind her diaphragm. Jail? Her hands shook as she picked up the mug of coffee and a large pool slopped onto the table. Becca went to the sink for a sponge and mopped the table.

"Darling, is this what teenagers do for fun these days? Make up stories to shock the older generation?"

"Mom said you'd probably pretend not to remember." Becca's green eyes were tinged with worry.

"What am I supposed to have been in jail for? Trespassing on the Minsky scrap heap?" Years of training allowed her to produce a mocking trilling laugh despite the giveaway trembling of her hands. "And what on earth does Piero have to do with it? The last I heard he was in New York closing out the Met production of *The Ghosts of Versailles*."

"You called him. Or somebody called him, and he called Daddy, who had to drive all the way into Chicago to get you. Daddy says he should have just let you rot there, it would have done you good."

"Oh, Jan—oh, good, you're up." Karen had come in and was washing mud off her hands at the sink. "We need to talk. About last night."

"Becca has been spinning me some kind of ghoulish teenage tale," she said lightly. "But I don't think you should encourage that kind of prank. And I don't think you need to involve yourself in my activities."

"Don't need to involve myself?" Pots as well as glassware rattled at Karen's shriek. "Piero Benedetti called us in the middle of the night after you had woken him at home. Don't you remember any of it? Look at me, and don't smirk in that oh-I'm-so-superior-to-you way! You made a spectacle of yourself at *La Bohème* last night. Even without the arrest, two of my neighbors already called to tell me. You hummed loudly throughout the first act, and then, deciding that the poor girl getting her chance to debut in a miserable community production didn't deserve to be the center of attention, you actually got up and sang over her voice in the third act. And now you sit here in my kitchen, eating my food, after dropping dirty towels all over the house, trying to pretend you don't remember a damned thing about it."

"I don't think she does remember, Mom. We read about it when we covered alcoholism in our health class this spring. You can be so drunk you can't remember what you did, especially if it was embarrassing."

"Becca! Are you—is it possible that you are calling *me* an alcoholic?"

"Oh, please!" Becca's eyes, which used to watch her in adulation, held so much misery she had to look away. "It just makes it so much worse when you lie, when everybody knows that's why you're in Chicago instead of New York. It's nothing to be ashamed of. You can't help it. It's a disease, and if you could only admit—"

She swept the dishes off the table, enjoying the crash and the alarm in Karen's and Becca's faces when they shattered. "If you've *quite* finished your *extraordinary* remarks, will you find some clean clothes for me to wear? I'll call someone to come out and pick me up."

"Be my guest. But you can't borrow any more of my clothes. You took my Donna Karan suit the last time you were here and when I finally got you to return it, you'd spilled something on it that the cleaners couldn't get out." Karen took a breath. "And Harry wants you to get a job. He's tired of supporting you."

"Does he want me to drive a truck at the scrap heap? Now that would be a sight worth seeing."

"Janice, you can do what every other retired diva does: you can—"

"My name is Luisa Montcrief, and I am not retired!" She wished she hadn't wasted the dishes on Becca's childish remark: her fury was real this time, and needed a physical vent. "I am just as eager to leave this town as you are for me to go, but my manager has so far been too lazy to get me the engagements I desire."

"Well, call him, and take something you *don't* desire."

"And have everyone join you in saying I'm a has-been? I think not!"

"Look, even if you're not retired, would it kill you to give a few lessons? There must be people in Chicago who think you have something worth saying about singing." Karen's tone didn't hold out much hope at the prospect.

"Very well: I will call my manager in the morning and remind him that I'm getting impatient." She swept from the room, every inch a diva.

"What were you doing making her tea? I thought I told you not to wait on her." Karen fetched the broom from the utility closet and stabbed at the broken crockery with it.

Becca pulled a strand of hair straight and sucked on it. "She misses all the attention."

"But it's not your job, miss, to be her maid-audience-secretary, or whatever it is she thinks she needs at the moment."

"She made the glasses ring for me," her daughter offered.

"It's just like your father to go off golfing and leave me to deal with her," Karen grumbled. "She's *his* twin, after all, not mine, I married *him* for better or worse, not her."

"She's your 'worse,' Mom, that's all. Anyway, Daddy did try to talk to her, but she locked herself in the bathroom for *hours*."

Karen forced her face into a tight smile. "I know, sweetie: your aunt makes me feel helpless and that brings out the worst in me."

"It was fun when she was famous," Becca said. "Remember when we got to have dinner with Jackie Onassis? Corie didn't believe me—I had to show him the photographs. You looked so tough in that red dress. Of course, I looked like a little porker, a seven-year-old porker with an Orphan Annie fright wig."

"Darling, you looked adorable. As you do this minute, although you know I'm not crazy about those combat boots."

"So why do you call her Janice when she hates it so much she changed it decades ago?"

"People have been encouraging your aunt to deny reality since she was seventeen. She doesn't need help from me along those lines—in fact, just the reverse. It's time she stopped playacting and faced up to her drinking problem."

"But even before she, well, stopped getting engagements, you and Daddy insisted on calling her Janice. Janice Minsky, what a name. I wouldn't be a star with that name, either. Not that someone like me will ever be a star. Why couldn't I take after her, or you, and be tall and skinny? Why do I have to look like Daddy, the short squatty toad side of the family?"

"What is with you and the animal kingdom today? First you look like a porker, and now Daddy is a squatty toad." Karen dumped the fragments into the waste can with a bang. "Minsky's good enough to pay for your riding lessons, young lady! If your aunt had been able to accept being a Minsky, maybe she wouldn't turn to gin to get her through what else she doesn't like about herself."

The diva swept back into the room in the rumpled black shantung. Karen tried not to notice the white blouse: it was out of her own closet, but she wasn't up to fighting her sister-in-law for possession.

"I called my car service. They should be here shortly."

"Do you have money to pay for that car?" Karen demanded, hands on her hips.

"Don't worry: it's not coming out of Becca's college fund. Someone will reimburse the man when I get back into town."

Becca sucked in her breath at the sight of the blue Rolls when it pulled into the drive. She ran upstairs to call Corie, to urge him to run over to watch her aunt's triumphal exit.

But when the diva got back to the city, the man she'd been staying with opened his apartment door only long enough to dump her suitcases outside. He would not pay for the limo. He would not "lend" her money to pay for it, let alone a hotel room: he knew what a deadbeat she was. And if she could get the money from her brother to pay him back, then she could just go to her brother and get it up front, right now. He had been beaten up by the police last night for trying to defend her honor when she'd made a total fool out of both of them. He didn't think his kidneys would ever be the same. He did not want to see her again.

She left the cases in the hall and went back down to the car. She was not an alcoholic, despite Becca's ill-natured remarks. Just the shock of the man's totally rude behavior made her want a drink to calm down. And now here was the driver demanding payment in a truly rude fashion. She would have to call her manager and tell him never to use this service again. Come to think of it, she needed her manager to give her an account number to charge the rental to. And her address book was in one of the cases still upstairs in the hall. It was all too complicated for words: Harry would have to pay for the car after all. Maybe for a place to spend the night as well. In the morning she would call New York and get them to wire her any new royalties that had come in on her recordings. Her manager ought to do something for her: she had made his career, after all. She gave the driver Harry's MasterCard number and told him to collect her bags and take her to the Ritz.

2

Resident in Purgatory

Utilization management is God, and Hanaper is its prophet. This morning paramedics brought in a guy who wanted to launch himself from the sixteenth floor of the State of Illinois building onto the atrium below. He thought he was a chicken and could fly—a secretary grabbed him as he was teetering on the railing. A homeless man who often wanders through State of Illinois building, the medics say.

Hanaper, conducting rounds, was called to emergency room, dragging me along since it was my patient we were seeing when he was paged. The ambulance crew filled Hanaper in on what had happened, told the great doctor they thought the guy was schizophrenic.

H cut them off: "Does either of you have a license to practice medicine? I thought not. I'm the head of psychiatry here at Midwest and don't need paramedics to make diagnoses for me."

The homeless man was sitting on a gurney, twitching, muttering, rolling his eyes in panic. Hanaper walked up to him. While nurses and other patients looked on, he bellowed, "You know you're not really a chicken, don't you, my man?"

Poor devil, frightened at surroundings, people staring, white man in doctor's gown shouting in his face, mumbled "no." Hanaper turned to the paramedics, told them there was nothing wrong with the guy, to take him home.

Paramedics said, man homeless. They didn't think he belonged on streets, couldn't look after himself—survives by foraging for scraps in garbage cans. And Hanaper, bless him for consistency, said that proved he knew how to find food.

All this time I'd hovered in the background, part of the scenery like one of the gurneys. But at that point I tried protesting. The meek stammering protests of a resident worried about his job? Or just of Lily's son, nervous of anyone in authority?

Either way it didn't matter. H. cut me off: "If you are willing to assume financial responsibility for this man, Dr. Tammuz, you may make all the diagnoses you want. If not, let's get back to the patients we pay you to look after."

And so on to the dreary round of trying to recommend hospitalizations that are too expensive and therefore unnecessary, or even worse, long-term outpatient psychotherapy. Even the hint of wanting to talk more to a patient brings out the Fear of Freud in Hanaper.

When I accepted this residency, thought of it as great opportunity to learn real psychotherapy on the job. Of course, Dr. Boten was still here then. Didn't know that he and Hanaper were engaged in great battle over direction of psych dept—the outcome never in doubt as the utilization management team was backing Hanaper. Now Boten is gone, forced to leave, concentrating on private practice. The hospital grudgingly runs outpatient clinic on Weds. afternoons. Group therapies on Friday nights, but they love those—big moneymakers, treating alcoholism among rich overworked businessmen. No room for the kind of patient who needs more than Prozac or a shot of Haldol.

Hector, writing in an upper bunk in the on-call room at the hospital, using a tiny reading light to keep from rousing his sleeping colleagues, put his pen down in sour memory of the day's frustrations. He and Hanaper had returned from the emergency room to the ward, where Melissa Demetrios, the senior resident, was waiting with a new rotation of medical students. They had stopped outside the room of a woman Hector had admitted the previous afternoon. A worried daughter brought her in when she found her mother with her possessions piled around her in the middle of the living room, saying only that she was gathering strength for the journey.

Hector recited the bare facts, then added, "Her cat died last month and that seems to have upset her, maybe heightened an existing sense of anomie. I've ordered a general workup to make sure she's not just suffering from a vitamin B deficiency or thyroid problems, but I would recommend talking to her several more times before—"

"Prozac, Tammuz. Have you ordered a trial dose for her?"

"Not until I have a better sense of—"

"Prozac is the recommended treatment for compulsive collectors and hoarders."

"She's not really a hoarder, sir; she's making these clay figurines, at least according to her daughter, or—"

"Writing on scraps of paper, isn't she, collecting them around herself? Sounds like an obsessive-compulsive disorder. Obsessive-compulsives respond well to antidepressants. Twenty milligrams a day, you'll find it effective."

And as Hector stood stubbornly in the hall Hanaper said impatiently, "Have you written that down, Tammuz?"

"I think it's premature, sir. What if her problem turns out to be—"

"When you're responsible for this ward you can make that decision. I want her started on twenty milligrams of Prozac. Stat!"

It was typical of Hanaper to punctuate routine pronouncements with medical jargon. Tammuz sometimes wondered if the department head had forged or stolen the diplomas ostentatiously framed in his office, learning the little he knew about medicine from medical shows on TV.

When Tammuz had still not written down the order on the woman's chart, Hanaper pulled him to one side for a confidential chat, making sure to speak loudly enough for the new students to overhear. "Dr. Tammuz. We have an obligation to cure people as fast as possible.

Contrary to your emotional pleas, that obligation is not just to the institution, or our management team, but to the patients themselves. And, really, Tammuz, if you could choose between a pill that solved your problems in ten days, versus an analysis that might take a decade, wouldn't you choose the pill? Oh, no, come to think of it, you wouldn't."

Hanaper gave the students a would-be hilarious account of Tammuz's interest in—"infatuation with"—psychoanalysis, then swept the group into the new patient's room, where he informed her with loud cheeriness that Dr. Tammuz would be giving her a pill that would make her feel good as new.

"Not that those big black eyes of his can't help you, too, eh?" And Tammuz, hating himself, had written out the order.

The woman, from the middle of a nest of torn-up paper towels on which she was writing, said, "I don't take pills. They're against my religion," and went back to rearranging the paper towels.

Tammuz had been unable to suppress a smile. Fortunately he was standing behind Hanaper. Melissa and the students stirred restively, not wanting any of the department head's wrath deflected toward them.

"I thought her name was Herstein." Hanaper whirled around to look at Tammuz. "Isn't she Jewish?"

The resident Jew. "I don't know, sir: you'd have to ask her."

"How can pills be against your religion if you're Jewish?" Hanaper asked one of the other students, not the patient, whom he typically discussed as if she weren't present.

"It's in the Mishnah," Mrs. Herstein said unexpectedly from behind her barricade. "You think you're an expert on life's vexing problems, young man, but you would do well to study the Mishnah."

Hanaper flustered to be called "young man," promptly takes it out on us. Melissa gets chastised for sending a patient to long-term care without running it past review panel: insurance denied, now what do we do, family may bring malpractice suit if she commits suicide after discharge as Melissa thinks she's in danger of doing.

A relief to go to afternoon clinic. At least people with anxiety disorders admit they have a problem.

At the end of his stint in the outpatient clinic, Hector tried to slide out of the hospital for a walk along the lakefront. He hoped that half an hour in the May sunlight would wake him up enough to get him through his looming on-call shift tonight. Melissa Demetrios intercepted him as he was heading to a back staircase.

"Dr. Stonds wants to take a look at our caseload," she said. "Hanaper likes all the residents to be present—in case Stonds blows up we can take the blame."

"Stonds?" After seven months at Midwest, Hector knew the neurosurgeon wielded enormous power in the hospital, but he didn't understand why Stonds cared about psychiatry cases.

"Dr. Stonds cares about everything that affects the well-being of Midwest Hospital and its patients," Melissa intoned, lowering her voice a register in an attempt to mimic Hanaper.

Hector laughed. "Yes—but does he look at all the admissions? When does he have time to scoop out brains?"

"I can't believe this is the first time we've been summoned to the master's office since you've been here." Melissa looked around to make sure they weren't in anyone's radar range. "Stonds's grandfather—the original Dr. Stonds—was one of the founders of this hospital, back in the 1890s, so the family has always had a lot of clout here. When Abraham—*our* Dr. Stonds—was a neurosurgery resident, neurology and psychiatry were one department, and they learned how to treat 'diseases of the nerves.' That's still how Abraham thinks of mental illness. Somehow he persuaded the hospital to let him review all the neurology and psychiatry cases."

"Oh, a kind of *droit du seigneur*," Hector said. "It fits in with the medieval atmosphere this whole hospital exudes."

"Droit du seigneur?" Melissa echoed. "Oh, you mean like barons getting to sleep with the peasants' daughters. I suppose. And he certainly likes to act like a grand seigneur. He lives in baronial splendor on the

Gold Coast, in a huge apartment on one of those quiet streets near the Cardinal's palace. You'll get invited there for dinner in the summer—he always has new residents in at the end of their first year. His older granddaughter is incredibly gorgeous, by the way, so if you could get her to fall in love with you, you'd never have to grovel to Hanaper again."

Hector snorted. "Yeah, but then I'd have to grovel to Stonds, which would probably be worse. Or the granddaughter, if she's anything like him. Is she a doctor?"

Melissa shook her head. "Nope. A lawyer. So the good news is that the Stonds empire will die out with the old man. The bad news is, even if he is seventy-seven everyone says he's still really sharp in the OR. And he shows no sign of wanting to step away from his fiefdom."

Melissa's beeper sounded. She read the number on the display. "Hanaper. Time to grovel. Hector, I know you really believe in psychotherapy, but try not to mention it this afternoon—it will make your residency so much easier."

Followed Melissa down the hall to join Hanaper and the other two psych residents on our procession to the surgery wing. Don't mention psychotherapy in discussing psychiatry patients—I'd laugh if it didn't make me cry. Or the other way around!

Watching Hanaper bow and scrape to Stonds is almost worse than watching him send a psychotic homeless man back onto the streets. Like all bullies he's obsequious to those with greater authority.

As the new kid on the block I had the privilege of having my work dissected by the Great White Chief. Hanaper brought up what he refers to as my "devotion to outmoded methods," so Melissa's advice was all for nought as I had to explain my belief in nonchemical therapies. Stonds is too full of his own greatness to share Hanaper's cheap sarcasm over the talking cure, but he rumbles good advice at me.

"In my day, young man, people were infatuated with Freud. They thought analysis would solve any and all psychiatric problems. But just look at the state modern society is in. A direct result of the permissiveness encouraged by letting people find excuses for their problems, ducking personal responsibility. Pharmacology is making important strides with some of these more intractable cases. The important thing is getting people up and working again."

I said the only thing possible under the circumstances: "Yes, sir."

Then Hanaper, as a parting joke, brought up my new patient's comment about the Mishnah. I thought Stonds was going to explode all over us. "These neurotic women who like to sit around reading ancient texts and pretending they know something about life. I don't want to hear any more about it, Hanaper. Get her out of the hospital. I'm sure someone who's really ill could use that bed."

The Great White Chief got up to leave. On his way out said, Oh, Hanaper, by the way, I want you to see someone for me. Hanaper tugs at his forelock: your wish is my command, O King.

Luisa Montcrief, the GWC says. A diva whose family is concerned about her. The Minsky family—they gave three hundred thousand to the cancer research pavilion after old Mrs. Minsky died here of a glioblastoma. We owe them some attention. I told poor Harry Minsky his sister could stop by your office at eleven on Friday.

Naturally Hanaper scrambles to rearrange his schedule, which means we all have to rearrange ours as well since H wants us to sit in, see how you really conduct a patient interview. But putting off our own patients is unimportant. After all, at the name of Stonds, every head must bow, every tongue confess him king of glory.

3

The Ugly Duckling

MAYBE EVERY TONGUE in the hospital paid lip-homage to Dr. Stonds, but it was a different story in his fifteen-room apartment on Graham Street. Well, yes, Mrs. Ephers, the doctor's housekeeper (his shadow, his executioner, young Mara muttered), certainly declared the doctor's glory. Mrs. Ephers had spent her adult life not exactly worshiping so much as building a temple around him, with herself as its high priestess.

And his elder granddaughter Harriet, the beauty, yes, she led her life according to his precepts. At thirty-two she had her reward, senior associate at Scandon and Atter, the dervish of a half-dozen clients, including the Hotel Pleiades, where she handled lawsuits by angry guests, trips and falls by careless employees, attempts by the city to duck responsibility for sidewalks in front of the building, doing it all with so much energy that during the day she's almost invisible, matter moving at the edge of light, a translucent pillar of color—turquoise today for the fabric of her suit.

But the doctor's wife and daughter, well, Mrs. Ephers could only say it was a blessing in disguise that they died while pursuing their separate unpleasant destinies. And as for Mara, the doctor's younger granddaughter—as she glowered at Mrs. Ephers across the dinner table, her large frame and wiry black hair a repulsive contrast to Harriet's pale petiteness—the housekeeper wished for the five thousandth time that she'd talked the doctor into putting Mara up for adoption when the child was dumped in their laps.

When Mara was little, she knew the Ugly Duckling turned into a Swan, that Cinderella got the handsome prince, that the poor homely sister who waited patiently by the hearth, taking abuse from the step-mother, would encounter a witch who showered her with gold, while the spoiled older sister found her brocaded gowns covered in pitch.

Mara was sure that one day she would look in the mirror and see her mass of rough curls transformed into long straight hair, soft as silk, just like Harriet's. It would still be black, not golden, but that was all right, for Snow White had hair the color of a raven's wing. But her skin would change from its muddy olive to Harriet's—Snow White's—Cinder-ella's—clear pinky-white. She would have a wide circle of friends and suitors, as Mara labeled her sister's boyfriends in her six-year-old, fairy-tale language, and be magically gifted in ballet or tennis.

And Harriet, well, Mara couldn't wish her magical sister evil, Har-riet wouldn't be permanently deformed, but something very bad would happen to her that would make her sorry for all the times she had ig-nored or ridiculed Mara, told on her to Grandfather or Mrs. Ephers. And then Mara, magnanimous in victory, would tell the witch that she for-gave her sister, to take the spell off her, please. And Harriet would be restored to her normal beauty, her normal circle of friends, but she would give them all up to look after Mara. I'm so sorry, she would say, curtseying low to the ground. Can you ever forgive me for all the pain you've suffered?

At that point, Mrs. Ephers appeared in the doorway of Mara's bed-room. Young lady, dinner is on the table. As it always is at this hour. You're big enough to tell time, you shouldn't need me to fetch you. Your grandfather is waiting for you. He works hard all day to make a nice home for you; the least you can do is be punctual at the dinner table. Are your hands washed? And did you even try to run a brush through that hair? Although a garden rake might be more useful.

Mara set herself secret goals and tests. If she could walk to school every morning for a week without once stepping on a crack . . . if she made Mephers smile and say "thank you" to her three days in a row (for the housekeeper could be wooed, with a cup of tea brought while she was ironing Grandfather's shirts—no laundry could be trusted to get them just right—or a bouquet of flowers, until some bigmouth complained they'd seen Mara picking them out of the Historical Society's garden) . . . if she got a perfect score on two spelling tests, or arithmetic, and Grandfather said, "Well done" . . . when she turned eight . . . But at no point did her hair straighten or her skin turn creamy pink. And when she got her first period, two weeks before her twelfth birthday, and no change occurred in her crackling bush of hair, she knew she was doomed for life.

The next thing everyone knew she was a moody teenager. What happened to you? Mrs. Ephers said. You were always so good at school; your grandfather is not going to be happy with this report card.

Long sessions with Grandfather, impatiently taking time from his crowded schedule to coach Mara. It's a quadratic equation—what does that mean? I know you know the answer to this, Mara: don't play stupid, it isn't cute. There's a big competitive world beyond these walls and I'm trying to prepare you to take part in it. You won't always be able to live here, you know.

"I know," she screamed one night. "I know you'll leave the apartment to Harriet, she gets everything, she even had her own father. You hate me for being born and now you want to prove I can't do anything right so that I kill myself or run away and leave you and Mrs. Ephers and Harriet in your little heaven here."

And slammed into her bedroom, in total defiance of the household law against slamming doors.

It was Harriet, getting ready for her bar exams, who came into Mara's room later that night. "They're old. They don't know how to talk to a teenager."

"So I'm supposed to feel sorry for them? They're always telling me how ugly I am. Nothing I do will ever be as good as what you did."

"You're not ugly. When you don't scowl you have a strong and interesting face. Godfrey was saying so last night." Godfrey Masters, the suitor of that particular era.

"He did?" Mara's dark brows met in suspicion, but her scowl lightened, even though strong and interesting was a poor second to beautiful and charming.

None of the suitors stayed around for long. Mara wondered if Harriet drove them away on purpose, fearing that if she married, she would follow their mother and grandmother into the ether.

First Grannie Selena, who got pregnant while Grandfather Stonds was finishing his residency. She could have waited—after all, he'd come home from a difficult war, to finish the medical training he interrupted to serve, but *selfish* was the first word you'd think of with her.

That was from Mrs. Ephers, who had known Selena since Dr. Stonds installed his bride in the family apartment in 1942. Even when he was in love with Selena, haunted by her quicksilver charm, he knew she'd never manage a house. So Mrs. Ephers arrived, not so much to spare Selena any worry (you couldn't imagine such a self-indulgent woman worrying about anyone else's comfort, anyway) as to make sure the doctor had nutritious meals waiting when he got home, and freshly ironed shirts morning and evening. For even at twenty-five, sweetly sick with love, Dr. Stonds liked an orderly schedule.

In those days the doctor's mother was still alive, but something about Selena drove her from her own home, Mrs. Ephers never did understand what exactly. Words were exchanged behind closed doors. Selena emerged with her secretive inward smile and old Mrs. Stonds, eyes still red from weeping, packed her things—including the Stonds family silver, a gift to her own husband's mother from Princess Marguerite, grateful for the treatment to her epileptic son—and moved out to Palm Springs where her married sister lived.

And then Mrs. Ephers had to put up with Selena for those two long years the doctor was overseas. Maybe Selena hoped to drive Mrs. Ephers away along with the doctor's mother, but the housekeeper was not one to turn her back on her friends, or leave a poor man like the doctor in the lurch. Selena, dreaming, head always in a book when the doctor was around, certainly didn't languish dreamily in the family temple during his war years. Mrs. Ephers could tell you a thing or two about Selena, if she weren't too well brought up to gossip.

No sooner did the doctor return, with his star for the Battle of the Bulge, and a suitcase full of Chanel No. 5 from his stint with the Army of Occupation, than Selena got herself pregnant. Mrs. Ephers well remembered his frustrated anger when Selena told him. She was in her fourth month and just beginning to show. He'd been furious, and who could blame him. I thought you used a diaphragm, he shouted. I lost it, Selena replied. When all the time it was in her dresser under the silk camisole she'd also stopped wearing when the doctor came home.

Mrs. Ephers pulled out the diaphragm and handed it to her after Dr. Stonds left the next morning: I didn't realize you were looking for this, Mrs. Stonds. And of course Selena hadn't known what to say. She should have known by then not to tell fibs around Mrs. Ephers—this with a meaningful look at Mara, prone to fibbing, to dramatizing herself and her orphan situation.

Well, Selena had a healthy girl, named her Beatrix—without consulting her husband, who planned on naming the baby for his own mother—nursed the infant for a time, and then, one day the poor doctor came home from the hospital, where he was already making a name for himself in neurosurgery despite his youth and two-year absence and whammo, there he was with a baby and no wife, just a note saying Selena had gone looking for something.

Mara knew this much because Mrs. Ephers told her, oh, about once a week, as a prelude to a lecture on getting off her lazy butt and helping out, doing her homework, practicing her ballet, after all, when Harriet was her age she was already—winning the Nobel prize in physics, dancing *Swan Lake* with Nureyev, winning Olympic medals for horseback riding—Mara would shout, to drown Mrs. Ephers's litany of her sister's accomplishments. But that wasn't until she was thirteen or fourteen, by which time well aware that compared to her sister—there was no comparison.

Where did Grannie Selena go? Mara used to ask Mrs. Ephers when she was little. Didn't my mommy ever hear from her? Is that why I never hear from my mommy? Trying to get some assurance against her terror, that Beatrix left because Mara was in some inherent way evil, that even as a baby it was so obvious that Beatrix fled from her.

Did I invite you to mind other people's business? Mrs. Ephers would respond. Your grandmother's life came to a fitting conclusion, and as for your mother, the less said, the better.

Beatrix means "the voyager." In her note Selena said she hoped her daughter would grow up to be a great adventurer, an explorer. And no, the note was no longer in existence: the doctor had chosen not to keep reminders of this painful episode.

At first Beatrix looked as though she was going to be a credit to Mrs. Ephers and the doctor. She went briefly to Smith—old Mrs. Stonds's school—before marrying one of her father's residents when she was nineteen. She set up housekeeping on the North Shore, gave birth to Harriet, busied herself with the Women's Board at the hospital, seemed primed for a life of home and service.

But then Harriet's father died, in a car accident toward the end of the Vietnam War, and Beatrix began to drift. She wandered into the hippie world, a little late in the day. The doctor started hearing ominous reports through the hospital gossip network, of booze and men, drugs and rock stars. Much as the doctor would like to believe in nurture over nature, Beatrix obviously had Bad Blood in her, or she wouldn't have made a mockery of his wonderful rearing of her.

Against his will Grandfather had to take Harriet in, poor little thing wouldn't have had a scrap to eat or wear if he hadn't come to the rescue. A disgrace, the way Beatrix left her alone at night in that big house up in Winnetka, and the filth—her husband's life insurance could have paid for a housekeeper, but Beatrix just put that money up her nose.

Dr. Stonds had already raised one child. Oh, well, Mrs. Ephers did the hands-on work—changed the diapers, nursed Beatrix through chicken pox, saw she had new shoes for school, and that she got her homework done on time—but his had been the guiding genius. After one girl on the premises without a mother, he didn't want another.

But what a doll Harriet turned out to be, what a perfect gem, taking to law and order like a proverbial duck flung into Lake Michigan. The doctor doted on Harriet. Mrs. Ephers doted on her. She let Harriet call her "Mephers," even though it was hard to imagine someone with so rigid a back unbending to a nickname. Harriet had curls like spun silk, she got straight A's all the way from Chicago Latin through Smith and then her University of Chicago law degree, she rode horseback, ice-skated, dated only socially acceptable men.

From age six to thirteen she and her grandfather led an idyllic life, Mrs. Ephers hovering around tying their shoes and combing their hair and generally singing celestial hymns morning, noon, and night, at least as Mara heard the story. Every now and then Beatrix popped in on them, but Harriet very properly turned her back on her mother's expensive gifts: they all knew where she'd found money to buy them, thank you very much.

Then one day, when Harriet was thirteen, Beatrix showed up nine months pregnant. After an eighteen-month stretch where she never even gave Harriet a phone call. What a mother. And Mara's father? Who knows who the man in question was, although, given the muddy skin and curly dark hair that the baby emerged with, one suspects the worst. Beatrix provided Harriet with an unwanted sister, and then, like her own mother, drifted off, never to be seen again.

"Drugs," Mrs. Ephers would say, brushing Mara's hair so hard her eyes teared. "Drugs and booze were all she cared about. 'Voyager.' Yes, she liked to laugh and say she was a voyager, that she had tripped out. . . . Stand still, missy, while I put a ribbon in your hair so you look nice for dinner. Harriet would stand like a little princess while I brushed her, and then give me a kiss and thanks for making her pretty. What do I get from you besides fussing and cussing? There's no doubt who your mother was, that's for sure. If it weren't for your grandfather I'd let you run around like the savage you want to be. He works hard to make it possible for you to live in this nice apartment, you do your part by looking pleasant and speaking nicely to him."

One afternoon when she was fifteen Mara went downtown to the

Herald-Star's offices and looked through back copies of the paper until she found her grandfather's wedding. Her grandmother wore a glossy veil that covered her shoulders and merged with the fabric of the wedding gown. The microfilm blurred the photograph; Mara couldn't tell if Selena had been dark or fair. She was almost as tall as Grandfather, who was five foot ten, and she was smiling, not in rapture like some of the brides, but inwardly, as if she knew some secret that you longed to learn.

Mara read the short text three or four times, looking for clues about her grandmother but finding none. Selena was given in marriage by her father, August Vatick, a professor of Assyriology at the University of Chicago. The newlyweds planned to honeymoon in Mexico before Grandfather raced back to his medical studies.

Mara scrolled forward, looking for any other family news. Her mother's birth was announced in the August 1946 paper, a Happy Event on the society pages, the column headed by a stork with a diaper in its mouth. Beatrix Vatick Stonds, seven pounds eight ounces at birth, home on Graham Street with Selena (Mrs. Abraham Stonds), both doing well.

In April 1947, the paper reported on a tragedy to the well-known Chicago Assyriologist August Vatick and his family. Wife and daughter dead with him in a snowstorm in the Taurus Mountains, where he had been looking for remains of a temple to the goddess Gula. Selena, his only child, dead as well, survived by famous doctor husband and baby Beatrix in Chicago.

Mara thought the *Herald-Star* overdid the account of Grandfather's grief at his wife's death: she couldn't imagine him caring enough about anyone to grieve for them. Maybe he was like Henry the First, a school friend suggested, burying his heart with his dead wife and never smiling again, but even someone with Mara's storytelling proclivities couldn't imagine Grandfather burying his heart anywhere but in himself.

By the time Harriet was born, the papers no longer had society pages. Neither Harriet nor Mara merited a line of type for entering the world. But Harriet's father's last name had been Caduke, so Mara searched for his death in 1972, to find if there was anything suspicious about it. Dr. Harold Caduke had died on Lake Shore Drive, the *Herald-*

Star reported, when the car he was driving crossed the median strip at the curve over the Chicago River and slammed into an oncoming station wagon. A medical student in the front seat with him was also killed in the collision. Ah ha! So Harriet's father had been cheating on their mother. But that didn't help Mara find out what became of their mother, or why Grannie Selena left Beatrix behind when she went to Iraq.

Mara looked up "Assyriology" in the dictionary: "the study of the language, history and antiquities of Assyria." Very helpful. Ancient history, maybe. Grandfather had a friend who studied that, a Professor Lontano, who often came to dinner on Graham Street, or went to the theater with Grandfather. Mara called her to see if she knew anything about Great-grandfather Vatick.

"I told Abraham not to wrap Selena in such a cloud of mystery," Professor Lontano said on the phone. "There was nothing mysterious about her or her family. Her father worked on the Assyrian Dictionary but his real love was excavation. He went back to Iraq as soon as the war was over. . . . No, not the Gulf War, what do they teach you in school, anyway? If it had been the Gulf War he'd still be alive today. World War Two. Your grandmother went out to see them after your mother was born. . . . No, I don't know why. I only met her briefly, Dr. Vatick was at my first dig, near Nippur, when Selena arrived. . . . But, Mara, I was a young student in philology, and he was a distinguished professor. We seldom spoke. . . . Your grandmother? Well, she was very beautiful, as I recall, perhaps somewhat willful, but we were really the slightest of acquaintances."

Sucking her teeth thoughtfully—which distended her cheeks into what Grandfather called her "chipmunk" look: not your most attractive expression, Mara, so that she took to doing it whenever she wanted to irritate him—Mara checked out a selection of books on the history of ancient Iraq.

Mrs. Ephers demanded to know what made her want to read about that? in a tone which told Mara that the Ancient Near East was a sensitive nerve on Graham Street. But Grandfather said nothing when Mrs. Ephers mentioned it at dinner. He only said it was high time Mara showed an aptitude for something, and maybe archeology ran in her blood. Disappointed not to rouse a more active response to Assyriology, Mara returned the books to the library and went back to irritating Grandfather by rewriting operas.

When she was eleven and Harriet was busy with law school, Grandfather started taking Mara to the symphony and the opera. Mara, not used to attention, proclaimed an enthusiasm for opera—so difficult for a child to understand and respond to, therefore so much more meritorious in her to like. In her teens, she found a kind of release in the extravagant emotions onstage. Luisa Montcrief, singing the "Willow Song" from *Otello,* carried Mara to the brink of suicide.

In her teens, too, she started calling herself a feminist, to annoy the doctor, who said that like all ideologies feminism was an excuse for mental sloth. Mara began fighting with him on all subjects relating to women, including opera. Why did the women always die, while their stupid lovers beat their chests in remorse? She wrote revisions of *Rigoletto* and *Madama Butterfly,* since she couldn't revise her family's history. Grandfather was disgusted: if you're going to start playing games with music as well as the rest of your life, we'll have to discontinue these outings. And so their brief rapport dissolved.

Mara muddled on through Chicago Latin. Although she didn't achieve Harriet's stellar grades, she performed brilliantly on the SAT and was easily accepted at college. But a wish to choose her own school, perhaps a big state university, couldn't stand up to the family tradition of Smith. After all, Harriet had gone there, had loved it. Mara knew by now she wouldn't develop straight hair or smooth white skin if she went to Smith, but she could still imagine a glittering circle of friends and lovers like her sister's.

But once there, away from the buckram of Grandfather Stonds to give her shape, she drifted, making few friends, finding no milieu, turning to alcohol as the easiest way to prove to one and all that, really, she was Beatrix Stonds's daughter even if she had no father to identify with. Until after her third semester, the college—not liking to offend the grandchild of a rich donor, but really left with no choice—kicked her out.

Back in Chicago she got out of bed to go to work, but spent long hours listening to music and writing in her journal. At night she meandered through the netherworld of the city, to the jazz clubs, the dyke bars, the places where other rootless people swirled.

Blood will tell, Grandfather said grimly to Mrs. Ephers. I was right to name her Mara: for the Lord has dealt very bitterly with me.

4

The Woman at the Wall

EVERY NIGHT when Mara climbed down the iron stairs that led from Michigan Avenue to the truck and bus routes below, the woman was in the same place. She sat cross-legged on a blanket, back against the wall, face hidden in the shadows. Some nights candle stubs, scavenged from the Dumpsters of nearby hotels, flickered in empty whiskey bottles in front of her. Between the candles lay a grimy photo of the Virgin Mary torn from a magazine. The woman leaned over it as if in prayer. Candlelight glinted gold from the icon in the photo, streaking the woman's gray-white face and hair with yellow. Light flickered over the damp crack in the bricks behind her head where a pipe was leaking and dripping.

Mara, drifting through the Underworld on her way to the jazz bars on the other side of Michigan, stopped to stare at her. Mrs. Ephers's warnings echoed in her head: You're following in your mother's footsteps. Be careful you don't end up in a trash bin with the rest of the garbage of Chicago.

Is that what happened to Beatrix? Mara demanded. They kept telling her Beatrix was dead, but in such a way that she never believed them: no details given, only a pursing up of the lips, and "too painful for your grandfather to talk about."

Harriet, when pushed, reported going to a funeral.

Did you see the body? Are you sure it was Mother? Mara persisted, only to have Harriet snap, don't be a ghoul. But Beatrix's death wasn't in the papers, under her married name or her birth name. Mara thought Grandfather and Mephers had thrown Beatrix out, but were ashamed to admit it. Her mother might be one of the army of street people marching unseen through the alleys and underground streets of the city.

Mara began to inspect every homeless white woman she came upon, searching for a resemblance to her grandfather or Harriet—not to her own face, which must have been taken from her father's mold, Mrs. Ephers often said, since no one ever saw a Stonds with those cheek-bones—trying to imagine Harriet wrinkled, gray-haired, that sleek golden beauty turned to ashes. Their mother would be only fifty or so if she were still alive, but everyone knew life on the streets aged you before your time.

Of course, only a terrible mother would abandon her children, and everyone agreed that Beatrix had been a terrible mother—look what she'd done to poor golden Harriet, after all. But Mara couldn't help thinking it was she herself, some particular defect in her that was obvious from the moment of her birth, that led their mother to disappear so completely. For, after all, until Mara was born, at least Beatrix came around from time to time. But no one had seen Beatrix since she drifted out of the apartment when her new baby was nine weeks old.

If you and Grandfather didn't want me, why didn't you put Beatrix in rehab and help her so she could have her own place with me? Mara asked Mrs. Ephers.

You can't help someone who doesn't want to be helped, Mara, she must have heard that saying three hundred thousand times or so in her nineteen years. We sent our bucket down into that well many times, probably too many, and it came up dry each time. Beatrix had to learn to come to grips with life herself. We prayed for her, but the Lord had other plans for all of us.

Mara waited for the day when Grandfather and Mrs. Ephers would throw her out to join Beatrix on the garbage heap of life. They did keep rumbling about how she needed to support herself, she shouldn't expect some trust fund was going to materialize to bail her out, not if she didn't show she was responsible enough to manage money. After she'd been home from college for three months, Grandfather put his foot down: you cannot go out drinking all night, then sit in your room all day long, young lady, pretending you're a writer. It would be one thing if you were in school, but as you've chosen to avoid education, I expect you to contribute to your living expenses.

Even Harriet chimed in, Going out to those bars isn't the smartest way to use your evenings. Why don't you register in one of the local writing programs if you don't want to go back to college? That way at least you'd have some focus.

And anyway, Harriet added, how do you get into those jazz bars? Don't you have to be twenty-one to drink in this state? Which of course Harriet knew, being a lawyer and knowing all the laws that ever were, those on the statute books as well as laws of conduct, of the jungle, even of gravity, since she'd been so good at physics in school along with every other subject.

Harriet tried to find Mara a job in the word processing room at her law firm, but Mara couldn't type fast enough, and she was always drifting into daydreams when she should have been transcribing some brilliant exposition of securities law.

Harriet next persuaded one of her clients, the Hotel Pleiades, to give Mara a job in their Special Events office. She could answer the phone, sound pleasant to prospective customers, book weddings and bar mitzvoth—surely that was within her capabilities? So Mara put on pantyhose and lipstick every day—Did you run a comb through that bush of yours, miss? Mrs. Ephers would call to her as she left the apartment in the morning—Try to remember it's not just your name that's injured if you make a bad impression. Your sister went out on a limb for you: don't you go hurting her career by making a mess of this job.

The Hotel Pleiades perched east of Michigan Avenue, one of the skyscrapers that had suddenly erupted from the empty lots around the train station. The hotel's white masonry and slate-colored glass shot thirty stories over the river, shutting out light from the old buildings on the avenue, but giving guests a clear view of Lake Michigan.

The hotel also sent down shoots to the Underworld, the shadow network of streets beneath the heart of downtown Chicago. The Pleiades parking garage opened onto Lower Wacker Drive, where delivery vans and garbage trucks bring supplies to downtown businesses, and ferry away their waste. Under rusting rebars in the roadbed to the bright city overhead, homeless people lived in makeshift boxes, protected from rain and snow, skin turning gray in the absence of light and air.

It was near the Pleiades garage that the woman at the wall camped. The exact location under the leaking pipe seemed important to her: one night, when Mara was climbing down the stairs to the Underworld, she saw a panhandler working a line of homebound office workers while they waited for one of the buses that had a terminus on Underground Wacker. The commuters stood in an unspeaking, unmoving line, as if by holding themselves completely still, the germ of homelessness would not infect them. When the bus arrived and the passengers surged through the doors in panicky relief, the panhandler snarled and moved up the street to the woman at the wall's usual spot.

The woman wasn't there. Watching the man unzip his pants to relieve himself against the bricks below the crack, Mara wondered if he'd forced the woman to leave, when she suddenly appeared at the corner of the building.

She drove him away, yelling curses at him: "The Mother of God knows you've defiled Her temple! She will curse you, She will wither your balls, She will turn your urine black!" The panhandler, twice her size, stumbled off without taking time to cover himself. Mara laughed. Street theater, performance art, right on, sister.

A couple who'd just left their car with the garage attendant backed away in horror, first from the panhandler, trying to zip himself together as he shuffled along, and then from the woman's curses which followed him down the street. As Mara walked past the garage she could hear the driver of the car complaining loudly to the garage manager: "Can't you do anything to keep the street clean down here?"

"It is clean, except for suburban scum who come and dirty it with their minds," Mara yelled.

She turned back to the homeless woman, who was rubbing a crumpled newspaper over the dark blotch left by the man's urine. Mara found a five-dollar bill in her wallet and handed it to her.

The woman interrupted her work to pocket the bill. "Thank you, ma'am, thank you. The Mother of God thanks you, too. Her face on the wall will smile at you. Her blood will cleanse you."

The woman finished her work and stuck her fingers against the crack in the bricks where water, stained red by the rusting pipes behind it, oozed out. She laid damp fingers on Mara's lips, then on her own. Mara tried not to grimace or draw away, but she couldn't help gagging at the woman's touch, and the taste of the chalky-sweet rust on her mouth.

As she walked back past the garage the manager was standing with the outraged couple, watching her. "Hey!" the manager yelled. "You! Do you know that woman?"

Mara scrunched her face into its most evil scowl. "She's my mother, dickhead. What's it to you?"

5

Offstage Performance

Made rounds early, ordered blood workup on Mrs. Herstein before her discharge, told her to come to clinic next week for results. She asked what would happen if she took the Prozac: "Will I have deeper insights?"

Into what, I asked. "The nature of life." Not one of the side effects ever reported in the literature—told her I didn't know, but that the drug might make her feel calmer, less like weeping. At that she got angry.

"I want to weep. Weeping gives you insight if you do it right."

Too tired to try to understand what's going on with her. Told her to come to clinic next week if she wanted to discuss further treatment when we have results of blood work.

Strange dream right before I woke up. Walked into room—large, light, empty, like a music room in a rich man's house, thought at first I was alone, then uneasily aware of presence, pulled a screen aside and saw Mrs. Herstein dressed in surgical scrubs, large butcher knife in one hand, stereo receiver in the other. She was going to do surgery on my brain, plant the receiver in it. I turned to run and found door blocked by Hanaper, smiling, saying, just let her do it, it will keep her happy.

Woke in sweat before she could begin operating. Is this some kind of substitution for my parents? What did I think Mom wanted to plant in my brain? But Hanaper as a stand-in for Dad doesn't make sense—I dislike H, dislike his bullying, his lack of interest in patients, while Dad was a peace-at-any-price kind of guy. Or does that equate to lack of interest in children—in me? Hanaper called me into his office this morning. . . .

"Dr. Tammuz. You're always complaining that we are more attentive to the needs of the hospital than we are the community."

Hector, the dream still heavy on his mind, eyed the department head warily. "Yes, sir?"

"An opportunity has come to me—to the hospital—to give something back. I think you would be ideal for the position."

"And what is that, sir?"

"The Lenore Foundation has designated a fund to send a psychiatric resident into the homeless community one day a week. As you know, since the mayor closed community mental clinics, all hospitals in the city have experienced a greatly increased load of mentally ill homeless patients."

Hector thought of the man who wanted to prove he was a chicken at the State of Illinois building, the one Hanaper had bullied into leaving the hospital so that he wouldn't add to their uninsured costs, and said, "I hadn't realized that, sir."

Hanaper squinted to see if he could read irony in his resident's face. "The man in charge of finding the right resident is Angus Boten. I think you met him when you came out for your interview. Unfortunately he wasn't able to stay with the department here, but he called me yesterday to see if I could recommend anyone. Of course I thought immediately of you."

Hanaper stared at me with a kind of cocky maliciousness. Does this mean he's aware of my disappointment at not being able to work with Boten? But if that were the case he wouldn't give me the opportunity to have even this modest association with B: H knows I am more interested in talking therapy than pharmaceuticals, and thinks it's his job to ridicule that nonsense out of me, wouldn't deliberately send me into a clinic where the emphasis would be on Boten's approach to treatment. More likely H has some knowledge about—poor—conditions of Lenore clinic: perhaps a cold cheerless room where an endless progression of smelly, psychotic men and women rant at me, much like Mrs. Herstein, only without benefit of soap.

Hector could see himself, ever shorter on sleep, writing prescriptions for Ativan, Prozac, Haldol, flinging drugs at the mentally ill the way GIs threw candy to children in war-torn countries. "I presume this means I can cut back on my on-call rotation, sir, since I'll have to be out of the hospital one day a week."

Hanaper was disconcerted, although only briefly. "The clinic will meet on Fridays, starting a week from today. We'll move your on-call rotation permanently to Friday night through Saturday, Tammuz. That way you can dictate your notes on your homeless clients while you're in the on-call room, save you some time so you don't have to be away from home any more than necessary. Although you don't have a wife yet, do you?"

Wanted to pick up the Steuben paperweight the bastard keeps on his desk and brain him with it. Wanted to sing, "Take this job and shove it." But of course I just meekly said, "No, sir," and got directions on when and where to start. Orleans Street Church has offered use of a room, since they run a homeless shelter there in an old coal basement. Hagar's House. Wasn't she the woman sent into the wilderness? So a fitting name: women out of the wilderness into the coal cellar.

Hard to remember why I wanted to become a doctor. Even if I finish my residency at this hellhole it will only mean signing on with some managed care group elsewhere and doing more of the same: relying on drugs, not therapy, having an average of fifteen minutes to spend with every patient, having to justify every admission to a committee of administrative baboons who know nothing about mental illness!

About to leave when Hanaper's secretary buzzed him; Luisa Montcrief had arrived. The diva Stonds told us about on Tuesday, whose family is worrying. Completely forgot about her, as H obviously had, too, but he was glad to sweep me along on his coattails, have secretary page Melissa so he could have bigger audience on his great therapeutic methods.

Bad news from the secretary: diva has no health insurance. Coverage lapsed after eighteen months of not paying premiums.

On first sight, Montcrief very striking—dark hair swept back from strong cheekbones, expensive-looking crimson dress. Another woman with her, sister-in-law we later learned, face tight with the kind of worry all care-taking relatives get after a while.

"Ms. Minsky? I'm Dr. Hanaper. Your brother says you've been having a few problems lately."

The diva turned mocking brows toward her sister-in-law, who said sharply, "He's speaking to you, Janice."

"But my dear Karen, I am not Ms. Minsky. You are the only person with that name in the room. Unless you have Becca concealed behind the arras?" Her voice was rich, like fresh coffee, and her laugh tingled the blood of the men in the room.

"She likes to think of herself as Madame Montcrief," Karen Minsky told Hanaper.

"I'm here in the room, Karen, and able to speak for myself. I like to think of myself as Madame Montcrief because that is my name. I paid a fee to a judge when I was twenty to have it legally changed. Not to 'Madame' of course; to Luisa Montcrief. 'Madame' is a courtesy title out of respect to my eminence in the world of music. So it is really never appropriate to call me anything else."

"Except when you want to use the Minsky money," Karen said sharply.

"Even though I changed my name I didn't have a DNA transplant: I am still Miriam and Herschel Minsky's daughter. I'm entitled to my share of their estate."

"She squandered her share of the inheritance—"

"Which included half the money our parents had to leave, but nothing from the profits of the scrap iron empire. I don't think I'm beyond my rights in wanting some of that cash flow."

"Harry has worked every day of his life since he was fifteen in that scrap yard. He's earned that money. You're ashamed to have anyone know you're a Minsky, even by DNA."

"When Harry sold my home in Campania—"

"To pay the debts you'd built up around the world—"

"Ah, ladies," Dr. Hanaper broke in, "you may both have valid points here, but let's try to see what is bothering Ms. Montcrief."

"There's nothing wrong with me that a better agent wouldn't cure," the diva said. "Harry and Karen are nervous about my not working, but they have no idea how I feel, a world-class opera star, not to have had an engagement for almost three years."

"People covered up for your drinking as long as they could," Karen said, her face flushed. "Longer than I would have. I don't know what hold you had over Piero Benedetti at the Met, but he brought you to New York to play Desdemona even after you were arrested in London for assaulting a member of the audience."

"Assault?" Hanaper asked. "With a weapon?"

"She threw a decanter at a woman. From the stage."

"The ridiculous creature was talking so loudly during the first act of *Tosca* I could barely hear my cues. I have perfect pitch, but I do need to know when someone else has finished singing so that I can time my entrance. By the time Scarpia was forcing me to sign my lover's death warrant the woman was so loud she spoiled my approach to 'Vissi d'arte.' After the performance my fellow cast members bought me dinner in gratitude for silencing her."

"Was that before or after the police came for you?" Karen asked with heavy sarcasm. "If you hadn't drunk most of a bottle of Scotch before going on in the second act you might have been more aware of the production than of the audience. Anyway, I don't think it was the woman's speaking—it was the boos from the balcony that interrupted your performance."

Karen turned to Hanaper. "Even then Piero Benedetti brought her back to the Met. That's where the end really came."

"Karen, it is pathetic that you are so resentful of me you have to slander me in front of total strangers." The diva smiled at Hanaper. "Her life has revolved around the house Harry built for her in Highland Park and her only child Rebecca. She's always been jealous of Becca's attachment to me: the poor child isn't exposed to culture, or glamour, and I provide her with both."

At this point I thought poor Karen Minsky was going to strangle Montcrief. Same thing must have occurred to Hanaper—not always lacking in insight: he suggested Karen wait outside while he finished talking to Madame Montcrief. The interview went on for half an hour, with the singer denying that she was anything but a social drinker, talking of the jealousies in the opera world that led to slanderous reports of her drinking.

"Your brother says you stole his credit cards and ran up quite a hotel bill this last month. That doesn't sound like slander, does it?" Hanaper said.

"Harry and I are twins, but we're not identical." She laughed heartily at her own joke. "We've never seen eye-to-eye on anything, even as children: he always preferred Queen Esther to Vashti, so that's who he married. Now he wants me banished."

Hanaper pounced on this, thinking he was getting a first true sign of delusions.

The diva threw up her hands—a theatrical gesture, yet somehow, from her, genuine as well. "Oh, dear: you really haven't heard of the Book of Esther, Doctor? There was a time when you could expect to carry on a cultivated conversation with a man of medicine. That's still true in Italy, you know: the most devoted fans of opera there are often in the medical ranks. Or the clerical. And if I had made such a statement to one of them, they would instantly have understood all the relationships in my brother's life. But I suppose with drugs and machines to rely on American doctors acquire a technician's approach to problem solving."

Wanted to applaud her, but engrossed myself in notes while Hanaper stared at me suspiciously. He summoned the sister-in-law, said "Tough love" the only thing to do in cases like this. Of course if diva had insurance he could recommend Midwest Hospital's in-patient alcohol dependency program, but if Mrs. Minsky wasn't prepared to pay the bill? Mrs. Minsky emphatically not ready to pay a twenty-thousand-dollar hospital bill.

Then, H advised, don't let her sponge off the family, give her one last chance, if she blows that then don't pick up the pieces again. And by the way you can give my secretary a check for two hundred fifty dollars. Melissa and I choked: poor Karen Minsky paying a seventy-five-dollar premium because Hanaper never read the Book of Esther.

After we slunk out as fast as we could Melissa said, "I would give up my residency if I thought I could ever dress and move like Luisa Montcrief." I'd give up my residency if I could find another way to pay my medical school debts, I said, and we all went off to our respective patients.

Dr. Stonds pounced on me as I was writing up my last orders at the end of the day. What had happened with Mme Montcrief? He and his granddaughter used to enjoy her performances at Lyric Opera.

Told him she seemed to be an alcoholic without any medical insurance, so tough love seemed to be the indicated treatment.

Stonds looked at me bleakly. Tough love is often the best treatment even in the presence of medical insurance, Dr.—Tammuz, is it? As you gain more experience you will be less willing to cry over the manipulators, the users, the abusers in the patient population. You need to develop a thicker skin, or you will be torn apart by your patients' woes.

Advice I've been hearing since I was five, I think, Mom telling me not to be a crybaby. Develop a thicker skin. Instead, over time, my skin gets sandpapered to translucence.

6

Hagar's House

"YOU SHOULD DO some volunteer work at Hagar's House," Mrs. Ephers told Mara one morning at breakfast. "Your heart bleeds over all these homeless women, but you should see what their lives are really like. Drunk, most of them, some from homes as nice as this one. Maybe it would give you more sympathy for their families, or at least stop you heading down the same road they're on."

Mara hunched a shoulder and left the table without answering. As a matter of fact, she had volunteered at the shelter a few times, without telling anyone at Graham Street, but she hated the shelter's director. The church had approved Patsy Wanachs not only because she spoke some Spanish, but because she was a member of the congregation whom everyone had known since childhood. Patsy shared the obsession with order and decorum that the Orleans Street Church prized, and could be counted on not to let the shelter move from the basement into the pews.

Mara hated the fact that women had to ask permission to get tampons or seconds at breakfast, or for an extra blanket if they were shivering. The rows of cots, four feet apart, allowed no privacy. Women could put their personal belongings in a locked office for the night, to protect them against theft from their sisters, but then had to come to one of the volunteers, Mara, for instance, to request access to their own possessions. A handful of private lockers could be "earned" by the inmates from points scored by good behavior.

Mara hated the way Patsy Wanachs looked at the women when they violated one of the shelter's rules, a secret pleasure in power shining through as she shook her head, made a note: LaBelle, or Caroline, if you become abusive we have to ask you to leave.

Mephers poured out her grievance to Harriet that evening: I tried to get Mara involved in something outside herself, but I might as well talk to the elevator here. In fact, I'd get more satisfaction out of it—at least the elevator comes when I call for it.

Harriet was tired. She wanted only to lie down before dinner, when she'd have to play hostess to some of Grandfather's surgical colleagues, but hearing Mara in the front room, trying to improvise on the piano, she took a breath and went in to talk to her sister. Mara was playing the same triad over and over with her left hand while fumbling with chords in the right.

Harriet couldn't understand why Patsy Wanachs's attitude troubled Mara. "They have to have rules. I know it seems dehumanizing, but in any group of people there are always a handful who would grab everything if we didn't have some restraints."

"Yeah, like your clients." Mara didn't look at Harriet, but she did stop fumbling with the keys. "They didn't get to own banks without stealing from other people."

Harriet refused to fight. "That's why they need me. Someone has to explain the rules to them and keep them out of jail if they've gotten too grabby. Well, Patsy is just explaining the rules to these women, so they don't have to spend the night on the street. It's a pretty rough job, you know, running an overnight shelter. The church is lucky she's willing to do it."

Mara twisted around on the piano bench to look at her sister. "But it's the look on her face when she makes a note in that log of hers. Like she's happy she gets to chew someone out."

"I think you're imagining that, Mara, because you always want to fight anyone with authority." Harriet spoke gently.

"And I suppose I'm just imagining that Rafe Lowrie is a sanctimonious hypocrite, too? Well, he's over there preaching at the women every

Wednesday night. Showing them their evil ways. He makes Cynthia go
with him and hand out Bibles. He has more money than God, his son
Jared is like the biggest most hideous rapist on the Gold Coast—"

"Mara!" Harriet spoke in her Do-you-have-proof-for-that-allega-
tion? voice.

"Talk to Tamara Jacoby!" Mara's skin flushed to a muddy red.
"Okay, so she's sleeping with him, but Cynthia says she's terrified of
him. It's like the classic battered wife syndrome: Tamara's paralyzed by
him, so she keeps coming back to him. But meanwhile, Cynthia has to
live like a nun, and Rafe talks to her in that rasping voice about what her
duty to God is. That's his phony way of saying 'Do everything exactly
like I say.' It's the same way he talks to the homeless women. That's why
I hate to go over to Hagar's House."

"He only agreed to run Bible study because of the dissension in the
congregation about whether to keep the shelter going at all. You know,
when Mrs. Thirkell found out that we had pimps hanging around outside
the church gates . . ."

Harriet sat on the bench next to her sister and imitated the outraged
Mrs. Thirkell. Mara had to giggle.

The Orleans Street Church had been built in 1893, on land donated
by a speculator who thought the wealth that moved across the Chicago
River after the famous 1871 fire would spread west as well as north.
Right after the fire, Geoffrey Lenore bought up useless chunks of land in
what became Irish and German slums, and when he finally admitted his
mistake gave three acres of it for the church. Lenore also endowed the
massive stone complex, built around an atrium so that his only daughter
could have a garden wedding the year the building and grounds were
completed. Besides a nave to rival Notre Dame's, the building included
twelve Sunday school classrooms and a giant hall where people could
have danced if church rules allowed.

When parishioners met a century later during the coffee hour, filled
with shock and titillation at the sight of women sleeping on the subway
grates at Chicago Avenue, they looked over their vast plant. The cellars
where coal used to be stored weren't really used for anything. They could

be cleaned out, turned into sleeping quarters, the church could install a kitchen so that women could get a hot meal before leaving in the morning. God clearly intended for them to do this great work. It would be like the early eighties, when they opened the building to El Salvadoran refugees—a very successful program, repaid with becoming gratitude by the various families when they'd been established in permanent homes.

Of course, without putting it in so many words, the parish council knew the shelter would be kept separate from the church: an outside entrance created on Hill Street where the old coal chutes used to be together with the private kitchen meant that no homeless woman need ever come upstairs to the main buildings.

Once Hagar's House was up and running, the reality of their client population dismayed many church members. For one thing, some of the women drank. When parishioners were singing hymns and laughing as they scrubbed the cellars, they had never imagined drunks—they'd pictured clean well-groomed women, down on their luck, humbly grateful to the church for providing them with shelter, praising Jesus and thanking His servants, the Orleans Street Church.

The parish council forbade alcohol within the shelter—it was never allowed on church property, anyway, not even for communion, when the elders served grape juice to the congregation—and they ordered Patsy Wanachs to bar the door to anyone who arrived drunk.

Even more shocking, some of the women were prostitutes: Patsy Wanachs reported that their pimps came around demanding to see them. The church's own doorman, faithful old Ronald Hemphill, was slapped one night by one of the pimps demanding entry at the main gate.

At that point there was a strong movement to shut the shelter altogether. The trouble was, Sylvia Lenore supported Hagar's House. The great-granddaughter of the original Geoffrey Lenore, Sylvia continued the family presence in the front center pew of the church, served on the parish council, and—as Rafe Lowrie grumbled to the head pastor—had depressingly progressive politics. If she'd had to earn that inheritance herself, Rafe and his cohorts agreed, she wouldn't be so free in handing it out.

Pastor Emerson was hard pressed to keep both the Lowrie and Lenore factions in his congregation satisfied. Like many large downtown churches, Orleans Street contained both young fundamentalists, who tended to be social conservatives, along with older members who were more liberal both in doctrine and on social issues.

Sylvia Lenore, who'd been baptized at Orleans Street fifty-six years ago, had been reared in a progressive tradition: her father marched with Dr. King in Memphis and Marquette Park, her grandmother ran a settlement house out of the church's Sunday school rooms. Sylvia and Rafe clashed over every issue before the parish, from Hagar's House to the organ fund.

One night, in a particularly heated discussion of Hagar's House, Sylvia preached (raved, Rafe Lowrie muttered) about the church's duty to the widow and orphan. Which brought Mrs. Ephers to her feet in turn: Are these widows? she demanded. They're like the woman in the Gospel of John, who had five so-called husbands, but was never married to any of them.

A ripple of laughter went through Lowrie's faction. Pastor Emerson got up to propose a compromise before Sylvia or any of her furious supporters could respond. He could ill afford to alienate Sylvia Lenore— her hundred-thousand-dollar annual pledge was an important part of the church's budget. Besides, in his heart, which he tried to keep hidden from the fifteen-hundred-plus members of the congregation, the pastor found Sylvia and her friends easier to work with than Rafe Lowrie. He didn't always agree with her, but Sylvia didn't phone him at two in the morning to harangue him when they differed. As Rafe had. Many times.

Keep Hagar's House open, the pastor urged: The congregation had put far too much into starting it to shut it so soon. Give the shelter a full year, but let someone try to bring the Gospel to the homeless.

After another half hour of dickering, the entire parish council agreed to the proposal and the pastor breathed more easily. Sylvia knew that the longer she could keep the shelter running, the harder it would be to close it down, while Rafe was ecstatic at the opportunity to show Emerson the right way to run a Bible study meeting.

Rafe's supporters also relaxed: If the women were praying regularly, and reading the Bible, they might find God—after all, He had demanded that Joshua spare Rahab the harlot, who was able to recognize a divine emissary. So, too, might the women in Hagar's House someday come to Jesus. Might even save the church from some danger, although that was added with a snicker.

"And you know," Mara said to Harriet, still next to her on the piano bench. "He makes Cynthia come along sometimes to hand out the Bibles and make coffee and shit. You know how hard he whipped her that time she came over to watch the new Madonna video with me?"

"But Grandfather had told you that you weren't to buy it: you know his feelings on that kind of pointless eroticism."

"So he had to tell Rafe. I'll never forgive him for that. I tried getting her to go to the emergency room, but Cynthia was afraid of what a doctor might say. Rafe's turning her into a little Stepford wife. He's joined that horrible bunch of hypocrites called Family Matters, you know, where men get together and learn to be men again, praying God to smite all the evil feminists in their midst and pick out Christian spouses for their children. Mrs. Lowrie left after he broke her arm all those years ago, but Cynthia's been terrorized into thinking she'll go to hell if she disobeys him."

Cynthia Lowrie and Mara Stonds had begun an improbable friendship when they met in Sunday school at the age of nine. Cynthia's mother had just run away with a computer repairman; Mara had no mother at all. Even in a world filled with divorce most girls had a mother. Mara and Cynthia were the only two in their whole Sunday school class who didn't.

Mara told Cynthia her grandfather had locked Mara's mother in the psychiatry wing at the hospital, even though nothing was wrong with her, and that he whipped Mara when she tried to smuggle a key to her mother. Cynthia's whippings made a big impression on Mara, which is why she added that particular detail to the story. Grandfather never actually beat her, although Mrs. Ephers, furious with having such a liar on her hands, smacked her across the face and washed her mouth with soap.

They made Mara apologize to Rafe for the story: I'm sorry, she said. My grandmother was kidnaped by the Russians after World War Two because Grandfather is a spy for the CIA. My mother died when she tried to go to Russia to rescue my grandmother. They were both shot by a firing squad.

No punishment could cure Mara of her storytelling, as Harriet labeled Mara's dramatic tales. Lies, Mephers said, and don't try to dress them up as something prettier.

Rafe and Dr. Stonds didn't agree on much, but they were united in wanting Cynthia and Mara to find other friends. Dr. Stonds hated the friendship because he thought Cynthia dragged Mara down: she ought to have friends who were ambitious for education and professional acclaim. After graduating from high school, Cynthia became a transcriber in the word processing center at a big insurance company. She was only going to work until Rafe found a good Christian mate for her.

For his part, Rafe tried to end the friendship because he thought Mara taught Cynthia to disobey him. Dr. Stonds let Mara talk back to him in a way that he, Rafe, would never tolerate. He'd made it clear that in his own home Mara was to treat him with the same respect Cynthia did. Now that she'd been thrown out of college, he hoped Cynthia could see what a slippery slope her friend was on. Cynthia would murmur, Yes, Daddy, No, I'm not seeing her these days, Daddy, not adding that they talked almost every day on the phone while Cynthia was at work.

"You know, now Rafe's got his undies in a bundle because the Lenore Family Foundation is bringing in a psychiatrist to counsel the homeless." Mara played chopsticks with her right hand. "It's only once a week, on Fridays, but apparently the resident they picked is a Jew. Rafe has been screeching about how a Christian church ought to be able to find a good Christian to work there. And they're letting men as well as women come to see the doctor, so the possibility exists that homeless people might have carnal relations. I mean, they're barely supposed to eat, they ought not be allowed to be together as men and women."

She hit a discordant seventh to emphasize her anger. "You know the asshole held up the start of the psych clinic for three weeks so Sylvia

Lenore could see if any Christian psychiatrists or social workers in the parish felt called to minister to the homeless? I guess Gilbert McIlvanie and Connie Trumaine needed CPR to recover from the shock of donating a day a week to *pro bono* work."

Harriet laughed, but shook her head. "Beebie, you take everything too hard. I know why you worry so much about homeless women, but sometimes I think Grandfather is right, that you're identifying too much with them."

Mara's face scrunched into lines of angry hurt. "Beebie" was Harriet's pet name for her, rarely used, and it always made Mara feel too hurt by the sense of love gone missing from her life. She loved Harriet. She hated Harriet. She saw the feelings running through her veins like two different-colored streams of blood that never mixed; she never could tell which one dominated.

Mara turned back to the piano. Harriet left the room, a momentary impulse to hug her sister replaced by a more typical irritation with her. Grandfather was right: Mara just never made any effort.

7

Open-air Clinic

Haven't written in several weeks. Been run ragged between work with street people for Lenore Foundation and regular hosp duties. Disappointed that work with Hagar's House doesn't include more time with Boten. He met with me before I started there, remembered me from my interview when I applied for residency, which was pleasing, but told me bluntly there wasn't going to be much scope for general therapy work. He will meet with me once a month to discuss patients and progress—if any—but no budget for him to play more active role. It's all on my shoulders.

So I've been going every Friday to a room in a converted coal cellar at the Orleans St. Church where men and women, mostly women, from different shelters come in and talk to me. More men without shelter than women, but women more willing—more eager—to see doctor, have someone to talk to, try to get help. No cost containment committee to limit sessions to fifteen minutes. On the other hand, after first week—where only two people showed up in five hours—numbers have been growing and I have to limit sessions based on my own stamina.

Another negative is the hostility of some of the church staff. Shelter and counseling room have a separate entrance, on Hill Street, but you can't just walk in: church is like a fortress, with pseudo-Gothic buildings behind eight-foot-high cast-iron fence. Intimidates me, no doubt worse for the mentally ill.

"The security discourages people who most need help," Hector said to Patsy Wanachs, the executive director at the shelter. "If you're paranoid, you're not likely to respond to a voice coming out of the wall demanding to know your business."

"Running a shelter in a church like Orleans Street involves a series of compromises, Dr. Tammuz," Patsy Wanachs told him, keeping one hand on her phone so he'd realize how busy she was. "A lot of our client base has serious problems with drugs and alcohol, as you surely realize. And we're a stone's throw from one of the city's most dangerous housing projects. Perhaps our security system keeps away some people who badly need help—but it also keeps out drug dealers and pimps."

She picked up the receiver as a sign of dismissal. One of the volunteers followed him to the hall.

"This isn't really the hostile place you're taking it for," she told Hector. "Women feel a sense of safety here, and that's important on the street. And we're one of the few places in the city where women can shower, and get a hot breakfast."

Suppose you can put up with a lot for safety, food and shower. Including prayer meetings or Bible study, whatever they call it.

Sessions led on Wednesday night by a forty-something commodities trader who's found Jesus and wants to bring him to the homeless women at Hagar's House. Rafe Lowrie. Raspy voiced, but smooth, well-dressed, no light of fanaticism in his eyes, maybe motivated by need to be in charge of everyone's life. He came along my second Friday to interrogate me about my methods and goals. Told me he doesn't want me undoing the good he's achieving with Hagar women through heightening their spiritual awareness.

Thinking of some of the visions my patients are seeing, I suggested to Lowrie that tamping down their spiritual awareness might be a good thing. He became very huffy, said he had warned the parish council that bringing a Jew in to work with the homeless not a good idea at all. Jesus cast out devils; if the Holy Spirit was really at work in the Orleans St Ch the parish ought to be able to pray these people well.

I said, anything that could cure schizophrenia was fine with me, whether prayer or Prolixin, or both together. He stared at me for a several minutes without speaking—probably thought he was looking like Clint Eastwood staring down Lee Van Cleef, but looked more like a man who's found a cockroach in his soup. Then in Eastwood style turned on his heel and slowly stomped off.

So at the hospital I have Hanaper telling me I'm like a witch doctor because I prefer therapy to drugs, and here at the shelter I have this born-again Lowrie telling me I'm a heathen—worse, a Jew—who believes in medicine instead of prayer.

Starting to have dreams in which I'm shaving, and my face comes loose. Sometimes behind the skin I'm a monster—a savage concoction of bone and blood. Sometimes I'm a woman. Always the question of—who am I really?

As Dr. Boten warned Hector, most people who came to the Orleans Street clinic were in state of acute crisis. What he wasn't expecting was the rough good humor with which many met life's most trying conditions. He found himself looking forward to the visits of a number of regulars, including two women who always seemed to travel together. Jacqui and Nanette didn't want separate sessions of therapy, just Hector's empathic ear. They told him bloodcurdling tales of life on the street: that most women who were out there any length of time were raped, sometimes by homeless men, even by cops, but just as often by white businessmen on their way home to suburbs, wife, and family.

Jacqui is black, Nanette white. Apparently on the streets racial differences stop mattering as much as they do aboveground. Last week, J & N told me they have a third friend, woman named Madeleine Carter, who has always had mental health problems, but now they're seriously worried about her. Took some doing to get the story out of them—they were afraid I would either laugh or tell them to take the tale to Jesus.

They say Madeleine thinks the Virgin Mary appeared to her on a wall on Underground Wacker. She won't leave wall now, even in the foulest weather. The three women used to sleep at Hagar's House, or sometimes, when they had enough money, rent an apartment together, but now Madeleine won't leave the street at all. J & N found a big crate that a generator came in around the corner from Madeleine's vision; when their money is short the two of them sometimes sleep there with her, and they fixed it up with blankets so Madeleine could get some shelter.

J & N tried to persuade Madeleine to come to me, but she won't leave her post at Virgin's side. So—they want me to go to her. After a lot of arguing with them—I'm stretched too thin to visit people on the streets, I say— This isn't just anyone, Doctor, she's our friend. Imagine dozens of their friends scattered around town, they prodding me into visiting all of them, but there's something about the friendship between J & N that moves me, so I agree to go, on Monday afternoon after finishing up at the hospital.

The woman at the wall was reading a Bible. When Hector arrived with her friends, Madeleine marked the place and put the book away in a plastic bag.

Before Hector could work his way into an interview Jacqui said, "This here is Dr. Tammuz, Madeleine. He's come to talk to you about your wall."

Madeleine turned and touched a crack in the concrete. Hector looked at it intently, but could see no Rorschach that looked like a face. The concrete was split by a line that looked like a flattened sine curve; by tilting his head to one side he supposed he could make out the shape of a woman's breasts, or a child's rendition of a bird in flight, but no face.

A faint reddish liquid oozed from the crack, rust from the rebars behind it. Madeleine dipped her fingers in it and sucked them. Hector tried not to let his disgust show in his face.

"Her blood," Madeleine explained to Hector. "The Mother of God weeps tears of blood. I was looking for the place in the Bible where it says it but I can't find it. All I can see is the place where Jezebel was murdered and her blood splashed on the wall. But I know this isn't Jezebel, this isn't the blood of a whore, I can tell by the taste."

She looked fiercely at Hector, as if expecting him to argue the point with her. Instead he asked her how long she had known the Virgin was present in the wall.

"Since She spoke to me one night when I was walking by. Some man had been doing his business on me and I came by here and She spoke to me out of this crack. She tells me I'm Her daughter, I'm as pure as She is, and She's crying because the rest of the world isn't pure enough, they won't listen to Her, but I listen to Her. I loved my own little girl, I wouldn't never leave her but they made me go. The Holy Mother says She loves me just that much as I love my own little girl."

"That's right, honey," Jacqui said. "You need the Virgin Mary to look after you, but you need to eat, too. You tell her, Doctor."

Persuaded her to go around the corner to their generator box to perform a cursory exam. M very frightened of men, understandable, if they've been "doing their business" on her, so Jacqui and Nanette promise to stand right outside, talk to her while I examine. Underneath the layers of coats and socks M a wraith, skin transparent from weeks out of the sun. Seems to be a case of acute schizophrenia, probably intensified by vitamin deficiencies, oh, not to mention lack of sleep, fear of rape, etc.

Ought to be hospitalized, but would mean a trip over to County, and she won't leave her "face." Under prodding from her friends agreed to an injection of Prolixin. Worry about ethics of dispensing medication in such a setting, how can she give an informed consent?

The next week Jacqui and Nanette came to Hector, ecstatic: the shot he'd given Madeleine had changed her dramatically. She was eating now, and would leave the wall sometimes to get some sunlight in the world overhead. She'd even spent the night at Hagar's House a few times. She was still guarding her "face" on the wall, but not drinking rusty water from the crack as much as she'd done before.

Jacqui and Nanette bought him a potted daisy at Woolworth's to show their gratitude. They also started spreading the word on the street that Hector was a miracle worker, a sympathetic man who would listen to their troubles, and give them the kind of drugs that could really help. The two women started bringing patients in to see him. Hector tried telling Jacqui that she shouldn't force anyone to come against their will.

Jacqui shook her head. "You're thinking of poor Ashley, Doctor. You don't know her life. She ran to the streets to get away from her mother's boyfriends, that was when she was thirteen, and she ran straight into the arms of a pimp who started working her over for his own gain. She's like a lot of people out here, thinks she's worthless, she wouldn't ever come see you on her own. Me and Nanette have to see she gets help, otherwise she'll be dead in six months. And even though she doesn't say anything to you, those pills you give her really help."

Ashley won't let me give her an injection, and won't take pills when she's on her own, so J brings her in every week and watches her swallow a handful of Haldol.

Funny how my eye for street people changed by working with them. Tough lives. In shelter have to follow strict set of rules, yet handle it all without losing dignity.

Am trying to learn from them how to put up with Hanaper's petty rules without losing my own dignity. Hanaper vastly entertained after looking over clinic sheets for last three months to see Mrs. Herstein, the compulsive hoarder, has been coming in every week. Daughter still with her. One of these nuclear families created by fission, turning into black hole that sucks in all joy, light.

"Ah, your black eyes, Dr. Tammuz, I knew Mrs. Herstein would find them irresistible. Cultivate her—she may be one of these demented women who keeps a fortune stuffed under the bedclothes. Where she apparently would like to reside with you."

The dark man in America, even if not from Africa, always has great sexual prowess. Foolish grandfather—thought by fleeing the Aryan nation could leave behind the greasy Jew of perverse sexuality.

But Hanaper's so-called banter good for me: makes me feel like vomiting, his image of sex with Mrs. H, and that in turn makes me try to figure out why my reaction so acute.

Dreamt last night that Jacqui, Nanette, and Madeleine were the three witches from Macbeth, stirring a pot on Underground Wacker. I came along to treat Madeleine's schizophrenia and the three turned to me—on me—and laughed. Madeleine flourished a gigantic wooden spoon and hissed, "Physician, heal thyself!" Then she turned into Mother, and the wooden spoon dissolved into a jar of face cream.

It frightened him sometimes, how much the homeless women knew about him—part from information gleaned from some informal street network, part from a hypersensitivity honed by life in the open, where they had to decide in an instant whether chance-met folk were friend or foe.

They knew Hector was unmarried, that he'd grown up out east, that he didn't get along with his boss.

"Seems to me you're running away, Doctor, running away from your family out east, from your boss, from everything you can't stand to face, so you've run to the last place you can find: the streets," Jacqui observed one morning. "One of these days you're going to have to stop running from and start running to."

If you were an ambitious, superstitious thane you would pay close attention to their words. But in their own eyes they were ordinary women with the usual concerns—for their children (Nanette had a son, in and out of prison on drug charges; Jacqui, two daughters raised by their grandmother, one of them a secretary in a law firm who made enough money to vacation in the Caribbean), or their hair, or even the men in Springfield and Washington who wanted to line their own pockets at the expense of education, of old people, and of the living breathing poor.

8

Rude Awakening

AGAIN IN HER SLEEP the double basses menaced her. Again the angry man approached, a chorus of angry men sang that she should be strangled, her voice silenced forever. She thrashed herself awake and blinked once more at a strange room. After years of waking in one city after another, she should be used to strange rooms, but instability mounted with time rather than diminishing. She longed to wake up always in the same place, to know exactly where she was.

No pictures by the bed to give her a clue, neither Becca as Queen Esther nor her own talisman, a signed photo of Rosa Ponselle (the legendary diva came to a student recital at Cincinnati when Luisa was nineteen, praised her voice, signed a photo, where was it now?).

Next to the lumpy bed a nightstand, rickety, scarred wood where someone had stubbed out cigarettes. Empty of anything but her own red-and-black scarf. It hung wantonly, ends trailing on the dusty floor.

"Clio should know better, a Valentino scarf, you don't throw three-hundred-dollar scarves on the floor," she grumbled.

Of course Clio stopped working the day she cashed her last paycheck. No one had any loyalty in this business, it was all look out for number one, even if you found them in tears fighting deportation, took care of their legal battles with the immigration service—okay, Leo found the right lawyer and did the day-to-day work, but she made it happen, she recognized Clio's genius the day the Greek woman handled Luisa's quick change in—in—her head was one searing mass of pain, why wasn't Clio there with a massage, her French *cachets*—the only reliable headache cure. Even those stupid bitches who looked down their noses at her, Dame This, Dame That, agreed that Luisa's *cachets blancs* were better than Alka-Seltzer.

That little chemist on the Rue Charpentier, his sour face lighting up when she came into his shop, "*Bonjour,* Madame! All Paris misses you when you are gone, and from the burst of sun on the Seine this morning I knew you had returned! You need another order of *cachets blancs,* Madame? *Mordieu,* that you with the voice of an angel should suffer these torments, it is an injustice, but I will make it right for you."

If she could only get to Paris the little chemist wouldn't allow Leo or Harry or Clio to torment her as they were doing now. Piero would book her a seat to Paris. Piero was the one person who didn't yell at her when she talked to him. He was still under her spell, he'd fallen in love with her when he heard her sing Violetta in Houston, oh, that Sunday in his apartment overlooking Central Park, yes, I knew as soon as I heard the opening bars of "Sempre libera" that the audition would be a formality, they are eating from your hands, *carina,* not since Tebaldi made her debut here—I was a third assistant stage manager then, only twenty-five, but that voice! Yours is the first I've heard since that approaches her lyricism, although it's darker, richer, you should sing Aida, not Violetta, but if he didn't want her to drink so much champagne why did he keep pouring it for her?

It wasn't true that she was a drunk, people kept saying that, it was that bitch Cesarini who started the rumor because she wanted to sing Fenena when they revived *Nabucco* at Covent Garden and couldn't stand it when Luisa got the role. She started telling everyone Luisa drank, as if the opera world was some kind of Teetotalers' Paradise, if Luisa had a dime for every time she'd found someone backstage with a bottle or a bag of white powder she could have built herself a villa in Campania instead of that tiny apartment Harry kept screaming about, only eight rooms and not even a private beach, she'd had to share it with the condo next door.

Harry would never understand that you can't compete in the opera world without a pied-à-terre in Italy, bastard sold the apartment, furniture, everything without talking to her, used the money to pay some bills that he probably made up, or maybe were Karen's, Karen always harping on how Luisa ruined some stupid suit or other, some off-the-rack Donna Karan, when Galanos himself used to pin the fabric of her concert dresses at her fittings—it takes your genius to carry off this gown, Luisa, the two of us together are making a symphony of sight, eh, to go with the symphony of sound you produce—what did she care about Karen's petulance?

She stumbled to her feet looking for her purse. Besides the bed and nightstand the room held only a chair and a lopsided dresser with a small mirror, a circle just big enough for her to see her face. But not with those lines grooved from nose to chin, the light here was abominable, why had Leo picked such a terrible hotel? Where was she, anyway?

She was ill, flu, too many performances, she'd lost track of time and place, she thought she was in Chicago, staying at Harry's in between engagements, but this little room looked like the dreadful place the taxi driver had taken her to in Istanbul. All that confusion at the airport, she wanted to fire Leo for not having a limo there to meet her, for making her spend the night in a fleabag just like this place—it was far too late for her to be finding her way around a strange city and the idiot taxi had dumped her and torn off with a great screeching of wheels—but Piero talked her out of it, these mistakes happen, *carina,* and Leo is the best, the best for a woman of your moods and sensitivity, your voice, he soothed. And look where that got her—Leo yelling at her now every time she phoned him—if she could get him to speak to her at all. Hiding, telling that bitch who worked for him to say he was out all the time.

Her purse was in the top drawer of the bureau, but her address book wasn't there. Surely she knew Piero's number by heart, though, it was he she had phoned from that miserable Turkish delight, reeling his number off by heart to the international operator, sobbing her woes to him collect, everything fixed by magic.

She sat on the bed and stretched an autonomic hand for the receiver. And realized there was no phone. She scrambled around the room, but there was no phone anywhere, not even under the bed. Panic swept through her, covered rapidly by anger. No phone, and no bathroom. She, Madame Montcrief, was expected to dress in this tiny hovel, with only that shocking mirror that distorted her face, and no private bath? And where was her robe? Her fingers shook as she found her suitcase, Clio, or maybe Karen, had stuffed her clothes in any old way, they were wrinkled, her gold silk Ungaro blouse had a long stain down the front, someone used it as a floor mop by the looks of it. She dug out her makeup case and robe and staggered down the hall looking for a bathroom.

The hall smelled of old cabbage, but the bathroom, when she found it, smelled worse. She picked up a newspaper that someone had left on the back of the toilet and spread the sheets on the floor around the rust-stained tub. Her name jumped at her from an inside page.

How dare Leo let the press print lies about her? It was high time he started earning his commission, twenty-five percent and what did she get in return? A sordid rooming house and this—this slander.

Police were called yesterday to break up a brawl at Six-fifty South Wabash. Not between rival gangs or outraged Bulls fans, but between a diva and her students. Chicago native Luisa Montcrief, on indefinite leave of absence from the opera world because of health problems, was giving a rare master class at the Midwest Conservatory of Music which, according to those present, degenerated into an ugly physical confrontation. Faculty aren't commenting, but students say Montcrief's remarks were crude and personal, having little to do with vocal technique, and that she sang over student performances in a voice that was loud but seldom in tune. The class was finally terminated when Montcrief picked up a student's flute and threw it at a window. The shattering glass injured pregnant Mildred Gomez, walking underneath with her husband Albert, so badly that Gomez required twenty-two stitches in her scalp and neck. It was not possible to reach the diva. Her spokesmen in New York did not return calls to this paper.

Becca's fingers plaited into a knot. "But where did you take her?"

"Daddy found a room for her in the city. She can't stay here, Becca, you know that. When she was drunk only occasionally it wasn't so bad, but for the last six months it's turned into a nightly occurrence. None of us can go on like this, her least of all. If she has any voice left it's a miracle."

"But what will she live on?"

"Social security. Daddy's lawyer looked into it all for her." Karen lifted her daughter's chin in a gentle hand. "Darling, she spent all of her share of the money Grandpa Minsky left her and Daddy. Years ago. She spent all the money she ever made from singing. Leo Golub advanced her thousands of dollars on her recording earnings and he'll never get any of it back. Since she returned to Chicago last year Daddy has, well, let her have over forty thousand dollars. We can't afford to support her on the scale that she spends. And every time she shows up here in Highland Park it blows holes in my relationship with your father. The last straw was this master class she conducted down at the Midwest Conservatory."

"Just because she came home from it a little drunk—"

"It wasn't *just* because of that." Karen Minsky dropped her hand; her voice sharpened to the knifepoint Becca couldn't stand. "And throwing up in the hall is not a *little* drunk. She was outrageous: she broke a window, she yelled unbelievable swear words at the students. I will not let her in this house one more time. That is final."

"She's in an SRO, isn't she? You could have asked me. If you don't want her here I'd let her live on my trust fund so she wouldn't have to be in a place like that."

"Darling, we're hoping if no one rescues her she'll finally realize she needs treatment. Dr. Hanaper told us tough love is the only solution to someone who is denying her problems the way your aunt is. And be honest: you don't like your friends here when she shows up, you told me that last week after she draped herself around Corie in the living room."

"But where is she? Where have you dumped her?"

The patience lines around Karen's mouth tightened. "We didn't dump her, darling. Your father found a place that she can afford on her social security."

"Money, money, that's all you and Daddy care about, you don't care that she's an artist, she's too sensitive to survive in an SRO." Becca, hiccuping with sobs, fled the kitchen so that her mother couldn't make her admit she was being unreasonable.

9

Bible Study

Rafe Lowrie asked—told?—me to come to a Wednesday night prayer session so I could see what he—in his words, what the Spirit—is trying to accomplish with women at H House. Stange experience—my only other experience of Christian church at weddings of friends, & those always formal occasions, with set ritual.

Rafe's meeting free-form prayer and Bible study, stressing a personal God who's wrapped up in individual lives and concerns. That certainty seems both ridiculous and enviable to me. How nice it must be to think that someone in the Universe cares about the hairs on your head. From where I sit it looks like a bleak and random place. Jesus save us from homelessness or rape, and if he doesn't, well, God's ways are not ours.

The ancients used to cast lots to find out what they had done to displease the gods. If you were Jonah and unlucky they threw you overboard where you were swallowed by a whale, but the great storm was stilled and everyone else was saved. Today they're doing the same thing, but in a less direct way: God is smiting us because of pregnant teenagers, or welfare mothers, or feminists or queers. Cast all those overboard and the seas of the Republic will be quiet again.

Lowrie's daughter came along to hand out Bibles, do whatever else the great man deems too menial for his own hands. She directed women to their seats, went around trying to hush ones who were carrying on private conversations. Stoop-shouldered, face drawn down, looked much older than nineteen (of course learned her age from Jacqui!).

The class or meeting or whatever it was began with Lowrie praying. His voice is hoarse after yelling all day in the commodities pits.

"Jesus, send Your Holy Spirit so that we may understand the Word You have given us. Make us worthy to receive that Word, let it lead our feet in the paths of righteousness for Your name's sake. Lord, many come to You like the woman in the Book of Joel, who sold her daughter for a bottle of wine, and then drank it, and yet even for her God promises salvation if she truly repents. Others are like the man in the tombs of Gerasenes, so violent from the force of the demons who possessed him that he could not be held even with chains, and yet through faith and through prayer the Lord cast out these demons.

"Let us pray that the Holy Spirit who already makes Himself felt and known within us, will empower us to cast out demons, for with faith are all things possible, even the curing of disease that baffles medical wisdom." Rafe concluded his prayer and opened his eyes to address the women on the subject of the Gospel's healing power. "Remember the woman in Mark's Gospel? She had a flow of blood that lasted twelve years, and spent all the money she had on physicians who were unable to cure her. Yet she had only to lay her hands in faith on Jesus' robes for the bleeding to stop."

Hector felt himself flush with anger. Lowrie had clearly insisted on Hector's coming to show him, or the women, or both, that psychiatry was not welcome at the Orleans Street Church.

"Some of you come here in torment, torment worse than that woman's in the Gospel, and you think that the power of medicine may heal you. But what has that power done for you, other than to take your money and send you into the streets, just as it did to her? And just as the mere touch of the robes of the Lord was enough to cure her, where doctors and their science had failed, so if you truly believe that the Holy Spirit is among us, you may also be made whole."

Don't know why Lowrie should feel competitive with me. I'm a struggling resident, working seventy hours a week for thirty-eight thousand a year, just enough to make my debt payment schedule for med school, rent on a four-room apt, no family (not forgetting Lily's presence looming over me) while he has a successful career, children, gracious living in one of those lofty apartments on Elm Street.

Jacqui, of course, gave me all these details before the prayer meeting. Asked her how she knew so much about my life, Lowrie's.

She threw back her head and laughed. "You think I'm psychic, Doctor? I'm only homeless, and black: you can't be more invisible than that in America. People talk around me, they think they're talking to the furniture. But why Rafe Lowrie is an unhappy man, that I can't tell you, not without I really was psychic. Maybe Jesus is trying his soul for some reason. But Jesus doesn't talk to me the way he talks to Brother Rafe."

"Thank You, Lord, yes, Lord," Cynthia Lowrie muttered at intervals. Some of the other women chimed in more loudly. "Yes, Jesus," "Praise Jesus," they murmured as Lowrie continued to badger them in his rasping voice.

Others, like Jacqui, sat expressionless. Hector wanted to think that Jacqui shared his distaste for the proceedings, but he had no idea what her beliefs were.

Madeleine Carter, the woman from the wall, was sitting between Jacqui and Nanette. Although the Prolixin Hector had given her calmed her most extreme symptoms, she still twitched badly. Her lips moved incessantly as she communed with presences invisible to Hector. Perhaps Brother Rafe, his mind attuned to the spiritual, knew what voices Madeleine heard. If he did, Rafe would no doubt dismiss them as demons, but what if they came from angels?

Looking at Madeleine's gray skin, the sharp points of bone in her cheeks and wrists—all of her body that was visible outside her swaddling of sweaters and dresses—Hector wished he'd given her a vitamin injection along with the antipsychotic drug. At least she'd left her wall for the evening.

"And the woman taken in adultery"—Lowrie had moved on to sexual themes while Hector's mind was wandering. "Jesus tells us that whoever is without sin may cast the first stone. Well, we become free of sin when we wrap ourselves in the mantle of His blood."

Making us free to throw stones? Hector wondered. The words set up other associations in Madeleine's mind.

"Jezebel's blood splattered on the wall," she cried, her hands kneading her outermost skirt. "The Holy Mother tried to speak through Jezebel but no one would listen. But She's at the wall now. We can all go there now and drink Her blood and be healed."

"Sh-sh." Jacqui took one of Madeleine's agitated hands and held it firmly. "No one wants to go out tonight, honey. We're going to stay here and sleep. But, Brother Rafe, maybe you could tone down talk about blood: it upsets Sister Madeleine here."

Brother Rafe narrowed his eyes: he is the only one in charge here. During the day tames the wild futures markets; at night tames the wild homeless women. Then presumably goes home to rule his children. The one who's here tonight looking white and terrified just at Jacqui's simple intervention. There's someone who could benefit from some therapy, but suppose it's pointless to suggest it.

Rafe decided to let Jacqui's challenge rest—maybe a little afraid of what Madeleine might do if he stirred her up too much. Instead grabbed M's hands and started to pray for her healing, but she didn't want to be touched uninvited, expecially by a man. She backed off, started to cry. Before I could jump in Nanette took her to one side, talked her down, while Rafe asked all the women to pray for their sister, that her demons might be cast out.

Guess he saw he was losing authority, so he quickly turned to a Bible lesson, out of First Samuel, where Hannah is praying for a son:

And Eli said to her, "How long will you be drunken? Put away your wine from you." But Hannah answered, "No, my lord, I am a woman sorely troubled; I have drunk neither wine nor strong drink, but I have been pouring out my soul before the Lord."

Lowrie wanted women to discuss the verse, to show them that God does not want women to drink. When I was growing up, Mom hated that passage, always read at High Holy Day services. Why are these women praying for sons, she would snarl at Dad and me on the way home. I'd give both of you for a daughter and throw in the dog as a bonus.

Felt a horrible helplessness as Lowrie directed and dissected Samuel. Of course it would be better if these women didn't drink or use drugs, but it seems so manipulative to take one passage out of context and use it to hammer on the homeless. Why not take up Isaiah instead. Not knowledgeable about the Bible myself—haven't even been to services since last Yom Kippur with Lily before coming west to school—but looked up "homelessness" in a Bible dictionary at the hospital library this afternoon, and Isaiah says God wants us to take the homeless poor into our houses! What would happen if I brought that up here at the church?

Couldn't get into a pissing contest with Lowrie on the Bible, although he kept looking at me off and on as if daring me to challenge him. Hate the feeling of voicelessness, or castration maybe it is, from not standing up to bullies, to Hanaper or Abraham Stonds, now Lowrie.

Just when I thought I couldn't endure his platitudes a second longer, and the women were shifting restlessly in their seats, some of them automatically whispering "thank you, Lord, yes, Lord," a newcomer showed up.

The group in the activities room could hear Patsy Wanachs, the shelter director, talking to a woman outside the door, and then the newcomer's rich voice, slurred from drink.

"Bible study? How quaint. No, no, I wouldn't dare inarupt praying women. The leader is a Bible expert? Then must ask his perfesh—professional opinion about something."

Luisa Montcrief appeared in the doorway of the meeting room, Patsy Wanachs at her elbow. "Brother Rafe? I'm sorry to interrupt, but this is a newcomer, Luisa Montcrief. She says she wants to sit in on your

session, but I've warned her that she isn't allowed to create a disturbance."

"Everyone who is striving for understanding is welcome here.
Come in, Sister—Luisa, is it?—and sit down."

Luisa was dressed as a parody of a diva, in a black silk suit whose
skirt had slit up one seam, black stockings that were a mass of ladders, and
a gold blouse soiled with food and a dried trail of vomit. She lurched on
her way in, and Hector saw that the bottom of one of her high heels had
broken off. Alcohol had flushed her cheeks and brought an angry glitter
to her eyes.

She swept over to Rafe Lowrie. "You in charge here? King Ahashu-
erus with his docile harem? You're an expert on the Bible, I understand."

Lowrie smiled. "Not an expert. Someone struggling to comprehend
it along with the other seekers in the room. Cynthia, get Sister Luisa into
a seat and give her a Bible so she can follow along in First Samuel. We're
discussing alcohol and women; you would benefit greatly from the text."

"Ah, yes. Alcohol and the Bible."

Luisa was very drunk; she almost fell when she leaned over the table
to pick up one of the cheaply bound Bibles the church had donated to
the shelter. She spoke more clearly than most people would at her stage
of drunkenness—after years on the stage good diction was automatic—
but Hector thought Lowrie was underestimating how close she was to
blacking out. She lurched to a chair, lost her balance and fell to the floor.

"The Bible and drunks, yes. Do not look upon the wine when it is
red. Isn't that in there someplace? You should stick to chardonnay." She
rocked with laughter.

"Sister Luisa!" Lowrie snapped. "Get up from the floor and sit in a
chair. If you can't listen with respect to what we're trying to do here, get
out."

Luisa cast him a reproachful look but climbed to her feet and managed to perch on one of the folding chairs. "I respect what you're saying.
Alcohol and the Bible. Lot's daughters, getting him drunk so he could
commit incest with impurity. Not impurity. Im—what's the word I
mean? Anyway, he wouldn't get punished. He gets to do what he wants

without getting punished. That's a beautiful story. If you're a man and in the Bible you get to do what you want and they make you a saint, but if you're a woman they banish you. Isn't that right, Mr. Preacher?"

Some of the women shifted uneasily, but one said, "She's telling it, Jesus."

"Cynthia, what are you doing just chewing on your hair? Get over there and quiet this woman down," Lowrie commanded.

His daughter, flushed with misery, stumbled over to Luisa. "We're not doing Genesis tonight. Let's look at what's in Samuel. It's an interesting book, too, don't you think?"

Luisa let Cynthia open the Bible to the relevant passage, but her outburst had upset the other women. One named Caroline, who'd been thumbing through her Bible looking up Lot, cried out, "Here it is, here's the place she's talking about, where Sodom and Gomorrah get destroyed, and oh my, look, first Lot was going to throw his daughters to the mob. Let the mob rape his own daughters just to keep them from attacking his house. Then he rapes them himself, pretending he's drunk and doesn't know what he's doing. How do you like that? What kind of Bible lesson is that?"

"And Jezebel." Madeleine stood up in her agitation. "They fed Jezebel to the dogs. Her blood splashed on the wall and they didn't care. The Mother of God weeps tears of blood, Her blood comes out of the wall, but nobody cares."

She started to cry. "I have to go back, I've left Her too long. The Holy Mother will think I'm like all the others, that I don't care what happens to Her."

Hector sprang to his feet and followed her from the room. "Madeleine, the Holy Mother knows you love Her day and night. And if She loves you, She wants the best for you. Isn't the best for you right now to let me take you to the hospital for a rest?"

"I'm not going, you can't make me leave Her. I never should have left Her tonight."

"Then let me give you another injection," Hector urged. "It will make you calmer."

"I don't want a shot, when you gave me that shot I couldn't hear Her so well. It made Her angry, that I was trying to turn away from Her."

Jacqui and Nanette came into the hallway. "Madeleine, you can't go back out there tonight. It's dark, it's too dangerous for you and we want to stay here to rest. You know there's a bed here for you tonight. You could even take a shower. Stay here with us."

Madeleine wrenched her hand from Nanette's and ran down the hall and out the door. Hector started after her.

"What are you going to do?" Jacqui demanded. "You can't make her come back. You can't force her to go to the hospital if she doesn't want to, even assuming they'd let her have a bed, which the word on Midwest Hospital is, most definitely not. It's only a mile and a half to that wall: she'll make it."

"I've had enough of Brother Rafe's preaching, although that drunk who just showed up is making the place more interesting," Nanette said. "Only I don't like watching Patsy Wanachs throw people out, and that's what's going to happen next. I'm going to get me a cup of coffee. You want one, Doctor?"

Under the shelter's rules, beds were available from ten o'clock until six the next morning. Until Bible study finished, no one could watch TV, because the class was held in the shelter's activities room, where television, art projects, and such games as the church didn't think involved gambling took place. If someone didn't care for Bible study, her only choice was not to come to the shelter until ten—when all the beds might already be allotted—or to sit in the refectory with a cup of coffee under the gaze of a bored volunteer, assigned to make sure the women didn't ransack the pantry.

Hector went back to the doorway of the activities room. Caroline, who'd found the passage where Lot slept with his daughters, was arguing with Rafe about the meaning of the passage he'd selected from First Samuel.

"It doesn't say women shouldn't drink, only that this priest, this Eli, thought Hannah was drunk."

"But we know if the word is in the Bible it is the true word of God, and a guide for us," Rafe said. "And it's clear that God, through Eli, is condemning drunkenness in women very specifically."

"But drunkenness in men is all right." Luisa, who'd been lolling on her chair, picking at the threads in her stockings, sat up. "When Shahwerwus—Shawer—Hasherus sent for Vashti you'd better believe he'd been drinking, yes, sir, golden goblets for the king. But she gets sent away and is condemned forever for not wanting to go to this drunk. Is this right, should she have to let him fuck her when he's drunk? It's not fair. Are you saying it's fair, you holy roller, whatever your name is, for kings to get drunk, but women can't?"

Lowrie's smile became fixed with the glue of anger. "The Bible is the just word of God. But it is never right for anyone to get drunk, least of all for you to show up here drunk and disrupt this class. If you cannot be—"

"Who's saying I'm drunk?" Luisa was on her feet, swaying. "It's that bitch Cesarini, isn't it, jealous because they wouldn't let her sing Fenena in Covent Garden—"

Patsy Wanachs shoved her way past Hector into the room. "Luisa! Come with me."

The shelter director grabbed Luisa's hand and yanked her into the hall. "I suggested that you might not be ready for Bible study, but you insisted you wanted to attend, that you wouldn't disrupt the meeting. Now look what's happened: Madeleine Carter leaving the shelter in hysterics, everyone in the room in an uproar, all because of you.

"We have rules here, as I told you when you came in. One is against drunkenness, two is against creating a disturbance. You've violated both of those. If you want to stay tonight you will sit quietly in the refectory until we can give you a bed. But if you ever return here in a drunken condition you will not be admitted. Do I make myself clear?"

"As a broken windowpane, my good woman." Luisa's disdain was hampered by her slurred consonants and her unsteady legs, but she followed the director down the hall to the refectory.

Hector decided he, too, had heard all he could take of Brother

Rafe's preaching. He made his way past the homeless women drifting into the shelter, some with shopping carts, most with all their belongings slung over their backs in plastic bags.

He sat in his car for a long time. A man came to the gate at one point and became furious at being denied admission. He stormed around and swore, threw a bottle at the fence, stomped down the street, then came back and tried to muscle his way through the gate in company with some of the entering women. One of the volunteers came out. Hector thought her very brave, to confront the man in person, but whatever she said was effective: he left the gate and took up observation across the street.

After Hector had been sitting for half an hour, Luisa lurched out. She was singing, in a very loud voice, "Sempre libera," Violetta's first-act aria from *La Traviata*.

10

Down for the Count

HARRIET FIRST LEARNED about the woman at the wall the day Mrs. Ephers had her heart attack. That's why she didn't bring her usual energy to the problem. The senior partners at Scandon and Atter couldn't believe it when the president of the Hotel Pleiades complained to them: Harriet had always given both clients and firm what they wanted in the past; no one could believe she wasn't doing it now.

"I E-mailed Harriet as soon as I heard about the situation," the hotel president told his superiors in the Olympus Hotel Group during one of those endless meetings corporations convene to avoid action and assign blame. "Apparently the garage people had a complaint earlier, got operations involved. They had the cops remove the woman once, but when she reappeared, Brian Cassidy at the garage thought corporate had decided she could stay as long as she kept a low profile. But that night . . ."

That night Luisa got thrown out of Hagar's House for breaking up the Bible study class. She leaned against the gate, muttering to herself, but when a man walked by, said, what's a fox like you doing out here alone? looks like you could use some company, she flagged a cab. In the dark the driver could see her imperious hand and the outlines of her expensive suit, not the torn and dirty details.

When the cab dropped her at Michigan and Wacker the driver was furious to discover she had no money. Leaving his car where he stopped—blocking two lanes of traffic—he jumped out to chase her. A horrible screech of metal on metal made him turn around: a bus had ripped off his open door.

A policeman strolled over from the far corner, demanding to know what the hell the driver meant, leaving his cab in the middle of the road. By the time he explained he'd been stiffed, Luisa had disappeared underground.

Those two homeless women had been very kind in their way. The diva clutched the railing to keep from tripping on the stairs. Philistines, not recognizing Violetta's great aria when Luisa started to sing it in the refectory, but sympathetic with her plight when that bitch who gave herself airs because she had a title objected to Luisa's impromptu concert. How pathetic people were in their neediness. Why should Luisa bow and scrape to a director of a homeless shelter, when her own name had been on dressing rooms in Milan and London? But when that idiot, that Warlocks or whoever she was, forced Luisa to leave, the two homeless women followed her to the door. The black one wrote down directions to a makeshift shelter they sometimes used on Underground Wacker.

A canceled engagement, was that it? Harry and Karen not home, was that it? For some reason she was in Chicago without a place to stay. She'd had a room, some wretched hovel that Harry shoved her into, always jealous of her, she couldn't even remember why, it went back so far into their childhood, and then something went wrong with the room. She was locked out, the ugly man at the desk demanding money for her to stay on. She explained that she never handled money, her manager did that, gave him Leo's number in New York, but he refused to call. Said he wasn't going to rack up a long-distance bill that she couldn't pay, but when she got her social security check on Tuesday she could come back, pay up, he'd hang on to her clothes until then. As if she would ever darken his doorstep again!

After that, she couldn't remember what happened. Needing a drink to steady her, not true that she was a drunk as that priss-ass Bible thumper was saying tonight, obviously listening to the gossip Cesarini and Donatelli were spreading about her, doesn't make you a drunk just because you want a little brandy when some oily Brown Shirt locks you out of your own room.

Finding a man who would part with some cash . . . No, cunt, I didn't pay to hear you sing, spread your legs, she must have seen that in a movie someplace, that hadn't happened to her, but she got the price of a quart. The woman at the liquor store was so rude, had to see her money before she'd even bring a bottle down from the shelf. Fat with three hairs on her chin, shave before you touch my bottle, Luisa said, I don't want to catch lice from you, and the woman so hostile, you're lucky I don't touch you over the head with this bottle, you drunken whore.

Chicago was a horrible city. Why had she come back here? Harry sold her beautiful little apartment in Campania, just because her account at Banco di Roma was the teeniest bit overdrawn, and she told the manager her brother was rich, he'd take care of the problem. And then Harry showed up in Italy, bellowing, not helpful at all. He was like all men, greedy, wanting money more than anything, how terrible for Becca to be growing up with a father like that.

And now here was this revolting taxi driver swearing at her. "My good man, it's been your privilege to carry the world's greatest soprano in your car. It is something you can tell your grandchildren, if any woman would ever come close enough to your ugly body to allow you to procreate." And then he was chasing her down the street.

She had to laugh when the door came off his cab, serve him right for swearing at her. When the cop came over, she should have gone and explained why the man deserved to be arrested. . . . But some survival instinct made her scuttle underground instead.

When she got to the bottom of the stairs she was supposed to go straight ahead along Wacker, then turn right at the second roadway. The black woman had written it all down for her on a napkin, so kind, even in Chicago you could still find enormous love for opera among the common people. Not like in Copenhagen or Berlin, of course, but heartening when the world seemed bent on burying her alive.

Turning into the second entryway she stopped, rage flooding her brain. A woman was waiting for her. Humiliating her. A mock stage set for *Otello*. Candles lit, a portrait of the Madonna between them, the woman kneeling before the portrait in ecstasy, no doubt singing *"Ave Maria, nell'ora della morte."*

Luisa lunged forward. "Who sent you here? Was it Leo or that stupid tenor, couldn't stand being upstaged, badmouthed me to the *New York Times*? Did those two homeless bitches set me up?"

She assumed a mock bass that bounced off the high concrete overpass. " 'Just go down below Michigan, Luisa: we have a crib you can hang out in.' And all the time waiting to set me up."

The woman in front of the Madonna screamed. "Don't come near me, Jezebel, the dogs will eat me if they see you near me."

Luisa whirled, lost her balance, sprawled in the street. "Where are the cameras? Where are all you paparazzi, panting to— You want to show me—show me—you hate me, I'm the best that ever was, Piero Benedetti said so, he heard my Violetta, *carissima,* that voice, that presence, I won't make you a queen—you are one already—but I will make the world acknowledge your majesty, he said that to me, not to Cesarini, or Donatelli, everyone knows she has to be miked to sing, but not me, not even in Covent Garden."

She lay in the road, howling. A car coming out of the Hotel Pleiades' garage almost hit her. The owner jumped out.

"You stupid bitch! What are you doing lying in the road like that?"

Luisa continued to sob. The man kicked her, tried to force her to the gutter.

"Don't do that." A small crowd had gathered, a few late workers waiting for their bus and some theatergoers on their way to collect their cars; one of the women shook off her husband's restraining hand to lecture the driver. "What if this woman is hurt? We ought to call an ambulance. Patrick—go into the garage and see if they'll phone 911."

The driver of the car ignored the theatergoer and yelled down at Luisa, "I ought to run over you, drunken cunt, get out of the street!"

He got back in his car and leaned on the horn. Luisa didn't move. Where was Leo, her lawyer, the police? She sniffled. The man reversed with a great squeal of rubber, revved his engine and drove forward, missing Luisa by a few inches.

As the honking went on Madeleine began to wail. "The Mother of God hates that sound. It's an abomination. She will punish you, She will rain curses of black blood on you for desecrating Her home."

The onlookers edged away from both Madeleine and Luisa. The three people waiting for a bus decided to go to upper Michigan and hail a cab, while the woman who'd initially intervened agreed with her husband that they were in over their heads—collect the car and head for home, besides, the baby-sitter needs to be relieved.

The parking attendants were already standing at the mouth of the garage, drawn by Luisa's diatribe, when night manager Brian Cassidy appeared. The honking hadn't roused him: it was commonplace in the city, but one of the hotel guests, waiting for a car, had come in to complain about the chaos outside.

"I always stay at the Pleiades because I feel safe here, but this kind of street warfare is intolerable. What am I supposed to do? Wear a bullet-proof vest just to come down to get my car?"

"Is not so bad, Mr. Cassidy," one of the attendants said. "No one shooting, no one has gun, only two poor drunken ladies, or maybe they crazy. They hurting no one, only man, driver, too much angry, almost run over that one."

"I want an escort up to the lobby," the angry guest said. "It's not safe down here. I don't want to be jumped by some street person."

"The elevators are inside the garage, ma'am, and they're secure. Why don't you let Nicolo here escort you to the lobby? He'll make sure no one's lurking in the elevator."

Nicolo flashed a smile, offered the woman his arm, but she refused to be mollified. Safe in her room she wrote out a detailed complaint, including how much business her company sent to the Olympus Group's hotels during a year and how she expected to be protected from incidents of this kind. Okay, maybe she fudged a few points. Maybe in her version the driver didn't kick Luisa and almost run the diva over; maybe in the angry businesswoman's story the woman at the wall started raining curses

on her, on all the guests at the garage. But that wasn't lying, it was only
an effort to make the hotel president see how serious the problem was.

At the garage Brian Cassidy ordered two of the attendants to pull
Luisa out of the road and stick her around the corner, out of sight of any
more hotel guests. The diva had passed out by then, and although she
hadn't eaten well for months, hers was a dead weight. The men grunted
as they shifted her down the roadway. They propped her against the
Westinghouse box, next to a man sucking on a can of Colt 45.

11

Past Upheaval

GIAN PALMETTO, president of the Hotel Pleiades, wants to know why they haven't heard back from their expensive lawyer at Scandon and Atter. Secretary phones secretary late in the day: a family emergency has summoned Ms. Stonds from the office.

Palmetto comes on the line in person—Sorry if Harriet has a personal crisis, but he needs advice, urgently, on how to dislodge a homeless woman from the sidewalk outside his garage. He spoke briefly to Harriet this morning; she promised to get on it. Will Harriet's secretary, for Christ's sake, find someone who knows what steps she's taken? No one knows? Surely Harriet isn't dragging her feet because she thinks the hotel mistreated her sister?

The secretary doesn't think so . . . the police?

Thank you, yes, he's been to the police. The sidewalk being public property the city won't arrest the damned woman for trespassing. The cops could cart her elsewhere, but they won't put her in jail. Someone suggested threats: rough the woman up a bit. Scare her into moving on. He could hardly order a subordinate to do that (wouldn't mind if it happened, but these days he can't order it: some busybody would find his E-mail or report him to the ACLU. And then, phht!—good-bye, career). Gian Palmetto needs other options. Given the three hundred dollars an hour he pays Scandon and Atter for Harriet's advice he'd appreciate a little activity.

"What kind of emergency?" he asks, wanting only to know how soon she'll be back in the office. "I didn't know Harriet had a family."

"The Stonds housekeeper, who's been with them a long time, had a heart attack this afternoon."

Family emergency. This conjures up a child falling from a swing, not a housekeeper with a heart attack. Gian Palmetto is understandably furious when he hangs up. Especially after the report he's received on Harriet's younger sister from the Special Events director. He goes out of his way to find a job for the sorriest specimen who's ever worked at the Pleiades, including dishwashers and laundry maids, and then the lawyer stiffs him because her housekeeper is sick. In the full flood of his anger he dictates a letter to senior partner Leigh Wilton.

Really, few people even at Scandon and Atter knew Harriet had a family. So burnished was her professional armor, so tightly did she keep all personal feelings locked in a remote chest, that her co-workers didn't know she was an orphan, that the housekeeper was as close as she could come to naming a mother. Not for her the chitchat with secretaries or associates on family matters. When Leigh Wilton complained about the lack of direction his children had, and how his two older sons had moved back home, Harriet shook her head in sympathy, but didn't share horror stories of Mara dropping out of Smith, hanging around in her bedroom or at bars, barely holding down a dead-end job at the Pleiades, then getting fired from that.

Yes, the hotel fired Mara, on Wednesday afternoon. Mrs. Ephers had her heart attack on Thursday. Before that she'd been in perfect health, aside from the occasional cold.

"We didn't know she had any heart disease," Grandfather Stonds told the cardiologist.

Didn't know she had a heart, Mara muttered to herself. They blamed her, Grandfather and Harriet. What did you do to her, Grandfather demanded, because Mrs. Ephers refused to go to the hospital until the doorman promised her that Mara would be kept out of the apartment until the doctor got home.

"What did she tell you?" Mara yelled at Grandfather, grabbing his arm, shaking it despite his icy anger at her for jarring his operating hand. "Did she give you the letter? Did you see the photograph? Who is it?"

Mara, seeing herself as the ugly lurching Caliban of the Graham Street apartment, secretly agreed she had caused Mephers's illness. Although her getting fired didn't bring on the attack—that only confirmed Mara as a failure, after all. Maybe Mephers's heart beat a little faster, with pleasure at seeing Mara flounder, but that wouldn't cause damage to the muscle.

No, it was Mephers's fury when she found Mara in her room going through her papers. The housekeeper pulled Mara to her feet, slapped her so hard that Mara had a black eye for six days, and then collapsed, clutching her left arm but refusing to cry out. She was eighty: hauling a nineteen-year-old, especially one as big as Mara, was too much exertion for her.

"They weren't her papers," Mara tried to tell her sister. "She had a letter about Grannie from somebody in France. It was written to Mother. And a photograph of a man who looks just like you."

Harriet stared at her. "Mara, I can't believe with Mephers in the hospital, seriously ill, you can have the temerity to make up more stories about Beatrix. You are old enough to stop this kind of playacting."

"It's not—I'm not!" Mara's muddy skin turned mahogany in fury. "Mephers always said we didn't have any pictures or documents or anything about Mother. Well, there was a letter to Mother from someone in France. And that picture, I'm telling you, that picture looked like you in drag!"

"Mephers is really ill, Mara. Don't go bothering me with stuff about Beatrix. Mephers is the only mother I ever had, or you, for that matter. You should be worrying about whether she's going to get well, not making up stories about Beatrix and France. If Mephers hadn't been worrying about you she wouldn't have been vulnerable to an attack."

Mara gasped at the injustice of Harriet's accusation. "Worrying about me? She never worried about me a day in her life. When I came home on Wednesday I found her in my room, reading my journal."

Harriet gave her most tight-lipped, Mrs. Ephers–imitation smile.

"You came home drunk after being fired. I heard about it from the president of the Pleiades Hotel. Mephers says she was trying to make some order out of the scrap heap you leave in your room—your desk, I might point out, looks like an ill-run recycling center—when you came in and started screaming at her. You may well have fancied Mephers was reading your journal as a drunken hallucination. The less said on the subject the better."

Grandfather said Hilda couldn't rest comfortably until she knew her privacy would be inviolate during her absence. The building super brought a locksmith up to the apartment and supervised the installation of a new dead bolt in the fat oak door to Mrs. Ephers's room. The super gave duplicate keys to Grandfather and Harriet, shook his head sadly at Mara, with whom he used to share Snickers bars in his basement apartment while they watched the Cubs, and left.

No one wanted to hear Mara's version of events. Yes, she had been fired. Yes, she was drinking at lunch. She hated the job, hated the stupid way they had to answer the phone: "Hotel Pleiades, soaring to new heights, how may I help you?" hated clients who screamed because centerpieces held daisies instead of chrysanthemums, hated having to say "I'm sorry you're disappointed, ma'am: the daisies are so bright and fresh, and the florist tells me the only mums we could get now would be wilted," when she wanted to pick up the centerpiece and brain the carp-faced woman. She hated above all the pointlessness of her own life, and often persuaded one of the waiters to bring her a double bourbon to brace her for the afternoon.

It was two-thirty when Mara had her termination interview. Two-hour lunches were not part of the job description for junior assistants in the Special Events office. You've been warned twice, as a courtesy to Ms. Stonds, the personnel director said, we have no choice now but to let you go. Turn in your pass, collect a week's pay in lieu of notice.

Home, because she didn't know where else to go. Entering stealthily, hoping to avoid Mrs. Ephers, still able at eighty to hear the cleaning woman break a cup in the kitchen while lying down for her afternoon nap.

The housekeeper was in Mara's room, making use of Mara's absence at work to hunt out her journal and read it. When Mara crept in the two stared at each other in shock. Mara gasped and backed away. She left the apartment and didn't reappear until three the next morning, when the household was asleep.

Mrs. Ephers took especial pleasure in rousing her at seven that day. "You're going to be late for work, miss, if you don't get going."

"Mind your own damned business for a change," Mara said, turning over.

"None of that from you, young lady." The housekeeper marched to the bed and shook Mara. "Do you want me to bring in your grandfather?"

Mara pictured the doctor as a battering ram, wielded by Mephers to shove her out of bed. "I've been fired. I have no job to go to. Why don't you race into the dining room and share the news with him? Then the two of you can exclaim how I'm just like Beatrix, you knew it all along, you should have put me in foster care instead of lavishing all your warmth and sweetness on such an unpromising specimen."

The doctor summoned Mara to his study after breakfast. I'm going to overlook your shocking language to Hilda. I'm most disappointed in you, young lady, for getting fired. What do you propose to do with yourself? You know I'm not going to support you forever. I learned my lesson with your mother. No, young lady, I don't want to hear anything about Harriet: she was an orphan just like you, but she's made the most of her opportunities. If you want to go back to college, just say the word: I'm sure we can find a school, a good school, that will let you start over again. After all, you don't lack for intelligence. But otherwise you must find another job by the end of the month.

Or what, Mara wondered? Or Grandfather would throw her out? Would she join the woman at the wall on Underground Wacker?

Mara dressed and went to the coffee shop across the street from the apartment. She had the seasick feeling that comes from too much wine and too little sleep. Her hands shook as she carried the large bowl of coffee to a stool by the window.

At nine she watched Grandfather walk down the street toward the city. It was his pride to walk the two miles to the hospital every morning, even in the bitterest snow. Although seventy-seven, he still put in a full week on surgical consulting and teaching. He'd stopped heading surgical teams when he turned seventy-two, not because he was any less confident, but because he wanted to stop while he still knew his hand was sure.

Mara thought he would die if they made him leave the hospital, even though many of the younger doctors were tired of his heavy authority on their cases. She imagined the funeral, Mrs. Ephers flinging herself into the grave in hysteria, and Beatrix and Selena suddenly appearing, having read about the doctor's demise in the paper. They shared a bottle of champagne with Mara to celebrate and the three went off to live in the south of France.

Darling, we're so sorry we left you with those two gargoyles all these years, Grannie said. Mara couldn't come up with a compelling reason for why her mother and grandmother, happily living together in this scenario, hadn't come for her sooner. Or how to overcome the published reports of Selena's death, although maybe Grandfather had forced the papers to print them—he had a lot of influence in Chicago.

Mara was on her third coffee, shaking now from the combination of caffeine and sleep deprivation, when Mrs. Ephers left the apartment, heading for the market at the hour when fish and produce would be freshest. Mara waited five minutes, in case Mrs. Ephers had forgotten something, not that the perfectly organized iron maiden ever did, and crossed the street again to the apartment.

Raymond, the doorman, who had known her since she was three, smiled and held the lobby door open in a grand gesture. "Not working today, Mara?"

Mara only smiled in return and hurried to the elevator. If Mrs. Ephers thought Mara's journal worth hunting out, maybe it was because she had desperate secrets of her own that she was trying to conceal. That inspiration came to Mara when she was drinking at Corona's, a jazz club on Kinzie, around midnight. What if the housekeeper really was Harriet's mother, for instance? Grandfather and Mephers having a fling in the master bedroom, Harriet conceived when the housekeeper was forty-eight—stranger things have happened.

The elevator opened onto the Stonds's private vestibule. Most people in the eight-story building left their front doors open during the day, figuring that Raymond and the locked elevator were sufficient deterrents even in these difficult times, but Mrs. Ephers believed that was an invitation to theft. Mara undid the locks and stopped in the entry hall to listen. Barbara, the cleaning woman, was busy in the kitchen.

Mara took off her shoes and slipped into the housekeeper's room. This was sacrilege, like jumping rope in the Garden of Gethsemane, for no one was ever allowed into Mrs. Ephers's private room, not even Harriet, unless especially invited. Mara's shiver of excited fear dispelled her seasickness.

Harriet's face stared at Mara, from the wall by the bed where she stood larger than life in her law school robes, from the dresser where she was ice-skating, dancing as the fairy queen in fourth grade, graduating from high school, riding her pony. The doctor joined his granddaughter and Mrs. Ephers on the nightstand at her Smith graduation. Mara wasted precious time searching for herself. Two cabinet photos, one at her own high school graduation, one formally groomed for her fourth birthday, grinning at the camera, wearing a blue velvet dress that she could still remember, the color of Harriet's eyes. Her own longing for blue eyes and cornsilk hair washed over her as if she were four again and fingering the fabric.

"You stupid fool," she whispered to her four-year-old face. "Why were you laughing while you waited to be slapped down, made a fool of?"

She picked up the silver frame, one of her own Christmas gifts to Mrs. Ephers, and put it on the floor where she was going to stomp on it, forgetting for a moment her stocking feet. Fear of Mrs. Ephers, the feeling that the housekeeper would know if she made the slightest mark in the room, let alone removed a picture, made her pick it up and replace it, next to the one of Harriet's tenth birthday party, a crowd of white-clad girls with balloons on the yacht of one of Dr. Stonds's important patients.

A dark-red secretary stood in one corner, its writing surface empty. Mrs. Ephers was no reader—a Bible, an old edition of Edna St. Vincent Millay, and a library biography of Queen Victoria stood rigidly to attention on the windowed shelves.

Mara glanced briefly in the drawers, where Harriet's school reports were neatly laid, next to old books of household accounts. She looked for her own report cards but couldn't find them. Her mouth puckered in hurt. She slammed the drawer shut, took a pin from the cushion on Mrs. Ephers's dressing table and dug a deep scratch along the secretary's glossy writing surface. Take that, you horrid old bag.

Mara slid open the dresser drawers, patted the underwear—white or beige, cotton briefs, formidable brassieres like breastplates—the neat stacks of cardigans, nightgowns—cotton for summer, flannel for winter—hard to imagine her seducing Grandfather Stonds in those.

The image of Mephers as Harriet's mother receded along with Mara's excitement. Her headache began to return and she started to feel ashamed. She heard Barbara slipslopping down the hall in her mules, and the door closing. Barbara left for the day at two. Had Mara been in here three hours? No. Barbara must be on her way to the cleaners, or some such errand.

Mara went to rub spit into the scratch she'd dug on the secretary. Now she'd really catch hell. She started to sniffle, unloved orphan, fired from her job, and now in deeper trouble for ruining a valuable piece of furniture.

As she rubbed she must have pressed a recessed catch; a drawer suddenly opened in the middle of the writing surface. Her self-pity vanished. Just like Nancy Drew: *The Secret of the Housekeeper's Secretary.* The girl detective doesn't hesitate but dives headfirst into the cache and pulls out a small bundle of papers.

On top was an old manila envelope addressed to *Mademoiselle, la Fille de Mme Selena Vatick Stonds,* in ink that had turned brown with age. Blue and gold stamps glowed brilliantly against the paper. Mara took it to the window: France. The postmark was blurred, so she couldn't read the date or town.

She sat down at the secretary and pulled out the contents, nervous about what she might find. There was a letter in French, in the same browning ink, addressed, like the envelope, to the daughter of Selena. Mara had neglected French in high school. Now she cursed herself for ignoring Grandfather's strictures: French the only language of a truly civilized person, speak it at mealtime until you show mastery. Mara had chosen instead to study Japanese, but much good that did her now.

She stumbled through the first few sentences. *Dear Mademoiselle Stonds, I am a woman very old and very something else, and the time for something is long past.* Selena Vatick Stonds and Nippur figured in the next paragraph, but Mara couldn't tell what they were up to. Frustrated, she wondered if she dare take the letter away to photocopy, but what if Mephers checked her cache every night? Said her prayers: Lord deliver me from Mara and deliver the doctor into my bed, and then fondled this letter to Beatrix?

Maybe Mara could copy the gist of it, to worry over later with a dictionary. She took it to the desk and turned on a light. That was when the picture slipped from between the pages, a black-and-white photo of a blond, with the kind of ironic smile women sold their souls for. He was wearing a tweedy double-breasted jacket cut in the style of the fifties.

What struck Mara more than the smile and the probable age of the picture was his resemblance to Harriet. She held the picture next to Harriet in her law school robes. The man's cheeks were broader, but around the eyes and nose the likeness was startling.

Mara jumped as Mephers dropped her purse in the doorway. "Just what are you doing in here, young lady?"

"Who is this man? How come you have this letter, when it was written to Mother?" Mara screamed. "What happened to Mother? You know where she is, don't you?"

The housekeeper snatched the picture from Mara, stuffed it into her bosom. When Mara lunged for it, Mrs. Ephers grabbed her and yanked her to her feet, slapped her hard enough to give the girl a black eye, then fell against the bed, clutching her own left arm. Her face turned a waxy gray and her breath came in shallow bursts.

"Get out of here," she whispered hoarsely. "Get out of here and call the doctor."

12

Are You Washed in the Blood?

Jacqui and Nanette waiting for me at the Orleans St. Church clinic this afternoon, troubled about Madeleine. Not because of visions or voices, but harassment. Seems her Wall is part of the foundation for the Pleiades Hotel, one of those ultramodern, pricey places that've cropped up east of Michigan near the river. I've never noticed it, but apparently hotel garage is close by M's vision. Management doesn't want homeless women ranting about the Virgin—or anything else—to disturb the slumber of any incumbent. Jacqui says last night hotel hosed down the Wall during the evening when M was sitting there.

So much wanted just to go home, go to bed for an hour before starting weekend on-call shift. Read once that you sleep in bits and pieces when you're overtired, even standing up or while talking to people. Wonder if that's what I'm doing with patients these days—often seem to get only fragments of their complaints.

I like Jacqui, but worry, too, she'll turn on me the way Mom used to: look at me when I'm talking to you, Hector—we named you for the bravest of all the Trojans, well, your father is always off on some engineering junket to the Middle East, it's time you acted up to your name and behaved like the man around the house. So I did her bidding. Jacqui's, that is, although almost always Lily's as well.

After his last patient shuffled out, around six-thirty, Hector went with Jacqui and Nanette to the wall. Madeleine was kneeling in front of her crack, weeping over her treasures. The hosing had turned her photo of the Virgin into a sodden mess. She was trying to dry her Bible over the open flame of a candle, but Hector doubted it could be saved—the pages were gummed together like a Kleenex that's been through the laundry.

When Hector went over to talk to her, she shrank back against the wall. He saw that the blanket she knelt on was also damp. He tried not to recoil from the smell of mold and must that rose from it, and gently asked if he could check her pulse. Although her eyes dilated and her breath came faster, she did let him hold her wrist. The pulse was feathery and irregular; he worried that she might have caught a chill from her dousing; her usual agitation seemed enhanced by fever.

As he was trying to talk to Madeleine, a man wearing a suit and tie came over to them. His enormous forearms strained his jacket sleeves. He introduced himself as Brian Cassidy, night manager of the hotel's garage.

"Are you responsible for this woman?" Cassidy demanded.

Hector said, "No. She's quite ill, but like all adults, she's responsible for herself. Are you the man who turned a hose on her last night?"

"I'm in charge of the garage. That includes keeping the street clean so that our guests are comfortable walking here."

"You destroyed her icon and her Bible. Was that essential for hotel hygiene?"

Unconsciously Hector's voice took on some of his mother's sarcastic inflection; the garage manager bristled defensively and leaned forward. "We asked her to move but she refused. I didn't have any choice, since I had to clean the wall and the sidewalk there."

Jacqui pointed at coffee cups and paper bags gray-brown with dirt that were packed along the curb. "Seems to me there's a lot of debris right in front of your garage. You going to get that garbage cleaned up tonight, or you need one of us homeless folk to sit there before the street looks dirty to you?"

The garage manager looked at her for the first time: until she spoke she hadn't been human.

Only I existed for him—because I'm white? A man? Well dressed? Anyway, he trotted out those tired old phrases of "following orders." All these years after Eichmann you'd think people would squirm in agony to hear themselves say it, but he seemed to think it was the most wholesome reason in the world for hosing down a homeless woman.

"Can't she move around to the other side?" Cassidy said. "We know she's sleeping there in that Westinghouse box, but it's not on our property, our guests can't see it, so we try to look the other way. We're not monsters here."

Jacqui and I put it to Madeleine. She got very agitated.

"I have to sit on the north side. It's written that the weeping women sit at the north gate. It's written in here—" flapping her damp Bible at me. "I have to stay here. This is where the Virgin is crying."

Felt acutely embarrassed to be associated with her, even in the eyes of the garage man. And that in turn embarrassed me more: mine is supposed to be a profession of empathy. I tried to shut out the man Cassidy and focus on Madeleine. Besides obvious mental problems she has chill, fever. Suggested she go into shelter so she wouldn't get seriously ill.

"I can't leave the Holy Mother now that She's under attack," Madeleine wailed.

"Madeleine, you're undernourished, and you seem feverish. If you don't get some help now, you'll end up in an emergency room and then you'll be away from your Holy Mother for a long time." Hector tried to sound caring, not impatient. "You need antibiotics, warmth, and lots of fluids."

"You listen to the doctor, Maddy," Jacqui put in. "He could be home, but he's come out here to look out for you because he cares whether you live or die."

"Let me at least give you another shot of Prolixin," Hector urged. "You know you do better with the drug: you feel safer and you come aboveground where you can get food and fresher air."

"No!" Madeleine screamed. "You're trying to cloud my mind.

When you gave me that shot I couldn't hear what the Virgin was telling me."

Cassidy rolled his eyes. "She's down here listening to the Virgin Mary?"

"The Holy Mother cries tears of blood, they come here through the wall." Madeleine put her fingers into the rusty water and showed them to Cassidy, who backed away in disgust.

"She's been down here for weeks," Hector said. "How come you suddenly felt the urge to clean her part of the sidewalk?"

Got a highly colored story of a drunk woman attacking hotel guests as they left the garage. Jacqui pursed her lips, pulled me to one side: said Cassidy might mean Luisa—J sent Luisa here to doss down in their old generator box when Patsy Wanachs threw her out. Would Luisa attack someone? Might have the desire but certainly not the strength: she's a pretty frail woman these days. More to the point, what's become of her? Cassidy didn't know, certainly didn't care.

Jacqui said, Doc, you may not know this, but sidewalk doesn't belong to hotel, belongs to the people. Can't stop someone hanging out on the sidewalk.

Kind of legal information you pick up if you're on the streets: I certainly would never have known about it. Cassidy, angry, trying to intimidate Jacqui, said the Pleiades had legal advice for what they'd done, did she want to sue the hotel? She just stared, didn't say anything, so he turned to me, his face swelling into a listen-to-me-young-man expression—he was serving me notice here and now that homeless women were not going to camp out at his garage. And if I was going to encourage them, he'd see that the hotel sued me. Took my name and my hospital affiliation. Wonder if I should notify Hanaper? And get lecture on overstepping my responsibilities. Why rush it? Will doubtless come in time.

On that cheerful note, returned to hospital. Stopped at the library to do a computer search to see if Madeleine had company in her quest for the Virgin. Apparently her delusion becoming quite common as we close in on millennium—in some tiny Kansas town a wall painting of the Lady of Guadalupe is crying tears of blood. Is happening in Italy as well. Started reading a long *New Yorker* story on how the Catholic church investigates these claims, until my first Friday night crisis called me to emergency room.

It seems truly incomprehensible that someone like Rafe Lowrie, running Orleans St. Church's Bible study, listening to God and repeating his words to anyone who will listen, is labeled a sane member of society, but Madeleine underground hearing messages from the Virgin is psychotic. Of course, she is psychotic, but why isn't he also?

13

Call for a Goddess

Mara was locked in her bedroom channeling the goddess Gula. Her grandfather and older sister tried to pretend they didn't know, didn't care, but every night when the incense started to seep down the hall to the sitting room they found themselves unable to read or talk or concentrate on anything but the smell. They couldn't really hear Mara— the doors in the apartment were too thick for sound to travel—but they sat tensed, straining for the rise and fall of her voice.

Dr. Stonds invited Professor Verna Lontano to dinner one evening to inform Mara how utterly spurious was her knowledge of ancient Sumer and its deities. Professor Lontano, an old friend of the doctor's, was the Assyriologist Mara phoned four years earlier, when she was trying to get information about Grannie Selena. Professor Lontano had spent her adult life on the literature of Sumerian deities, and had nothing but withering contempt for New Age goddess worship.

"You young women are intellectual slovens," she said in her precise, accented English. "You want to imagine a gyno-centric universe and so you totally pervert historical reality by assigning to the old goddesses a supremacy they never held. You are unwilling to do the hard work, the research"—pronounced with a great rolling of r's that spattered the table like semiautomatic bullets—"to find out what the ancients actually said and believed. So you take a few translated texts and build a whole theology from them. Why? Why not stick to the gods you know—money, sex, the usual deities of your generation of American?"

To Harriet's intense embarrassment, Mara bent her head, pulled her legs up to sit yoga-style on the dining room chair, and began a high-pitched wordless wail. After howling for a minute or two she began to chant in the same high nasal:

"The goddess speaks through her unworthy vessel. O Maiden, weak thou art but full of yearning for the truth, for the healing rays that Gula sheds on sick humanity, how many thousand years have I waited, bound in silence, weakening ever, until one came who could hear my Voice."

"Mara! We've had enough of your showing off. Put your feet back on the floor and converse like a normal human being." Dr. Stonds's sharp voice usually silenced blethering subordinates, but Mara continued to wail as though her trance were too intense to acknowledge human speech.

"She's not going to listen to you, *Grand-père,*" Harriet said. "Why don't we take our coffee across to the sitting room. As soon as her audience has disappeared she'll quiet down fast enough."

"This is what she does every night?" Professor Lontano stopped to admire the Louise Nevelson marble in the hall as they crossed to the living room. "She sounds intensely lonely. I'm surprised she's taking Mrs. Ephers's illness so hard—I never thought they got along. What's the word from the rehabilitation hospital?"

"Oh, Mephers is recovering well," Harriet said. "They say she can come home in another week, but of course we don't want her to be under any stress, and if Mara is going to be difficult . . ."

She left the sentence hanging, but the doctor said, "She'll have to leave. This was Hilda's—Mrs. Ephers's—home thirty years before Mara was ever thought of. I'm not sending Hilda to a nursing home because my own granddaughter is so ill-bred as to make life miserable for her. And, of course, to a certain extent we hold Mara responsible for the heart attack to begin with."

Harriet thought the wailing in the dining room behind them stopped momentarily at that, like an electric current briefly dipping, but the maid from the temporary agency brought coffee in just then and the clatter of cups covered the texture of Mara's chant. As soon as the woman withdrew, Harriet pulled the sliding doors shut.

"Out of curiosity," she asked the professor, "who is Gula?"

"The Sumerian goddess of healing. Curious that Mara should have fixed on her—feminists usually choose Inanna because she was the most important female deity. They try to promote her to head the pantheon and go through some convoluted rigmarole showing the creation of patriarchy through the loss of power by the female gods."

"Oh, Mara isn't a feminist," Dr. Stonds snorted. "She's just a confused young woman who picks up ideologies as a cloak for her unhappiness."

Professor Lontano looked around for a place to set down her coffee cup. The marquetry table next to her was clearly an art object. Harriet rose with her usual precise movements and put the cup on the tray.

"I didn't know Mara was interested in Sumer," Lontano said. "She did call me once, three or four years ago, to ask if I'd known Selena's father."

"I don't believe you ever mentioned this. What did you say?" The doctor frowned.

Lontano shrugged. "There wasn't much I could say, except what you've always known—that I met Selena briefly at the dig near Nippur. I sat in on a seminar Professor Vatick ran, but in those days we had very formal notions about the distinction between faculty and students—I didn't know him or his family socially. Anyway, Mara wasn't interested in him—she only wondered if there was any doubt about her grandmother's death. At the time she called me I thought she was trying to cloak those stories she used to make up about Selena and Beatrix in some reality. She never brought up the matter again."

"I wish Mara would cloak herself in reality," Harriet said. "She claims she found a letter in Mephers's room addressed to our mother, from someone in France, but her story was all gibberish. Mephers found Mara in there rummaging through her things. That was what brought on her heart attack, so I suppose Mara had to make up something to convince herself she wasn't to blame for Mephers's illness. I have to confess I was curious, so I looked myself. Of course there was nothing there."

"She's been nothing but trouble since the day she was born," the doctor snorted. "But since getting kicked out of Smith she's been intolerable."

"I don't think we should have made her go there when she'd set her heart on Michigan," Harriet remarked, forcing up a smile, "but that's an old story. Even though Mephers's heart attack rattled Mara, she only started this chanting after—after—well, I was relating a problem at dinner that we're having with a homeless woman."

She stopped, uncomfortable at the memory. They'd been eating carry-out food, with Mephers out of commission and no one from the agency in place yet to take over the meals, and Harriet had mentioned the Pleiades' problem to Grandfather.

"One of your residents from the psych department is championing the psychotic woman at the garage wall. The garage manager couldn't remember his name but I thought you should know about it."

And then she'd looked at Mara, muddy skin pale green with fury, cheeks swelled out in what Grandfather called her chipmunk face. "You're cheering your fascist clients for hosing down a woman just because she's hearing voices from the Virgin Mary? That could be Mother! This woman is homeless, which is good enough reason to be crazy, and you're happy because you're making her even more miserable. You two think you're so perfect, but no one else can stand you. It's no surprise to me that none of the suitors ever wanted to marry you, cold cruel bitch like you would freeze their balls off in five minutes."

On that line Mara fled the table, fled the house. Grandfather had a serious talk with her the next day. You cannot stay here, young woman, if you are going to enact these kinds of hysterical scenes. You betrayed your sister's trust by drinking on the job and getting fired. You almost killed Hilda with your unwarranted invasion of her room. You are walking very close to a precipice now. Either buckle down, get going on a job and an education, or look for someplace else to live.

The next day Mara took the commuter train down to Hyde Park.

She holed up at the Oriental Institute and studied translations of ancient texts. She found a few scholarly papers written by her grandmother's father and read those. Although they were for the most part impenetrable philological essays, he had translated a few incantations to Gula for warding off disease. Mara memorized those, then announced at dinner that the goddess Gula was speaking to her, and was most unhappy with Harriet's coldness.

Harriet thought she hadn't minded, except, of course, for the irritation one always felt with Mara's histrionics. But now, talking with Professor Lontano, she wondered if she really was a cold person.

"Don't you still attend the Orleans Street Church, Abraham?" Professor Lontano asked. "Why not have your minister talk to Mara? Surely a Christian ought not worship a goddess. I believe the Bible is full of women who brought down Jehovah's wrath by putting up altars to the old goddesses."

"The fewer people I advertise her stupidity to the happier I'll be," Grandfather snapped.

"Anyway, I doubt Mara would listen to Pastor Emerson," Harriet said, leaning back in her chair. "She thinks all men in positions of authority are only trying to control women and that religious leaders are worse than most."

"But you don't agree with her feminist diatribes?" the professor asked.

"I'm not unhappy." Harriet smiled. "I don't need ideologies. But Mara is blaming herself for Mephers's—illness—and it's leading her into greater extremes than are typical even for her."

"In my day we sent unhappy girls to visit relatives in the Dolomites. Hikes in the mountain air were supposed to cure you," Dr. Lontano commented, remembering an older sister drenched in misery from a disastrous love affair. "If that failed, parents resorted to enemas. Then we had the war, and all that excitement and misery cured my generation of melancholy."

"Mara seems to think she's at war," Dr. Stonds said. "With me as the convenient whipping boy for the world around her. When I was a young man I believed ardently in the effect of environment on human morality. But I raised three girls in the identical milieu, same school, same home, same housekeeper. One became a drunk and a waster, and Mara seems determined to follow in her steps. In my old age I've become convinced of genetics. *The Bell Curve* has a lot of truth to it, despite the cries from the liberal establishment."

Harriet's smile became strained. "Darling, I hate to think that everything I've been able to accomplish was predetermined by my DNA. Surely my personality had *something* to do with it. And to be honest, my memories of life with—with Mother are vague, but so painful they've driven me to make sure I never live that way. Poor Mara keeps wishing she had a mother."

Dr. Stonds snorted. "Don't start spouting pseudo-Freudian claptrap at me, Harriet. We have a young resident on the psychiatry service who's been infected with those ideas. Fortunately Hanaper can be relied on to keep him in line."

Professor Lontano's wide mouth twisted in sardonic amusement. "My dear Abraham—I've no more patience than you with women who fancy themselves unwell and lie on a couch to talk to a doctor about their troubles—but surely a psychiatrist should be expected to believe in Freudian claptrap?"

She left a few minutes later. It was curious that the two sisters were so unalike. Or maybe not. She thought back to her own sister Constanzia, the one who'd been sent to the Dolomites when Lontano was seven—they didn't have much in common, and they'd had the same father.

Why did Mara and Harriet both still live with Abraham? As beautiful as Harriet was, Professor Lontano used to assume her marriage would take place at any moment. Not that a woman needed a husband—after all, she, Lontano, had led a most satisfying life without one.

Although there had been a time—and then when she came to Chicago, she had thought, with Selena dead—but it was Abraham himself who proved unwilling, uninterested. He didn't need a wife, not even to look after baby Beatrix, since he had a resident housekeeper. They enjoyed evenings at the opera, discussions of art or politics, dinner at the Drake Hotel, but not love. Already in those days a great surgeon, Stonds demanded as much devotion from those at home as he found in the operating theater, and he could not accept a lover who placed her own work above his. Sumerian literature, he would laugh. How many lives has it saved this week?

And she hadn't really cared. After Emil—Lontano tried to push the thought away, but Harriet's face tonight, a certain look, in the lamp-light—what photo did that dreadful Hilda Ephers keep locked in her angry bosom?

14

Barroom Balladeer

"Don't tell me it's for my own good. It's for yours, yours and Mephers's. You've been dying to throw me out ever since I was born and now you have the perfect excuse. Mrs. Ephers is old and fragile and needs quiet. Let's get rid of the last trace of the evil Beatrix and her loathsome mother Selena. Their genes somehow bypassed the perfect golden Harriet, but we need to root them out when they crop up again in Mara."

Once again Grandfather had called Mara into his study. If she didn't stop her chanting and find a job—or, better yet, go back to school—she would have to move. That was an ultimatum.

"I'm not ordering you to leave, although you are not attractive to live with. But it's time you learned that your actions have consequences. Having to look after yourself in your own apartment might be a good experience for you—it would teach you how much Hilda has done for you over the years." Grandfather spoke coldly. "Not to mention me. Perhaps we made a mistake in allowing you to think you always had a room here."

"How much rent does Harriet pay you? I suppose it's a lot, since she makes a bundle at the firm and you gave her that three-room suite."

Mara's cheeks, swollen with misery and anger, made Dr. Stonds feel even less charitably toward her. "Yours and Harriet's situations are very different. If you showed the same desire to make the most of your opportunities as she has, I'd be glad to give you a suite like hers. But if you mean, how are you going to afford a home as nice as this one, you should have thought of that before you started on your current disastrous course. I am prepared to help you pay rent on a decent apartment elsewhere. Provided you find a job to take care of your remaining expenses. And, of course, there is no need for you to leave at all if you will start living like a civilized person."

"I'll behave like your version of a civilized person if you'll behave like my version of a truthful one," Mara said. "I found a letter to Mother from someone in France in Mephers's room, along with a photograph of some man who looks just like Harriet. I want to know where Mother really—"

"I've had enough of your self-dramatizing." The doctor's face reddened. "Your mother is dead. I have told you that many times, but you refuse to listen. Mrs. Ephers will be released from the rehabilitation hospital on Thursday. That gives you two days to decide on your course of behavior."

A bell tinkled in the background: the cook from the agency had dinner ready. She would have to stay on when Hilda returned, the doctor realized: he and Harriet needed to make sure Hilda didn't overdo it. She had always sacrificed her own well-being for his, ever since he left her alone with Selena when he was in the army. After Selena and Beatrix, Hilda didn't deserve Mara. Maybe send Mara to see Hanaper? Stonds didn't believe in psychotherapy as a rule, but someone needed to straighten her out.

A hot spot started to burn under his rib cage as he thought of the many times Mara had behaved abominably, the tantrums as a child, a blue velvet dress she had cut to ribbons when she was four, flowers stolen from the Historical Society garden, files deleted from his computer when he was finishing a paper for the American College of Neurosurgeons. He used to take her to the opera, when he'd far rather have gone with Verna Lontano or some other intelligent adult, and Mara repaid him by making up ludicrous parodies at a dinner with the opera's artistic director. He sent her to the same camps and after-school activities they'd given Harriet; Mara responded by being expelled from college. He had punished, bribed, pleaded. Nothing had any effect on her. Bad blood would always tell.

"It's dinnertime, Mara. Try to get those nuts out of your cheeks so that you look like a human being and not a chipmunk at the dinner table."

"I have plans for dinner elsewhere." She got up to leave, hoping Grandfather couldn't see her trembling hands, hoping she wouldn't start to cry in front of him.

In her mind she swept from the room, velvet skirts swirling around her in a graceful eddy. In her mind she was beautiful, coarse dark hair long and shiny, pulled into a chignon, waist so slender a man could span it with his hands.

Grandfather was like Aunt Reed in *Jane Eyre*. Or maybe he was the bullying cousin; Mrs. Ephers, the ever-effervescent, could be a ringer for Aunt Reed, playing favorites with her children, letting them tell lies and then punishing Jane for them. But Jane was small, birdlike, slipped in and out of rooms unnoticed. As Mara bumped against a table, knocking over a stack of papers, Grandfather said, you've made your point sufficiently, you don't need to vandalize this room. Or should I have it padlocked as well?

Referring to Mrs. Ephers's locked room, which Mara had entered by crawling along the outside wall, like Cary Grant in *To Catch a Thief,* easy, really, because of the balconies, but then she had made too much noise breaking the window. I want to prove to you that these papers are here, Mara told Harriet, when her sister and Grandfather came running to the housekeeper's room, but of course the secret drawer in the secretary was empty. Mrs. Ephers had moved them, or told Grandfather or Harriet to do so. Mara's only hope, and she didn't put real stock in it, was for a vision from the goddess Gula that would lead her to the papers.

Maybe Grandfather had locked Beatrix in the psych ward at the hospital. That was why he stayed on teaching and operating, to make sure she didn't escape. He wanted to lock Mara up alongside her mother, so he was trying to make people think Mara was crazy, that she imagined papers that didn't exist. Maybe she was crazy. Or would be soon if she stayed much longer in this mausoleum.

She shut herself in her bedroom and phoned Cynthia Lowrie to pour out her tale of woe. Fortunately Cynthia answered the phone herself. Her father wasn't home, so she could talk, for a short time: if her brother Jared knew she was talking to Mara, Jared would tell Rafe and then Cynthia would be in trouble again.

"Maybe it would be a good thing if you did move out, Mara. You know you're not happy there. I'd be happy if I could have my own apartment."

"Why don't we get a place together?" Mara said. "You'd get away from your father and your asshole brother. You'd never have to hand out Bibles to homeless women again or clean whiskers out of the bathroom sink."

Cynthia snorted. "You going to clean the bathroom if we get a place? I'd like to see you clean anything. Anyway, Daddy would never let me move out, not unless it was to get married, I mean—he's getting all wound up by Family Matters, you know, that group where men get together to prove they're really in charge of their families. Some of them even go and pick husbands for their daughters. Daddy started a chapter at the church, which you would know if you ever showed up there. He says he could rest easy if he knew I was going to a good Christian home, not off with some guy who'd encourage all my worst faults."

"You don't have to marry anyone you don't want to," Mara said hotly. "Anyway, if we got a place together what could Rafe do to you? He might be totally pissed off, but so what? They're pissed off with me all the time around here."

"Oh, Mara, it's not the same, you know it's not. . . . Help, I think he just came in, gotta go." She dropped the receiver clumsily into the switch hook.

Mara walked the two miles downtown to Corona's on Kinzie. She supposed Cynthia was even worse off than she was, although she grudged the ceding of any misery to her friend. But she had to be honest—no one would let Cynthia shag out to a bar. Grandfather might rant at her, but he didn't lock her in her room or beat her.

At Corona's, Jake the bouncer knew he was supposed to card her, knew she was too young, but he accepted her ten, her sad-girl grin, and let her in.

"You know it's Tuesday, Mara: slim pickings tonight."

"Yeah, I know, Jake, but my blues are good enough to fill in even for a voiceless white chick."

He laughed. "That's just what we have on tap for you tonight: a voiceless white chick. Go over to the Gold Star and listen to Patricia Barber."

Mara went on in. They always carded her at the Gold Star—she'd never been able to bribe the doorman there. The hostess showed her to a table near the door and brought her a bourbon while a white woman with a thin reedy voice sang "Bottom of My Soul" as if the distance from bottom to top were a micron wide. When she left the stage, to polite applause, the painist doodled variations on "Bottom of My Soul," speaking into the mike above the piano as he did so.

"It's not amateur night at Corona's, you know that. When you pay your five bucks at the door and buy those pricey drinks, Queenie treats you right, doesn't palm cheap imitations off on you. But tonight we have an unexpected guest here in the club, a singer, and she's offered to do a song or two for us. I want you to welcome Chicago's own . . . Luisa Montcrief."

Mara sat up. Luisa Montcrief, the diva? Surely not in a jazz dive. But when an aquiline woman in a crimson dress climbed the short step to the stage Mara recognized her as the singer who'd ravished her as Aida, Desdemona, and a dozen other heroines over the years.

Luisa looked alert and regal. Even though she was too thin, so that the dress hung on her, her presence made the small stage seem overcrowded. So it wasn't true, what Grandfather told her—that Madame Montcrief's family brought her into see that slimeball Hanaper because the diva was drunk and incompetent. Liar, liar, he lied about everything.

The diva put a hand on the piano, raking the crowd with an imperious glance. At the spindly-legged tables patrons were talking, softly, it's true, but Luisa was used to the silence of awe when she walked onstage. When a trio of men continued their conversation—one of them giving a loud shout of laughter—Madame Montcrief leaned forward.

"If you would like your conversation to be part of the performance, could you kindly join me here on the stage? Otherwise, have the courtesy to be silent while I sing."

A few people clapped, but the three men got up to leave. The hostess ran after them, trying to collect their money, but they were offended: they didn't come into Corona's to be insulted, and that by some singer who wasn't even on the advertised program.

"Oh, go back to whatever two-bit town you come from," Mara called. "Luisa Montcrief is one of the greatest singers in the world. No one wants to listen to your chatter about football or computer sales or whatever boring topic is so important to you. You'd have to pay a hundred dollars to get this close to her at the opera. Maybe more."

"No one lectures me on how to act in public." The biggest of the three men came over to Mara's table and glared down at her.

"What a pity." The diva spoke from the stage. "You have so much to learn."

The pianist began playing variations on "Troubled in Mind." "Let's have a few songs, Luisa, while Minnie settles things at the door. She's an expert at sorting things out, you're an expert at singing, so you leave the sorting out to her."

Luisa was reluctant to abandon the battlefield, but still sober enough to realize her audience agreed with the pianist. She bowed again to their applause and began singing. She'd sung a lot of ballads and Broadway in her student days, and pulled "Careless Love" from her old repertoire. An intelligent performer, she muted her big voice to fit the small room, and reached into her lower register for a smoky undertone. The audience, suspicious at first, began to respond, clapping hard as the last notes melted past the bar.

Luisa paused to drink most of a glass of amber liquid, then sang Maria's song from *West Side Story*. As she began her third song, the three loud men worked something out with Minnie and returned to their table. They immediately began laughing, emphasizing their humor by slapping the table. When Luisa finished "Thievin' Boy," they applauded loudly and whistled.

"I see our cretinous friends here have decided to join the party," Luisa announced. "Perhaps I should sing a song just for them, and loudly enough for them to make it out."

She began singing in German, using her full voice, which was so powerful, it set up a whistling feedback in the sound system. The piano player gamely followed her, although Mara could tell from his expression that he was annoyed. The three men continued their loud, staged remarks, but no one could hear them over the diva in full throttle.

When she finished the song there was a smattering of doubtful clapping. "Ah—since that was in German, and our friends here can barely understand English, I had best translate. It is, of course, by Hugo Wolf, from his famous *Italienisches Liederbuch*—for the ignorant, the '*Italian Songbook*'—and it means:

> *Who called you? Who invited you here? Who told you to come, if it's such a burden to you? Go where your fancy calls, I'll willingly forgo your coming to me.*

So, you troglodytes, like Hugo Wolf I gladly forgo your presence here. Leave now so I can continue this concert."

One of the men stood and cupped his hands to bellow, "Hey, you snot-nosed bitch, we came here for music by American singers with American words. Go back to whatever foreign rock you crawled out of."

"She is American, you great ape," Mara yelled from her table. "If I was as stupid as you I'd stay home instead of coming and showing it off in public."

Some of the crowd was laughing, but others began to gather up their handbags and briefcases, preparatory to departing. The hostess hurried over to Luisa and started a whispered entreaty that she ignore the men and return to pop music. Luisa turned a shoulder to her, and began singing, again at full voice, "Sempre libera," from *La Traviata*.

Minnie ran around behind Luisa to the sound system and turned off Luisa's mike. Even without it her voice filled the room, but Minnie went to the pianist's mike and was able to speak over the diva.

"I'm sorry, folks, but we have a temporary malfunction of the sound system. You'll be getting drinks on the house while we sort it out." She hustled Luisa from the stage.

The three men applauded, giving loud sports cheers. Mara stomped over to their table. She picked up a drink with either hand and dashed the liquor in their faces.

They sat frozen for a moment, then roared with fury and jumped her. She was on the floor, kicking and squirming, when the bouncer pulled the men from her. He tossed the trio from the bar.

Jake came back inside, his breathing only slightly hurried. "And as for you, Mara, out you go. You know Queenie doesn't tolerate any nonsense in her club. If she was here you might be barred permanently, so you're lucky she's not."

"Okay, Jake, okay. Can I clean up first? They'll kill me if I come home like this."

Unlike the bouncer Mara was panting hard. She was wet and dirty from being rolled around on the floor. Her feet were sticky inside her high-heeled sandals. In the dim toilet light she saw a bruise forming below her left eye and blood on her left arm. Her tank top had a tear under one arm.

"Huh. I look like that woman at the wall."

She washed off what parts of her arms and face she could fit in the tiny sink and let Jake escort her outside. The diva was there, arguing with Minnie about getting Corona's to give her cab fare.

"Ah, the little heroine." Luisa grabbed Mara's arm and stood on tiptoe to plant European kisses on both cheeks. "How brave you were, and how kind, to come to my support amidst that band of Philistines."

Her breath stank of whiskies past and present.

"I've been an admirer of yours for years," Mara muttered. "It's too bad Queenie wasn't here tonight. She's a pretty cool head, she wouldn't have let those guys get out of hand the way they did."

"I pay no attention to the *canaglia*." Luisa snorted, like Harriet's horse, Mara thought, suppressing a giggle. "Chicago is a vulgar town with no regard for artistry. My own brother is the *example par excellence* of that. A cretin, more at home on a scrap metal heap than a concert hall. Can you believe we shared a womb? I was born first: I couldn't wait to leave him. Even *in utero* I knew him for a Philistine."

This time Mara couldn't help giggling, but she said, "I hope you don't think everyone in Chicago is as ignorant as those guys. I love your singing. I own all your recordings. I bet I've listened to your *Tosca* a thousand times."

Luisa bridled again, this time with pleasure. "You are young to have such an appreciation for opera. I could use an amanuensis in this town. My dresser, my agent, they have all abandoned me; my own brother threw me out on the street. I'm reduced to making appearances in night-clubs, and that *malandrina*—excuse me—robber—I've lived so many years in Italy that their language comes first to me—wouldn't even give me cab fare, after agreeing to pay me for my performance."

"I live with my grandfather," Mara said. "He threatened to throw me out because I got fired from my job. Also because he doesn't want to admit he knows what happened to my mother."

"Hah! These men and their fixation about jobs. My brother would be happy to see me teaching music to kindergartners. I, who sing routinely at the Met and the Berlin Staatsoper, I who got fifteen curtain calls at La Scala after my debut as Carmen—" She lost the thread of her declamation. "He thinks only of money, and of scrap metal. Come! You may take me home with you."

"I'm not going home tonight. They had to choose between me and the housekeeper, so they chose the housekeeper." Mara gulped down a sob of self-pity. "I'm going to teach them a lesson."

15

Tossed in the Tank

"HARRIET, WHAT IN HELL do you think I pay your firm three hundred dollars an hour for? A paralegal who tells the garage manager to hose down the wall? That did absolutely nothing except generate more trouble for us. Some snooty doctor was down there last week protesting to Brian Cassidy, and last night—last night—"

"I know about last night," Harriet said. "The police woke me at three this morning. That was my sister you had arrested."

"I don't care if it was the pope," Gian Palmetto snapped. "What in hell was she doing creating a riot at my garage?"

Channeling for the goddess Gula. Entertaining Luisa Montcrief. Sticking it to Harriet. Enraging Grandfather. Yes, all of the above, and who knew what else besides.

"And furthermore, she says *you* advised her that the sidewalk was public property. Whose side are you on, anyway? I've got a good mind to take this up with Leigh Wilton. You've been giving us only half your attention these days."

It wasn't true she'd told Mara that the sidewalk was public property. In fact, when Harriet raised the issue at dinner last week, it was only to pass on Brian Cassidy's complaint about Hector.

Grandfather said he'd talked to Hanaper, but urged Harriet to have the woman at the wall arrested for trespassing.

It's not that simple, she'd responded: the wall belongs to the hotel, but the sidewalk is the city's, and that makes it tricky, especially if someone is advising the women on their legal rights. The hotel can't afford the negative publicity they'll get if some hotshot civil rights lawyer takes up the woman's cause.

And then Mara blew up at her and fled the house, leaving Harriet both angry and unaccountably forlorn. The sisters had not spoken since, except to grunt "excuse me" if they encountered each other in a hallway.

Harriet's head was aching. She didn't want to try to explain why Mara thought she should champion Madeleine Carter—even if Harriet understood what went through her sister's mind, which she didn't.

When the call came from the assistant state's attorney Grandfather insisted on going to the police station with Harriet; the rest of the night had been spent in a series of scenes with him and her sister.

If this *charade*—Grandfather gave the word its French pronunciation as he yelled at Mara—was designed to make me reconsider my ultimatum, you mistook your tactics badly, young lady, very badly. By then they were back in the Graham Street apartment and it was almost five. I want you out of this apartment today, and I will take steps to make sure you leave.

Goose steps, Mara said, green eyes smoldering.

How dare you! Grandfather's bellow rocked the chandelier. If you had seen the sights I did in Europe you would never use that expression so flippantly. I risked my life to create a world in which a pampered self-indulgent miss like you not only gets arrested for disturbing the peace, but can come home to hurl insults at me.

You risked your life to fight the Nazis, Mara said, but you run this house like a totalitarian state. Grannie couldn't live according to your petty rules, so she left. Then you drove your own daughter away. Only Harriet is too scared not to do every little thing you say—

Harriet, scared? You ignorant bottom-feeder, you're just smart enough to be jealous of her, but not smart enough to emulate her. Harriet doesn't know the meaning of fear.

And then he called to her, his golden girl, the apple of his eye, and demanded that she find Mara an apartment and have her installed in it by noon the following day: tonight is to be her last night under my roof. He was almost purple with fury.

Harriet was wobbly from interrupted sleep, from rage with her sister for getting involved with the woman at the wall, from worry over Mephers, from worry over herself (was she really cold, as Mara kept saying? was she really scared?), but when she looked at Mara's swollen face she felt a twinge of sadness.

It was her own photograph that dominated Mephers's bedroom, Grandfather's study. No one ever had time for Mara, not from the day Beatrix dumped her at Graham Street. She was desperate for attention. So she cococted the outrageous story about Mephers hiding a letter for Beatrix.

When Harriet didn't pay attention to her latest fabrication, Mara created a disturbance on Underground Wacker. Mara's behavior throughout had been totally inappropriate—okay, unbelievably sick—but how could Harriet continue to inhabit—rent free—her elegant suite, with her meals provided by Grandfather's cook, and send her sister off to some dismal apartment on her own?

Mara needs help, she told Grandfather. She needs love, and our support. Maybe she should see a therapist.

Don't you start in on me with that sob sister nonsense, Grandfather shouted, forgetting that he'd been considering the same notion. Every day at the hospital I see some patient who's never grown up despite years of therapy, sniveling about how their mothers didn't love them or their fathers raped them, so they're not responsible for their own acts. Look at Luisa Montcrief, ruined a brilliant career through petulant self-indulgence. That brother of hers is right: tough love is the way to handle this kind of problem. He says Hanaper advised it—good man, Hanaper, not like that idiot resident of his, mewling on about therapy.

Harry Minsky and Grandfather had encountered each other at the police station that morning. Of course, they had met many years earlier, when Grandfather removed a glioblastoma from Harry's mother's brain, but Grandfather had been a surgeon then, not a person but the priest in whose hands lay the auguries of life and death. Harry hadn't existed for

Grandfather then, either: he'd been one of the doctor's many supplicants from a world of prayers and tears. But at the First District police station in the middle of the night, Harry Minsky and Abraham Stonds were simply two men terribly aggrieved by their female relations.

Harry roared into Chicago after Luisa's fourth phone call, the one she made to Becca's room on Becca's personal line. When his daughter came in to wake him—Daddy, Aunt Luisa's in trouble, she's been arrested, she says you just want her to rot in jail—he rose in a fury so intense, he could hardly control his body. Let her rot there, a year in jail would be a year of peace in our lives.

His arms flailing, he pulled on whatever clothes lay to hand, stuffed his feet sockless into loafers, tore down the drive in his Mercedes with such a squealing of rubber that Karen ran down to the road—in her nightgown—to make sure the car hadn't turned over. He intended to go into Chicago and demand that the police hold his sister without bail, without trial, send her to the Château d'If for the rest of her life, which he prayed would be short.

Becca sat up in her bed, afraid he was going to murder Aunt Luisa. No, not that, but he was driving so wildly, what if he turned the car over, or hit someone? Or killed a dog? Around five she went into her mother and poured her terrors out to her.

Karen was worried, too, but her fears were more specific: that Harry would come home with his sister, unable, when the crunch came, to stand up to her. So when Becca spilled her fears for what her father might do, Karen, cords standing out in her neck, snapped she was more afraid of what Luisa might do.

"You're so unfair," Becca wailed. "She's a great artist and you stuck her in a nasty little hole of an apartment."

"She's a great drunk," Karen said. "Do you know she hit someone over the head with a whiskey bottle tonight? And when your father talked to the police sergeant, the man said she dragged some teenage girl into trouble with her."

"But does that mean she has to go to jail? Why can't Daddy bail her out? If you're worried about the money I can use the CD I got from your mother for my bat mitzvah."

"Darling, no. It's not the money." Karen pulled Becca to her. "Our only chance—your aunt's only chance—is that if no one rescues her, she'll finally realize she needs treatment. Dr. Hanaper told us tough love is the only solution for someone who denies her problems the way Janice does. What would you do if your father brought her home in the condition she was in when she called you?"

Becca couldn't answer that: it was a typical unfair adult question, designed to make you feel wrong. She called her dog Dusty and took him back upstairs to bed with her, determined to stay awake until Daddy was safely home. Clutching Dusty's fur, she wondered what teenage girl her aunt had taken up with. She felt a strange burst of jealousy and resentment, that Aunt Luisa preferred some other girl to her. She tried to imagine what Daddy and Mother would do if she had been arrested with her aunt, if she had called them in the middle of the night. Maybe this other girl lived with such understanding parents that they wouldn't scream over the phone at her.

Becca couldn't know that Mara Stonds expected so little empathy at home that she had refused to call Grandfather at all. An assistant state's attorney did that when the police brought her to the station. Mara told the state's attorney she'd just as soon go to jail, thank you very much, but he ignored her.

"Mara Stonds? Any relation to Harriet? Your sister? We went to law school together. Believe me, Mara, you wouldn't like jail at all: hookers and drug addicts. They'll tear the skin off your eyeballs. Seriously. Why don't you give Harriet a call? No? I understand, you're too embarrassed: I'll phone for you."

Mara saw the shine in his eyes and realized he was a would-be suitor of her sister's. She thought about telling him that rescuing her would not endear him to Harriet—that he'd earn more points by incarcerating her, but felt too apathetic to get engaged in conversation.

By the time she and Luisa were booked, Mara was feeling frightened by her own actions. What had been going through her mind? Maybe

Grandfather was right, maybe she had inherited some gene of disease and degradation. Perhaps it wasn't Mara's inborn evilness that drove Beatrix away (one sight of that ugly baby, never mind that she was as bald as most babies, the mother could foresee the bush of springy coarse curls, that outward sign of an inward spiritual death, and took off from the infant as fast as she could). Maybe Beatrix recognized her own weakness in Mara's baby face, was frightened at the idea she had perpetuated her monstrousness in her second child, and fled in terror from her own reflected image. Mara, sitting next to Luisa in the station, wept from desolation.

When they left Corona's, Luisa followed Mara along Kinzie Street as it ducked under Michigan, through the maze of underground loading bays, to the foundations of the Hotel Pleiades. On the way they passed an all-night liquor store, where Luisa insisted that Mara buy her a bottle of whiskey. The man at the counter carded Mara, so she gave Luisa a ten, which bought a quart of Four Roses. Luisa sucked from it as they threaded their way past Dumpsters and homeless men wrapped in old coats. By the time they reached the woman at the wall, Luisa was lurching on her high heels, but Mara kept an arm around the diva's waist to steer her past the worst holes in the pavement.

Madeleine Carter was in her usual place. The sidewalk and wall behind her were still damp from the hosing Brian Cassidy now gave them nightly. As soon as one of the maintenance men appeared, Madeleine would leap up, gather her bundle, and move around the corner, but by and by they would stop spraying and she would return. Her first act was always to stick her fingers in the crack and make sure they still came away red. With that reassurance she would sit down again, try to read the gummy pages in her Bible, and talk to the Holy Mother under her breath.

"Uh-huh, they're trying to scare me away, trying to torture You, but we're both still here, I'm a rock that no one can move, yes on this rock You can build Your church. I see Your tears, don't worry about that, I know all these days You've tried to speak, no one would listen, but I'm here, I hear You, oh, yes, I hear You, Mother, kiss me, hold me, taste me, my tears are bloody just like Yours."

Every now and then Brian Cassidy would come to the garage mouth and stare at Madeleine. He made sure a squad car drove by every so often to pin her with its spotlight. She would quiver then in terror, stand on tiptoe to place her lips against the crack, cling to the grimy concrete as if it were a human frame, until the car moved on.

The squad car passed Mara and Luisa as they reached the mouth of the garage. The night light drained the dirt from Mara's face and clothes; in silhouette they looked like a respectable mother and daughter, Luisa in her crimson cocktail dress, Mara in jeans, on their way home from the theater. The squad car moved on. Brian Cassidy returned to his office behind the cashier's window.

Mara squatted down next to Madeleine. Madeleine shielded her face with her Bible.

"Cowards, cowards, quitters, they're all cowards, Blessed Mother, cowards who want to destroy You. They will go away and leave me here, they're fools and evil spirits, but You will take care of me."

"I won't hurt you," Mara said. "We're here to help protect the wall and to sing the goddess's praises."

When Madeleine continued to whimper Mara scooted further from her, until the homeless woman relaxed enough to lower her Bible. Mara crossed her legs, shut her eyes, and began a loud incantation to Gula:

"O Goddess, we your unworthy servants call to you to appear in power and majesty. Drive away these men who oppress us. Remind them that life and death are in your hands. Your tears on this wall are a sign. Woe to those who ignore it, pestilence will rain upon them like hail, their testicles will wither up and rot, their urine will turn black."

Madeleine started to get excited. "It will. Their urine will turn black. They come and spray on the wall, they do their business on me, but the Holy Mother turns their urine black."

The two garage attendants who worked the graveyard shift came out to the street to watch. The garage stayed open all night so that hotel guests could come and go at any hour, but for the most part it was a long dull shift: action on the street livened things up.

If Brian Cassidy knew about it, he would make them get out the hose and drive the newcomers away, but the two attendants, earning minimum wage and barely getting by, didn't like tormenting a homeless woman. They had to, mind you, if they were ordered, because they didn't want to end up on the streets themselves, but they'd just as soon the manager stayed inside his office.

Anyway, the new girl who was shouting next to the bag lady was young and, like any young woman, attractive. A little plump, but Nicolo liked to see a young woman who wasn't afraid to eat. Working at a pricey hotel you saw so much food going to waste because all these rich women liked to prove how skinny they were by eating one lettuce leaf and throwing away a whole plate of salmon or pasta. It was shocking. Naturally homeless people hung out around the hotel's Dumpsters: they could be sure of four-star leftovers most nights.

Luisa, leaning against the wall as she pulled on her bottle, was still angry with the manager at Corona's for supporting those men against her. She was a diva; she had offered the finest jewel in her repertoire, the Violetta which had charmed Piero Benedetti and brought Europe as well as New York to her feet, and those Chicago morons, those beer-drinking Mammon worshipers, had thrown her out on the street. Just like her brother. In fact, the boors at the bar were probably her brother's hirelings, sent to watch for her and make sure that no matter where she tried to sing in Chicago she would be humiliated.

She became aware of the two garage attendants. There had been three men at Corona's, but only one had been truly insulting: these must be his friends, come to make amends. She put the bottle down, steadied herself with a hand against the wall, and again belted full-throttle into "Sempre libera."

Her voice was no longer the liquid gold that had bathed Benedetti twenty years ago. She wobbled in her upper register, cracked on the notes in the changeover, but she hadn't lost any of her power. The noise floated past the cashier's station to Brian Cassidy's box of an office.

He came out, muscles moving easily under his suit jacket. "Nicolo, what's going on out here? How come you're just standing by while these broads create a disturbance?"

Nicolo held out his hands. "Boss, they hurting nobody. So she drunk, she singing, who hearing her?"

"I am. So is anybody using the garage. I want them out of here."

As if summoned by his words, a Lincoln Town Car pulled into the bay, and a couple got out. The man tossed his keys to Nicolo; the woman took a brief look at Luisa and scuttled into the garage.

"A new service, Cassidy?" the man said. "Concerts for the guests while they wait for their cars?"

Brian Cassidy licked his lips. "Sorry, sir. I'm about to handle the situation."

He went back into his office to call the police while Nicolo filled out the man's garage slip. When Brian came back the couple was gone and Nicolo was parking the car.

Brian walked over to Luisa and shook her arm. "Can it, lady, before people start throwing old boots at you."

"You impertinent ape, how dare you touch me?" Luisa blazed back.

"Listen, broad, you've got five minutes before the cops show. If you can still walk, make tracks and take your two pals with you."

Mara was on her feet. "Who died and left you in charge, you Nazi? This sidewalk is a public place. Did you ever hear of the First Amendment?"

"Yeah, and it tells me speech is not free to mouthy broads like you." He slapped her face with the back of his hand.

"Help!" Mara screamed. "Help! Fire!"

She kicked Brian's shins. He grabbed her and slammed her head against the wall. She collapsed to the pavement and started kicking at his crotch. He seized her left foot and started to pull her across the pavement, but she twisted and managed to wrap herself around his legs. He was a solid man; she couldn't budge him, but he couldn't get a purchase on her, either. Luisa looked on for a moment, her face haughty at the insults he'd hurled, but she suddenly thought of her whiskey bottle. Making sure the cap was screwed on tightly she tapped him on the back of the head with it. He let go of Mara and turned to punch Luisa.

At that moment the squad car returned. After a quick consultation with Brian Cassidy, the patrolmen wrapped up Luisa and Mara, scooped Madeleine up from the sidewalk, and cuffed the three women together in the back of the car.

16

Lost in Space

Mara was in a spaceship sailing through the blackness of space. Strapped into the seat next to her was Beatrix. At the controls, her back turned to them, sat a woman in a bridal gown: only the white gown and veil were visible, but Mara knew it was Grannie Selena, because that was how she was dressed in her 1942 newspaper photo.

"Where are you taking us, Grannie?" she asked. "To Iraq?"

The woman at the controls didn't speak, but Beatrix laughed. "Grandfather has dropped you down a black hole, didn't you know? You'll never find your way back up to land."

Mara looked at her mother. It was a familiar face, from photographs Mara had found in Harriet's desk when Harriet was at college. As in the photographs, Beatrix's face was flat, without any human depth to it. As Mara looked the eyes turned into empty sockets. The hollow head continued to laugh: Mara was a ludicrous object, not lovable, uproariously funny only because she was unaware how absurd she was.

Mara wanted to get away from the two women, but the straps bound her tightly in place. She wanted to cry for help, but she couldn't speak, and even if she did, in the vastness of outer space who would hear her?

17

Thunder and Lightning from the Great White Chief

I wonder if training at Midwest Hospital is designed to turn psych residents psychotic: if you can find your way back to sanity after your residency you're qualified to treat the mentally ill. Don't even know how to tell what happened. The Queen ordered Alice, begin at the beginning, which was . . . clinic, I guess, today being Wednesday.

Always a chaotic scene: receptionists sit at a desk, with glass panels in front and metal dividers to give individual patients illusion of privacy. What really happens is the patient immediately feels isolated. Anomie is heightened by attitude of clerks. Hanaper's contempt for patients and staff translates to clerks, who treat patients with reflected disdain. Our Weds clinic treats psych and neurology outpatients. First you wait in line, then you get to the clerk, Charmaine for neurology, Gretchen for psychiatry.

Charmaine says, "You're not on the list for Dr. Szemanski. You're sure you have a neurology consultation? Oh, you're here for the psychiatry clinic. Dr. Tammuz or Dr. Demetrios? You need to check in at Booth Three. No, I can't check you in here. Didn't I just finish explaining this is the neurology check-in? As the sign clearly says?" Pointing to a small sign on wall behind her. And the person has to go to end of other line. Melissa Demetrios, as senior resident, has tried to make Gretchen and Charmaine exchange information and check in patients reciprocally, but no sale. Diminishes their sense of power—they couldn't boss so many people around.

I go to Gretchen's workstation after lunch to look at my schedule. Twelve people already waiting, for me, Melissa, or Szemanski. They look up with that strained hopefulness of the waiting room: Is the doctor here? Will it be my turn soon? Will I get good news?

A young woman is sitting at Charmaine's desk: she looks ill, unkempt, hasn't slept well. "I want to see Dr. Tammuz."

Charmaine goes through her routine—this the neurology line, blah, blah.

"That's okay, Charmaine." He turned to the young woman, touched by the misery in her face. "I'm Dr. Tammuz and I'm about to start seeing people. Do you have an appointment?"

The young woman muttered she had no appointment, and no, no referral, that she'd walked in from the street.

"I'll be glad to talk to you this afternoon, but it will have to be after I've seen all the people with appointments, okay? So why don't you give Gretchen here your details," Hector said.

"My details?" the woman whispered.

"Name, insurance, that's all. It's a hospital; we have to know how to charge for the service."

"I'll pay cash," she said. "I—there are reasons for me not to say my name out here."

"Dr. Tammuz," Gretchen butted in, eager to take part. "People are waiting for you. I'll take care of the administrative details."

Gretchen got up from behind her counter and followed Hector to the tiny consulting room assigned to him on Wednesday afternoons. She shut the door and lectured him on how he couldn't just add people to the clinic list on his own whim, because it totally disrupted the accounting in the unit.

"She said she'd pay cash. I'd think Midwest would be thrilled to take her on."

"It's not the money for one person per se, Doctor, but we get assigned rooms for so many hours, me and Charmaine work so many hours on Wednesday based on the patient load. It all gets out of kilter if we just let people walk in off the street assuming they can see a doctor for the asking."

"I see," Hector said. "So we should turn away people in trouble?"

"Oh, people who come in here think they're in trouble. They should try raising four children alone on a clerk's salary while their old man is on permanent disability, if they want to know what trouble is all about."

A key to what bugs her. Obviously needs to be on the other side of the desk getting succor, resents having to give it. When I try to respond empathically, though, she bites my head off. Does agree to add young woman to this afternoon's roster, though, and retreats to her workstation to send in the first of my waiting clients.

In the middle of my second appointment Gretchen buzzes me. I ignore her; she hits buzzer again, several times, rattling both me and my patient. At the end of our allotted fifteen minutes I find out Dr. Stonds is paging me.

"He wants to see you immediately," Gretchen says, assuming a posture of virtue that makes me uneasy.

Tell her I can't possibly go now, with so many patients to see.

"I called Dr. Hanaper when you didn't respond to my first buzz. He thinks you should finish clinic after you've seen Dr. Stonds."

Furious, with Stonds, for thinking he owns us all, and with Hanaper, for acquiescing. Furious at my own impotence. Apologize to waiting patients and head down to the surgery offices, where the god reigns en suite. Great contrast to our barren consulting rooms in clinic, with one plastic chair for patient, another for doctor, and a tiny metal desk for writing notes. Stonds sits in a huge office, with an antique grandfather clock, mahogany bookshelves. His personal secretary works in an ante-chamber as big as my whole apartment. Behind her is his private library–conference room, where he reviewed our psych cases a few weeks ago.

After conferring with the deity, his secretary sends me into the throne room.

"Well, Dr. Tammuz? Well? What do you have to say for yourself?"

Abraham Stonds greeted Hector from behind his leather-covered desk. Brocade drapes drawn across the window blocked out the summer sun. The curtains, the desk leather and the walls were all in green; in the shadows created by the only lamp that was switched on, Hector felt as though he had walked into the bottom of an aquarium.

"About what, sir?" Hector, irritated at having to leave his patients on a whim of the old man's, was thrown off balance by his opening question.

"Don't play the fool with me, Dr. Tammuz. What were you proposing to do with my granddaughter? After the events of last night you have one hell of a nerve attempting to see her."

Hector could feel his lower jaw droop slackly. He wondered if the old man was exhibiting dementia symptoms that his staff was concealing from the rest of the hospital.

"Last night, sir?" he said, trying to move cautiously. "I'm afraid I—"

"Are you a damned parrot, Tammuz, echoing everything I say? Yes, last night. When my granddaughter was arrested, thanks in large part to your officious meddling in matters totally beyond your expertise. And now you try to see her in your clinic on the sly? You think you can make a fool out of me? I'll teach you who's the fool here, young man!" And Dr. Stonds smacked the leather desktop with his open palm.

Hector became convinced the surgeon had suffered some kind of infarct. His own head splintered with colliding fears—that even if the old man was crazy, he could destroy Hector's career; that Hector ought to summon help; that he needed to soothe Stonds and make his escape as fast as he possibly could.

"Uh, sir, I wonder if you're confusing me with someone else. I've never met Ms. Stonds."

"How dare you?" In the dim light Stonds's face seemed to swell like a giant shark in front of a stranded sailor. "When you told your clinic clerk to add her to your patient roster, that you'd see her without an appointment!"

"That was your granddaughter? I had no idea—she didn't tell me her name—I'd never seen her before."

Hector felt ill. After the events of last night . . . Had someone assaulted the Stonds girl? Had she come up with his name somehow, and decided to finger him for it?

"Hector Tammuz? That's your name, isn't it? Recommended by Dr. Hanaper to work at the Lenore Foundation's clinic for the homeless?"

"Yes, sir, but—"

"And you've taken it upon yourself to get involved with a psychotic woman living around the foundation to the Hotel Pleiades, and to advise her on her legal rights?"

"No, sir. I know nothing about the law and would never give anyone legal advice." Hector's lips felt stiff and clumsy, as though they had been soaked in formaldehyde. "I have tried, unsuccessfully, to treat the woman for symptoms of acute schizophrenia and paranoia. I have tried to get her to leave the wall where she is living and come aboveground, but have failed in my efforts. That is the limit of my connection to her."

"Don't lie to me, young man!" Dr. Stonds hit his desktop again. "You gave your name to the man at the hotel garage. He told us he heard you advising this woman. He told us you said that the sidewalk was public property and the hotel could not force her to leave."

In the middle of his fears Hector tried to remember the scene at the hotel garage. He spoke to so many people about so many things that the evening already belonged to the distant past. His clearest image was of the garage manager's arm muscles bulging against his jacket sleeves as he tried to justify the hotel's harassment of Madeleine.

"I see you didn't expect a witness to speak up, Dr. Tammuz."

Dr. Stonds's triumphant bark goaded Hector into speech. "One of the street people who brought me to see Madeleine Carter—the schizo-

phrenic woman—made the point about the sidewalk being public property. I didn't know that was the case. The guy from the garage probably
thinks it was I who said it, because to him those women were ciphers.
They're homeless, one is black, so his memory is playing a kind of trick
on him, putting information on the lips of the only person he recognized. I suppose you could call it a form of projection."

Hector was amazed that he could speak so lucidly while the room
rocked and bucked around him. Or maybe gibberish was coming out and
he was too distraught to hear it. "But, sir, what does this have to do with
your—with Ms. Stonds?"

"Don't be insolent with me, young man! I've been hearing about
you from Dr. Hanaper, that you're a whiny crybaby who ducks his
responsibilities, and I see how right he is: you try to pass off your own
malfeasance onto a psychotic creature who wouldn't know one end of
the law from the other. . . ."

As the diatribe continued Hector began calculating his debts, a technique for dissociation, since he made the same reckoning a dozen times a
week. Ninety-seven thousand for education took first place, but there
were lesser ones, including five grand for a used Honda. Rent was over
six hundred a month. By the time he paid utilities, insurance, and his
loans he had about two hundred dollars left for food, clothes, and entertainment—for those occasions when he could stay awake long enough to
be entertained. If Stonds fired him, how long would it be before he
joined Madeleine Carter under the crack in the wall? In fact, if he still
had a job at the end of the afternoon, maybe he should invest in a
sleeping bag so he wouldn't have to wrap up in an old coat.

Dr. Stonds moved from Hector's feeble character and inadequate
training to a description of his own sufferings at the First District police
station. "Do you have any idea what it feels like to be roused in the
middle of the night with the news that your granddaughter has been
arrested for disturbing the peace?"

Of course I don't, you stupid fart, Hector thought, when I haven't
got a child, let alone a granddaughter. "It must have been dreadful, sir,

but I don't understand what that has to do with me, or with Madeleine Carter."

"Who the hell is Madeleine Carter?"

Hector tried to keep a hysterical scream out of his voice. "She's the schizophrenic woman living by the Hotel Pleiades garage. The reason you wanted to see me."

"Don't you listen to anything anyone says, Tammuz? She got my granddaughter arrested. Thanks to your interference in matters you should stay well away from."

Hector felt like a shipwrecked sailor, with land in sight but such swirling seas he couldn't keep track of what direction to swim. "What did she—Ms. Carter—do? She's very disturbed; she's afraid of strangers and isn't able to engage with people. Someone who isn't accustomed to psychosis might be upset by her behavior. But, honestly, sir—I don't know what happened last night. Why was your granddaughter arrested? And what happened to Madeleine Carter? Was she arrested as well?"

Hector imagined Madeleine offering the Virgin's blood to Stonds's granddaughter. When a psychotic homeless woman held out her rust- (or maybe blood-) stained fingers, the Stonds girl ran to the police screaming that Madeleine had attacked her.

"You claim to know something about the human mind." Stonds changed tack, leaning across his desk in a plea for empathy. "You tell me why a girl given every advantage—*every advantage*"—slapping the desk again for emphasis—"of education, attention, money, would think she had to make a public spectacle of herself in order to humiliate me."

Hector didn't say anything.

"She went down to your wall, to your precious psychopath, to embarrass her older sister, the most talented, accomplished young woman in Chicago. And to try to embarrass me. She got embroiled with that damned singer, poor Harry Minsky's sister, she assaulted the garage manager, and had herself arrested. Then came to the clinic just now to brag about it to you. And you still deny all knowledge of her?"

Hector made a feeble effort to speak. "Sir, the brief glimpse I had of Ms. Stonds in the clinic was the first time I ever saw her, and at that moment I had no idea she was your granddaughter. I didn't know she was arrested last night. But she didn't look like someone coming in to brag: she looked like a very unhappy girl who badly needed someone to talk to."

His hands were shaking from the effort of speaking up to the old man. He stuck them in his pockets.

Stonds scowled at him. "You are not to talk to her. That is an order. I've scheduled an appointment for her with Hanaper: I can rely on him to give me an honest evaluation of her mental state, not to encourage her to wallow in self-pity."

"Sir, with respect, she came to see me. Shouldn't she—"

"I've had enough of your insolence, Tammuz. As long as I'm part of this hospital, patients will see who I think is best for them, even if they are my own family."

Would have been funny if he hadn't been so deadly serious. Meanwhile, I was too confused to say anything else. Probably said way more than I should have, anyway, at least if I want to finish residency. The power these men have over our lives—hospitals are little totalitarian states in the midst of the republic.

Suddenly Stonds barked, "Well, what are you waiting for now?"

Pulled myself together as best I could and made my way back to clinic. Scene there chaotic—patients backed up at desk, waiting to be checked in, ones already registered understandably distraught at long delay. Interrupted Melissa Demetrios long enough to give her a thumbnail sketch of why I'd been gone. Couldn't see Stonds girl in the mob, but decided I'd better get to work on the people waiting for me first.

Worried about Madeleine—was she arrested as well? Wish I knew what the Stonds girl did last night. Harry Minsky's sister must be the drunk diva, but don't know how to track down people who are in police hands.

A real job to keep focused on the woes of patients, but after the long delays they'd suffered they were in a state of terrible anxiety and needed my best work. Knew I couldn't possibly accomplish anything in the fifteen minutes allowed by cost containment committee, so ignored clock, spent over half an hour with each. Gretchen kept buzzing me to remind me "time was up." Unplugged phone after third interruption. By good fortune a power surge just then crashed the computer. This kept all the penny-counters so busy they couldn't monitor what I was doing.

18

Reception Room in Hell

WHEN MARA WAS LITTLE she liked to go to the hospital with Grandfather on Saturdays. The medical students let her listen to their hearts through their stethoscopes; after he finished rounds, Grandfather took her to the animal labs where she could pet the rabbits. Everywhere they went people stood respectfully to one side to let them pass, or displayed intense interest in the little girl because she was attached to Dr. Stonds.

When she was little, the respect he received made Grandfather even more important to her. Yes, she was scared of him when he got angry, but he was so important he was worth all the attention and fear he generated. She once told some dinner guests that her grandfather owned Midwest Hospital; everyone laughed, and Grandfather himself ruffled her thick curls with delight. That was during Harriet's absence at Smith, when Grandfather briefly turned to Mara for a reflection of his glory.

Today, though, when she tried to see Dr. Tammuz, she hated Grandfather for owning the hospital. It meant she had no privacy on a most private errand. Although she slid into the building sideways, with a group of clerks returning from lunch, she felt as though at any moment a voice would bellow over the intercom: "Dr. Stonds, your granddaughter has entered the hospital. She is now on the second floor of the Kobold Pavilion, heading south."

Since her last visit five years ago, the hospital had ballooned, much as she felt her body had, into an ungainly place with unexpected useless lumps. She had trouble finding the psychiatry clinic, but wouldn't ask directions in case someone recognized her.

Her caution proved useless. Despite her effort to resist, the admissions clerk bullied Mara into giving her real name. The next thing she knew, Grandfather was on the phone bellowing at her for washing the family's dirty clothes in public: it's not enough that you drag me down to a police station, where I have to endure a lecture from a fat desk cop on poor discipline in the modern American family. Now you have to humiliate me in front of my colleagues and students. Including Hector Tammuz of all people, the weakest resident we've had at Midwest in twenty years, flaunts the advice of people with enough experience to teach him. I forbid you to see him.

What good could Dr. Tammuz do her, anyway? She'd only gone because of the dream about her mother in the spaceship. When she woke up she felt unbearably bereft. The recollection of herself with Luisa, the diva's drunkenness, her own theatrical chant to the goddess, and the distress of that poor woman who heard the Virgin speaking, made her writhe with self-hatred.

She went into the bathroom to shower, and caught sight of herself in the full-length mirror on the door. Usually she immediately glanced away, but now she made herself stare. Hulking body, large brown breasts, coarse black hair at crotch and armpit. You loathsome lump, she whispered to the mirror. The wide cheeks twisted into sobs; she slapped her face. What do you have to cry over, you blubber ball?

She showered, scrubbing herself with fury, and then, desperate for reassurance, called Cynthia Lowrie at her desk in the insurance company. "Grandfather wants to throw me out of the apartment. He says I can't be here tomorrow when Mephers comes back from the rehabilitation clinic."

"You can't come live with me, Mara, you know my dad would never let me invite you."

"I don't want to live with your stupid father. He's even worse than Grandfather. But—but Cynthia, what am I going to do?"

She poured out the whole story of the previous night's adventure. Cynthia was shocked, but envious: Mara had so much courage, even if it led her into really stupid actions. It wasn't the first time Mara had called after getting in trouble from her impulsive exploits, but this was the most extreme act she'd ever reported.

"Do you think I might be crazy? Grandfather talks so much about my bad blood, I'm starting to wonder if he's right, if there's something wrong that everyone who meets me can tell by looking at me."

"You are crazy, Mara, to go squatting under a wall pretending you're talking to some old goddess. But you know what you should do, you should talk to a psychiatrist and find out the truth. There's a guy at your grandfather's hospital who comes to Hagar's House to counsel the homeless women. Daddy says your grandfather doesn't like him much, and that's why he was picked for such a thankless job. Daddy hates him, on account of he's a Jew, or maybe because he looks down on him, on Daddy, I mean, but that wouldn't bother you, would it? Him being a Jew, I mean. And he's really cute."

When Mara called the hospital she learned that Hector was seeing patients that very afternoon in the psychiatry clinic. Synchronicity. Maybe the goddess Gula really was guiding her steps.

Dr. Tammuz was cute, Mara had to agree when he stopped to talk to her in the waiting room. And he had a very kind face. Mara imagined talking to him, telling him about Harriet and Grandfather; he would fall in love with Harriet just from hearing her described. Like the assistant state's attorney last night, he would help Mara in the hopes of getting close to her sister. And Harriet, ignoring all the suitors from Orleans Street Church, all the Christian young men who'd been Grandfather's students or at law school with her, would see that Mara had a crush on Dr. Tammuz and marry him just to spite her. By the time Grandfather started yelling at her on Gretchen's phone—the receiver stuffed through the hole in the bottom of the glass where patients slid their insurance documents for photocopying—Mara was sniffing at the picture of herself, Cindermara, forgotten in some garret while Harriet and Dr. Tammuz honeymooned on a Greek island.

"I don't know what to do with you, young lady," Grandfather concluded. "If I set you up in your own apartment you'll lie around all day drinking, without lifting a finger to find a job. You're too old for boarding school. You refuse to go to college. What do you suggest?"

"You should have let me stay in jail. At least you'd be happy," she flashed through her tears.

"Don't be melodramatic with me, young lady, I'm not in the humor for it. You are seriously disturbed; it may be that hospitalization will help you. Dr. Tammuz is hardly competent to evaluate your mental state, but since you're already here in the hospital I'm asking Dr. Hanaper to examine you."

"No! I won't." Dr. Hanaper was a regular dinner guest at the Graham Street apartment. Mara hated him for the coldness in his eyes while his mouth smiled at Grandfather and Harriet. "He's just one of your flunkeys, he'll put me on the locked ward if he thinks that's what you want. That's where my mother is, isn't it? You got tired of her and had her committed so she—"

"That's enough, Mara. My mind is made up. I'm going to make sure he talks to you this afternoon. Put that clerk back on the line."

Mara dropped the phone and ran from the clinic.

Plenty there for Gretchen and Charmaine to talk over. The line of patients waiting to check in, which had swelled while Mara used Gretchen's phone (Charmaine listening in on her extension), ground to a complete halt as the two clerks retreated to the file cabinets to dissect the conversation—from which they were roused only by Dr. Stonds's summons of Dr. Tammuz.

When Hector finished with his last scheduled patient, a few minutes before five, Gretchen and Charmaine were talking to each other while they cleared their desks for the day. They ignored Hector, who was standing in front of Gretchen, waiting for a break in the flow.

Finally, furious, he said, "Gretchen, what became of Ms. Stonds?"

She looked up at him. "Doctor, the computer system crashed. Me and Charmaine were so busy trying to bring it back up we didn't have time to keep track of walk-ins."

"Why did you call Dr. Stonds, when she was trying to make an appointment with me?"

Gretchen glanced at Charmaine. "The problem with America today is the breakdown of the family. Everybody knows that. I couldn't let an uninsured minor sign up for health care without informing her parent or guardian: it wouldn't be right."

"In other words, you were afraid Dr. Stonds might find out you knew she had come to the clinic, and you were determined to stand in good with him. Very right. You can't afford to be too careful about your job in these cost-cutting days. Do you know if Dr. Hanaper saw her?"

Gretchen's round cheeks were pulled away from her teeth in a rictus of venom. "I suggest you ask him, *Doctor* Tammuz. He thinks you're so special I'm sure he'd be glad to tell you all his patients' secrets. Now, if that's all, Doctor, I have a baby-sitter who charges me double time after six p.m. I don't suppose that matters to a doctor, but it does to a lowly reception clerk."

She slammed her drawers shut, locked them ostentatiously, and stormed out of the office, Charmaine in her wake. All Hector could think was that now he'd never get any cooperation from them.

He slumped in one of the waiting room chairs, his bones aching from the confrontations of the afternoon. Gretchen was right about one thing: he ought to find out whether Hanaper had examined Ms. Stonds, but the thought of talking to his department chairman was more than Hector could bear. He wanted to go home to bed, but he needed to find out if Madeleine Carter was still in jail.

He had no idea how to approach the police. Perhaps Mara Stonds might be able to tell him where the police had taken Madeleine.

He went back to the office he shared with the other psychiatry residents to dictate his notes from the afternoon's sessions, and saw the hospital directory out on Melissa Demetrios's desk. It gave Stonds's home address and phone number. Feeling a little queasy, he dialed the number. When a woman answered in a cool, remote voice he felt even more nervous, but he identified himself, and asked for Ms. Stonds.

19

The Ice Queen in the Underworld

Harriet wasn't usually home so early in the evening. Client meetings, discovery, consultations with her senior partner Leigh Wilton, usually carried her workday past seven, often later. Lack of sleep and worry about Mara sent her home early today.

She'd had another hysterical call from Gian Palmetto after lunch. The president of the Hotel Pleiades wanted to know what steps she was taking to guarantee that her sister wouldn't create a disturbance again outside the garage.

"I don't know, Gian," she said, trying to fight back fatigue and irritation, to speak with calm attentiveness. "Let's take a look at this wall and see what your options are."

Her afternoons were usually scheduled so solidly that it was hard to find time to eat. It was part of her pleasure in her skills that she could turn from a sanitary engineer at two-thirty to a ballerina at three-fifteen, and show the same clarity in understanding the problems of both. Today she was having trouble remembering who she was speaking to at any given moment, let alone what troubles brought them into their lawyer's office.

Everything about the day had been difficult, starting with the phone call that summoned her to the police department, but the hardest part had been saying "no" to *Grand-père,* that she wouldn't find an apartment for Mara. And then Mara gave her no thanks of any kind for this support.

Now here was Gian Palmetto howling in her ear, as if Harriet had sent Mara there on purpose to harass him.

She smacked the phone with the flat of her hand, wishing it were Gian's face, no, really Mara's face, and told her secretary to reschedule her remaining appointments; she was going over to the Pleiades to get a handle on their crisis, and then home.

"I'm too ill today to do my clients justice. If anyone's desperate, ask one of the other associates to see them."

Her secretary paused fractionally before agreeing: competitive young lawyers like Harriet normally guard their client lists with the ferocity of junkyard dogs. Either Harriet was ill, or she'd lost her fighting edge. In the latter case, the secretary would look for a new assignment: Harriet's only grace as a boss was that she was a winner, which meant she brought glory to her overworked, underthanked staff. If she'd lost her will to win, there was no reason to stay with her.

Once on the street, Harriet started to get into a cab, then waved the driver away. Maybe if she walked the mile to the hotel her head would clear.

The July air was warm. In her office, the seasons passed in reverse: the building's heating system made the rooms so toasty in winter that woolen clothes chafed her skin, while in summer she had to wear long sleeves and jackets against the cold. Outside, her dress, with its suggestion of a military cape in the back and long epauletted sleeves, clung to her like a plastic glove. Not for her tennis shoes on the street, that sloppy look that turned women into unprofessional slatterns. As she walked east her toes began to hurt inside her high heels.

Her route took her along the Chicago River, and she stopped near one of the bridges to rest her feet. A lake-bound boat, packed with tourists, passed below her. She couldn't imagine finding pleasure in such an outing, crammed among strangers, breathing diesel fumes mixed with stale grease from frying food in the galley. And yet her own vacations, passed in solitude at ski resorts or remote islands, did they bring her greater pleasure than these people experienced?

Was Mara right? Was she a cold person who lived in fear of Grandfather? Well, maybe she did fear him, but Mara didn't understand the nature of Harriet's dread: not that he would bellow at her, as he did at his students or Mara, but that Harriet would somehow be reduced in his eyes, that he would see her as less, and lose his affection for her. She called him "*Grand-père*," and often spoke to him in French to bolster his opinion of himself as a cosmopolitan man—setting herself further apart from Mara, who refused to learn the language.

Since the time he and Mephers took her in, Harriet knew she had to be as different from Beatrix as possible if she was going to be allowed to stay there. After the arrival of the baby, that little sister she feared might unseat her in the throne of *Grand-père*'s affections, she had tried harder still to attain perfection. If she wasn't the best in an activity, such as tennis or horseback riding, she gave it up. Failure was too risky.

The tour boat hooted a warning to a smaller craft. Harriet looked at her watch in alarm: she'd dawdled there at the bridge for seven minutes without once thinking of her client's legal problems. She shoved her feet back into her shoes and hurried over to the hotel.

By the time she reached the Pleiades, her feet were swollen and her hair was clinging to her neck in limp, sticky strands. The melancholy insights she'd had at the river vanished as her sore feet dominated her mind. She was demeaning herself in front of Gian Palmetto, leaving her office to meet him at his tiresome garage wall; damn Mara, anyway, for being so self-centered, so volatile, as to create last night's scene.

The air-conditioning in the lobby blew through the wet armpits of her dress; she was shivering when she reached Palmetto's office. His secretary gave her a cardigan and a cup of coffee with the bright promise that Mr. Palmetto would be with her soon.

Harriet's irritation deepened: she hated feeling like a supplicant in a client's office. It was typical that clients waited for her as she whirled from meeting to meeting, not for her to sit looking as bedraggled as an immigrant from a cleaning service while Palmetto made her dangle her heels.

She pulled her mobile phone from her purse and began making calls. When Palmetto finally emerged she was too engrossed to notice him. After a lengthy discussion of the exact meaning of paragraph seven, section two, of the Illinois Commerce Commission's opinion on waste haulers' liability for road contamination, she put the phone away, and affected to see him for the first time.

"Gian! Been waiting long? I'm sorry—but I had to shunt a lot of people to one side to come here, and everyone seems to be feeling the same urgency about their problems today. Must be the weather, making us all edgy. . . . Now, what's the story on this garage wall? Why has it become such a focal point for action?"

"Damned if I know. We'll get Brian Cassidy to meet us down there. He's the night manager at the garage, but he should be over in the operations room—he usually gets here at three-thirty for a briefing before his shift."

Brian Cassidy was glad to meet Harriet, hoped she'd be able to get this problem resolved. God knew he wasn't eager to attack women, even crazy bag ladies, but this broad—excuse me, Ms. Stonds, this—gal—was seriously getting under his skin.

Like Hector, Harriet noticed Cassidy's muscles straining his jacket sleeves. Mara had said this morning that Cassidy knocked her over, slammed her head into the wall; thinking of that, Harriet's mood toward her sister veered again. Poor baby sister, getting beaten up by a monster. Mara was big for a woman, but no match for a gorilla, which is what Cassidy looked like, short forehead over small blue eyes, snub nose lost in the expanse of round red face.

"My paralegal tells me you've been hosing the wall down every night. That isn't discouraging the woman?"

Her voice was crisp and cold, like shaved ice, and the garage manager fingered his tie, wondering if it was crooked. "She runs away until we're done, then she's right back there, lighting candles, carrying on like she thinks she's in church. All these homeless people down there get on my nerves, they watch you from the shadows like spooks, but this crazy one is the worst. It's hard to run a garage down there with that kind of shit—excuse me—disturbance going on all the time. Women hate it most—we had a major complaint last week from one of our best customers."

"Madeleine Carter is loitering," Harriet said calmly. "We ought to be able to get her picked up any time she camps out here."

"But that doctor who was here last week, he—I guess he was trying to give her an injection and get her to leave—but at the same time he said the sidewalk was public property, we didn't have any authority over her if she was on the sidewalk."

Harriet smiled. "I wonder who this doctor is. Would he want me giving his patients medical advice? The sidewalk is not hotel property, that's true. But Carter is still loitering, and can be made to leave. Let's go take a look at the space, while she's still in jail."

Harriet had called the state's attorney before leaving her office: they were letting Madeleine and Luisa cool their heels for a few days. Luisa had been slugged by a sister prisoner sick of listening to "Sempre libera" echoing down the corridors outside the holding cells. The state was trying to have Madeleine admitted to County, but might not be able to swing it. Harriet didn't bother her client with this information—if the state's attorney couldn't force Madeleine to accept hospitalization, Palmetto would spend the rest of the summer wanting to know why Harriet didn't do something about it.

Brian Cassidy led the way to the service elevator. When they reached the street outside the garage entrance Harriet suddenly felt nervous, wondering if Mara might have returned to the garage. Her sister would think Harriet was spying on her; her cheeks would puff out in that ugly swollen way and she would create a scene in front of a client. To Harriet's relief, there was no one at the wall, neither Mara nor any homeless women.

From Brian Cassidy's words, Harriet had pictured a little enclave of people in cardboard houses and sleeping bags. Instead, the sidewalk was filled with homebound commuters. Harriet was surprised—she lived in a world of limos and taxis and never thought about how most people got to work. Brian Cassidy pointed at the bus stop on the corner: three city routes started there.

When she asked where all the homeless people were, he took Harriet down an alley near the east end of the garage. They walked underneath an entrance ramp for Lake Shore Drive. An old wooden crate, slats torn randomly from its surface, was wedged between a pair of low-lying pylons.

"Our woman sleeps there some of the time. And there are some of the others."

Cassidy flicked his flashlight on a heap of blankets, like a zoo curator showing a snakepit to a visitor. After a moment Harriet saw the rags move, and realized that what she'd mistaken for an extra rag was actually a human head. She turned sharply and walked back to the garage.

The roadbed overhead seemed to press down on her. The street wasn't dirty, not in the sense of being filled with garbage, but the gray walks and walls, the absence of daylight, made her feel as though she were walking through grime. A dull buzzing seemed to fill her head. She spoke loudly, trying to assert herself against the pressure of the underground world.

"Can you show me exactly where this woman comes? Is it to the same place every day?"

Brian Cassidy went over near the crack. "I think it's about here."

He shone a flashlight around the area; Harriet saw bits of wax on the sidewalk, the residue of the woman's little altar. The smell of urine made her blench. She pictured Mara on that filthy ground, singing her idiotic chant, and backed away in distaste.

"Is there something about this area that makes it attractive to Madeleine Carter? Does the proximity to the garage give her greater access to lucrative panhandling? Or is it a feeling of greater security?"

Brian Cassidy said it was probably a good spot to beg, but Nicolo, the garage attendant, who was hovering in the background said, "No, boss. She never beg for money or nothing. She sit here because this—this hole. She think hole special, blood of Mother of God come out this hole."

Harriet hadn't noticed the crack in the wall. She took Brian Cassidy's flashlight to see it better. It was just a break in the concrete where rusty water oozed out.

"How do you know?" the hotel president asked Nicolo.

"When we taking people's cars, or now, when boss telling us, wash this wall, she cry. She put fingers so"—he stuck his hand into the crack—"then into mouth, and tell everybody, here is blood of Mother of God."

Harriet recoiled from the red on Nicolo's hands. "That isn't blood, is it?"

Brian Cassidy laughed. "No, ma'am. Probably rust. Must be some pipe in there leaking a bit."

"Cement it over," Harriet said. "The wall is your property: you don't have to leave it open like that if that's what's attracting her. Break up the box she sleeps in. There are plenty of shelters in the city to give her a bed: you don't have to. Keep someone from your security force down here to escort her away if she comes back. If she persists, call the city and have her arrested."

"And you guarantee your sister won't come back to create a bigger disturbance?" Gian Palmetto said.

Harriet's shoulders sagged. "I can't guarantee anything about Mara. But if she's loitering here or creating a disturbance, you don't need—the fact that she's my sister—" She couldn't get the words out and finally settled for saying, "She needs to learn that her actions have measurable consequences."

"As long as she doesn't bring the media in," Palmetto said. "I can't afford the negative publicity of looking like I'm harassing homeless people."

"I thought you couldn't afford the negative publicity of this woman worshiping the Virgin Mary down here. Your choices are somewhat limited. Cover up this crack, since that's the attraction that draws her, and make it unpleasant for her to come around. Or tolerate her sitting there with her candles, howling about the Mother of God."

Gian Palmetto wanted something else, something magical, the woman wafted away by Harriet's chanting sections of the Illinois Criminal Code that would bring the gods of justice to life here on Underground Wacker. He spent twenty minutes trying to argue her into some other suggestions. In the cab going home she phoned the firm's word processing center to dictate a report, along with her billable hours for the Pleiades time sheet. In her irritation she charged Palmetto for the seven minutes she'd spent watching the tourist boat.

20

The Ice Queen Adrift

W HEN HECTOR PHONED, Harriet was standing in the living room looking at the street. She arrived home determined to have things out with Mara once and for all, although what things she couldn't specify. She was furious with Mara for creating a hideous public spectacle, but at the same time felt guilty for ignoring the baby sister all those years ago. She wished Mara would move away, leave her in peace with Mephers and Grandfather. She wanted to beat up Mara at the same time as she pictured herself wrapping her little sister in a warm blanket and nursing her.

But when she rapped on Mara's door and sharply called her name she got no reply. Her anger rising, she called more loudly. Damned brat, pretending not to hear her! The woman from the cleaning service emerged from the kitchen. She told Harriet in her halting English that Mara wasn't home. She had come in, yes, and left again in maybe thirty minutes, with—Barbara struggled for the word and finally imitated someone walking with a burden—yes, a backpack. No, Mara had not left any message.

Harriet unlocked the door to Mephers's room and checked that everything was ready for the housekeeper's return in the morning. The sheets were clean, the few books standing at military attention, just as Mephers had left them. A conservator at the Art Institute, grateful to

Grand-père for saving her husband's life, had repaired the damage to the secretary.

Maybe when Mephers returned the apartment would feel more inviting. But Mara—she was like the warning buzz of violins in a horror movie: fearful things followed in her wake.

Harriet went into her sister's room, flinching as always from the disarray—drawers open with shirts and bras dangling over the edges, paper everywhere, books piled next to the bed, a musty smell from unwashed sheets. Mara had left her computer turned on. Harriet touched the mouse, resolving the screen saver back to text.

> *Dear Harriet,*
>
> *I know you hate me for messing up in front of your client. I'm sorry, even though I think the hotel is a pig and a bully for terrorizing that homeless woman. I know you and Grandfather want me gone since Mephers is coming tomorrow, that she's more important than I am so I'm leaving before Grandfather puts me in the locked ward. Maybe I'll find Mother, or maybe I'll just turn into her. Do you think—oh, fuck, what's the use*

Harriet looked around her sister's room, wondering if she'd finished the letter in a different file and printed it out. After searching the visible surfaces, and checking in her own room to see if she'd overlooked a note, she decided Mara had started to write, been unable to finish, and left her machine on so that Harriet would see the message. Back in Mara's room, she printed out the letter, saved the file, turned off the machine.

Self-dramatizing brat. A good thing she'd taken off: they could use some peace in the apartment. Off to find their mother? When would Mara believe that Beatrix was dead? Three weeks before Harriet turned fifteen, as she was planning a birthday party for friends from school, writing out the invitations, proud of her spiky handwriting: Grandfather telling her Beatrix had an accident in her bath—always be careful climbing in and out of the tub.

What Harriet remembered most clearly about that day, besides her bold black script on the white cardboard notes, was her arms, slender against the navy of her school skirt as Grandfather explained to her: Beatrix had been living with terrible people, so terrible, Grandfather would prefer Harriet never knew the exact circumstances. He had made sure the papers wouldn't print the story, so she needn't fear nosy questions at school. No church funeral—Beatrix had been estranged too long from her family—just a quiet service in a funeral home. Mara, two at the time, didn't understand, and later never believed.

Harriet went to her suite at the other end of the hall and took off her caped dress. With her usual precise motions she folded it into a bag for Barbara to take to the dry cleaners. She stood under the shower, washing the grime from Underground Wacker from her hair and her skin, standing there long after she was clean, thinking of—nothing.

When she emerged she still couldn't get her mind to work. If Mara had run away, it solved the problem. Mephers would return home, she and Grandfather and Harriet would resume the life Mara had interrupted nineteen years ago. She would be Grandfather's only princess once again. Grandfather's Ice Queen.

Hector's phone call came in while she was pushing her hands against her diaphragm, feeling how empty she was. When his unfamiliar voice asked hesitantly for Ms. Stonds, Harriet tensed, thinking she was about to hear of some fresh disaster of Mara's. But she said yes, she was Ms. Stonds.

Hector apologized for not seeing her in clinic that afternoon. "I don't want to go behind your grandfather's back, but if you'd like to talk to me I'd be happy to set up an appointment."

"You've made a mistake, Doctor—I'm Ms. Harriet Stonds. Were you looking for my sister Mara?"

Hector, nervous to begin with, grew more flustered by her cool tone. Was it Mara who had come into the clinic? Should he have known there was a sister? Was Harriet going to report him to the doctor?

"Mara's gone out, Doctor—what did you say your name was?— Tammuz. I'm afraid I don't know when she might return but shall I take a message?"

Harriet's voice sounded like water one degree above the freezing point. She didn't know that, didn't know that her polished surfaces were cold, like jade, to the touch; she only knew that in her empty state she couldn't summon the energy to respond to a stranger.

At the other end of the line poor frozen Hector could barely curve his tongue to shape vowels, but he managed to stammer that he was concerned about Ms. Stonds, that is, Ms. Mara Stonds, but also—he had learned she'd been arrested last night, in company with a psychotic homeless woman he was trying to treat; he hoped Ms. Stonds might know where the woman had been taken.

"Oh." Harriet's voice dropped into the low Kelvin range. "You're the doctor who's been handing out legal advice to street people. I remember now: my grandfather, Dr. Stonds, has spoken of you."

Hector, hunched over the phone at Melissa's desk, started to feel seasick again, as he had in Stonds's office earlier that day. That made him angry: he was damned if he was going to let another Stonds reduce him to drivel.

"Ms. Stonds, I have not given any legal advice to anyone. I don't know anything about the law, but did we get rid of the idea that people are innocent until they're proved guilty? I did not encourage your sister to stage a sit-in with Madeleine Carter, in fact, I saw your sister for the first time this afternoon, and we exchanged about a dozen words, all relating to her desire to schedule an appointment with me."

"That wall where your psychotic homeless woman sits belongs to one of my clients," Harriet said, surprising herself by offering him an explanation. "I am a lawyer. The garage manager—oh, what difference does it make, anyway, who said what to whom? I bailed my sister out early this morning. Your patient and the other woman, the singer, no one was there to speak for them. They're being held at County Jail for a few days. The state wants to admit your patient to County Hospital."

"I see. So I should call over to the jail?" Hector said, wondering where it was.

"Do you know anything about how to get information out of the courts? You need the woman's case number. Call my secretary: she should still be at her desk. She'll get it for you. My sister has run away from home. I don't know where she is. I'm a bit concerned about her."

Her voice hadn't changed in color or warmth. Hector couldn't know she had violated her own standards of privacy and confidentiality in what she'd said. He thanked her for her advice in a voice as aloof and formal as he could manage and hung up.

At the other end Harriet felt bereft and then angry. She'd reached out to him, told him her private business, smoothed his path with the courts. For no reason at all, except that his hesitant soft voice sounded vulnerable—and he hung up on her. She started to weep, which made her angrier, but she couldn't seem to stop.

A key turned in the door. She retreated to the shadows at the end of the room. Grandfather hated all displays of emotion, except, of course, his own. She waited for his tread to echo down the hall, the door to his room to shut while he changed clothes, and slipped into her own suite to clean her face. When she came out to greet him she looked calm as usual.

"Home early, my dear?" He kissed her cheek and looked at her old clothes. "You planning to go out with some of your friends?"

In deference to his formal attitude she usually wore a dress to dinner. "No, darling. I'm just tired, after this morning's *contretemps,* and wanted to be comfortable."

"Hmm. Well, you look a good deal better in your jeans than your sister, but it does seem odd. You're coming with me to pick up Hilda in the morning, right? I know that will make her feel strong enough to return here. This afternoon she suggested moving into a retirement community, to avoid friction with Mara, but I told her not to be ridiculous. This has been her home for—my God, has the time gone?—fifty-five years."

"Mara thinks you want to hospitalize her," Harriet said.

"Best solution," he grunted. "She's very disturbed. Wouldn't last a day if we put her in her own apartment, won't go to school, needs help that she refuses to get. She tried to turn to that prize loser Tammuz. I stopped that nonsense in a hurry, you can believe."

Harriet, who had planned to tell Grandfather about Hector's phone call, found herself responding only with a neutral "oh," adding the news that Mara seemed to have run away.

"Oh, damn her, anyway!" Grandfather snapped, not questioning how Harriet knew. "Now we'll be faced with some other dramatic crisis, just when Hilda is in the middle of her recovery. Where'd she go?"

"I don't know. I thought I'd phone Cynthia Lowrie after dinner to see if she knows." Harriet played with a tassel on the lamp next to her, not sure how to ask a question about her mother. "You know, *Grandpère*, Mara is terrified that she's like Beatrix. Did you ever hospitalize her?"

"Scared about turning out like her mother? She damned well should be. The only thing we've been spared so far is a reprise of Beatrix's indiscriminate sexual proclivities. No doubt they will appear next."

"You never tried getting Beatrix medical help?"

Grandfather's frown turned his face into a terrifying mask. "Don't tell me you're going to start second-guessing my judgment now, too. I thought you at least knew that we were well rid of her."

Of course she was well rid of Beatrix. She knew that catechism by heart, because Grandfather or Mephers said it at least once a week all the time she was growing up, congratulating themselves on their good deed in saving Harriet. For the first time, though, she wondered if she was well off with Grandfather. Better off than with Beatrix, certainly, she wouldn't disagree, but couldn't she have had a little warmth along with the French lessons, the vacations in Europe, and the quiet good taste on Graham Street?

21

Saint Becca Slays a Dragon

I T H A D A L L S E E M E D so clear to Becca when she left the house. Her mother, hearing the side door, had come outside and asked where she was going. To Northbrook Court with Kim and Mimi, Becca said. Karen frowned with sleep-heavy eyes. She didn't believe her daughter, but was too tired to start another battle. Be home in time for supper, was all she said, besides the usual, who's driving (Kim's mom, Becca said quickly) and don't charge more than twenty-five dollars, you've maxed out your credit for the month.

Karen was afraid her daughter was going off to pour her woes on her boyfriend Corie's chest. She was afraid that Becca's anger and confusion over her aunt could quickly turn into a more resolvable passion, and she didn't want her daughter to have sex so young. If she'd known that Becca, picking up her bike, was riding neither to Corie's nor Kim's, but to the train station, that she was on the 11:49 to Chicago—well, how could it have made her more worried than the idea of inexpert teen gropings, no condoms, no pill, nothing between Becca and a baby but the laws of chance?

After her outburst at her mother's cruelty in not wanting to bail Luisa out of jail and bring her home, Becca had returned to her own room. She planned to keep vigil until her father's return, but fell immediately asleep, waking only when Harry's Mercedes crunched on the gravel below her window at nine-thirty. She ran downstairs to eavesdrop outside the breakfast room.

"Dr. Stonds was at the station, too," Daddy was saying. "You probably don't remember, but he operated on Mother's brain tumor."

Mom's voice, a murmur telling Daddy that Becca was sleeping. Daddy's rasping voice dropping to a husky whisper. Stonds's granddaughter . . . crazy homeless woman . . . (then, exasperated, more loudly) oh, who in hell knows what Janice thought she was doing? Yes, she was drunk. No, I left her in jail. You don't need bail, disturbing the peace they let you out on your own word, but they're holding her a few days until she dries out . . . hospitalization . . . fed up . . .

Becca crept back upstairs. Aunt Luisa in jail. His own sister. If she had a sister . . . No, she'd have a brother, he'd be in line to inherit Minsky Scrap Iron, to be crowned the new King of Scrap, as Aunt Luisa liked to call Daddy. There was nothing wrong with owning a scrap business, it was good for the planet, recycling other people's rusty junk that they didn't care enough to look after. When she first met Corie she almost beat him up for making fun of Daddy's work. The kids in her school, their fathers were lawyers or doctors, they didn't understand the value of meeting a payroll, but there was only Becca, and Daddy didn't think he was being prejudiced, but, sweetheart, I just can't see a girl in that rough neighborhood. It's hard enough on me. Your grandfather never needed to use a gun, and I've had to take up marksmanship, not a job for a nice Jewish boy, let alone a girl.

Becca was going to be a veterinarian. Besides her dog Dusty she looked after a trio of hamsters, a tank of goldfish, and two cats. Once, when Dusty cut his paw on a broken bottle that some jerk dropped in the park, Becca held him while Dr. Kalnikov stitched him up. Dr. Kalnikov said she had a natural rapport with animals.

If she had a brother, she wouldn't leave him in jail, especially if he was a sensitive artist, used to pampering. Mom was right, Becca hated Aunt Luisa showing up drunk, but Luisa needed looking after. Prostitutes with knives, she'd seen that on TV, women's prison was no joke. What if someone cut Luisa in the throat and she was never able to sing again?

Because of the Holocaust it was very important always to support human rights and civil rights; Harry and Karen gave a lot of money to groups like the ACLU and the First Freedoms Forum, but what about Luisa's civil rights?

It was at that point that Becca decided to take the train to Chicago. She looked up the First Freedoms Forum address and set out. By the time she reached the city her confidence began to wane. She had been to Chicago, of course, many times—to shows with her parents, down to the South Side to visit the scrap yard—but she'd never come alone. When she was with Karen the crowds seemed exciting, but buffeted now in the cross-tides of commuters she felt frightened. She had never noticed how dirty the station was, either, with its unwashed floors, litter dropped everywhere. The vaulted ceiling was miles away. Some tired designer had stuck particleboard cubicles into the enormous space to house fast-food restaurants. They looked like the toys of an unkempt giant, dropped randomly between the benches and ticket counters.

Becca thought about turning tail and running home, but Aunt Luisa was still in jail. She had to show there was one Minsky with compassion. She gritted her teeth and asked a cop how to find LaSalle Street.

Her courage ebbed still further as she waited in a cramped ante-chamber for someone to be willing to talk to her. When a young man in khaki pants and a rumpled white shirt finally came out, he did nothing to set her at ease. He stood over her with his arms crossed, looking at his watch, his files, anything but her, until she could barely get out any words.

Before she finished he told her she should be at a legal aid clinic if she couldn't afford a lawyer. Triple-F only took cases with some constitutional significance. Like what? Oh, free speech, illegal search and seizure, that kind of thing.

"Well, my aunt's free speech rights were violated," Becca said wildly, picturing Luisa singing one of her arias in public, and being told to shut up.

The young man gave an exaggerated sigh, and said that Luisa's behavior constituted a public nuisance, not protected speech. Becca by this time was close to tears.

Another attorney, a woman about her mother's age, stopped to listen to them. "Just call over to the station for her, Stefan. Or I'll do it if you're busy. . . . Luisa Montcrief? The diva? Are you sure she was arrested, honey?"

"Yes, she's my aunt." And to her own embarrassment Becca started to sob.

Stefan scuttled away as from an open sewer, which made the woman smile. "They sure don't like any PDEs, do they? Oh—displays of emotion. Public or private depending on the circumstance. Stay here and I'll make a couple of calls for you."

She handed Becca a box of tissues and disappeared into the inner offices, where she was gone for some time. Becca excused herself shyly to the receptionist and was directed to a ladies' room. She washed her face and carefully outlined her mouth again in the black lipstick Karen hated.

When Becca returned to the reception area, the woman was waiting for her. She had a man with her, an older one, who looked more like Becca's idea of a lawyer than the young man: his hair was gray, he wore a suit, and he had a serious face with intense eyes. In fact, he looked at Becca so seriously that she thought at first he might be going to chew her out for wasting their time.

The woman introduced him: Maurice Pekiel, a senior attorney, free speech expert. She herself was called Judith Ohana. Judith had persuaded the state's attorney to release Madame Montcrief, but, looking Becca in the eyes, your aunt is quite ill; to be blunt she's suffering delirium as the result of alcohol withdrawal. It would be quite unpleasant for Becca to see her now. In fact, the state's attorney had released Madame Montcrief to a bed at County Hospital until they could calm down her seizures. After that, well, it would be up to Becca and her family to decide whether they felt like bringing her home.

Becca flushed with misery . . . for her impulsiveness in riding downtown; for exposing herself, her family, to public scrutiny; for taking Judith Ohana's time on a problem which now looked tawdry, not urgent;

for being fourteen and not knowing what she thought or felt about anything in the world around her. She got up to leave, trying to mumble a thank-you so they wouldn't think she cared about their opinion.

"But you've brought a pretty little problem to our attention," Judith said. "Mr. Pekiel wants to look into it. The woman who was arrested with your aunt was having a religious vision at that hotel garage. We might want to support her. It could be that her religious liberty takes precedence over issues of public disturbance—well, not to bother you with technical language—but it could be she has a right to be down there, if that's the only place she can practice her religion. So we wanted to thank you for letting us know about such an interesting situation. And can you give us your phone number? It's always possible we might need to get in touch with you."

By the time Becca got home she had forgotten both her fight with her mother and her airy lie about going to Northbrook Court.

"I got Aunt Luisa out of jail. And she's in the hospital, so don't worry, she isn't coming here."

A furious Karen demanded the whole story. By the time it came to an end, Becca was grounded for three days. She stalked to her room, haughty, a princess among commoners, then raced to call Corie and Kim, to show off what a heroine she'd been.

22

Free at Last?

WHEN MARA WAS SMALL, she hid clean underwear in her doll's crib, along with nickels saved from her allowance, so that when she felt especially hurt and misunderstood she'd be ready to run away. She actually fled as far as the corner once, the first summer Harriet came home from college, when her efforts to dress up in front of her grown-up sister led Grandfather to hold Mara under the kitchen sink while Mephers scrubbed her face. Later, while they were fawning over Harriet, Mara rode down the service elevator on her trike. Raymond, the doorman, phoned up to Mephers, who caught Mara as she was starting to cross North Avenue.

Mara had imagined running so many times that she packed quickly when the moment came: a few clean shirts, socks and underpants, tampons, toothbrush and deodorant, her passport. Instead of the nickels from her allowance she'd need real money. She'd saved over a thousand dollars from her job at the Pleiades, but she'd never had to pay bills, she had no idea how much or how little twelve hundred and forty-two dollars could buy. When she looked at apartments for rent in the paper, she was appalled by how much even the simplest place cost. She'd need to take a sleeping bag, so that she could sleep in the parks, her small flashlight, and a few other camping necessities.

She tried to write to Harriet, started, deleted, started again, and finally abandoned the attempt. In the kitchen, her backpack over her shoulders, she helped herself to fruit and a few staples. Down on the street she joked with Raymond, who assumed she was heading on a camping trip, and teased her about running away. She wondered if she would ever see him again, and pressed a five-dollar tip in his hand, although she turned down his offer of a cab.

She hadn't figured out where to spend the night. Her first idea was Hagar's House, since she was among the homeless now, even with her twelve-hundred-dollar bank balance. But Patsy Wanachs would only report her to Grandfather and Harriet. Cynthia had said, absolutely do not come to my place, and anyway, she couldn't stay overnight with Rafe Lowrie and that prize creep Jared.

The thought of the Westinghouse box near the crack in the wall passed through her mind, but she cringed from the memory of the previous night with Luisa and Madeleine, the arrest, the humiliations of the day. Luisa drunk . . . if that was what Beatrix had been like . . . of course, Grandfather probably made that up, he made up lies about Mara, probably about Beatrix as well. If Beatrix had defied him . . . but then why hadn't she taken baby Mara with her? Harriet said when she lived with Beatrix after her father's death, they lived on Spam and Bloody Mary mix. Mara wasn't like that, not really, she got high out of misery, not out of the craving for alcohol that gripped Luisa, squeezing her until she turned mad with desire.

Mara would go to Iraq and find out the truth about Grannie Selena's death. What if Grandfather was lying about that, too, and Grannie Selena was really still alive, unable to come home because the doctor refused to send her airfare, or maybe had denounced her to the State Department as a spy for Saddam Hussein.

Mara had read books about women who disguised themselves as men and traveled through Middle Eastern countries. Would those large breasts of hers lie down quietly beneath a man's white tunic? She was sharing coffee in a desert tent, the men laughing at her jokes, as she quickly became fluent in Arabic. And then a telltale red stain destroyed the white quiet of the sands. She was stripped, and her breasts tumbled out like swollen cantaloupes.

At a travel agency on Michigan Avenue she was surprised to learn that she couldn't even go to Iraq. Since the Gulf War no one from any country in the world could go there, except as part of some special medical mission.

"But my grandmother is in Iraq; she's disappeared and someone has to find her," Mara said.

The travel agent didn't care about Mara's grandmother, what she might have done to be stuck in the Middle East. She tried to interest Mara in Israel or Turkey instead, but in face of Mara's escalating fury, told her to go to the State Department, and gave her directions to the federal building downtown.

Mara climbed onto a southbound bus—unlike Harriet she knew the buses, rode the L, part of her feeble effort to set up an identity separate from her sister. It was rush hour. People glared at her as she squeezed into the aisle, her backpack bumping against glasses and shoulders. She could see herself as larger than ever, her body ballooning across the aisle until it seemed as though her arms were touching the windows on either side.

Finally escaping at Adams Street, trying to pick her way carefully through the crowd, stepping on feet, bumping a man with a briefcase who swore at her, all that misery only to find that the State Department offices closed at four.

She began to believe her own story, that despite the newspaper report she'd read when she was fifteen, certainly despite Mephers's tight-lipped assurances that Selena was most definitely dead, her grandmother was still alive. Maybe her mother, too. After all, Beatrix's death had not even been in the paper at all.

If she could find Grannie Selena, everything would be all right. Mara's body would assume a proper shape, her life a real direction. She took a train to the University of Chicago, down to the Oriental Institute, the museum where she'd done her research on Great-grandfather Vatick. That was as close as she could get to her grannie tonight, but it was better than returning to Graham Street.

Behind the museum lay landscaped grounds for the university

chapel, a stone Gothic building as big as a cathedral. Among those bushes and plants she could set up her sleeping bag unnoticed.

She wandered the streets until dark, the backpack cutting into her shoulders, her hair and clothes matting with sweat in the close air. She hadn't thought about how she might keep herself clean on the streets.

Students passed, talking about grades and class requirements, couples went by with baby carriages or dogs. Mara felt more and more isolated, with no friend to call on for help, no relatives. She felt as though she'd come unbound from the planet itself.

The midwestern summer does not ease at night. When dark came and Mara unrolled her sleeping bag near the chapel, the air pressed around her, warm and wet. Even so, she zipped the sleeping bag up to her chin, as though its thin down could keep the bigness of the night from crushing her. She lay stiffly, heart pounding, unable to relax. A furry shape brushed against her face and she gasped with fear. Her hands trembled so much she could hardly use them, but she managed to find her flashlight. A cat stared into her light with impersonal malignancy, then spat at her and ran.

23

The Fatherless Orphan

OVER THE NEXT SEVERAL DAYS, Grandfather kept commenting at dinner on how wonderful Hilda—Mrs. Ephers—looked, and how pleasant it was that Mara had chosen to go away for a few days, to let Hilda settle in again. When Harriet wanted to tell Mephers the truth, that Mara had run away, Grandfather ordered her not to: the less Mrs. Ephers has to worry about right now, the better.

It troubled Harriet that the doctor showed no interest in Mara's whereabouts. Perhaps it was age: he couldn't take histrionics, so he gave an indifferent shrug, oh, she's gone to join Beatrix on the road to perdition. That's what he said to Harriet in private when she suggested reporting Mara's disappearance to the police, or hiring a detective to trace her.

Mephers never asked where Mara was, or even mentioned the episode that had precipitated her heart attack. Infarct, Grandfather called it, heart attack is an unnecessarily dramatic expression and not descriptive. Infarct sounded vaguely obscene, Harriet thought, evoking bodily functions she couldn't associate with the housekeeper's iron posture.

Mephers had lost fifteen pounds in her time away, but otherwise seemed unchanged. Despite her age she suffered no lessening of her powers, except to need a longer nap in the afternoons. In the mornings, after she'd overseen the start of the household for the day, she went to the rooftop pool and swam for half an hour. Dr. Stonds forbade her to do any heavy work, but it was clear to both him and Harriet that running their home was essential to Mephers's well-being. Barbara, the woman from the agency who took care of their fifteen rooms, their food and laundry, without supervision during Mephers's absence, quit the third day after the housekeeper's return. Mexican, Mephers said with grim satisfaction. No work ethic. And made the agency send her a Pole.

Harriet was surprised to find she wasn't as happy to have Mephers at home as she'd expected. She kept wanting to ask about the letter Mara claimed she'd found, and the photograph of a man who looked like Harriet. Did you have a letter to Mother from France? Did Beatrix give it to you? Or did you intercept it in the mail and never show it to anyone?

Harriet had argued with Mara, told her she was only imagining the photograph. Now she found herself wondering why she'd never noticed Mephers's secretive air of triumph as she surveyed the apartment. Selena was gone, Beatrix was gone, Mara had disappeared. Only Harriet remained between Grandfather and Hilda Ephers. She began to feel vulnerable, as she had when she was seven: she needed to be on her best behavior or the two of them would make her leave.

Harriet had phoned Cynthia Lowrie, hoping at some unconscious level to hear a friendly voice discuss her sister. Since it was Wednesday night, Cynthia was at Hagar's House, distributing Bibles. Lowrie's son, Harriet couldn't remember his name, told her that with an unpleasant sneer in his voice. He grudgingly agreed to leave a message for his sister.

At the shelter, Cynthia was watching the study meeting with a pained, anxious face in case any of the homeless women challenged or contradicted Rafe. Last week, after Luisa had disrupted the Bible class, Rafe yelled at Cynthia all the way home: you useless moron, I'll never get you off my hands, what man would ever want to marry someone as lazy and stupid as you, Jared's right, you look like a retarded cow, the kind of creature I buy and sell futures in all day long, you're pathetic.

Once inside their own door she'd tried to run to her bedroom, but he grabbed her and shoved her against the doorway, so hard that her right

cheekbone was cut open to the bone. Cynthia stayed home from work
the next two days, but didn't try to see a doctor.

Cynthia was starting to hate the whole idea of Jesus, since worshiping Him and praising His name brought her so much personal misery.
On Bible study nights before going to the church she couldn't eat.
What's in these potatoes that you're not eating them, ground glass? that
from Jared, home from college for the summer. Of course on your best
days your cooking is kind of poisonous but I thought you were immune
to it. By the time she and Rafe left for church she was usually on the
verge of tears.

Tonight's session had been calm, calm for the setting, that is, for one
of the women fell asleep in the middle of Rafe's homily, while LaBelle
kept crying over the fate of the dismembered concubine in Judges, refusing to believe that the passage was merely allegorical: the twelve pieces
standing for the twelve tribes of Israel, who didn't listen to God, and
forfeited their place at His right hand to the twelve Apostles.

Rafe repeated this allegorical meaning to LaBelle over and over, but
she kept wailing, it almost happened to me, my boyfriend cut on me so
hard I thought he was going to cut me into twelve pieces; I almost died,
they had to put two hundred seventy-three stitches in me, the doctor, he
said he never seen someone cut on so bad and still living.

But tonight no one challenged Rafe's authority outright. Despite
Cynthia's fears he felt a pitying superiority to the cut-up woman, rather
than anger over her cries, so the ride home wasn't marred by his hoarse
shouts.

When they got in, Jared, watching the White Sox on TV in the
family room with his girlfriend Tamara, yelled, "That snooty sister of
your friend Mara phoned for you."

"Hu–Harriet?" Cynthia gasped, looking at her father. "What—
what does she want?"

"How should I know? She doesn't talk to peons like me." He
assumed a phony British accent to characterize Harriet: "Oh, could you
take a message for me? Ask her to call Ms. Harriet Stonds when she
returns."

Tamara, trained in obedience to Jared's whims, laughed at his imitation and patted his thigh. Tamara was a nervous young woman, inclined to anorexia; Cynthia felt little jealousy of her glossy dark hair or skinny prettiness, since Tamara often sported more bruises than Cynthia herself.

"Oh." Cynthia looked at Rafe. "Do you mind—I wonder if something's wrong—is it all right if I call?"

"Suit yourself." He opened the refrigerator in the family room. "We're out of club soda in here, Cynthia: can you check the supplies occasionally, instead of spending your life mooning around? Go ahead and call Harriet Stonds, but don't imagine I'm letting you go on any outings with them, because the answer in advance is 'no.' "

Cynthia brought a six-pack of club soda from the kitchen pantry down to the family room. She waited until Rafe had poured himself a bourbon and soda and settled in front of the game with Jared and Tamara. The Sox were behind by two runs, she noticed, wishing they would start scoring before Jared and Rafe got too upset.

When she phoned, from the kitchen extension, her whispery breathlessness irritated Harriet. What possible attraction did this dreary creature hold for Mara? After a prolonged catechism, Harriet got Cynthia to reveal the substance of Mara's conversation with her that afternoon. (I know she called you, Cynthia: you two have spent the last ten years encouraging each other to imagine you were ill-used at home, Harriet's cold voice making Cynthia teeter once more on the brink of tears.)

Yes, she sniffled, yes, she would let Harriet know if Mara phoned again; and she'd better run now, Daddy didn't like her to tie up the phone at night. When she hung up Texas had scored another three runs. She tiptoed into her bedroom and wedged a dictionary between the dresser and the door to hold it shut.

At the other end, Harriet frowned into the receiver. Maybe Mara was right, maybe Rafe Lowrie did beat up Cynthia. It wasn't natural for a nineteen-year-old girl to be so terrified of her father. Mara ought to live Cynthia's life for a week or two, then maybe she'd know she was well off with *Grand-père*.

During the week, after the bustle surrounding Mephers's return wore off, Harriet became more uneasy about her sister. On Friday she had a call from Gian Palmetto at the Pleiades Hotel—just wanted to tell you that we cemented over that crack in the wall, and that homeless woman hasn't been back. On the other hand, Brian Cassidy in the garage thinks he saw your sister there last night.

Harriet drove around the wall on Friday and Saturday night, but saw no one, not even two homeless women hunting for Madeleine Carter in the recesses of the underground roads. As Harriet slowed her Acura to inspect the wall, Jacqui and Nanette slid into the shadows with practiced ease.

On Sunday, accompanying Mephers to the eleven o'clock service at Orleans Street, Harriet waylaid Cynthia Lowrie outside the young singles Sunday school class. Cynthia, keeping a nervous eye out for Rafe, said no, she hadn't seen Mara, her daddy didn't like her hanging out with Mara since she got thrown out of Smith.

Harriet, used to dealing with lying and nervous witnesses, thought Cynthia knew more than she was saying, and finally—using more gentleness than she usually mustered—got Cynthia to admit to a second phone call from Mara, to her office, Friday after lunch.

"She was upset—she thought she could go to Iraq to look for her—your—I guess she's yours, too—grandmother. She says your grandmother is really alive, she thinks Dr. Stonds paid off the newspaper to print a false report of her death. Only apparently you can't go to Iraq these days. So next Mara wanted me to try to find a detective for her, someone who could hunt for your mother, who she says is also alive. Only of course I couldn't."

Mara, you want a detective you go hire one, Cynthia told her on the phone, angry at the freedom her friend seemed to be enjoying. I'm going to get fired if they catch me making more personal calls here. Well, what about me? Mara demanded. I have to use a public phone in the park, I can't even find a phone book.

No, Cynthia told Harriet, Mara hadn't said where she was staying, only that she'd had a difficult time at the State Department, where they wanted to know every detail of her private life: didn't she know there was an international boycott of Iraq? what was her grandmother doing there, anyway? And Mara, terrified that they would report her to Dr. Stonds, had fled the building without giving her name, and phoned Cynthia.

Harriet felt her shoulders sag: why couldn't her sister know someone more focused? Not that Mara was so focused, either. Imagine going off the deep end like that, getting so wrapped up in her fantasies about Selena that she actually thought she could find her in Iraq.

"Please, Cynthia, if she calls you again, will you let me know right away? I'm really worried about her. You and Mara always have indulged in dramatic fantasies, but this isn't a game, you know."

And Cynthia, with a rare flash of spirit, retorted, "I know it's not a game, Harriet. You and Dr. Stonds want to lock her in an insane asylum. How would you feel if that was you?"

Harriet flushed. "Don't be impertinent with me, Cynthia. All he wants is for someone competent to evaluate Mara. Naturally, she—and you—turned that into a threat of forced hospitalization."

Patsy Wanachs, the director of Hagar's House, came down the hall just then. She was surprised to see Harriet in agitated private talk with Cynthia Lowrie. She made a pretext for stopping, to discuss the Family Matters seminar Rafe wanted to run at the church in early August.

"I know it's a spirituality session for businessmen, but I wonder if your father should invite some of the homeless men who come to Dr. Tammuz's Friday clinic. It could show them some realistic options for taking charge of their lives." And then broke off. "Oh, I'm sorry, Harriet—I didn't realize you were in the middle of something important with Cynthia. This can wait."

"We're finished." Harriet turned on her heel and walked back to join Mephers in the sanctuary.

Mephers didn't so much have friends in the congregation as sycophantic well-wishers. These were clustered around her in the Stonds family's traditional pew. Harriet took her seat and tried to attend to the sermon. The text, from the seventh chapter of Jeremiah, said that God would know Israel had amended her ways if she stopped oppressing the widow and the fatherless orphan, and stopped worshiping Baal and other foreign gods.

Pastor Emerson preached for half an hour, with his usual sincere eloquence, on the many Baals Americans turned to: sex, money, power. "It's not surprising that some women have revived the real Baals, or the Asherim, that the prophet preached against. Money and sex are poor substitutes for the living God. At the same time, truly taking on a commitment to Jesus is too hard for some, so they turn to goddess worship as an easy way out. Faith is a gift; grace is a gift; but they are not ours just for the asking, if we discard them as a spoiled child does his toys when they don't do exactly what he demands. We need to strengthen each other in our quest for faith. Brother Lowrie thinks he has a way to help some of the men in the congregation on their spiritual journey. We all know Brother Lowrie's a persuasive salesman—well, he's persuaded me to let him hold a seminar here in the church, but he hasn't got me to understand exactly what it's about, so I'm going to let him tell you. Brother Lowrie?"

Rafe bustled up the chancel stairs, furious with the pastor for his patronizing tone: if he ran this church, things would be different. He climbed up in the pulpit and began to wax eloquent on the Family Matters group. Men need to reclaim the home . . . Children don't respect fathers, because fathers have ceded all authority . . .

Harriet's attention quickly wandered, back to her sister, this time thinking about Mara's chants to the goddess Gula. The text for the sermon, on looking after the fatherless orphan, and not worshiping foreign gods—Jeremiah would probably warn Mara that she was going to bring serious wrath on her head, but wasn't Mara—wasn't Harriet herself—a fatherless orphan? Shouldn't she receive compassion as well as wrath?

24

Breaking Camp

"Do you know this girl, Professor?" The campus security officer shoved Mara into Professor Lontano's office.

Verna Lontano looked up from her computer. "Certainly, Officer. It's Mara Stonds. What are you doing down here, Mara? Catching up on your goddess studies?"

"She was camping on the grounds, ma'am, and claimed to be a student of yours."

The professor's ironic eyes took in Mara's dishevelment—the sleeping bag trailing from the sides of her backpack, her uncombed hair and heavy eyes—and sent the cop on his way. "You may safely leave her in my care, Officer."

There was a brief ceremony, the cop asking the professor to sign a form, the professor thanking him with a flourish, and then he shut the door on them.

"Well, Mara? Did the air-conditioning break down on Graham Street, that you needed to seek refuge in the wide-open spaces of the South Side?"

An hour before Mara's head had been full of the buzzing that comes from too many days away from human contact. Now she felt a roaring from too much contact as fear, anger, embarrassment, chased each other through her mind.

When the cop picked her up, Mara was sitting on her sleeping bag with her back against the museum, arms around her knees, rocking herself. After five nights under the bushes near the chapel she was feverish from lack of sleep, and lack of conversation. She couldn't think clearly, couldn't remember why she thought Grannie Selena or her mother might still be alive.

Her first two days on the run she had tried to keep clean, using the bathroom in one of the classroom buildings on campus. She tried to make a plan for tracking down either Beatrix or Selena. Then that woman at the State Department started acting like Mara was some kind of spy, like Mara wanted to sneak into Iraq and work for Saddam Hussein. Thanks a bunch, she felt like saying: travel eight thousand miles to work for another man on a heavy authority trip, just like Grandfather, except Saddam had a whole country full of places to lock people up in, instead of only the psych ward in a hospital. Instead, afraid that the official would call Dr. Stonds if Mara said too much, she took to her heels.

If she couldn't go to Iraq, couldn't prove Grandfather lied about Grannie Selena, then Mara would find out the truth about her own mother. They all said Beatrix died when Mara was two. If that was so, how come her death hadn't been written up in the papers the way everyone else's was: hated daughter of Abraham, discarded mother of Harriet.

Harriet always snapped at Mara, yes she's dead, you stupid brat, I was at the funeral. Did you see her body in the coffin, Mara would persist, are you sure it was Beatrix they buried? Of course Harriet hadn't seen the body: Grandfather had too much taste to expose everyone to the vulgarity of an open coffin.

But that meant Beatrix might still be alive. It would be like Grandfather to dust his hands off, well, we're rid of her, when his own daughter was still wandering the streets looking for food. But how could Mara possibly find her mother, after so many years? She didn't even know the names of her mother's friends, let alone the man who'd gone to bed with Beatrix the night Mara started her journey from ovum to unhappy teenager.

Cynthia wouldn't help her find a private detective—Cynthia thought she was playing a game. Or was jealous because Mara was finally taking steps. All those years they'd talked over how they would find Beatrix, or get rid of Rafe and move in with Cynthia's mother, and Mara was actually doing—what? Dramatizing herself as Harriet and Mephers and Grandfather always said. Chanting to the goddess Gula, Mara knew deep down that was only to annoy Grandfather. But why couldn't he believe her about that photograph she'd seen in Mephers's room? Why did it always have to be Mephers or Harriet he listened to? She hugged her knees and rocked harder.

"You know you're trespassing on private property, young lady?" A black man in a police uniform loomed over her.

She gaped at him, suddenly aware of the empty potato chip bags strewn around her sleeping bag, of her grimy body, unwashed for several days, and the used tampons she'd stuck in her abandoned juice cartons.

"I'm—I'm a student," she stammered.

"Then let's see your ID, miss."

"I don't have it on me. Anyway, I'm not a student here, I'm a private student of Professor Lontano's, Verna Lontano in the Oriental Institute. She's an expert on Sumerian goddesses, you know, and—I'm testing some of the Sumerian chants. They have to be done under a full moon."

Her heart was thudding so hard, she thought it might rise in her chest to choke her. She'd be taken to the police station. Another scene with Harriet, Grandfather arriving triumphant to lock her in the psych wing. Maybe she could give a fake name, and spend time in jail—unless one of Harriet's suitors was in court, as would probably be the case again.

But to the cop, sent over to investigate a report by the dean that there was a vagrant on the chapel grounds, Mara looked like many of the unkempt students who casually dropped their litter across campus. Her tangled coarse hair, so out of place on Graham Street, was normal here. It was only her nervousness that made him doubt her; he radioed his commander, who told him to get Professor Lontano to check the girl's story.

"Why do you think Selena might still be alive?" Professor Lontano asked her, when they were alone.

"They're always lying to me, Grandfather and Mephers, they hate me, they hated Selena, you can tell by how they talk about her. I thought—" Mara flushed and stumbled on her words. It did sound ridiculous to say it out loud: Grandfather bribed the paper to print the news of her death.

"The goddess Gula supplied you with this information, no doubt?" The professor saw Mara was about to cry, so she quickly added: "Your grandmother is really dead, Mara. I was in Nippur at the time. It was a terrible disaster, that expedition to the Taurus Mountains. A whole Iraqi family who'd gone along to do cooking and help with the rough digging was killed, buried in snow. Your grandmother, and her mother and father, starved to death before anyone could rescue them."

Mara felt her body swell and grow ungainly. In the grim lines around Lontano's mouth she read not the painful memories of a young student on her first expedition hearing about the death of an admired teacher—but contempt. She hates me, too, Mara thought, wanting only to flee the office, not to have those mocking gray eyes bore into her mind any longer.

Lontano shook her head, shaking herself out of the waters of the past, and looked at the disheveled young woman in front of her. "I never thought you were a coward, Mara, but here you are running away because you're afraid to see Mrs. Ephers now that you made her ill."

Mara's cheeks puffed out in her fury. "It's not like that. It's because of the lies, all the lies. I found a secret letter Mephers was keeping locked away, it was written to my mother in French, at least, it was written to the daughter of Madame Selena Vatick Stonds, I can't read much French but even I could tell that, and there was a picture of a man who looks like Harriet, but no one believes me, they only listen to Mephers. But Grandfather must know. Where is my mother? Was that a photograph of Harriet's real father? Why doesn't Grandfather want me to know, unless it's something really awful?"

When Lontano didn't say anything Mara cried, "You know who it is, don't you?"

The professor leaned across her desk and spoke crisply, but not without sympathy. "Sometimes you can know too much, Mara. That's strange advice from a woman who's spent her life digging into the secrets of people long dead, you're saying to yourself. But the nearer dead, surely they have a right to their privacy, don't you think?

"Why don't you go home, eh? You can't camp out on the university grounds any longer, and you have a beautiful home, even if Abraham is not always an easy man to live with. Or go to university yourself, then you'd have a place of your own to live. Why don't I get that young security cop to come get you, give you a ride back to Graham Street. When you're calmer you can come see me again and talk about your education."

Professor Lontano was Grandfather's friend; she only wanted to send Mara back into his clutches. Mara lurched out of her chair, knocking it over. She ran down the wide stone steps, certain that Lontano would have the museum ringed by campus security before she got to the exit. She shoved the heavy door open and made it to the street without anyone trying to stop her. She ran down the street, past the old brick houses and narrow yards, the women with baby buggies, the knots of students, without seeing any of them, and finally, hot and gasping for air, onto the platform for the train.

At the South Water station, end of the line for the train, she stood at the sink in the washroom and poured water over her head, then, keeping an eye on the entrance, stripped herself in sections and washed her whole body. All her clothes were dirty now. It didn't occur to her to sneak into Grandfather's apartment while everyone was out to get something clean: Graham Street seemed to belong to a different city than the one she now inhabited, too far away for her to reach by ordinary means.

When she wandered out of the train station she was underground, only a block from the foundation of the Hotel Pleiades. For want of a better destination she walked over to the garage and looked at the wall. Someone had patched it over without repairing the damaged pipe behind the crack: a rusty stain was spreading around the edges of the cement. She walked around the corner, hunting for the woman at the wall. The splintered boards of the Westinghouse generator box were all that remained of Madeleine Carter's refuge.

Mara sat among the splinters. Her head ached. She was tired. She knew she should get something to eat. Perhaps she should check into a motel for a few days so she could take a proper shower, get a good sleep and find a job. The thought flickered in her head like a falling star, quickly obliterated by the denseness of her fatigue and isolation.

She imagined Professor Lontano calling Grandfather to tell him about Mara's visit. Grandfather was terrified that Mara was on the track of his wife and daughter: he had murdered them both. Lontano and Mephers were accomplices; they were sure they had obliterated all traces of their crime, but now the doctor panicked, thinking his granddaughter was going to find him out. He called the police, urged them to arrest Mara as a dangerous criminal, and shoved her into the locked wing at Midwest Hospital before she had a chance to denounce him.

But perhaps Harriet would come to her rescue. Instead of the police descending on her, her sister would arrive, her normal calm shattered, her beautiful blue eyes red with sobbing: Mara, dearest, how sorry I am I doubted you. You were right all along about Grandfather and Mephers—they're indescribably monstrous. Mara leaned against a pillar and slept.

25

Digging Up the Past

Professor Lontano had not even thought of calling Dr. Stonds. She was almost seventy-five and her mind was back in Iraq, her first winter in Nippur. One never thought of cold in the Middle East, but winters in Iraq were sufficiently bitter. The deliciousness of making love inside a sleeping bag, while the wind drove snow through the chinks in the mud walls of her one-room house. The professor smiled to herself: you could only enjoy that when young. In old age one wanted a proper bed, warmth, and no worries that an angry wife might appear.

A letter in French to Beatrix? With a photograph of a man who looked like Harriet. Why had she never noticed that? Human perversity, the things one refused to acknowledge. She was not immune to that disease, but it was always a shock to realize it. Now that she thought of it, the likeness was extraordinary. Perhaps a lack of sensuality in Harriet's face caused Lontano to overlook the resemblance all these years. More likely, though, it was the desire not to know. The professor made a face—the irony that intimidated Mara not spared in looking at her own self.

But who could have written Beatrix, and how did that gargoyle of a housekeeper come to hold the letter and the photo? Had the Ephers woman told Abraham about it? Probably not: his pride wouldn't survive such news. Who had written, not knowing Beatrix was dead, for dead she surely was, despite Mara's wishes to find her among the living. How long had that been now, since that blustery March day she'd gone with Abraham to a funeral chapel on the remote northwest side of the city: he refused to let anyone at the Orleans Street Church participate in the service, or have a church ceremony at all.

Years melted into each other. Lontano used to remember them by sharp events, a particular lover, an amazing linguistic discovery, but now, all occasions seemed equally remote.

At any rate, she had been at the funeral, Harriet and Mrs. Ephers the only other—not mourners, participants. Mara must still have been a baby, perhaps left with a sitter—Lontano couldn't remember her in the chapel. What she remembered most about the occasion was Abraham's fury, his refusal to talk about his daughter, his angry satisfaction in having silenced the papers: she isn't going to embarrass me beyond the grave.

Lontano never understood why Beatrix's death infuriated Abraham so much: in a way, he had almost chosen it. But the professor acquiesced in his desire to keep the matter secret—it was his family, she wasn't going to pretend she understood all the complicated emotions that held families together or tore them apart. By then, by whenever it was—she remembered suddenly wondering during the funeral about the plumbing in her Polish apartment; that was the spring she went to Krakow to lecture, instead of returning to Padua, as she usually did in the spring. So seventeen years ago. By that time, anyway, she had no illusions left about Abraham, the possibility of romance: he was utterly self-absorbed, past the point where he could see anyone except as a reflection of his own desires.

They were all like that: it's the male condition. Helen Vatick used to say that—Selena's mother, lecturing the wives in Nippur when they complained that their husbands cared for nothing but clay pots and inscriptions. *They're wrapped in their small worlds,* Helen said, *so jealous of Jehovah who made this great earth that they attempt to create their own universes. Or is that why they invented a god like Jehovah? They say we create gods in our own image, and from what I see of the Sumerian gods, humans have always expected their deities to be as small-minded and territorial as we are ourselves.*

And Lontano, overhearing this, felt superior for being herself absorbed in pots and inscriptions, not a whiny wife with too little to do in the desert, unless one became like Sabine Tholuck, taking on her husband's job so vehemently that she expected to be called "Frau Professor" by young students like Lontano. But Lontano also felt curiously unfeminine in Helen Vatick's presence, unable to sit with the company of women and share their easy gossip about husbands and children. A very feminine woman, that was how Lontano remembered Mrs. Vatick. Selena, too, although a different type altogether.

Oh, what was the point of this maundering through recent history? The distant past was where she belonged, where she knew what to think, what conclusions to draw. Before she returned there, though, she should call Harriet, let her know where Mara was. Perhaps probe, delicately, to see what story Abraham had told his granddaughters about Beatrix's death.

When Lontano phoned, Harriet was trying to get ready for a meeting. Lauren, her secretary, refused at first to interrupt her, but the professor persisted and Lauren, curious about the current upheavals in Harriet's life, summoned her young boss to the phone.

Harriet was abrupt, her mind on a long-distance waste hauler who faced toxic-dumping charges. So Mara was taking her annoyances to the University of Chicago now? Many thanks for the news.

Lontano was startled by her brusquerie. "Harriet, Mara doesn't look well. She's been sleeping in the open. Can't you do something to make it possible for her to come home?"

"She's welcome to return any time she chooses, as long as she stops behaving like a prima donna in a soap opera." Harriet looked at her desk clock: her clients would arrive in three minutes.

"She thinks Abraham is lying to her about your mother's death. I think—I hope—I persuaded her that Selena really perished back in 1947. But can't you make her realize that Beatrix is gone as well? I'm worried about her. I wouldn't have thought she could become, well, deranged, but she's got it in her mind that she should find Beatrix. If you talked to her, told her the truth?"

"I've told her many times. I was at the funeral. Mara just won't believe me, she claims because I didn't see her face. But even if Grandfather would have tolerated an open coffin, he said Beatrix drowned in her bath, and her face looked all swollen and disfigured." Harriet broke off: she used to have nightmares about that swollen body rising from the coffin and coming to snatch her, to take her to a horrible underworld where they lived among broken furniture and rats.

"Mara says she found a letter to Beatrix written in French," Harriet found herself blurting out to the professor. "And a photograph of some man who looked like me. Do you know who that was?"

As soon as she'd spoken Harriet wished the words unsaid. There was no man. Or maybe Harold Caduke wasn't really her father—was that so awful? She hardly remembered him, anyway. Although she had always felt superior to Mara, for many reasons, but including the fact that unlike Mara she could name her father.

She was upset enough with herself for asking that she didn't notice the pause at the other end of the phone and the unnatural voice in which the professor said, no, she had no idea, and she really thought Harriet should persuade Mara to get help.

"I'm one of your grandfather's oldest friends, and I take a special interest in you and your sister. It isn't good—for either of you—that she's running around the city as upset as she is now."

Lauren came back into Harriet's office: the client, whose annual bill ran to six figures, was getting impatient. Harriet hung up. She wanted to go home and pull out her photographs of her parents, find a likeness in her own face to her father. More than that, she wanted to find Mara and punch her in the mouth: why couldn't she keep the family's private business private?

In response to Lauren's impatient cough, Harriet got up and went to the conference room. She found herself unable to pull her mind together to think about rights-of-way or Superfund exposures. It frightened her, that she couldn't remember the substance of recent conversations or documents. What did it mean, for her to fragment in this way? Was she, too, an inheritor of Beatrix's bad blood, in abeyance all these years but suddenly showing up at the first real stress in her life?

After her meeting, she worked on reports demonically through lunch. Leigh Wilton had suddenly dumped two tricky new problems on her, one demanding an answer before a three o'clock meeting on the other side of town. She drove her two paralegals to exhaustion with the demands she made for data and kept them at their desks, alongside her, through lunch, determined to prove that she was Grandfather's girl, up to any challenge.

As she turned to her computer she heard one of the paralegals mutter, PMS. The second snickered. Harriet affected not to hear. PMS. Post-Mara Syndrome. It had been affecting her all day. Maybe all her life. Or perhaps it was the weather, the unrelenting closeness of the air. At three, when she left the building with Leigh, she saw thunderheads building over the lake, great towers that stretched like the parapets of a giant's castle. God's chess pieces.

Her father—was he her father?—had called them that. The memory slipped over Leigh Wilton's discourse on Rapelec's patent fights in Malaysia: she couldn't have been more than four or five. They were by the lake (where? not their Winnetka home, the country someplace) and her parents were fighting. She could still hear her mother's horrific sobs— Harriet thought at first she was laughing, and had danced up and down in excitement. Her mother hit her across the mouth, furious at Harriet's mocking of her grief, and Daddy swept Harriet into his arms, walked down the lake shore with her, pointed to the white pillars spiraling overhead and said: God's chess pieces. When he's bored with running the universe he settles down for a game. The archangels always lose; this makes them mad and they throw the pieces down. That causes thunder.

Once again she couldn't keep her mind on the client and his problems. She kept wondering why she never thought about her father. Was that distant quarrel between her parents over who Harriet's real father was? He slept around, Harold Caduke, she didn't like to admit that, but it was true: he'd been with some other woman the night he died. It was more likely that someone else was her mother—no, that was impossible. Mara was infecting Harriet with her hysterical fantasies. It didn't matter whether Harold Caduke was Harriet's father or not: Grandfather had adopted her, legally, when she was nine, and her name was Stonds. And she possessed Grandfather's incisive mind, not the mush that lay between Mara's ears! The many times Mephers had smacked Mara for fibbing— no blows had ever fallen on Harriet!

Back in the office she forced her paralegals to work on the follow-up to the afternoon meeting, until one of them wailed, I have tickets to the Who; do you know how hard those are to get? Harriet raised pale brows: and this job, was that easy to find as well? But she relented, let the two women leave at seven-thirty. At eleven, she realized in despair that she had read the same essay on company law in Indonesia three times without being able to figure out how to apply it to Leigh Wilton's client, a recording studio in Tel Aviv.

Thunder was rumbling across the lake. She went to the window. If she craned her neck and squinted, she could see lightning flaring and dimming over the Chicago River. Maybe the storm would break, and with it end her own nervous fragmentation.

Not moving from the window, she played the messages on her voice mail. The fourth was from Grandfather, who'd called a little before eight. His austere voice wondered where she was and what she was doing about dinner: you are usually more thoughtful than this, my dear; it hurts Hilda when you forget to call to let her know your plans.

She didn't play the rest of the messages, but jerked herself from the window, picked her umbrella off the hook by the door, and left the office. As she stood in the street, waiting for a cab, she could picture her arrival home. She would walk in the door, nerves jangling, respond to Grandfather's raised brows with some tale about a difficult client, present her cheek for his dry lips, plant her own chaste kiss on Mephers, retire to her ivory-curtained suite and try to cry the tears that seldom came to her.

What would happen if she asked about Beatrix, about Mara, about who their fathers were? Grandfather would retreat into a thin-lipped huff: my dear Harriet, I was hoping your calm rationality would rub off on Mara—not that she would infect you with her idiocies.

The first drops of rain, thick and wobbly like bags of plasma, were hitting her when a cab responded to her outstretched arm. On an impulse, she told the driver to swing first through Underground Wacker, to the Hotel Pleiades garage, on their way to Graham Street.

26

Deluge

FLASHING BLUE STROBES lit up Underground Wacker. A police car blocked the intersection with Stetson; a patrolman with the superior air officers assume at the scene of a crime was blowing his whistle and ordering cars to make U-turns back to Wacker.

"I have to get through here," Harriet told the cabbie.

He flung up his arms. "Is not possible, missus. You seeing cop? You wanting I run over him?"

"I want you to stop and let me talk to him."

The policeman whistled peremptorily at the cab. "Let's move it, buddy, let's move it."

"See?" the driver said. "No stopping."

Harriet rolled down her window. "Officer! I'm the lawyer for—"

"Save it, lady. Get this cab turned around."

Harriet opened the door just as the cab driver whipped into a U-turn. "You ignorant cretin, stop at once! You could have killed me!"

He stood on his brakes. "Get out, bitch. You bitches all same. Go home, not go home. Stop here, no stop here. Now you starting trouble on me with police. Get out. Keep money, I not wanting him!"

Harriet scribbled down his name and medallion number: a call to the commissioner's office would be her first act in the morning. She warned the cabbie to expect an official censure. He roared down the street so fast he nearly collided with an oncoming squad car, whose

driver wheeled around and brought the cab to a standstill. Harriet paid
no attention, was unaware of the cabdriver dancing up and down in his
fury, waving an arm in her direction, screaming imprecations. She
walked past the police barricades, imperious, ignoring whistles and yells
from the cops there, heading to the garage.

Water was pouring into the street. At first she thought it was the
storm overhead, pounding out rain so hard it penetrated the upper roadbed. She tried to step around the freshets, for her Italian high heels
wouldn't survive a soaking, but water lay in a sheet across the sidewalk
and poured into the gutter.

The center of the street was filled with city vehicles. A blue truck
from Streets and Sanitation, flanked by five squad cars, was positioned
near the Pleiades garage, next to the disputed wall. The mass of police
and city workers made it impossible for Harriet to see what was actually
happening.

A Fire Department ambulance waited next to the curb, its red lights
mixing with police blues. Walkie-talkies crackled. A knot of uniformed
men huddled by the back door of the ambulance, which was open.
Craning her neck around the mob of men, Harriet saw a stretcher on the
sidewalk, wheels lifting it above the flood.

Three women waited near the stretcher, their faces shining in the
flashing lights, their expressions unreadable. From the layers of dresses and
sweaters draping two of them, Harriet assumed they were homeless. The
third stood slightly aloof, yet was clearly with them. She wore a black suit
whose silhouette proclaimed something cut by a couturier. What was she
doing with those two?

A crowd of spectators had gathered on the perimeter: commuters,
hotel guests, theatergoers, huddling out of the storm on the underground
streets and drawn here by the strobes and the hope for vicarious gore.
Some probably hoped to be on TV, for Minicams, sound techs, and
reporters had cascaded into the street on the tide of water. Harriet
scanned the crowd for her sister's distinctive bush of hair, but it was hard
to see anything now that she was inside the circle of lights.

Hovering near the crowd at the ambulance was Brian Cassidy, the garage manager. His thickly muscled arms looked too big, as though they had grown on him without his knowledge and he now was at a loss how to use them. Harriet walked over to him just as a policeman tried to tell her she had no business inside the barricade.

"Ms. Stonds!" Cassidy greeted her in relief. "She's our lawyer, Officer. How did you find out what happened? I only just called Mr. Palmetto five minutes ago."

She shook her head. "A coincidence. I stopped by to look for—to check on things. What's going on?"

He swung one of his big arms in a meaningless gesture. "That damned bitch—sorry, but you know, that psycho homeless woman! She left us in peace for a few days, but then she showed again tonight. We cemented over the wall, like you said, and when she saw that she started howling like it was the end of the world. Then these other three—well, women—show up, and I see one of them is that damned twat who was bellowing her head off the other night, thinking she was some kind of singer."

So was the woman in the couture suit Luisa Montcrief? Harriet hadn't seen the diva in court when she bailed out her sister last week; she'd only listened to Harry Minsky's lament. And sympathized, having a sister herself.

"So the psycho, not that they aren't all crazy, she starts howling that the Mother of God will never forgive her, and the singer, she starts braying some wop music or other."

In fact it had been Verdi's "Madre, pietosa Vergine"—most merciful virgin mother—one of Luisa's hallmark arias. She'd made her European debut as Leonora, at the opera house in Venice, how sad that such a beautiful place burned to the ground, although when she read about it she laughed: imagine a building burning in the middle of Venice. All that water, so much that the city is sinking into the sea, and the opera house burns to the ground. She'd been at an admirer's apartment when she saw the story in the *Herald-Star,* and the man—what had his name been?—winced as she laughed, her full-throated enchanting laugh, that's how Tyrone Bennet from the London *Independent* described it. The admirer, a cretin after all, said, must you make such a god-awful racket at the break-fast table? He must have been hung over: one had to be charitable with a drunk, and, after all, he'd been good enough to put her up for a few weeks, even if he proved to be spiteful in the end. Thank goodness she had never had that kind of problem with drugs or liquor. Of course, it was rare for a Jew to be an alcoholic—she herself was proof of that, only needing a drink now and then to steady her nerves, but never dependent on it the way so many sad souls were.

It was funny that a Jewish woman would spend so much of her life singing piteous pleas to the virgin mother of Jesus. If it wasn't "Madre, pietosa Vergine," it was "Ave" upon "Ave Maria" or Gounod's "Angels pure and bright"; you'd think she'd spent her childhood in convent schools. When she told Piero that, he put his finger on her lips: don't go around announcing that you're Jewish, *cara,* this is still an ugly world and your career isn't established. You look like a Roman, and "Montcrief" is not a Jewish name, after all. Maybe I should buy you a rosary for luck, but it hadn't been lucky, she'd been carrying it as she always did that night at the Met, and—and her head was aching abominably.

What was she doing here, anyway, with this crazy woman who thought the Virgin was bleeding through the wall at her? That brutal man at the *pension* this morning, throwing her out, you vomited all over the front hall, I'm not running a flophouse here, throwing her luggage down the stairs. She'd only just left her sickbed, a terrible flu, she couldn't remember ever being so sick—she'd actually been in the hospital until yesterday, with no notion how she got there. No wonder her breath control wasn't right: she shouldn't have been singing so soon after being ill, that's probably why she threw up, but would that idiot listen to her? Probably on Harry's payroll, paid to make her life a misery.

She'd had to leave her luggage at the Civic Opera House, even though she wasn't engaged to sing there. What a struggle that had been, just to leave a suitcase, you'd think she was some street person, not a diva who had received eight curtain calls for her Aida in that same building, thank you very much. It wasn't even as though anyone was using the place. It was July, no rehearsals, all she asked was an empty practice room.

Then Alessandro had appeared, kissed her hand, Madame, you need a practice room? What, you are thinking of a comeback? That would be glorious news indeed. And let her have a key to one of the rooms on the eighth floor, with a concert grand in perfect tune ready for her accompanist. The feel of the key where she'd tucked it against her breasts reassured her. She was still a diva, she could still get into the great opera houses of the world.

Then the thunder began. She tried to get into the shelter at the church, but that bitch in charge, that Patsy Warlocks, wouldn't let her in: we have rules here, Luisa, I told you two weeks ago not to show up here again if you were drunk. My good woman, I just got out of my sickbed. Doesn't your god, your Jesus that you turn to, to get your mind off the fact that no living man wants that cold stiff body of yours, doesn't he tell you to take in sick people when they need shelter?

And all she got in return was a furious scream: Don't try to come here again, I'm having your name permanently struck from the rolls.

So she returned to Underground Wacker, hoping to find the little shack where the black woman said she could sleep if she was desperate, and came instead upon the most dreary chaos: the crazy woman, the black woman, the white friend, all wailing around a crack in the wall. The only crack here is in your head, Luisa said, but they told her it had been cemented over.

The crazy woman was imploring the Virgin for help, so Luisa thought she would give her some support, show her the right way to address the Virgin: in Italian, to the strains of Verdi. In the middle of her aria out came these goons, must be Callas's claque, following her everywhere, getting her location from Harry and Karen so they could humiliate her.

My good ape, Luisa had interrupted her song to talk to the ringleader, his arms looked like an orangutan's, I know exactly what you're up to. Have the goodness to wait until I'm singing in a proper venue before you start your harassment: we'll see then who sings the final note.

While he was arguing with her, the black woman pulled a knife from some recess in her layers of garments and poked at the cement. She cried out, look here, Maddy, you can still see the Virgin's blood, it's still coming through. The ape turned from Luisa to the black woman, yelling that he'd have the police on them if they touched the wall again, get out of here, you stupid bitches, when suddenly water started pouring over them, a cataract that almost knocked the crazy woman off her feet. At first Luisa thought it was the storm: she could hear the thunder pounding overhead, but then she saw water cascading from the wall. She had to laugh, the ape looked so ridiculous with his hair plastered to his head, trying to rub his eyes clear, and listen to him now, claiming that the black woman had started the flood, Luisa had to laugh again.

The raucous sound made Harriet's teeth tingle. She looked in irritation at Luisa, but the diva was as impervious to glares as she was to threats of violence.

Harriet's stockings were soaked now inside her high heels, which made her more irritable. "Surely poking at the cement couldn't cause this flood."

"No?" Cassidy said. "Well, I'd like to know what else could have done it. The city says we must have broke the pipe hammering on the concrete, but no such thing. In fact, the boys from maintenance didn't even take out the old stuff, which I told them they'd better do if they want the patch to hold. They just cemented over it. They sure didn't pound on it. Nobody else so much as touched it until these bitches—excuse me, these homeless women—arrived. And then the crazy one screams, 'the Mother of God has forgiven me.' Next she goes and sticks her head into the waterfall and almost drowns."

"Is that why the ambulance is there?"

"Yeah. Stupid bastard Nicolo called 911, even though I ordered him not to. Would have solved a lot of problems if he'd just let her go. About time he looked for another job. Guess he don't remember who's signing his paycheck."

Harriet looked at him in astonishment. "You can't make that kind of statement in public, Cassidy. I'm the hotel's lawyer, so no one can force me to repeat it, but I'd hate to have to defend you on an employee dismissal charge because your carhop saved a woman's life."

She turned away from him and went over to the ambulance, where she had to raise her voice to a shout to be heard over the water, the walkie-talkies, and the bellows of the different work crews. "I'm the hotel's lawyer: how is this woman doing?"

The driver, impressed by her air of authority, was starting to answer when a plantation of mikes sprouted under Harriet's nose: she'd spoken loudly enough for the camera crews to hear her, also. Hot lights blinded her as the technicians converged, like a flock of pigeons all seeing a bag of popcorn at the same time.

What was her name? Why had the hotel cemented over the crack? Did she believe the possibility of a miraculous appearance by the Virgin? And didn't Madeleine Carter have a right to worship the Virgin there? What had caused the geyser? Did she support the hotel's decision not to pay for Madeleine Carter's hospital care? What if Ms. Carter contracted pneumonia and died?

Harriet, very aware of her water-soaked shoes and uncombed hair, tried to smile in a friendly way: she knew how bad it would look for her clients if she, their lawyer, appeared surly on television. "We won't know anything until we get some structural engineers down here to determine the cause of the leak. We'll organize that as soon as I can return to my office. And I don't know anything about this woman Madeleine Carter, or her condition. I was just about to get that information from the paramedics when you converged on me."

She turned to the medical crew. The cameras hovered nearby for a minute or so longer, but suddenly all left at the same time. They'd been underground for forty minutes; except for the lawyer showing up—a good tidbit, as she'd look attractive on tape—they weren't going to get anything new. They already knew what had happened to Madeleine Carter—that she'd stuck her face into the spouting water and almost drowned, that the paramedics wanted her hospitalized but couldn't find a bed. Like a flock of pigeons suddenly taking flight together, the camera crews rushed to the next disaster, a ten-car pileup on the Kennedy.

Another gush of water coursed over Harriet's feet. Three-hundred-dollar kidskin, ruined. The water was up to her ankles now. In the lights from the ambulance it looked like blood. She shuddered and backed away, trying to escape the growing torrent. Whatever the city workers were doing was causing more, not less, flooding: the whole wall seemed to be spewing water.

Damn Mara, anyway, for drawing her into this chaotic scene. Let the cops, the hotel, the doctors, and all the other men sort this out on their own. She was going to bed, in her own home.

Her first impulse, to find a cab, was useless. She saw a set of stairs leading away from the chaos and tried to get to them, but her way was blocked partly by the mass of spectators, and partly by the barricades that the police had erected. With the disappearance of the camera crews, the crowds pushed in closer.

Harriet turned back to the ambulance, and asked the driver if she could climb in next to him out of the water.

"Against regulations, ma'am, but you can perch on the tailgate, as long as that's open, and no one will bother you while we wait for word on what to do with our patient."

The paramedics shifted to make room for her. They were drinking coffee from a thermos and taking turns staying next to the stretcher on the sidewalk, monitoring their patient, trying to protect her face from the water swirling around the stretcher wheels.

Harriet looked at the homeless women. They stood on the far side of the gurney like cattle, stolid in a rainstorm. The diva, thinking the flood a very good joke, started singing what she could remember of Britten's operetta based on the story of Noah. Her voice was so out of shape that the sound was hardly recognizable as music.

Harriet accepted coffee from one of the medics. When she looked up again, a fourth woman had joined the diva and the other two by the stretcher. Where had she come from? The police were letting no one through, and anyway, Harriet hadn't noticed her approach. At first, seeing only an outline of wild hair, Harriet thought it was her sister. She jumped from the tailgate into the water and splashed to the curb, torn between relief and anger.

When she reached the stretcher she recoiled in disgust at her mistake. The woman was a horrible specimen. Her hair was piled in a massive pompadour that looked like snakes, but Harriet was more re-volted by her breasts. The newcomer was naked from the waist up, and her breasts looked so enormous, Harriet had the fantasy that they were reaching across the sidewalk to suffocate her.

The crackling from the walkie-talkies grew more excited as one group after another noticed the woman. Men poked each other, made obscene jokes. Their faces glowed purple in the blue strobes.

The diva caught sight of the newcomer and stopped singing. "Queen Vashti?" she croaked, touching one naked arm uncertainly.

On the stretcher next to her Madeleine Carter struggled to sit up. "Holy Mother," she choked. "You've come to save me."

A hand tugged on Harriet's sleeve. She shuddered, still feeling the weight of those breasts, and was astonished to find Mara at her side.

"Harriet, did you come to find me? Harriet, look at her hair. It's like mine. Harriet, it's Mother!"

27

Starr

Ominous weather all day. Masses of sparrows huddled on asphalt in front of hospital to stay clear of the rising wind. On locked ward, patients agitated, splintering—the brain breaks into a thousand crystal shards as the atmosphere descends.

About midnight the storm broke. A monster. People flooded the emergency room to escape the torrents. One woman hid under a gurney and screamed every time thunder sounded, rigid with fear—took four men to remove her.

Then in came the car wrecks, new head cases, new spinal fractures from would-be immortals who roared down expressways at eighty on slick roads. Left those to the knife-happy neurosurgeons, retreated to residents bunkroom, an hour of blissful sleep when I got beeped to the locked ward: teenage boy had cut open his left wrist. Wondered what he'd got hold of, then saw he'd chewed through the veins.

They kept paging me to the phone while I was with the poor kid. Almost an hour before I could leave the boy, though, and then it was to a disaster with Madeleine Carter. Paramedics were phoning to say Madeleine attempted suicide, by sticking her head into a broken main. Imagined gas, but they said no, broken water pipe, she was in bad shape, semiconscious, feverish, but needed authorization to bring her to hospital: no beds anywhere in area. Knew if I actually went to admissions to discuss they would say absolutely not, so I told them bring her in.

Ambulance arrived with an entourage attached, like that Russian peasant tale of the woman dangling from the heavens by an onion, with all the damned clinging to her: in this case, Jacqui, Nanette, Luisa Montcrief.

And also—

Every time he tried to write about the fourth woman with Madeleine his skin curled, like a sea anemone poked with a stick. He tried to calm his mind, to force himself to confront what it was that so repelled him—was it the woman, or the excitement she created in him—but it was too painful. He couldn't think about it.

"Dr. Tammuz, what in hell were you up to last night? How did a simple patient consultation deteriorate into a brawl that put Millie Regier's neck into a brace, landed us with work comp claims for her and one of the security guards, and all, I might add, for three unfunded patients?" Hanaper was swelling with fury, his face a round red ball that might explode at any second, brains, blood all over the room.

Hector, thankful to turn his attention to the purely practical, murmured, "We may be able to get the city or the Hotel Pleiades to pay for Madeleine Carter, sir."

"Oh, well, if you got it down to *two* unfunded patients, that would make a difference, Dr. Tammuz, an enormous difference. The cost containment committee will be glad to know of your thoughtfulness."

Hanaper, bowing across his vast walnut desk (where has the hospital come up with funds for this antique monster, when it cannot afford patients without insurance?), at his most insufferable in irony. Hector imagined him in restraints, tied to his black captain's chair with the Harvard University seal. Perhaps when he bought his diplomas, framed like Old Masters behind his head, the school threw in a captain's chair as a bonus.

Wanted to ask, have you ever worked in a psychiatric hospital during the kind of storm we had last night? Have you ever been on call for thirty-six hours when everyone in town was disintegrating? Were you ever on call anywhere where people were in anguish?

Like the Red Sea under Moses' hands, the waves of psychotics would flee at Hanaper's approach—Hector saw them flinging themselves from the casements in hordes, rather than endure Hanaper's brusque contempt.

"For someone who believes in the talking cure you don't seem to have much to say, Tammuz. Will it help if I tell you that Millie Regier says you were on the verge of improper contact with one of the women, an aphasiac patient?"

"Millie was rattled last night, sir. She doesn't usually slap patients, or rush them into restraints. But we were both exhausted. One of the women was the opera singer, Luisa Montcrief, whom we saw here a few months ago. She was so drunk I don't know how she stayed upright, let alone spoke. The paramedics thought she belonged in a detox unit, which is why they brought her. And the other one—"

"Arrived naked. Yes, I heard about that from three different people before Millie came to see me this morning."

Naked from the waist up until one of the orderlies found an old T-shirt for her. Her breasts were large and golden, like ripe gourds, the nipples glowing cherries. Even after Millie Regier, the psychiatric charge nurse, managed to cover them—a struggle, since the woman's hair was piled high with heavily waxed curls that looked like horns; she was tall, too, so that Millie, panting and heaving, maneuvering long bronze arms into sleeves, stretching to pull over curls and braids, the woman not resisting, but not helping, staring around at the attendants, the machinery, Tammuz himself—even after those dugs, which looked as though they might suckle the whole world, were covered, Tammuz found his gaze returning to the woman's bosom, looking past the red cotton, with its gaudy pictures of athletes, basketballs, trophies, seeing those ruby nipples.

Millie coughed warningly. Hector flushed. With an effort—a man pulling his legs from a tar pit—he withdrew his gaze, looked at the woman's face. Hawk's eyes, under brows like overhanging cliffs, he had the uneasy fancy that they stared with merciless amusement into his soul.

Angry at the notion—the result of exhaustion merely—he lost his carefully constructed professional demeanor (detached compassion, to impose trust without attachment), and snapped, "What were you doing with Madeleine, Ms. Montcrief?"

To his fury, the diva clapped her hands ecstatically. "My dear boy, how wonderful that you know me. You saw my Aida? Or was it Leonora?"

"I met you here, in Dr. Hanaper's office, two months ago. I'm one of his residents. I've never seen you perform."

Her face crunched up like a disappointed child's. "I was—I *am*—the greatest interpreter of Verdi of this century. *Die Zeit* wrote that. In German, of course. You have, I presume, heard of Verdi, Doctor? You know what opera is? You should take the time to listen to music: it will expand your mind, turn you into a more rounded polished person than your Dr. Hanaper—a vulgar ignoramus, I'm sorry if he's a friend of yours. And Verdi in particular is the richest of all composers."

Taking a breath she began to bellow "Sempre libera." Hector, whose mind it's true had never been expanded by Verdi, couldn't believe such noise had ever won international acclaim.

Millie Regier leaned across the Amazon and slapped Luisa's mouth. "A dozen people are waiting for a chance to see the doctor. We don't have time for playacting."

Luisa drew herself haughtily up. "I am not playacting, my good woman. Nor am I trying to steal the doctor's affections from you—yes, I see you're in love with him. Twenty-five years in professional opera, with all the loves and hates and jealousies, I know it when I see it—"

"Ms. Montcrief—can you spell your name?" Hector interrupted, before Millie snapped completely. "One *f*, thank you. We'll try to find a bed for you in detox—Millie, call up there, will you?—but in the meantime—"

Color surged into the veins around the drunk's nose. "I am not an alcoholic! Who has been spreading lies to you? Was it my ultra-pious sister-in-law? I've seen her knock back her share of martinis, whey-faced butter-won't-melt-in-my-mouth bitch! Or was it Cesarini, always angry because—"

In the midst of that outburst the Amazon grunted, seemed to grunt in some purposeful way, at least the drunken diva interpreted it so, for she pulled herself up midsentence. "It's not worth wasting breath on," she finished regally. "Suffice it to say I do not go into any detox unit— what an ugly word, conjures up rows and rows of bureaucrats all thinking of ways to demean one, start with the language, turn it into harsh insulting sounds, and everyone lines up obediently to take orders. The Nazis were like that, you know, Doctor: I presume you have heard of the Nazis?"

"If you cannot be quiet and pay attention to the doctor's questions we will have to put you in restraints." Millie couldn't contain herself; still furious at the secret of her heart being blasted out loud by this woman, smelling of stale vomit and Scotch, her yellow silk blouse so stained it looked like dried mustard.

"Millie, thank you, but let's try to get through this interview without that, so that we can move on to some of our other customers." Hector trying to smile, through lips wobbly with the effort of holding himself upright. "Can we start with Madeleine Carter? Do you know what happened to her?"

Luisa leaned forward and spoke to him behind a cupped hand. "She's a poor, sad creature, Doctor: mad, delusional. She thinks the Virgin Mary is speaking to her through some crack in the wall. The Virgin Mary haunts my life, you know. I made a career out of singing her praises, and then—then—"

She clutched her head, as if in a spasm of pain, and Jacqui spoke from the doorway. "Something went wrong down there, Doctor. Maybe Maddy is right, and that wall is haunted. Because Nanette here saw the rust, you know, that Maddy thinks is blood, was still oozing out around that cement the hotel put on her crack. So I dug at it a little with my knife, and the whole wall started pouring out water. It was like the rock that Moses struck. Then poor Maddy stuck her head in it, I don't know why, maybe she was trying to drink the blood or something. But she almost drowned. That Brian Cassidy from the hotel, he was going to just let her die right there, but a Good Samaritan in the garage, he sometimes feeds her on the sly when Mr. Cassidy isn't watching, he called for an ambulance."

"The storm was terrible," Nanette ventured—she rarely spoke, seemed to shelter herself behind Jacqui's stronger personality. "It was thundering the whole time, and we was wondering what to do with Maddy, on account of they'd gone and chopped up our little house, our Westinghouse box. Then, this woman came"—she gestured toward the terrifying stranger without looking at her—"and Maddy, well, Maddy thought—"

"She thought it was the Virgin," Luisa cut in, almost smacking her lips with excitement. "To me she looked like Vashti, but Maddy, or whatever her name is, screamed, 'The Blessed Mother is here, She has appeared to me, She forgives me and is calling me Her own pure daughter."

Hector shuddered, Luisa so perfectly re-created Madeleine—not just her voice, with its nasal whine and singsong intonation, but also her jerking uncoordinated movements.

Delighted with his reaction, Luisa got to her feet, her flopping arms sweeping Hector's papers to the floor.

"So Luisa Minsky knocked your papers off the desk, Tammuz—that seems like a minor irritant to set off a major catastrophe, a major violation of professional standards. You're going to have to do more to persuade me that you are capable of carrying out your duties."

But hard put to explain it to myself, let alone him. Not the first time we had a patient, or even a staff member, out of control. So why was this so much worse?

The Amazon never spoke. I wondered if she might be aphasiac, but Millie thought she was involved in some elaborate con with Luisa, because the singer seemed to interpret her grunts, give meaning to them. It started when I asked Amazon for a name. She stared at me, then grunted—a guttural noise, not a word at all, but Luisa piped up, "Her name is Starr."

"Stop playing games with us, Luisa, it's a busy night in an over-worked hospital," Millie snapped, when Luisa began instructing Hector that the name had two *r*'s. "You and your friend may think it's funny to come up with this kind of routine—"

"I wouldn't call her my friend," Luisa said.

"Where does she live?" Hector demanded.

"Dear boy—Doctor—I don't know. I suppose someplace on Underground Wacker, since that's where she appeared. But I never saw her before tonight."

"Then I'd like to know how she communicates with you. So far she has not spoken an intelligible sentence. How do you know her name?"

"She told me. In the ambulance when we were riding over here." Luisa cocked her head. "You need to know how to *listen*, Doctor. Surely that's the first thing they teach a psychiatrist when you start training. *Listen.* I have perfect pitch, so I understand her from the tone of her voice."

Millie couldn't contain herself any longer. "Hector—Dr. Tammuz—either do a proper exam or put them back on the street where they belong!"

This outburst totally unlike Millie, usually the most empathic, least judgmental of nurses. Startled me into losing what was left of my poise. I turned to Starr, said we needed to check her reflexes, see if she had brain damage, do some blood work to check for drugs. Luisa on edge of desk, swinging one leg, eyes drooping, suddenly perked up at this, said, No need, nothing wrong with Starr's brain, but Millie and I ignored her.

Bracing himself, his hand on the back of Starr's head, the mass of coiled braided hair like a nest of snakes, the breasts brushing his arm, a tightening across his groin which embarrassed him; he tried to forget the weight of flesh touching him through the fabric of her T-shirt, his hospital coat, his shirt sleeve, his skin.

He shone his flashlight into the hawk's eyes. Starr jerked her head away and uttered a noise—a word in some language she alone spoke, or the grunt of an outraged animal, he was far too tired, too near the edge of his own collapse to know, but the sound was loud, unexpected, and he dropped the flashlight.

Starr picked it up, inspected it as though she had never seen one before, played it over his face, Luisa's and Madeleine's; as the light reached her eyes Madeleine whimpered and tried to sit up. Hector moved over to make sure she didn't fall from the gurney.

A couple of orderlies arrived to wheel Madeleine to a bed. Millie snapped at them to help her with Starr first, to put her in a chair so Millie could get a blood sample. The orderlies, big gentle men, not like some on the service who liked to throw their weight around, usually kidded with Millie. Tonight her edginess startled them.

"I don't think that's a good idea, Millie," Hector tried to interject, but she overrode him.

Since he was a transient—just the resident on call—while she had been the night charge nurse for eight years, the orderlies followed her directive, not Hector's. They took Starr's elbows and shifted her gently to the chair on the far side of the small desk. The hawk eyes were frowning, wary, but she offered no active resistance until Millie tied a length of rubber tubing around her biceps and advanced with a needle.

Starr knocked the syringe away, ripped the tube from her arm, picked up the chair and dashed it to the floor; rubbery plastic, it bounced but didn't break. Madeleine howled from her gurney. Hector and the orderlies, trying to seize the aphasiac's flailing arms, were buffeted about the head with a boxer's fists. Millie raced off to summon security.

From the cart Madeleine suddenly spoke in her nasal singsong. "They want your blood. Next they scan your brain to see whether you have waves or pulses there, they study you for aluminum, bitumen, chromium, your brain is like the fender of a car."

The aphasiac stopped flailing; she seemed intent on Madeleine's voice. She grunted. Hector felt the hairs on his neck stand up, as if she had delivered a personal warning to him.

"You can't take her blood." Luisa, who had been cackling at the battle, suddenly spoke. "It's some kind of religious thing, I don't know what. She isn't allowed to give you her blood."

I felt like smacking Montcrief myself; she was carrying on as if we were putting on an entertainment for her. Managed to restrain myself, just.

Millie returned with two security guards. She ordered the guards to put Starr into a Posey. The furies of a moment earlier were nothing compared to the battle that erupted then. The Amazon hurled herself on Millie and tried to strangle her, but the guards and orderlies managed among the four of them to wrestle her into a restraining jacket. Usually I hate these damned dehumanizing Poseys, they humiliate the patients, restrict their arm movements so they can't even feed themselves un-aided. Tonight I felt a most horrible surge of savagery, an exultation to have power while she sat helpless in her swaddling clothes; I was glad to be the one to tie her to a wheelchair.

I injected the Amazon, Haldol and Ativan, guessing at her weight—over-guessing, in my bestial gladness—pleased instead of dismayed with the power to sedate.

As they started to wheel Starr away the drunk flung herself onto Starr's lap. Put her arms around her neck, weeping against the Posey. So disgusted with both of them I told the orderlies to take the drunk to the locked ward along with the aphasiac.

28

Escape from the Booby Hatch

A hot summer day in the thirties, driving down a dusty farm road in the South. At first the scene ordinary, bucolic: high crops on either side block any view. No people—insects buzzing in underbrush the only life besides me. Road unpaved, dust billowing around me. I'm driving an old black jalopy.

Feel uneasy in the car, and realize that I'm fleeing someone very dangerous. Who or what not specified, but my car will go only seven miles an hour and my pursuer is in a modern car, doing ninety and gaining on me.

I drive into the field, thinking the plants will shelter my little car from view. And there in front of me, rising from the soil, are Jacqui and Nanette. Come, they say, Starr is waiting for you. They lead me to a glade, where Starr is lying at her ease. She offers me her breast. She says, Drink, you're very thirsty. I kneel beside, but my pursuers are upon us. She sees them over my shoulder, and vanishes, leaving me kneeling there, my mouth open, begging for her milk. And then whoever was following me is filling my nose and mouth with dirt.

He woke choking, wet with sweat. It was three in the morning. He was shaking, aching, as though he had a fever in his joints. He came back to the room only slowly, discovered he was wearing his clothes, vaguely remembered coming home at six, thinking he would lie down for just half an hour before eating supper. His belt buckle was digging into his belly and his tie, which he'd loosened without removing, had twisted itself behind his ear. Maybe that had led to a dream of choking.

He sat up in bed, but was so thick with the dream that he couldn't even move enough to undress. He hugged himself, rocking, needing some basic comfort that no one could give him.

"Starr," he whispered in the dark, tears swelling out, covering his face like glass. "Starr."

She had disappeared, along with the diva, and he felt unaccountably bereft. When he remembered his own behavior—was it only twenty-four hours ago?—stuffing her full of Haldol and Ativan, waves of shame swept through him. He sobbed as he had not since he was a child.

That morning, when he followed Hanaper up to the locked ward, they found Dr. Stonds in angry conversation with Venetra Marceau, the ward head. Marceau was black, so dark that the planes of her face were swallowed by the neon lights. Next to her Stonds looked pale and insubstantial.

"Because this hospital lets you get away with acting like Jesus Christ up on the cross," the ward head was saying as Hector drew within earshot, "I had to send two patients down to see you. Any other doctor in this hospital would have come up here. If you can make it now, to chew me out, why couldn't you come two hours ago? Then we might still have them on the premises."

"How dare you speak to me in that tone, young woman? I hold you responsible for the fact that no proper escort was sent with them. Two orderlies must accompany any patient leaving this ward. Is that not hospital policy?" Stonds shook an open policy manual under the ward head's nose.

"Two orderlies?" She slapped the manual onto the counter of the nurses' station. "We have three orderlies for this whole floor in the mornings, thanks to the brilliant insights of the hospital finance committee, and all three were occupied when your summons came."

Hanaper stood on one leg, like an anxious stork, while we waited for the great man to notice our arrival. Venetra saw us first. She must be the only person at Midwest who tells Stonds what she thinks of him; why he hasn't had her fired I don't know. Maybe he's scared of her, too.

She snapped out a question to H, who assumed a lofty tone to hide his own dis-ease: we're here to examine the women young Tammuz saw fit to admit last night.

"That's what Dr. Stonds and I are discussing right now," the ward head snapped. "He wanted to interview them, and he got one of my poor overworked nurses to agree to send them down to his office with only herself in attendance."

The nurse was huddled behind Venetra, eyes red, still sniffling. She couldn't explain how it happened. They were moving slowly, Starr, who was still groggy with antipsychotics, in a wheelchair, Luisa walking next to her. When the elevator started moving, Starr seemed to panic. She got out of the chair and knelt on the floor, almost as though she was trying to steady the elevator cage. The nurse tried to lift her back into her chair, but Starr was much stronger than her attendant. When the elevator stopped, the two patients shoved the nurse aside and disappeared down a stairwell.

"Disappeared?" Hector echoed foolishly.

"Yes, Dr. Tammuz. As in gone, vanished," Marceau said. "This hospital being a labyrinth like every other old hospital I've ever served in, there are fifty ways to get in and out, assuming these women weren't too disoriented to find one of them."

Hector was already close to swooning from fatigue. The loss of Starr made him feel as though he were falling through space. He'd been counting on the sight of Starr to vindicate him in Hanaper's eyes. Her overwhelming sexuality would unnerve Hanaper as it had Hector; the department head would shrink quietly away to his office, with no more talk about putting his junior resident on probation. Now the disappointment of losing his prize exhibit made Hector's knees buckle. He only stayed upright by clutching the counter.

Hector tried to pay attention to the argument between Stonds and Marceau, because Hanaper was bound to throw the blame on him, but they sounded far away, like ducks quacking on a distant pond: women were dangerous . . . knocked nurse over leaving elevator . . . security hunting . . . Chicago police notified . . . might harm someone . . . might harm selves . . . liability of hospital.

"Dr. Tammuz said the aphasiac was something special," Hanaper said, his lips glistening with anticipation.

Marceau flicked a glance in his direction. "That could be, Doctor. I only saw her when she was drugged."

Special. Hector was furious when he realized his chief was hoping for a peep show. Step right up, see nipples that glow in the dark, free to a man with a badge on his gown. Starr, I'll protect you from those greedy eyes, and then he was awash with longing, wanting to bury his face in her breasts and so lose all bonds of fear, of adulthood, of responsibility. He thought he could feel her flesh, warm and firm, but yielding to his tongue.

"Dr. Tammuz admitted them. Maybe he knows something of their associates."

The mention of his name startled Hector. Stonds and Marceau weren't quacking ducks, but barking wolves in need of raw meat. Hanaper would throw his junior resident into the fight just for the pleasure of seeing him devoured.

"Dr. Tammuz, have you lost your senses?" Dr. Stonds was beside himself with fury, and the naked longing on the resident's face only enraged him further.

"Sorry, sir: it's been forty hours since I was last in bed." Hector's voice came out in a husky whisper. "If you could let me know why you want to interview the women maybe I could help?"

"Where has your mind been these past twenty minutes, Tammuz?" Hanaper said. "Dr. Stonds wants to interrogate these women about his granddaughter. She's been missing for nearly a week, as you should know."

Why should he know? Hector was about to ask, then remembered his conversation with the glacial elder granddaughter. Her younger sister, who'd tried to see him in clinic last Wednesday. She'd run away.

"But I don't think Starr or Luisa could help locate her," he said aloud. "I know some of their behavior last night seemed as though they might be psychic, but Starr doesn't talk at all, and Luisa was falling-down drunk."

And then Hanaper and Stonds boiled over on me at the same time. I was an ignorant jackass, a fool, God knows what else, for not knowing that the Stonds girl had been present at the wall last night with Starr, Luisa and Madeleine. Harriet the Glacier had seen her sister, and tried to talk her into going home, but the kid, presumably sick of living with an iceberg and a rottweiler, took to her heels. Stonds actually thought one of the three women who disintegrated so totally last night might have paid attention to a stranger on their perimeter.

Then Hanaper said, well, the night charge nurse Millie says a couple of homeless women accompanied Madeleine and Starr to the ER last night—where are they now? Hanaper and Stonds ordered me to go back to the Hotel Pleiades and see if I could find Jacqui and Nanette, and bring them in to talk to Stonds. A bird dog, go into the swamp, Hector, and fetch us some homeless women.

I went down to the hotel garage. They were building a barricade in front of it, shoring it up, the garage manager told me. It looked like a medieval fortress, with great spikes sticking out of it. No one would get close to the wall now—those spears would impale them first.

I looked around the area but saw no signs of any of my crazy ladies, Starr or Luisa, Jacqui or Nanette. Or Mara Stonds, for that matter. Nothing but the shattered remains of the Westinghouse box where I examined Madeleine last month. I asked the garage manager how the box came to be destroyed. A sly look crossed his face. "We were getting complaints about rats. Someone was storing food back there and it was attracting vermin." I was too tired to take up the matter. Tired, chicken, I don't know. Hector the bravest of all the Trojans.

He staggered punch-drunk toward the stairs to the upper world, his body weightless, barely connecting to the ground with each step he took. As he grasped the handrail he felt as though he were flying, skimming the surface of the earth.

"Doctor! Wake up!" Jacqui was shaking him as he leaned against the stairwell. "Haven't you been in bed?"

He blinked at her, not sure if she was part of a dream. He thought he'd just been searching for her in this very spot.

"We know how to hide," she said briefly, and then he saw Nanette at her elbow. "What are we going to do about Maddy, Doctor? She's really going to lose her mind when she gets out of the hospital and sees these spikes. You can't even touch the wall, they're so long."

"Is anyone else with you?" He felt a surge of eagerness. "Luisa, or Mara Stonds—or—or Starr?"

"We can't take on that drunk Luisa, and certainly not Starr. Wherever she is people get too stirred up. It's hard enough looking after Maddy, but at least she's got a sweet temper."

I had to tell them that Hanaper was releasing Madeleine in a few hours. I'd visited her before leaving the hospital. Very frail. Don't know how long she'll live if she's back on the streets. Trying to get a social worker involved, but it's the same damned story. Since she's uninsured, cost containment won't allow hospital's social services. Spent an hour calling different social agencies, talking to Patsy Wanachs at Hagar's House, to a woman at the Lenore Foundation, but nothing will happen fast—if it happens at all.

Jacqui and Nanette told me various places where Luisa might have gone. They don't know her, don't know her habits, but suggested some of the drop-in shelters, some of the coffee shops where women can sit for a few hours nursing a single cup of coffee.

I wandered the city searching, but heard no tale of anyone like Starr. Reached home a little before six and fell into bed without undressing.

29

Big Sister Lets Go

"AUNT LUISA'S ON TELEVISION," Becca Minsky called to her mother.

Becca was perched on a kitchen stool, waiting for Kim Nagel to pick her up for a sailing party with Kim's family. Karen had the little kitchen set turned to the five o'clock news while she did laundry and started supper.

Karen turned from the washing machine to look. She was expecting some old clip of her sister-in-law, not the flood scene from Underground Wacker. Channel 13's Don Sandstrom was explaining what had happened at the Hotel Pleiades, using footage his crew had shot during the height of last night's deluge. Luisa—Janice—was standing in the background. Judging by the tilt of her jaw she was singing.

"What's she doing there?" Becca demanded.

"Singing in the rain." Karen couldn't get Becca to smile.

"Apparently the trouble began over a crack in the concrete," Sandstrom was saying. "A group of homeless women believe the Virgin Mary's blood has appeared in a crack on this wall. The hotel cemented it over, but last night, in an effort to get back to what the homeless women claim is blood, they chipped away the cement and managed to start a geyser. No one is sure yet what happened, although the hotel's lawyer, Harriet Stonds, assured Channel 13 that the stains on the wall are just rust from a leaking pipe, not blood as the women assert. Joining them in their protest was Chicago opera great Luisa Montcrief."

The camera zoomed briefly on Luisa's face. She seemed thin and ill to Becca. Before she could point this out to her mother, the picture shifted to Harriet's office. The lawyer sat behind her burled desk, wearing a royal blue suit that matched her eyes, but looking formidable despite an earnest smile.

"We're concerned about structural damage, of course. To minimize any risk to the public we've had engineers on the scene today constructing a cradle to hold the wall in place until any underlying damage can be ascertained. I would like to note that three requests we sent to the city to have the pipe repaired were ignored."

"Out of curiosity, Ms. Stonds," Sandstrom asked from behind the camera, "did you test the fluid coming out of the wall?"

The film switched to a shot of Harriet last night at the wall, talking to the cameras while the water swirled around her.

"To see whether it was blood?" Harriet's smile tightened. "We were all ankle-deep in water last night. I think the fire department and the city water engineers would have realized fast enough if ten thousand gallons of blood had been spilling on us."

The picture returned to the hotel wall and the spiked girders that were being screwed into position. "The hotel's foundation here is built into bedrock, so guests should not be worried that the building will collapse. Reporting live from Underground Wacker, I'm Don Sandstrom, Channel 13 news."

"That must be Dr. Stonds's granddaughter," Karen said. "You wouldn't know him, but he was the surgeon who operated on your Grandmother Minsky. She's beautiful, isn't she? Totally unlike her sister—the other granddaughter—she was arrested with your aunt last week."

"I know: you told me then," Becca said, in the universal adolescent tone that indicates adult stupidity. "Aunt Luisa doesn't look very well. They shouldn't have let her out of the hospital."

"They couldn't keep her."

"Because she doesn't have insurance and her family doesn't care if she dies."

Karen turned back to the towels. "Let's not fight that war again. Even if she had insurance they would have discharged her. Your aunt's only hope is to acknowledge her alcoholism and get help. We've got to agree on that as a family if she's ever going to change."

"I know she's an alcoholic, but you're thrilled to see her career in ruins. You loved it last year at my bat mitzvah when I talked about responsibility to the homeless and the orphan, but you're a hypocrite, you don't want to see me actually doing anything about a real homeless person, because you hate her." Becca slid off the stool and ran from the kitchen.

"If you are planning on going into the city to rescue her, you'd better stop in your tracks because I will not permit it," Karen yelled after her, wondering what she would do if her daughter disobeyed her.

Becca's feet pounded on the stairs; the house shook as she slammed her door. Karen stood in the hall, holding her breath, waiting for what Becca might do next. Her daughter made her feel helpless, like a reed bowing in the wind, and yet Becca was such a fundamentally good child—teenager—young woman—whatever it was she was these days. Not into drugs, or sullen depressions, the kinds of things that really bedevil a household. Still, Karen shouldn't be standing tensely in the hall: Becca should be huddled in her room wondering how to appease her mother, not the other way around.

The mother returned to the laundry, the back of her head aching with the strain of listening. Then she heard a click and a buzz from the kitchen extension and relaxed: Becca's private line and the house line were imperfectly separated, so you were always aware when one or the other was in use. Becca was telling someone her woes—probably Corie, since she was about to go out with Kim.

Karen might not have been so sanguine if she'd known her daughter was talking to Judith Ohana at the First Freedoms Forum: did you see the news? Doesn't this mean the hotel violated Aunt Luisa's civil rights, and did the same to all those women who were with her?

Harriet Stonds wouldn't have been pleased by Becca's call, either: she didn't want any action that would keep the Pleiades in the spotlight. Harriet hadn't slept much the night before, but she felt almost exalted with happiness. All the indecision she'd been experiencing since her sister ran off—no, since Mephers's heart attack—had dropped away. She spent the morning with engineers, going over specs to the wall for the Hotel Pleiades garage, the survey lines for the hotel's property, and the specs for the pipes. Her mind was once more alert, handling ten different clients, a dozen unrelated details, putting them together like a child solving a Rubik's cube: thirty seconds, with the adults dazzled to see it come together under their noses.

Her paralegals and many of her colleagues had watched her on the early morning news. You looked wonderful; you're so poised, I would have been too scared to open my mouth; you got caught in that storm last night? No one would have guessed it by looking at your hair when they showed you in front of the wall. And you look radiant today.

As if she'd been laid, her paralegals muttered to each other, hoping to be well out of earshot. Harriet heard them, but didn't mind. Sex? Sex never left her feeling this free. She felt Mara dropping away from her as though she were standing at the gates of Paradise losing all her earthly troubles. Mara's grimy face last night, trying to connect Harriet to that bestial woman who'd appeared at the wall, as if Harriet's mother looked anything like that bloated, obscene creature, the swollen monster of Harriet's nightmares.

Which had been more repulsive—the naked woman or Mara's suggestion that the creature was their mother? It didn't matter. In that moment Harriet withdrew from her completely. She dashed Mara's fingers from her arm. It's time to end the play, Mara, and come home, she said. You're not going to drag my name in the mud with some disgusting homeless woman you've dug up.

Her sister stammered, I didn't dig her up, she just appeared, but I've been longing for Mother or for Grannie Selena. I think she felt me wanting her and showed up.

Grandfather had been right all along. Mara was a self-dramatizing brat. Harriet, her face as rigid as carved jade, offered Mara two choices—either admit she was playacting, and come home, get a job, and grow up; or admit she was seriously disturbed and get the kind of help she clearly needed, and that Grandfather was loving enough to want to give her. And Mara, her own face a mask of pain, screamed something and ran off into the maze of alleys behind the garage.

As if Harriet cared enough to give chase. She went home to her lavender-scented sheets, almost singing, despite having to walk two miles in her ruined heels because she couldn't find a taxi. In the morning she stayed in to have breakfast with Grandfather, instead of going to the gym for her usual early morning workout. She kissed him warmly, and apologized for her abstraction during the last week.

"I let Mara suck me into her fantasy world for a while there. But I saw her last night: she seems to be hanging out with some homeless women down by the Hotel Pleiades. I don't know whether it's because the hotel fired her, and she's trying to embarrass them, or because they're my clients and she wants to embarrass me. But either way, I've had it. Let her act it out, let it run its course."

When Grandfather got the whole story of last night's events, he said he thought he owed it to the brat to make a push to rescue her. You know, Harriet, it could be that these women are taking advantage of her, of her instability. Maybe they know her family has money and think they can extort some from us through her. Since the women Mara had hooked up with had been taken to Midwest Hospital, he'd interrogate them, find out what they were up to.

She kissed him again: that's typical of your generosity, she'd said, or something to that effect, and called down to Raymond to find a cab for her. Her good mood lasted through lunch, which she ate at the Saddle Club, with three of the partners and the engineering firm that was one of their most important clients. Instead of the undressed green salad that was her usual meal she ate real food, fish with a sauce, roasted potatoes, green beans with butter. She would get up an hour earlier tomorrow and do double duty on the treadmill before work.

She had another full night and half a day of bliss, before Gian Palmetto called her back to misery.

30

A Night at the Opera

IN HER PRACTICE ROOM high above the street at the opera house, Luisa played the piano for Starr. She wanted music, but her throat was too parched for her to risk her voice. Luisa wasn't skilled on the keyboard—she'd only ever learned enough to pick out accompaniments to vocal pieces she was studying, but today she felt the music in her fingers. After a time Starr began to sing.

The words, if they were words, were in a language Luisa didn't know. The gutturals were harsh and Starr's voice was strong without being melodic, but Luisa listened as intently as if Mozart himself were performing. The rough voice seemed to blend with Luisa's playing, with half-forgotten chords to half-remembered arias. The diva forgot her sore throat, her grievances against Harry and Karen, against her agent and the director of the Met. All her being was concentrated in her ear.

As she played, as Starr sang, Luisa's head was shot through with images, a slide show, where the pictures came slowly at first: a river; a gated city with brick towers; then a long and difficult journey by boat, carrying books of law, with an angry father in pursuit. Luisa's fingers picked out passages from Schubert's *Elf King,* and its urgent pounding of pursuit through the night.

The mood of Starr's singing seemed to shift. Luisa found herself returning to her beloved Verdi while pictures cascaded more wildly through her brain.

The sky was the brilliant blue that arched over her villa in Campania. She sat under a tree whose long green branches curved and swayed
like arms stretching to embrace her. A bird in the middle of the tree
mocked her, fluttering just beyond her reach when she tried to drive it
off. A man appeared, a ruddy man, who caught and removed the bird.

King David was described like that in the Bible: a ruddy man. Luisa
had always thought that meant reddened, coarse, but she saw now it
meant someone so vital that his skin glowed from the coursing of his
blood.

She barely had time to realize that when she was lying with him on
a giant wooden bed, riding him in an ecstasy she'd never known, urging
him in language she couldn't imagine uttering: plow me, plow my vulva,
she was saying, but it wasn't she riding, it was Starr, and there was no
ruddy man, only herself, Luisa, so that her fingers left the keyboard, and
sought Starr's breasts, warm and firm as rising bread, and Starr's lips were
on her, glowing coals that burned her, froze her, then melted her again,
and gold came pouring from her, cleansing her, creating her new.

She tried to twine her legs around Starr, but she was too small. Starr
grew bigger and bigger, her black coiled hair became the horns of a wild
cow, her nostrils expelled fire, and the earth itself was not as large as
those breasts. Luisa clung to her, sobbing through her parched throat; her
arms and legs too frail for the ride, clutching at the horns, fearing to let
go, until the horns were suddenly clumps of sweaty hair, the fire breath
only garlic, and the two women slept in a heap beneath the grand piano.

31

A Death for the Virgin

PERCHED IN THE CROTCH of an iron girder, Mara watched the spikes go up on the wall. The garage manager, Brian Cassidy, stood almost directly below her, directing the operation.

Mara's sleeping bag and few remaining clothes were stuffed into a plastic garbage bag at her feet. A man had stolen her backpack in the early hours of the morning. She woke from a restless half-sleep to feel him jerking the pack from beneath her head. When she tried to fight him he punched her in the mouth so hard, one of her front teeth broke. Her bank card was safe in her jeans, but she couldn't squander money on a new backpack. She went from Dumpster to Dumpster until she found a thick black bag.

What would happen if she went to the family dentist? Would he report her to Grandfather, or would he let her bathe and then repair her tooth? She had only been on the streets for a week, but she couldn't imagine how it felt to be clean.

It must be at Harriet's command that the spikes were going up. Harriet, who hated her. She'd seen it in her sister's face last night: revulsion, masked for nineteen years behind the gauze of Harriet's perfect deportment, lay in front of Mara like the stage at the opera with the scrim pulled suddenly back.

Mara saw fragments of her own life, all those years of longing for Harriet's love—Harriet's first summer home from Smith, Mara riding her tricycle up and down in front of the building for hours, wanting to be the first to greet her sister, wearing makeup from Harriet's dressing table, her five-year-old body suddenly snatched up by Mephers—don't you know better than to break into other people's rooms and steal their things?—whisked upstairs to be held and scrubbed under the kitchen tap, her cries of, I'm waiting for Hehwie, I want to look like Hehwie, ignored and drowned under the sluicing.

She was a fool. How could she have been so stupid her whole life long? It wasn't enough that she was big and clumsy with hair that came from who knew what man, certainly nothing in the Stonds family tree would give rise to it. Harriet didn't want her love—she wanted Mara gone. Now Harriet was exacting her revenge for all those years of living with a sister she hated by pounding spikes into the wall.

Mara's blind dumb following of Harriet brought a flash of shame that made her skin prickle even now, as she perched on the girder. It was why she had run away from Harriet into the maze of alleys, why she had missed the departure of Jacqui, Madeleine, and the diva. And the woman with masses of black hair, bigger than Mara's untamed bush, blacker, wilder, the woman who might be Mother.

Now she needed to find that woman. If it was Mother, she'd tell Mara why she'd left her alone with Grandfather. Not because of you, little daughter, but because—nothing credible came to her hurt, tired mind. Because Beatrix was too involved in drugs, as Mephers always said, to care about her baby—maybe that was the best Mara could hope for.

But the woman last night hadn't looked like the druggies Mara saw around her on the streets every day. She held herself upright, her bright eyes assured, almost cocky (how can you know, she could hear Mephers ask, you only saw her for thirty seconds). But never mind, the woman would embrace Mara: little daughter, they haven't looked after you well. From a nest within those bronze arms Mara heard the woman lecture Mephers and Grandfather, and then a special scolding for Harriet: how could you turn away from this little sister who only adored you?

The image made Mara's eyes sting with tears. She cried, clutching the bumpy edge of the girder, and fell into a doze.

Madeleine's howl jerked her awake some hours later. Mara looked over the side of her perch. Madeleine stood in front of the spiked cradle, wailing with misery at being blocked from her wall. After last night's deluge the wall sported a whole network of hairline fractures, but Madeleine knew—or thought she knew—which was her original, the crack of the Blessed Virgin.

Mara couldn't make out any words in the high-pitched mewling. But Brian Cassidy had been waiting for this moment. He almost ran from his lair in the garage, coattails flapping.

"This wall is off limits to you and your kind. Look at what you did, look at all the trouble and expense you've cost the hotel. Now get your ugly crazy face out of here or I'll make you sorry you didn't leave under your own steam." He grabbed Madeleine's shoulders and shook her.

The homeless woman dangled from his arms like a puppet, her skinny legs jerking up and down beneath the layers of her skirts. She panted with the effort to free herself, her breath coming in puffs, in rhythm to his shaking. When she couldn't get away from him she spat at him. Cassidy dropped her and smashed her face with the flat of his hand. Mara sucked on her fingers in horror. Commuters on their way to the bus stop averted their eyes and crossed to the other side of the street.

Lying on the ground, Madeleine brandished her Bible at Cassidy. "You are an abomination, a desecration. The Holy Mother loathes all who deface Her temple, She will rain showers of curses on you. She will bring confusion and frustration to all that you do. She will smite you with the boils of Egypt, and with ulcers and scurvy and the itch. She will smite you on the knees and on the legs with grievous boils, of which you cannot be healed."

"I'll take my chances on that, cunt. Meanwhile, vamoose! Out! Am-scray." Cassidy bent over her and grabbed her right arm with the Bible in it and twisted it back. "If you don't, trust me: the street sweepers will be picking your dead body out of the rubble in back of the hotel tomorrow morning. And nobody's going to cry over your flea-bitten carcass."

He stood over her while she crawled to the curb, hugging her Bible to her chest and weeping silently. He was about to kick her when he realized that a number of homebound commuters had stopped to watch. He turned abruptly and went back to the garage, where impatient customers snapped at him, wondering why he was lounging at his ease when they were waiting for their cars.

When Brian Cassidy vanished inside the garage, the commuters scuttled on to the bus stop. No one wanted to get involved with a specimen like Madeleine, with her filthy clothes and matted hair, muttering over her Bible.

Mara, ashamed of her own cowardice in not trying to intervene, climbed down from the girder and ran to Madeleine. She fished in her bag for something to wipe the other woman's face, but could only come up with a pair of soiled underpants. She had a bottle of orange juice that still had a few swallows left in it, and finally persuaded Madeleine to drink some.

"We should get you some help. Maybe Jacqui and Nanette . . . Do you know where they are?"

Madeleine didn't answer, only rocked on her heels and wept that the Mother of God would never forgive her for abandoning the wall. "I let the doctor give me a shot, and that made me forget Her. Now they ruined Her wall. She'll curse me the same as She curses him."

"It's not your fault, Maddy; it's my sister who did this. The—the Holy Mother"—Mara stumbled on the phrase, feeling like a hypocrite— "She knows you love Her. Let's go over to the shelter and get a night's sleep. We can figure something out in the morning if we've had some real sleep."

She couldn't get Madeleine to move, but the idea of a real night's sleep grew vivid in Mara's mind. If she got to Hagar's House early enough, there would still be beds available. And a shower. She'd find Jacqui and Nanette and they'd tell her what to do to make Madeleine leave the wall. And they would know what had become of the woman with the hair.

Her heart beat harder as she slid through the underground streets. Past Corona's and the other jazz bars on Kinzie and Hubbard, where people flattened back as she passed: wild hair, unwashed body, she carried a terrible contamination on her, the germ of uncertainty.

When she used to walk that route from her job at the hotel, she'd watch the way people shrank from Madeleine or the other homeless and think contemptuously, homelessness isn't a disease, they're not going to infect you. She saw now the repugnance ran deeper: if those secure in shelter and job acknowledged that someone like—like Mara, all right, like she herself, with her broken tooth and smelly clothes—if Mara was a person, then they'd have to believe that life was uncertain. It was a wild bull in a rodeo where you got on but couldn't control where or how you were flung off. Plans and schedules, diets, workouts, and investments could disappear if a homeless person was human. That was too scary. So they had to look at Mara and say, we don't see her. Or: she's a problem child whom we can't fix—let her go, let her follow her mother into that black hole of loneliness.

She stopped in front of a store that had little mirrored panels in its window frame and frowned at herself. She was still recognizably Mara. It was the hair. Patsy Wanachs would know her in a second, and then, if Grandfather or Harriet had put out a warning (must be shot on sight. Shot full of Haldol and stuffed into a psychiatry ward) . . .

She went into a convenience store on the corner to see if she could find something that would disguise her face. It was a tawdry little store that hadn't given in yet to the renewal of the area, but with its dirty aisles and half-bare shelves it wouldn't survive much longer. The Lebanese clerk watched her indifferently—she could have stolen anything had she wanted to.

She finally bought a pair of knee-high stockings. Seventy-nine cents. Ten days ago she spent triple that on a cup of coffee without thinking. Now it made her anxious. That money could have gone for food.

She pulled one of the stockings over her hair and stopped to study herself in the mirrored panel. She looked—like a terrorist. A turnip. No, once the shock at the change was over, she was startled to find she had a face, cheekbones: gaunt now from a week of bad food and bad sleep, but a real face that she hadn't known lay behind her messy curls. Her own mother wouldn't know her, she burlesqued herself. And with her front tooth broken off . . .

You had to give a name through the intercom at Hagar's House. She hadn't thought about it. She couldn't use "Mara": it was too unusual; anyone on the staff would think immediately of Mara Stonds. Too bad Grandfather hadn't called her Sue. Selena, she said quickly, in answer to the scratchy query. Selena Vatick.

She had to have an interview, with one of the volunteers, fortunately, not with Patsy, who would have seen through the stocking disguise in a second. Some friend of Sylvia Lenore's was working tonight. Mara knew her by sight, from years of seeing her at church meetings, but the woman gave no sign of recognizing her.

Selena was new here, wasn't she? The rules: no drugs or booze on the premises, no disruptive noise, no men. Where the bathroom was, if she needed to make a phone call, if she needed help finding permanent lodging, if she was eligible for social security, if she wanted clothes where the community grab bag was. If she needed counseling, Dr. Tammuz came on Fridays; if her feet hurt, a podiatrist on Thursdays; if her soul ached, there was Wednesday Bible study. Tonight was Tuesday, so no activities were planned. Beds became available at ten; she was assigned twenty-three, out of twenty-seven—she'd arrived in the nick of time— but she could shower now if she wanted to.

Like a puppy wriggling with pleasure under the touch of a hand, Mara squirmed under the shower. She rinsed out her underwear and her second T-shirt, helped herself to a clean sweatshirt from the clothing bag, debating between too-small jeans and too-large sweatpants, and finally, imagining herself on the girder, chose the sweats under the watchful eye of another volunteer: two pieces per woman per month, her name carefully written in the register; Vatick—that's unusual—what nationality? Mara scowled below her stockinged head. Sumerian. The volunteer retreated, stopped trying out overtures.

In the activities room Mara found Jacqui and Nanette. She poured out Madeleine's newest woes, begged for news of the strange woman, learned her name was Starr. Starr was at the hospital with Luisa and Maddy, but if they had released Maddy, then maybe the other two were gone as well. And, baby, we're tired. We were at the hospital until three this morning. We have to let Maddy take her chances tonight—we need a bed. We'll go to the wall first thing in the morning.

At ten Mara fell into bed twenty-three, a narrow aluminum cot like all the others. When the church bought them three years ago Mara had protested hotly. Who could sleep on such a thing? Now she knew—those who were weary and heavy-laden. She didn't stir, even when Caroline and LaBelle got into one of their endless quarrels, when Ashley howled at a phantom, or LaBelle's pimp tried breaking in at three o'clock. She slept until six-thirty, when a volunteer shook her awake. Breakfast, Selena, and then you have to leave.

In the morning, when she accompanied Jacqui and Nanette back to the wall, they found the area once again ringed by police: early morning commuters had discovered Madeleine's body dangling among the spikes of the protective cradle.

32

Ulcers and Scurvy and the Itch

Brian Cassidy left the hotel at six Wednesday morning, when his shift ended, to sleep or drink, or find a hooker on west Madison before doing either. Off and on during the night he stepped outside to make sure the crazy woman was obeying his injunction. If he saw Madeleine Carter climbing the scaffolding, taking off the belt that held her many skirts to her body, wrapping it around her neck, he might have nodded in satisfaction and returned to his office. If he saw her do those things, he never said. He was gone before the first pale commuter ran into the garage, sick from what she'd seen, demanding police, ambulance, first aid.

Madeleine had committed suicide: there was no doubt about it, the paramedic said so to the cop, although final judgment was reserved for the medical examiner.

"But the garage manager threatened her last night. I heard him. He said if she didn't leave the wall the street cleaners would be picking up her dead body." Mara was trying to break in on the policeman and the medic, but they brushed her off, a buzzing mosquito that they couldn't see. "He hit her, too, and threw her to the ground. I was watching."

Jacqui took her arm and steered her gently away. "He's not going to listen to you, baby. You're homeless—no one cares what you think. Poor Madeleine. Those voices of hers did her in."

Madeleine lay one more time, one final time, on a stretcher along-

side the curb. Jacqui knelt next to her. Her rough hands smoothed the
thin cheeks, now blood-swollen, death-mottled. County morgue Madeleine's penultimate destination. A perfunctory autopsy. A waiting for
someone to claim the body; if no one came, the unmarked grave of
Cook County's unwanted poor.

"Nanette, she's gone off to phone the doctor. Maybe he can get
them to bring her to him." As though Hector Tammuz, powerless in his
own department, could move Midwest Hospital's pathologists to act.

Anger swelled up inside Mara, like yeast blowing up flour. This was
Harriet's doing, this death of Madeleine, Harriet egging on Brian Cassidy. For once, Harriet and Brian, Grandfather and Mephers, weren't
going to step on someone and pay no consequences.

Mara stumbled up the stairs to the upper world as the paramedics
lifted the stretcher: a featherweight, the load barely noticeable. She didn't
see Starr watching from the shadows, black eyes wet with tears as if she'd
known the dead woman personally, Luisa, at her shoulder, shaking with
thirst.

Mara found a phone in the lobby of one of the office buildings and
started calling reporters. She didn't worry about finding change—she
billed the calls to Grandfather's credit card. Don Sandstrom at Channel
13, Ray Gibson at the *Tribune,* Murray Ryerson at the *Herald-Star:* This is
Mara Stonds. You may know my grandfather, the neurosurgeon, or my
sister, the lawyer. I'm afraid there's been a terrible accident to a homeless
woman on the premises of one of my sister's clients.

Conversations within news rooms: Is this a story? The Stonds girl is
saying dead homeless woman, visions of the Virgin, threats from the
garage manager. Phone calls to the First Freedoms Forum, Maurice
Pekiel conferring with Judith Ohana: Is this something to do with that
kid who called you yesterday? The niece of that alcoholic singer, Luisa
Montcrief? Harriet Stonds very able lawyer, very able. Abraham Stonds,
prominent in this community, very prominent, can't tread on toes. Send
Judith to the hotel to make a few discreet inquiries.

At the hotel a belligerent Mara, pacing up and down in front of the
scaffolding with a sign: ASK ME WHY THIS HOTEL MURDERED MADELEINE.

The garage attendants looking on, Brian Cassidy inside because Don Sandstrom there with a camera (earlier Cassidy came outside to threaten Mara, but her anger, her accusations—I saw you, I heard you—made him uneasy, kept him from dragging her away as he had first intended).

What do you think happened here, Ms. Stonds? the reporter asks.

Mara trying hard not to sound like a fanatic. (Jacqui's advice: If you're going to do this thing, girl, don't sound crazy. Bad enough you look crazy. Clean clothes from a thrift shop, hair trimmed by Jacqui: I'm not going to march, but I'll help you look decent.)

"Madeleine Carter believed the Virgin was bleeding through a crack in this wall," Mara tells the reporter. "She never hassled anyone, she never panhandled, but she frightened Brian Cassidy—he's the garage manager—he got so scared he hosed her down every night, poured water on her Bible, and when that didn't stop her beliefs, he put all this scaffolding over the wall to keep her away. My sister, the lawyer Harriet Stonds, was actually the person to tell him to put up all the scaffolding. I guess this one skinny little homeless woman seemed too scary to all of them. Last night I was standing by that girder there, Cassidy didn't see me, but he hit her so hard it knocked her to the ground. He's huge, you can see him cowering inside there, and she was a tiny bit of a thing."

Judith Ohana, not ready to speak to a camera, watched near the entrance to the garage. Watched the Channel 13 crew try to interview Brian Cassidy. Saw him take the private elevator up to the lobby. It's not a sign of guilt to be wary of speaking on a camera, but the hotel wasn't going to look very good on the screen.

When the cameras were gone, Ohana talked to Mara. Ohana didn't much like the girl—sulky adolescent with a chip on her shoulder about her family, she told Maurice Pekiel back at the Triple-F office. Possibly a First Amendment case. Not something she wanted to make a priority right now, but keep track of the situation in case it developed. A file with a green tab set up to hold Becca Minsky's and Mara Stonds's phone messages, Judith's dictated notes.

When the four o'clock news showed Mara's speech and Brian Cassidy hiding from the cameras, Harriet was in a meeting. It was a tricky consultation with her long-haul trucker who'd run afoul of the EPA for toxic dumping in Mississippi. Harriet, performing her old legerdemain with a skill that exhilarated her, wasn't pleased when her secretary summoned her to talk to Gian Palmetto.

"He'll have to take his turn like a big boy, Lauren. I can't believe you don't understand how to tell him that."

"I know how to do my job, Ms. Stonds. A homeless woman died this morning over by the Pleiades. When Channel 13 called at one-thirty to ask for your version of the story I didn't think it was important enough to disturb you. But your sister was on the four o'clock news making charges against the hotel, accusing them of murder. If you don't think that's important I apologize for interrupting."

Harriet saw Lauren dimly, knew her to be angry, knew the secretary should be placated. But more present to her was Mara. An anger just as boiling as her sister's possessed her.

Ever since Mara was old enough to walk, the damned brat had been a menace to Harriet's work, her possessions, her aloof private self. At three she'd taken a red Magic Marker and drawn all over Harriet's social studies term paper. I'm helping, Hehwie, look, I'm helping you. That was before computers were everywhere; she'd had to retype the whole damned thing from the beginning by hand. And not even Grandfather's warnings or a swatting by Mephers could stop Mara from ruining Harriet's makeup or playing her records and tapes, scratching a Taj Mahal release beyond use, breaking tapes and sitting with the pieces around her, sobbing, as she ineffectually tried to glue them back together. And now she wanted to destroy Harriet's career, make her look like a useless fool in front of Leigh Wilton just when she was about to be made partner.

"Get me the details," Harriet said to her secretary. "I can't leave this meeting. These guys have a hearing in the morning before a federal magistrate and the strategy is tricky. Tell Gian . . . I don't know. Send in—no, let me talk to Leigh Wilton, see if one of the partners can get up to speed on my truckers, in case there's a real crisis over at the hotel. And find out what the accusations are . . . Oh, you've got them? Of course. I know no one is more reliable than you, Lauren, really I do. Or more

unreliable than my sister. She belongs in a mental hospital. In fact"—
scanning the secretary's typed notes—"she's picketing outside the Pleiades garage? Get me Dr. Stonds, see if he can find a way to bring her into
the hospital." Imagining Mara a cumbersome moth, Grandfather with a
large net to catch and dispose of her. "And get someone to tape the
newscasts for the rest of the afternoon."

Back to her meeting, her head fragmenting again, the exaltation of
the last two days evaporating as though it had never been. She had to ask
her clients to repeat statements, and still couldn't absorb them on the
second or third try.

At seven-thirty Harriet finally finished the session with the truckers.
Back in her office she went over her messages. A message from Grandfather: please call him at home to discuss her sister.

He was drinking sherry when she phoned, and feeling sorry for
himself because of the horrible women and useless residents fate doled
out to him.

He sent that prize loser Tammuz down to find Mara, he told Harriet; Tammuz, a half-wit, never returned to the hospital, Grandfather
waited for him until seven. They could bring the police into it, say Mara
posed an imminent danger to herself or those around her, have her
brought in by force, but there might be too much publicity if he did that.

Harriet agreed: leave the police out of it for now, although personally she felt like strangling the brat with her bare hands. Grandfather
clucked in sympathy, hoped Leigh Wilton wasn't going to blame Harriet
for a situation she couldn't control, and when would she be home?

Harriet had seven messages from Gian Palmetto: very upset, Lauren
noted on the first. Even more upset. Screaming—demanded to talk to
Leigh Wilton, who calmed him down (a duty of the senior partner).

Various partners were waiting around to talk to her. Some offered
support, but Leigh Wilton frowned as though Harriet had deliberately
sought such notoriety: had it really been in the client's best interest to put
those spikes up on the wall?

Harriet tried not to snap at her boss. "The flood Monday night
might have caused structural damage. We had to brace the wall. If we

hadn't put the spikes there, to keep those homeless women out, and the wall had fallen over on them, what would our exposure have been then?"

Various partners had various ideas, and, lawyer-like, each wanted a half hour of undivided attention in which to expound them. She finally managed to sit down with a video of the news. One of her paralegals had taped all the channels and edited their coverage of the hotel into one master tape. Harriet watched it four times. As First Freedoms' Judith Ohana had predicted, Brian Cassidy looked bad, like a mob heavy fleeing justice.

At least the hotel's vice-president for operations had agreed to be interviewed. He did a good job: "Mara Stonds worked here for three months. We had to fire her because she drank on the job, so I'm not surprised to learn that she's making accusations against the hotel. Fired workers often hold a grudge, although they don't usually get a chance to flaunt it on television."

"But the dead woman, Madeleine Carter," Channel 13's Don Sandstrom persisted, "is it true that the hotel harassed her because she had a vision of the Virgin Mary near your garage?"

The vice-president smiled easily. "I don't think it's harassment to try to keep someone from bothering our guests."

"So you didn't spray her with a high-pressure hose?"

"We use a hose to clean the sidewalks down there. If she refused to move, it's possible she got a soaking."

That didn't sound so good. Worse, Harriet thought, the notion that the Virgin was bleeding through a crack in the wall would bring hysterical women down there, and that would generate more media. Mara had been picketing alone this afternoon. Harriet stopped the tape on a close-up of her sister's face. Mara's cheeks were swollen in her pugnacious look; her broken front tooth made her look not only raffish, but older. The revulsion Harriet felt against her sister on Monday night intensified.

Harriet phoned the hotel. Gian Palmetto had canceled dinner with the mayor to stay at his desk. Harriet told him she needed to speak to Brian Cassidy.

"He had to go to the hospital."

"Whose idea was that? He can't hide, Gian: he looked bad on the news. Faking an illness is a really stupid thing to do right now."

"He's not faking, Harriet. Guy broke out in hives all over his body, even on the soles of his feet. I saw him—they came on in my office. He was in agony, couldn't stand, couldn't sit, was having trouble breathing. They shot him full of something to calm down the itching, but he's really sick."

Harriet sucked in her breath in exasperation: the most macho men always seemed to collapse first. "He needs to make some kind of statement. Mara is claiming that he threatened the dead woman. What does he say about it?"

"Come on, Harriet—bunch of homeless people, crackpots, and your sister, frankly—sorry to say it, she's ninety watts short of a bulb. Do you really take her accusation against Brian seriously?"

"It's not what I take seriously that matters. Don't you realize this will be picked up by the wires? What are you going to tell your corporate masters when they call tomorrow to ask if your garage manager murdered a homeless woman? Brian needs to make a statement. I'll go to the hospital as soon as we get through with this conversation."

Harriet's cool voice infuriated her client: he might lose his job and she sounded like frozen snot on a polar bear's nose. "Get off the rag, Harriet. Guy can't talk. His lungs are blistered, they're filled with fluid, he's on a respirator. Get it? Not everyone has your balls, okay?"

She flushed, but her voice became even more remote. "Gian, what are you going to do tomorrow if a crowd of hyperthyroid women swarm to that wall wanting the Virgin's blood?"

He hadn't considered it and ranted for some time about how he'd have a cop on every square of concrete to bar access, he'd have squadrols ready to haul off the bodies, he'd have fire hoses, guns, dogs.

Harriet timed him for four minutes, which she added to his billing sheet. "You want to do all that on camera? That would be totally stupid if this turns into a big story. . . . My advice? First, you should post the area. Get signs out there ASAP saying 'Danger: Wall Unstable, May Collapse.' Rope off the sidewalk, so access to the garage isn't affected if you do get a mob, and station some respectful young men in hotel uniforms down there to explain that it's too dangerous to get close to the wall, but people can take pictures, or whatever they want. They can't touch it because of the risk of injury. You might even bring down some chairs and a coffee cart, so that visitors see you are doing your utmost to be helpful."

"Just the thing for gawking tourists, but not my clientele," Palmetto grumbled. "They're used to discretion, quiet and—"

"I've read the marketing brochures. How much quiet are they going to get if we have an armed confrontation at the garage?"

Palmetto was angry with Harriet: damned broad cost him three hundred dollars an hour. Between her and her stupid loser sister they'd gotten the hotel neck-deep in shit. He was fucked if he was going to jump again just because she was holding up a hoop.

"I'll run it by our in-house people, see what they say." He slammed the receiver in her ear.

Massaging her stiff shoulders, Harriet slowly collected the documents she would need for her morning hearing before the magistrate. She didn't want a long discussion of Mara's iniquities with Grandfather—that clearly lay ahead—so she took her time, fussing with federal statutes, touching up her makeup, ambling to the elevators.

Damn Gian Palmetto anyway. He was more trouble than all her other clients put together. Let him get the advice of in-house counsel. Let the Olympus group handle the whole wretched mess. She'd be glad never to think about it again.

Long before Gian Palmetto could get his corporate review process under way, Harriet's more dire predictions were realized. By midnight the wall was besieged.

33

The Great White Chief's Errand Boy

ALL THAT DAY in the hospital Hector kept looking for Starr. On rounds he would glimpse her out of the corner of his eye, but when he turned he saw only a nurse with a medication cart, or no one at all. At one point he infuriated Hanaper by leaving a patient's bed and running down the hall, so sure he was that Starr had passed the door.

In the cafeteria he thought he saw her sitting at a far table. He shoved his way through the line, knocking the tray from the hands of one of the senior neurologists, bumping a little girl carrying a glass of milk so that it spilled down her dress, ignoring all the outraged cries behind him in his haste to get to the corner of the room. The woman sitting there, her black hair piled high on her head, scalloped around her ears, was a janitor. He felt so let down that he retreated to the residents' bunkroom, emerging only when he heard himself paged to the outpatient clinic. He had forgotten it was Wednesday: his usual roster of therapy patients was waiting for their fifteen minutes of succor.

Hector was just finishing with his last patient when Dr. Stonds summoned him. Gretchen came to get him, disappointed that she didn't have to interrupt a therapy session, but hoping the neurosurgeon was going to tear into Tammuz for his unprofessional conduct in the emergency room Monday night.

The hospital gossip network had overheated from the load of stories about Hector and Starr. Gretchen and Charmaine believed the most lurid: Hector had tried to rape someone in the ER, and then beat up Millie Regier, the night charge nurse, when she tried to stop him. Millie was suing; he'd be lucky if he didn't lose his license. Gretchen and Charmaine watched with anticipatory glee as he rushed from the clinic.

Hector thought Stonds was summoning him because they'd found Starr. He didn't wonder why Stonds was bothering to let him know, but he was so afraid Hanaper might be there—Hanaper with his lascivious lips drooling with desire—that he ran all the way from the clinics to the surgery office wing.

"Yes, sir," he gasped for breath. "Is she here?"

Dr. Stonds was too absorbed in his own concerns to find Hector's eagerness odd. Indeed, the surgeon was accustomed to people treating his affairs as more important than their own.

"No, Tammuz. She's down at that damned garage she seems to think is home these days. She's a menace, to herself if not to others, and I want you to get her to come in for a thorough examination."

"Yes, sir, of course. What has she done? She isn't carrying a gun or a knife, is she?"

Stonds fiddled self-consciously with his desk set. "Not that I know of. But she's physically very strong: she almost killed my housekeeper."

Hector blinked at the thought of Starr in Stonds's house. Why hadn't he thought to look there on his quest last night? What had she made of the glacial granddaughter? And behind all the wonderings the secret gloating image: she was strong, she would fight, he would have to take her in his arms to subdue her.

He got up to go. "Does Dr. Hanaper know we're bringing her in, sir? Will he approve the admission for me?"

"What the hell is going through your mind, young man? I don't need Hanaper's approval to bring my own granddaughter into this hospital."

"Your granddaughter?" Hector faltered.

"Dr. Tammuz, Dr. Hanaper has complained to me about you, and I have had reason to talk to you myself. If you cannot pay proper attention to the welfare of the people entrusted to your care, or to the instructions of senior staff, we will have to rethink your employment at this hospital. My granddaughter Mara. Who the hell else would I undertake so serious an errand for?"

"Starr," Hector managed to say. "And Luisa, of course. The two missing patients you sent me out to find yesterday."

"This isn't County Hospital, Tammuz. I know you've been assigned to the homeless clinic the Lenore Foundation is running at the church, but you need to separate what you're doing there from what you're doing here. You'd better be on your way."

Hector stumbled from the room, dizzy as he always seemed to be after talking to Stonds, as if slapped by converging waves. Through the half-formed thoughts: will they fire me . . . damned self-absorbed jagoff . . . what had Mara done to the housekeeper . . . lay the hope Starr would return to the wall. He walked the mile and a half to the hotel, on legs that wobbled with desire.

Starr wasn't there. The only person in sight was Mara Stonds, slumped on the curb in front of the scaffolding. Her picket sign lay upside down in the street. A half-eaten apple dangled from her hand. Nicolo, the kindly garage attendant, had brought her the apple after Brian Cassidy was taken to the hospital: he not come back to bother you, very sick, cannot—pantomiming inhaling—yes, cannot brease.

Mara had trouble with the apple because of her broken tooth. Besides, she felt too apathetic to want food. Her anger had subsided. She was only very tired. She couldn't go home now: Harriet would never forgive her. What had possessed her to accuse her sister in front of all those news people? She'd wanted to chase the revulsion from Harriet's face, but now Harriet would be her implacable enemy for life.

As long as Brian Cassidy was yelling insults at her she was able to stay angry, but he hadn't been back since the television crews chased him into the garage. Mara giggled at the time, his simian arms useless against a camera, but with his disappearance, and the end of the excitement of talking to the reporters, she fell into a lethargy so bleak that she couldn't even summon the energy to stand.

Hector sat next to her on the curb. She looked at him listlessly when he softly said her name. She didn't remember him from her brief glimpse at the hospital a week ago, but assumed he might be a hotel employee trying to talk her into leaving—there had been several such conversations this afternoon, including one with an old buddy from the convention office who used to drink with her.

"I'm Dr. Tammuz, Ms. Stonds: we spoke briefly at the hospital last week. Your grandfather says you're not feeling well."

"How does he know? He hasn't seen me in over a week."

Her misery made him temporarily forget his longing for Starr. "He says you got upset and hurt his housekeeper. Do you want to tell me about it?"

She looked at him suspiciously. "Are you here to put me in the locked wing on his orders, or because you want to know what went on with Mrs. Ephers?"

"No one has said anything about the locked wing, Ms. Stonds. Your grandfather just wants me to talk to you in the hospital, where we can see whether there's some problem we might be able to help you with."

"He wants to lock me up, don't lie to me, I hate liars more than anything on this planet."

"He says you tried to kill his housekeeper. Is that a lie, too?"

"She had a heart attack." Mara was on her feet, shouting at him. "She had a heart attack because she was mad at me for finding some old papers. She's like Grandfather's familiar, she slips around the place guarding his secrets. Everyone on the planet but me bows down when he passes, so don't you pretend you aren't here on his orders. 'Oh, we'll just go to the hospital to talk,' oh, sure, and then when I'm stupid enough to believe you he'll shoot me full of some shit and pat you on the back. Well, screw you, *Doctor.* I'm not that big a fool."

She picked up her plastic bag of possessions and fled, before he could even ask her about Starr. He stayed on the curb, too tired to give chase. Not wanting to give chase, anyway. Despite her ugly outburst he felt sorry for her. Stonds was hard to work for, imagine what he'd be like to live with—Hector didn't blame Mara for running away from home.

He couldn't face Dr. Stonds again tonight, his seal-like bark: What is wrong with you, young man? I send you on a simple errand, any fool could go to Underground Wacker and force my granddaughter to come into the hospital, so you must be lower than a fool. Maybe Stonds would make Hanaper fire Hector for failing to retrieve Mara. The thought failed to frighten him. At least then he'd be able to sleep as much as he wanted.

34

Once More unto the Breach, Dear Friends

Patsy Wanachs realized early in the evening that she would have her hands full this Wednesday. Most nights, Hagar's House didn't open until seven-thirty, to make sure all the youth activities had ended before any homeless women crossed the threshold. True, the women had a separate entrance, true, they were in the basement, not the main body of the church, but parents, with visions of homeless women or their pimps luring their children away to perform demonic rites, or giving them lice, insisted that their paths not cross.

On Wednesdays, because of Bible study, the shelter opened an hour earlier. Around six women began gathering on the sidewalk outside the shelter's entrance, jostling for places in line before all the beds were handed out.

Tonight Jacqui and Nanette arrived first. As other women started showing up, the two began to pour out the tale of Madeleine's death.

Some of the women had seen Mara on the news. Was it true that the garage man had threatened Maddy's life? Nicole demanded. All true, Nanette said. Only because she was having herself a vision there. Poor Maddy and her voices, Jacqui added.

But was it really the Virgin's blood? LaBelle wanted to know. Did it perform miracles?

No, no, that was all in poor Maddy's head, Jacqui said—if the wall performed miracles, Maddy would be alive now, she'd be well now.

But had anyone ever actually tried asking for something, something direct, LaBelle persisted. Maybe Maddy never tested it. LaBelle thought they should go over and test the wall, no, not straightaway, she wasn't giving up her place in line, thank you very much: she'd been walking all day. But in the morning.

And what would she ask for? Nicole asked derisively. A house, with a hundred beds and plenty of food? Oh, and a manicurist to fix up their feet, not to mention some clothes?

You don't ask the Virgin for that kind of stuff, LaBelle said. She heals wounded souls, She doesn't mess around with houses and clothes.

Oh, what do you know about that? Caroline snorted. You was never a virgin, which was almost true, technically, since the first time one of her uncles raped LaBelle she was six, and by the time she was thirteen her mother was trading her daughter's body for drugs two or three times a week.

Before the two of them could start fighting in earnest, Patsy Wanachs came out to open the gate. LaBelle asked her if she'd seen the news, seen that girl talking about how the hotel killed Maddy.

Patsy snorted. "Mara Stonds was born a troublemaker and she'll probably die one. I wouldn't believe her if she told me this church was on Orleans Street."

"But it is on Orleans Street," LaBelle said, a worried crease between her eyes.

"That's her point, but I don't think little Mara is a troublemaker—she's only troubled," Jacqui said, maybe the only person who'd ever seen Mara as small, thinking of her as young, scared like all of them were. "Yes, she's a troubled girl, but she was brave to stand out there today, stand up to that garage man. He's a mean man and a big one."

Patsy frowned at Jacqui as she swept the women up the side path to the basement entrance. "Mara's grandfather, who's been looking after her since she was born, has never had anything but heartache for his pains. He's trying to get her medical help now, but she's running around on the streets because she's too sick to know it's for her own good. If you run into her you should persuade her to check herself into the hospital."

All the women fell silent at that. The idea of someone going out of their way to offer medical care—that sounded good on the surface, but below the surface of hot meals and hospital beds lay forcible injections and incarcerations, surrounded by the howling damned.

Patsy Wanachs had seen Mara on the news, and had a call from Dr. Stonds besides: if Mara shows up there as she might—with her penchant for self-dramatization now picturing herself among society's outcasts—let me know. When Mara showed up, though, Patsy didn't recognize her. She was looking for that bush of wild hair, not a baldheaded girl with a broken front tooth.

When she ran from Hector, Mara managed only a block and a half at a dead run before she had to stop for breath. A week's malnutrition and sleep deprivation had weakened muscles which used to move her easily around basketball or tennis courts. Her bag banging into her side further slowed her down. She lurked under the loading dock of a building that backed onto the Pleiades for five minutes, but neither the doctor nor police seemed to be behind her, so she emerged and headed in the vague direction of Hagar's House.

If she got there early and got another night's sleep, maybe in the morning she'd be able to figure out what to do. Dr. Tammuz claimed Grandfather wasn't talking about the locked ward, but she didn't believe him. Grandfather probably told the resident to lie to her, to lure her into the hospital, and then he'd put her in restraints. That meant she needed to disguise herself, even out on the street, let alone at Hagar's House. She took the stocking out of her plastic bag and pulled it down over her ears, then frowned at her image in a store window. If Patsy Wanachs took it into her head to inspect the women closely, she might easily yank the stocking from Mara's head and tell her to stop playing games. And then, swollen with righteousness, call Grandfather.

Mara wandered on down Grand Avenue, kicking at loose pieces of pavement. Near the corner of Wells she passed a dingy barbershop. Maybe it was her throbbing tooth clouding her mind that made her think shaving her head would be a good idea. Anyway, the old black man who was alone in the shop didn't blink at her request. True, he demanded to be paid up front. Seven-fifty. About what Harriet tipped the man who styled her hair every Thursday morning.

When she saw herself in the mirror behind the chair Mara was shocked. She looked like a boy, and her head felt cold and unprotected, despite the muggy air.

Patsy Wanachs, glancing cursorily at Mara's face when she checked in, didn't recognize her, but Cynthia Lowrie did. Cynthia was handing out Bibles for Rafe in the activities room when Mara sidled in. Cynthia dropped the Bibles, her hand over her mouth, until Rafe asked if she'd lost the few wits she'd been born with, and to get busy.

Caroline and a woman named Ashley drew the metal folding chairs into a large semicircle—they got an extra clothes ration for helping out—while Cynthia went back to distributing Bibles. Cynthia tried shepherding the group into chairs, but they were still agitated about Madeleine and the hotel, and only sat down when Rafe, looking up from a low-voiced consultation with Patsy Wanachs, barked out an order to them. They were used to responding to his authority, and they did so again, although many of them muttered angrily as they broke up their conversations.

Cynthia took a chair next to Mara. She was afraid to speak to her, in case Rafe noticed, but she kept staring at her friend's bald head. When she'd seen Mara on the six o'clock news, her hair was as shaggy as ever.

"We'll start with a prayer. Cynthia, will you stop mooning about and join us in asking for Jesus' guidance in understanding life and its problems? . . . Lord, open our hearts to understanding Your will, and to receiving instruction from Your Holy Word. We may not always understand the guidance You are giving us, but we know You are acting out of perfect goodness, as a father looks after his children with perfect love."

Here Mara stepped on Cynthia's foot, but Cynthia refused to respond, except with a nervous glance at Rafe.

"We know that some of our sisters are distressed about the death of one of their company. Sister Natalie was sadly afflicted in mind, and it was Your will to keep her mind clouded, but—"

"Madeleine," Mara said, her anger starting to rise again. "Her name was Madeleine. And it's never God's will for someone to be as unhappy as she was."

Cynthia clutched Mara's hand: don't make him mad, the pressure in her fingers begged, he only takes it out on me.

"If you have a contribution to make, wait until I'm through with the prayer, young woman. I presume someone on the staff checked that you *are* a woman?"

"I'm a woman, all right," Mara said, feeling an enormous shield of anonymity protecting her from Rafe, "but did they check into your species? Are you really a member of the human race? If we stripped you, would we find a space alien? You were praying for a woman who died in a horrible way, and you got her name wrong. It's Madeleine, not Natalie, and if it was God's will that she was homeless and heard voices, then He's a piss-poor god."

"How dare you?" Rafe was on his feet, his husky voice raw with rage. "The rules of this session are stated clearly up front: you cannot disrupt the prayer meeting. If you say one more thing without being invited to speak I will have you thrown out of the shelter."

Jacqui moved over next to Mara. "Don't carry on so, girl: Maddy's at peace now, and she wouldn't want you giving up your bed just because Brother Rafe got her name wrong. Wherever she is, she's proud of you for standing up for her, so let it go, okay?"

Rafe breathed heavily for a few seconds, but when it was clear Mara had submitted to his will he sat back down and resumed his prayer. The day's study passage came from First Kings, where the prophet Elijah raised the widow's son from the dead, but then fled in terror from the threats of Jezebel. Rafe said, of course only Jesus could raise souls from the dead, so it was the power of Jesus working through Elijah that healed the widow's son; Elijah's mere mortal state was proven by his fear of Jezebel, the harlot, who made him flee Judea for a cave in the mountains.

"So how come there are no prophets around these days like Elijah to raise you from the dead?" LaBelle asked, thinking of Madeleine, thinking of her own father who had died when she was two, leaving her with her mother and her uncles: if Jesus could bring the dead to life, how come He let her father lie there dead, knowing what lay ahead for her?

"We will all be raised at the last day, if we have faith," Rafe answered. "And revelation ended with the Resurrection: we don't need new prophets—we need to follow the Word as incarnated in Jesus."

"We'll get pie in the sky when we die, is that it?" Mara demanded.

"Young woman, you may think you are being funny, but blasphemy is the sin against the Holy Spirit, the one sin that cannot be forgiven."

"But what if Maddy was a prophet?" LaBelle persisted. "What if she was a prophet from the Mother of God? Women never got any prophets like that, so maybe the Mother of God is speaking to us now, like Maddy thought, through that crack in the wall. You know, like women talk in real life, through cracks."

"Let it go, LaBelle," Jacqui said gruffly. "Like Brother Rafe said, she's at peace now. Let her lie in peace."

"And don't bring talk about prophets of the Mother of God into church," Rafe said. "That comes perilously close to witchcraft. As does talk about blood coming out of a wall. It's been on the news the last two days—there was a rusty pipe down there, and Natalie was an unstable woman who couldn't tell the difference between rust and blood."

"Her name was Madeleine. Don't you ever listen to anything a woman tells you?" Mara snapped.

"And did you go down there and look at that crack yourself?" LaBelle said. "You think because you have a lot of money God talks to you but not to us? That's not what it says in Scripture, in Scripture it says it's easier for a camel to go through the eye of a needle than for a rich man to get into heaven."

"You think we care about what you have to say?" Nicole added. "You know as well as me we only sit through these sessions because otherwise we can't get a bed on Wednesday nights."

"What does he know about Scripture that we can't find out on our own?" Caroline put in.

"Oh, why are we bothering with Madeleine?" the woman Ashley, who had helped set up the chairs, exclaimed. "No one wants to admit the truth—she was crazy. Let's finish the Bible lesson so we can get to bed."

The room erupted into argument, as Nanette leapt from her seat to argue with Ashley. Maddy was murdered, she said, by that hotel.

LaBelle and Caroline continued their fight about whether Maddy's wall might contain miracles, while others thought the point of the furor was a vote on whether they even wanted Bible study. Ashley repeated that she just wanted to go on with the text so they could get to bed. Two women actually were asleep, so worn by their day's trudging from drop-in point to drop-in point that not even the fight in the room could rouse them.

Rafe Lowrie was furious with them. He was on his feet again, yelling at top volume, but the voice that controlled the cattle pit had no effect on the women. Most of them were on their feet as well, all the insults of life on the streets—the rapes they'd experienced, the beatings and robberies, the daily humiliations, the sore feet, the unwashed clothes—finding expression in their furor over Madeleine's death.

Cynthia was so white that a pimple on her forehead glowed red. Mara, glancing at her, knew that as soon as he was alone with her Rafe would vent his furies on her. Suddenly, without thinking of anything except that she ought to do something to protect Cynthia, she climbed up on her wobbly metal chair. One or two people looked at her, but the rest kept up their arguments.

Patsy Wanachs, drawn by the furor, ran into the room. She took a police whistle from around her neck and blew into it, a long shrill blast that momentarily lulled the noise.

Into that relative silence Mara called, "The wall does perform miracles. On Tuesday night Madeleine cursed the garage manager, I heard her curse him with a plague of boils. This afternoon they took him to the hospital. One of the parking attendants told me: he broke out all over his body, he couldn't even breathe, they were in his lungs."

"It works." LaBelle's eyes were shining. "Praise Jesus! Praise Mary!

I'm going down there. Maybe She'll heal me or cure my bad knees. Nicole—you got female problems. Let's see what She can maybe do."

Mara grabbed Cynthia's hand and dragged her into the buzzing heart of the swarm.

35

Wailing Wall

Looking for Starr through the streets beneath Michigan Avenue, or even in clay tunnels dug deep in the earth. The darkness so complete that it denies the presence of light in the world, but find my way without groping, as though the blood in my veins divines the route.

Suddenly the wall of the hotel appears, and Starr is there, at the far end of the scaffolding, the diva at her side like a cat belonging to a witch. Starr beckons, not with word, or even gesture, but some expression in her eyes, apparent even in the dark. The distance between overcome, the people between, milling chanting homeless women, miracle-seeking suburbanites, only shadows that can't see or hear. The real miracle, that sweet inwardness, enveloping as if it were the earth itself, the underground tunnels, covering but not suffocating, home, I'm home, I'm—

He woke with the words on his lips. He was in his own bed, again at three in the morning, weeping with despair at the loss of the dream. He had been with her, in her, how could he be only here alone in bed?

He couldn't remember leaving the hotel and returning to his apartment. He had stayed at the Pleiades garage long after Mara Stonds ran from him, long after the first miracle seeker appeared, drawn as Harriet feared by the television report.

Sat on the curb, too tired to move, expecting at any minute the simian Mr. Cassidy to emerge to confront me. Could picture him with his firehose, spraying me as he had Madeleine Carter. By and by one of the garage attendants came out. Recognized me from previous visits: was I the doctor who had looked after the poor *loca ingenua*? It was a shame, a terrible shame, what had happened to her. But the boss, he was ill. Maybe stricken down by God, in response to his cruelty to the *ingenua*?

I never knew God to pay such intimate attention to the homeless and mentally ill, but maybe Madeleine special in divine eyes because of her attention to the Virgin Mary. Found out later that Cassidy was brought to Midwest Hospital, with severe asthma attack & hives—broke out after he was chased by TV cameras into hotel president's office. He has history of asthma and allergies, and excitement or fear triggered the attack—as often happens without God's involvement.

Garage attendant bustled off to deal with a car that was stopping at the garage entrance. A sightseer, drawn by television report of Madeleine's wall. Sightseer, a long lean woman of forty-something, in jeans and a Notre Dame T-shirt, eyes bulging from hyperthyroidism. Assumed since I was sitting on curb I knew something about this miracle-producing crack. Tried to disclaim all knowledge, but garage guy said, oh, yes, this man doctor, he look after poor dead woman.

She tells me she is protected by the blue aura of Mary: "My husband didn't want me coming here. Underneath Chicago? he says, It's bad enough on the lighted streets. We live out in Downers Grove, you know, where we don't really have any black people" (scrutinizing my Semitic features in the dim light to make sure she hasn't committed a blunder), "but I told him the blue aura would look after me. If this wall is authentic my prayer circle will be out tomorrow to pray the rosary as a group. But why is the scaffolding up here? What were you thinking, to let someone block off what may be a sacred site?"

She tries to insinuate herself past spikes, gets T-shirt caught in one of them, but manages to touch the wall. The garage man, uselessly helpful, tells her the poor *ingenua* always sat further down, shows the sightseer a

place ten feet further from the garage: "Isn't that right, *senor medico?*"
Maybe that was where Madeleine used to sit, I don't know.

Hector couldn't bring himself to move from the curb. As the evening deepened into night, other miracle seekers drifted by to inspect the
wall. The woman protected by Mary's blue aura stayed most of the evening, directing newcomers to the crack that Nicolo, the garage man, had
shown her, then pointing out Hector. He was her doctor, he knows
more than he's telling.

What Hector couldn't tell, wouldn't tell himself, hidden in that
underside of mind he didn't want to inspect, was the reason he stayed at
the curb: if he sat there long enough Starr might appear, as she had—was
it only two nights ago? The winds of his emotional storms so buffeted
him that every hour took on the weight of many days.

Around nine Nicolo brought me a plate of hot beans and rice. As I
sat poking at food a great swarm of women arrived on foot. Was shrink-
ing into shadows—couldn't take another band of miracle seekers—when
Jacqui emerged from the pack to hug me.

"Doctor! I knew you were a true friend of Maddy's. How like you to
be sitting in vigil for her."

How unlike me. My thoughts have never been so little on the ill and
halt entrusted to my care. I'm like a large raw patch of neediness, so
much so that even the embrace of a middle-aged, overweight homeless
woman feels like the clasp of true friendship.

Some fifteen or twenty women from Hagar's House were suddenly
filled with the Spirit, and led here to the wall. Jacqui's partner Nanette
was with her, Mara Stonds—pointed out to me by Jacqui—didn't recognize her: she'd shaved her head bald sometime between six, when I
talked to her, and now. And with her, looking terrified, the unfortunate
daughter of Rafe Lowrie, whom I met two weeks ago dispensing Bibles at
his study group.

The women didn't know why they'd come—a surge of anger, or

fear, over Madeleine's suicide: they had to come to the spot, they couldn't forget her, lest they themselves be consigned to oblivion.

The women began chanting conflicting demands: free beds for the homeless; arrest the killers of Madeleine Carter; let us get to the Virgin's wall. LaBelle was so overcome with the desire to get to the wall, to feel the Virgin's saving power wrapped around her, that she began to tug on the spikes, trying to tear them loose.

Nicolo, the garage attendant, seconded her enthusiastically. "What it will hurt, we take off this one small area belonging to the *ingenua*?"

He bustled into the back of the garage, emerging a few minutes later with a pipe wrench. He unscrewed a few spikes, enough for the women to go one at a time to the wall, bent over almost double, and touch the bleeding crack.

Tourists continue to come by in dribs and drabs, an almost festive air of protest. By and by the tumult rouses someone from aboveground. Or maybe one of the hotel guests complains in the upper lobby: not everyone enamored of the scene. Square-faced man in suit and black Infiniti yells angrily for Nicolo. I'm paying for garage time, not a fucking carnival. Nicolo instantly changes: withdraws into himself, almost touches his forelock, smiles, ingratiating, so sorry, sir.

Anyway, around ten or so management arrives, bringing the cops (a patrol car has cruised by a few times without stopping). Now six or seven cars swarm to the scene. They love to turn on their flashing strobes, to gather, be a group of comrades, swashbuckling, gang members, the toughest gang. They turn to me, the white man on the spot, as if I knew anything. But I tell them these women are praying for a dead friend, woman who committed suicide here.

Some man from the hotel demands the cops round up and arrest the women. If it were just the homeless maybe they would, but apparently the hyperthyroid woman protected by blue aura of Mary has some kind of important connection—brother a bishop, she a big donor to Holy Name Cathedral—so for now the police just stand by, watching.

Around ten the lights and everything must have woken the birds, confused them into thinking it was day.

The sparrows began chattering, swooping from the rafters to perch on the scaffolding, their cheeping so loud it drowned the women's shouts and the static on the police walkie-talkies. Hector, looking up to see the bars darkened by the mass of birds, caught sight of Starr at the edge of the wall. His mind had tricked him so many times that day that he looked away, shut his eyes, held his breath, counted twenty, but when he turned she was still there, Luisa at her elbow.

36

Operatic Performance

UNDER THE LEGS of the grand piano Luisa's dreams became feverish. At first she had been back at her apartment in Campania, nestled on soft grass in the garden. Suddenly the earth gave way and she was deep underground, bleeding from breasts and vulva. She tried to wipe the blood away, but found she was chained and couldn't move her hands. Great copper shields bound her breasts to her body and a copper girdle encircled her vulva.

A chattering group passed, a happy family outing—the ruddy man carrying a great wooden bed, his parents and his own two sons at his side. She struggled through her drugged sleep to call to them, but in the nature of dreams could make no sound, and they did not see her.

Behind them came a procession, column upon column of drooping weary people, shuffling, not marching, heads bowed, each carrying a pitcher of beer. Luisa's throat was raw; she yearned for that beer more than for life or freedom. As she watched, the people poured their beer in front of a giant crucifix. The earth opened and swallowed the family and the bed. The fissure was spreading across the ground to where she lay helplessly bound.

Boulders tumbled down from high cliffs, crashing and echoing, and then their booming turned into the threatening hum of violins and she was in her familiar nightmare: kneeling in front of the Madonna, bass viols, red-faced man threatening to kill her, world whirling as she shrieked for help, her voice in danger, the Madonna leering at her with hawk's eyes under a horrific wig with cow's horns. She woke, thrashing in Starr's arms, to a pounding on the door.

"Who is in here! What's going on in here?" The voice was muffled by the heavy door.

Luisa struggled upright. The familiar bile rose in her throat. In the dark, windowless room she scrabbled for a cup or waste can to catch the greenish dribble but could find nothing but her silk jacket. She wiped her face on the sleeve.

The man pounded on the door again, and then turned a key in the lock. Flashlight sprayed the room, bounced off the piano, found the two figures underneath.

"Who the hell let you in here? What are you doing here? Get out of the opera house. You hear me?" It was the night watchman.

The diva's full-voiced scream as she dreamt had echoed eerily down the hall, bringing him running on clumsy feet to the practice room. He'd imagined horrors, someone held hostage, rape, murder, and had already pressed the alarm button on his phone to summon help, seeing himself in the morning paper: hero saves tourist.

Well, there were horrors here aplenty, but none that would get him a mayor's medal. Food scraps and an empty beer bottle on the floor, a smell of stale vomit, two naked women, so flushed with sleep and sex that his own stomach churned with mixed loathing and desire.

He slapped the light on. "Get your clothes on. Sluts! How'd you get into the opera house, anyway? Get dressed and get out!"

"I am Madame Montcrief, my good ape." Luisa spoke haughtily from her pile of clothes. "Have the common courtesy to get out of my practice room."

"Madam? I'll say you're a madam. Get back to your whorehouse."

The watchman was shrieking with embarrassment; he couldn't bring himself even to think the words of what had been going on between the women, both naked, one with the largest breasts he'd ever seen, even in surreptitious studies of porn magazines. Those breasts were brushing the shoulders of the scrawny one who'd spoken to him, while the look of satiation on the large woman's face—it was terrible, that two women could . . . His own wife's face flashed in his mind, lying beneath him in bed, her expression as empty as if she were washing dishes, what if his wife and another woman—this woman—were—how would she look?

He longed to seize those giant breasts, but they filled him with fear as much as longing; he hovered over her, his hands out. The big woman looked at him and laughed, so harshly that his desire withered, turned to shame, and then to a greater anger. He yanked the scrawny one from under the piano, thrust her into the hall, kicked the clothes after her.

"Get dressed, get these clothes on, you bitch."

The big woman, still laughing, climbed easily to her feet and pulled on a skirt and a T-shirt. Once she was clothed, he saw she was really quite an ordinary size, no taller than he was himself. It was only that ridiculous hair, sticking out around her head like the horns of a wild cow, that made her seem so large.

"I can't believe the opera would hire a cretin like you. How dare you?" Luisa hooked her bra with shaking fingers. "When I've talked to the management you'll be lucky if you still have a job. Singers are not to be disturbed in their practice rooms. I am Luisa Montcrief, a name which doubtless means nothing to an imbecile like you. I am preparing my comeback. I had planned to make it in Chicago, but if this is how Lyric Opera treats its stars, it will be a cold day in hell before I return."

She picked up the gold blouse, now a mass of stains and rips, the black Valentino suit turned gray and shapeless from vomit, dust, nights of sleeping in it. She wouldn't be bringing Clio back, either, not when the ungrateful bitch let her clothes get into this disgraceful shape.

The elevator pinged in the distance and heavy feet pounded up the hall toward them: a patrolman responding to the alarm, which the watchman had forgotten sending. The watchman waved his flashlight at the trash in the practice room, told the patrolman what he'd found: homeless women breaking into the opera house. And look at that, he shouted, seeing for the first time a pool of liquid inside the piano: the bitches poured beer into this Steinway. Seventy-thousand-dollar piano and the cunts trashed it.

They were everywhere, like rats, the patrolman agreed. Seeing Luisa naked from the waist down, you juice this one?

I think they were, you know, doing it together, the watchman's face crimson. That one—pointing at Starr—you've never seen tits like that.

Doing it together? The patrolman's eyes glistened: he'd always imagined, never seen. Maybe they need to see what a real man is like.

Pinning Luisa against the wall—asking for it, stupid bitch, standing there waving her bush in his face—unzipping his uniform pants; the watchman giving a warning as the other one came up behind him, kissing the back of his shirt with those breasts. One at a time, girls, he started to say, there's plenty for everyone, when a weight—later, in his report, he claimed the woman had a stone, a boulder: it couldn't have been her bare hands pushing him against the wall, shoving him to the floor, as the watchman stood with his mouth agape, too stupid to come to his help.

Luisa pulled on her clothes while Starr stood over the prone cop. Starr didn't do anything else, just stood there roaring out that rasping mocking laugh, but in the morning, called to the First District to verify an assault of a police officer in the performance of his duties, the opera house watchman couldn't remember Starr's passive stance, positively saw her holding a weapon, yes, a slab of concrete, must have found it in the rubble around the side of the building. And then the one who said she was a singer, she picked up her suitcase and the two of them took off. No, he didn't follow them, he was too worried about the cop, although the officer got back on his feet without any trouble once the stairwell door banged shut on the women.

Starr and Luisa followed the river as it curved north and east through the city, stepping around sleeping bodies, bags of garbage, discarded refuse of every description. At Michigan Avenue they turned south and tracked through the maze of alleys to the Hotel Pleiades.

37

Princess in Trouble

"FOR THE LAST THREE WEEKS, miracle seekers as well as ordinary sightseers from all over America have been flocking to this unprepossessing spot below Michigan Avenue to discover whether a homeless woman's hope was true. Madeleine Carter believed with all her heart that the Virgin Mary was weeping tears of blood through a crack on this wall. So intense was her faith that she kept returning to this spot despite the most strenuous efforts of the hotel that owns it to drive her away."

Don Sandstrom's chiseled good looks were replaced on the television screen by a photograph of Madeleine Carter. Harriet, watching on the firm's television, had already seen the snapshot: a copy was in the file that Scandon and Atter's investigators were putting together for the hotel's defense. The photograph showed Madeleine twelve years earlier, in between her second and third pregnancies, holding her year-old son while her two-year-old daughter clutched her hand. Madeleine's hair was neatly combed, her dark sweater buttoned up to the throat. She was smiling for the camera, but there was a strained, anxious look around her eyes that made her appear older than twenty-three.

Harriet had started her file on Madeleine Carter the previous Friday, when Judith Ohana from the First Freedoms Forum filed suit on behalf of Mara Stonds, Jacqui Dotson et al., to require the Hotel Pleiades to maintain the garage wall as a place where people could worship the

Virgin. Among the statements in the suit that the hotel—and Harriet—planned to contest was that the hotel had driven Madeleine Carter to kill herself because of the Pleiades' extreme opposition to constitutionally protected expressive activity—in this case, worshiping at the wall.

Harriet foresaw no difficulty in proving Madeleine Carter's psychosis to a jury, if it got that far: she'd found that Madeleine's delusional episodes began when she was twenty and pregnant with her first child. After four children in seven years, a number of hospitalizations, and a deteriorating home life, her husband divorced her. Madeleine lived for a time with her parents, but when her mother died, her father found it impossible to care for his troubled daughter.

During the next few years she was fired from a series of low-skilled jobs, while passing in and out of mental hospitals. She had no medical insurance; in the absence of publicly funded mental health programs or useful halfway houses, she'd ended up on the streets, where she managed to survive another three years. She was dead now at thirty-five: three years older than Harriet. Curiously, although husband and father had both abandoned Madeleine years before, both were anxious parties to the Triple-F suit. The husband had found the snapshot of Madeleine with her children stuck in a drawer in the utility room.

Harriet saw herself, in navy gabardine, presenting all this information to a jury: she would be pitying but understanding—a wasted life, four children left behind, a woman who couldn't tell fact from fantasy living out her last days under a leaking pipe. The hotel's tolerance until the flood, when they had to shore up the wall for the safety of passersby; the tragedy of a woman so disturbed, she couldn't understand that there was a danger her beloved wall might start shelling her with masonry.

Harriet's optimism wasn't shared by her senior partner. Leigh Wilton pointed to the flock of miracle seekers, and told Harriet that a jury would be swayed by their intense religious faith—the hotel would look like a rich bully trying to stop women from worshiping the Virgin. Leigh was angry with Harriet for not handling the situation more tactfully from the outset. What was all this about hosing down the wall to try to drive Madeleine away? Why couldn't they have let her worship in peace?

Harriet flushed, stammered that Madeleine was hurting the client's business, that she'd attracted a crowd of rowdy people (including your sister, Leigh Wilton snapped) who made it hard for the hotel's guests to use the garage. And hadn't that been Leigh's own advice, that the hotel make the garage wall too unpleasant for Madeleine to stay there?

Not at all, the senior partner said, at his coldest. Harriet's paralegal had done that unilaterally, while Harriet was away from the office, failing to attend to her clients, not giving her staff appropriate supervision. Harriet was left to gape at him. The past is always rewritten to serve the needs of the present, but she had never been aware of it before.

For the first time since Grandfather rescued her from Beatrix all those years ago, Harriet felt herself awash in disapproval. Her mother used to terrify her: Beatrix drunk, smelling of cigarette smoke (probably also marijuana, but the little Harriet wouldn't have known that), dark hair hanging tangled down her back, leaning over her daughter's bed, crooning snatches of lullabies intermixed with muttered threats against her husband: when I find him I'll cut off that dangling piece of meat so he can't stick it anywhere anymore.

Then Grandfather appeared, heroic, miraculous, calling Beatrix a drunken disgrace, turning that overpowering creature into something small and weak. Harriet, dressed in blue the color of her eyes, Mephers combing her silky hair until it shone, allied herself completely with Grandfather. Beatrix showed up from time to time, laden with gifts, which Harriet politely studied and put down: *Grand-père* gives me everything I need, thank you very much. No, thank you, I'm not allowed chocolates, they're bad for my teeth and hair. No, thank you, I don't wish to go to the movies . . . the zoo . . . shopping for a new dress. Especially I don't want a new baby sister, but that apparently was the one surprise she couldn't turn down.

Excelling at Chicago Latin and at tennis, charming Grandfather's dinner guests, his colleagues, Mephers, knowing that if she smiled, never complained, was always tidy and well dressed, and most of all, worked hard and did her tasks (homework, a few household chores to make sure she wasn't spoiled, later her job) perfectly, that no one would ever show her the disdain Grandfather felt for his only child, her mother.

And now Leigh Wilton, who had always treated her with an indulgent courtesy like Grandfather's own, was warning her about her work.

Even Grandfather was angry. Of course she had often seen him angry with Beatrix, or Mara, or his junior colleagues, but now his fury with Mara was spilling over onto Harriet.

I'm embarrassed to walk the halls of my own hospital. People are pitying me—pitying *me,* the man who made that hospital the modern surgical benchmark that it is. Mara on television accusing you, accusing us, of mistreating the poor. That psychotic woman was yours to manage, Harriet. I hate to criticize you, but you mishandled this one badly.

And Harriet, stung for the first time into snapping back at him: your precious hospital had a chance to treat Madeleine Carter, but because of your obsession with cost containment, you released her back to the streets. In worse shape than when she entered.

Harriet was shocked by her own outburst: Grandfather, protector, stern only with those who threw away life's chances, not with the good and hardworking. Feeling herself changing, changing physically, turning into something large and coarse like Beatrix or Mara, the feeling so intense that she ran to the health club and worked on the machines until she was a small focused body again.

Only Mephers, usually a mirror of Grandfather's feelings and opinions, continued to put the blame exactly where it belonged, on Mara's head: another dramatic production from young Mara Bernhardt, Mephers called it.

Instead of cheering Harriet, Mephers's criticism left her feeling hollow and confused. Mara was right about one thing: Mephers was cold. Whatever feeling she had for Harriet was a small thin bar from a space heater, not enough to warm either of them.

Mephers learned from Patsy Wanachs at the church how Mara had swept the women out of the shelter and stormed down to the wall: an intolerable embarrassment to her two icons, the doctor and the granddaughter. In an emergency meeting of the parish council, Mrs. Ephers urged the Orleans Street Church to ban from Hagar's House anyone who showed up at the garage. Many of the shelter's clients, like LaBelle, Jacqui, and Nanette, were spending their days at the wall, then turning up at the shelter at night.

The council agreed with the housekeeper: this wanton behavior was an insult to Rafe Lowrie, as well as to Dr. Stonds. Once they had made this decision, the council sent Patsy Wanachs to Underground Wacker to promulgate it. Patsy on a bullhorn told the women that someone from the church would be there—Rafe's son, Jared, volunteering to video the group—to see who attended the protests at the wall. After today, anyone who visited the wall would be barred admission to Hagar's House. Most of the homeless women promptly left, although LaBelle, still hoping that the Virgin might heal her, stayed on. Mara, of course, had no choice but to remain. Now that Patsy knew her with her bald head she couldn't possibly go back to Orleans Street.

Cynthia was already gone, shocked by a single night on the streets into returning to Rafe. She didn't know why she'd let Mara drag her away from Bible study to begin with. Her shout at Mara: you got me in trouble one more time. Daddy was right, he warned me not to talk to you. You got me beat up so many times when we were kids, now look— I've lost my home because of you.

You can have my sleeping bag, Mara told her. Or go over to Graham Street. If you tell Grandfather and Harriet how awful I am, how I got you in trouble, they'll probably let you have my bedroom. Anyway, don't you have a job? Can't you rent a place? And learned to her jaw-dropping contempt that Cynthia gave her paycheck to Rafe, who decided how much money she needed and doled it out to her every Monday.

Starr, whom Mara greeted with a rapturous cry—look, it's my mother, look Cyn—appalled Cynthia. If that's your mother no wonder your grandfather threw her out on the street. She looks like the whore of Babylon, dripping with the blood of the saints. The two friends had a terrible argument and Cynthia left as soon as it got light. She returned to work, and then home.

Home to Jared and Rafe, and even on Sunday she couldn't walk well enough to come to church: home sick, Rafe said, bad eye infection—her right eye being swollen shut. Then Rafe came up to Abraham Stonds after the service, and lectured him, in front of Pastor Emerson, on how Stonds didn't know how to keep order in his own house. You let that girl of yours run wild, and look what's happened: she led my daughter and a whole lot of innocent homeless women partway to hell.

As Grandfather and Harriet walked home from church—Mrs. Ephers staying behind for the meeting of the parish council—the doctor started snapping at Harriet again, criticizing her management of the hotel, her dress—that yellow is a poor color on you, makes you look old, and the neckline is a little indiscreet for church—even the arrangement of flowers in the vestibule of the Graham Street apartment: why red? Totally out of tune with my mood these days. Until Harriet suddenly for the first time began to wonder if not only Mara, but her own mother—maybe even her own grandmother—had a right to a grievance against Dr. Stonds.

Harriet slipped out to look at the garage wall Sunday night, hoping that Patsy Wanachs's decree would have cleared the street enough for the hotel to reclaim it. Unfortunately, miracle seekers were starting to arrive from around the world as the story got picked up by the networks and CNN. While most of the homeless women had left, the numbers of people in front of the garage remained high. And from the hotel's viewpoint, the newcomers were more troublesome: street people could be moved off without much difficulty—the Orleans Street Church's action had scarcely disturbed an electron on the airwaves. But tourists were another and more bothersome story—if you threatened them, they appeared on *Oprah* or *Jenny Jones* to discuss it.

Mara was at the wall, but the sisters looked at each other without speaking. Harriet was furious with Mara, that went without saying: calling in the television cameras, siccing the First Freedoms Forum onto her, maybe even ruining Harriet's career, who could tell? But when she saw the hollows in her sister's face, her naked head—all that coarse black hair poor Mara had hated for so long, tried to straighten, to tame into braids, vanished so that she looked like a new-hatched ostrich—Harriet also found herself wishing she could be sure her sister had a place to sleep, and that she could bring her that great stack of bread and butter she used to wolf down at dinner. She tried to forget what Patsy Wanachs had told her about homeless women, that rape was a given in their lives if they were on the street for more than a few weeks.

In the office on Monday, Harriet couldn't escape her sister, the wall, or the barrage of criticism into her handling of the Pleiades' problems. When she arrived, her secretary had a message for her from Leigh Wilton: He expected a report by noon on how she proposed to handle First Freedoms' lawsuit on Madeleine's death. It was a sign of Harriet's plummeting status that Leigh sent the message through his secretary to hers, instead of phoning her directly.

Harriet gave no sign that she felt the sting, smiling smoothly, asking her secretary about the day's appointments, summoning her paralegals to prepare tapes for her on everything that had been said about the wall on air this weekend. Internally her feelings toward Mara veered once again from compassion to fury. The author of her current discord . . . she realized she'd watched twenty minutes of tape without registering anything, and felt even angrier with her sister for breaking her mental poise. She rewound the cassette.

"Monsignor Alvin Mulvaney, an expert on miraculous expression for Chicago's Roman Catholic Archdiocese, has assured Channel 13 that the red substance on the wall is not blood. It is rust. Why it continues to come through the wall now that the city has repaired the pipe which broke here no one can say," Don Sandstrom intoned from the screen in front of her.

"But for the women on Underground Wacker, this wall possesses special healing powers. One says that years of hemorrhaging stopped after a night spent under the crack, another claims to have conceived a child after years of infertility treatments—although it may be too early to be sure—while still a third says she had a spontaneous miscarriage of an unwanted pregnancy (Harriet, making notes, wanting names, medical documentation).

"The Hotel Pleiades says they have no desire to keep devout women from worshiping at the wall, but want their garage accessible to their clients. They also want the area kept clean, which, given the rat population down here, is a reasonable request."

Here the camera drew back to show the street. It looked like a fairground after most of the rides had packed up: a few dozen women and a handful of men were milling around. Some had children. Three women, from the Downer's Grove prayer group, were kneeling on the walk praying the rosary, as they had every day since Madeleine's death.

The hotel had removed enough of the scaffolding around Madeleine's crack to form a primitive grotto, where three or four people at a time, depending on girth, could test the healing powers of the rusty seepage. Some carried signs, either attesting to the Virgin, or protesting the hotel's treatment of Madeleine. Food wrappers and coffee cups were liberally strewn around the curb. The personal belongings of the homeless in the group were tied up in bags.

Sandstrom continued, "Some think one woman more than others, more even than Madeleine Carter, lies at the heart of the controversy."

Harriet held her breath, waiting for Mara's face to appear on the screen. Instead she saw the revolting creature who had been there the night of the flood, the one Mara screamed was Beatrix. The camera, zooming in on Starr, flattened her cheekbones and dulled the hawk's eyes. The mouth glowed red, disturbingly sensual, against the greenish patina of skin shot with strobes in dim light. Harriet felt her toes curling inside her high heels as she retreated from the image on the screen. Next to Starr, although not clearly focused in the picture, were Mara, Luisa Montcrief, and a young teenager with a corona of hair not unlike Mara's own, before she shaved her head.

"Some of the women claim that the wall's miraculous properties are only felt when this woman, whom they call Starr, is present," Sandstrom explained. "Starr seems to be a sort of idiot savant, incapable of speech except in grunts. A local celebrity, Luisa Montcrief, the opera diva now in temporary retirement" (an old concert photo of Luisa in a flame-colored gown, briefly superimposed on the current raddled face) "inter-prets for her.

"However, Dr. Clyde Hanaper, chief of psychiatry at the Midwest Hospital, says Starr and Montcrief have both been patients at the hospital and there is no indication that they are anything more than a couple of drunks trying out a scam in the hopes of achieving celebrity status in our media-driven society. Furthermore, Monsignor Mulvaney of the local archdiocese says he has tested the wall both in Starr's presence and in her absence, and there is no alteration in the chemistry or the electrical charge at the wall whether Starr is there or not.

"Whatever the truth of the women's claims, one thing is certain: Madeleine Carter may be dead, but the spirit the Hotel Pleiades tried to quench with fire hoses and scaffolding is alive and well. Reporting live from Underground Wacker, Don Sandstrom, Channel 13, First Report News."

38

The Amusement Car-Park

U P IN HIGHLAND PARK, Karen Minsky watched the same newscast. Like Harriet she was scanning the crowd of women, looking not for Mara but for her daughter.

Kim Nagel's mother had called Karen around three-thirty. I thought you might like to know—the words that presage something you absolutely do not wish to hear. Mrs. Nagel went on to report a confession her own daughter Kim had just made, worried about Becca because she'd been trying to phone all afternoon—Becca wasn't home, was she?

No, Becca wasn't home. Karen assumed when she left the house this morning she was joining Kim at the beach.

Well, Mrs. Nagel just thought Karen should know about a dare the kids had put to Becca. You know your own business best, Mrs. Nagel said, but we would never let our Kimmie go into Chicago alone the way you do Becca.

Karen's stomach fell, remembering her fight with her daughter at breakfast yesterday morning. Madeleine Carter and her wall were on the front page of the Sunday *Herald-Star*'s Metro section. Becca never used to read the paper, but since Luisa's arrest she'd studied it, hoping for a sign that Triple-F was doing something for Luisa. Becca gave an excited squeak when she came on the story.

The First Freedoms Forum's Judith Ohana says the Hotel Pleiades is in violation of the First Amendment's protection of public
expressive activity when it makes it hard for women to worship at
the crumbling masonry on Underground Wacker Drive.

"Just because laboratory tests show the substance in the wall to
be rust does not mean worshipers cannot also believe it is the blood
of the Virgin Mary. After all, laboratory tests of communion wine
might prove that it has the chemical composition of wine, not of
blood, but that would not deter Catholics from believing it to be the
blood of Christ." She added that Triple-F was enjoining the hotel
from blocking access to the wall for anyone who wanted to pray
there.

Mara Stonds, a spokeswoman for the women who are protesting at the wall, said, "The hotel, in putting significant barricades
in the path of Carter's worship—ranging from spraying her with a
fire hose to putting a spiked scaffolding in front of the wall—threw
this mentally ill woman into such despair that she committed suicide."

"Look at this!" Becca thrust the paper in front of her mother. "That
hotel where they arrested Aunt Luisa pushed a homeless woman into
committing suicide. Now the Freedoms Forum is filing a lawsuit against
them to make them keep the wall available to anyone who wants to
worship there."

"I read the story," Karen said shortly. "That's in Mara Stonds's
opinion. She's a very troubled girl who's causing her family a lot of grief.
Can you imagine, embarrassing her sister like that, in front of her clients?
And she looks terrible. What was she thinking of to shave her head bald?
The sister is so beautiful—didn't you think so when she was on TV?
Funny that they should both be from the same family."

"No, it's not. Daddy and Aunt Luisa don't look anything alike and
they're twins. I think Mara looks dramatic, like Joan of Arc: I dare you to
arrest me and take me off to the stake."

"I see that your aunt's dramatic ability isn't going to die with her."
Karen returned to an interview with Germaine Greer in the Arts section.

"You'd like Aunt Luisa to die, wouldn't you? It would be so convenient, if only that garage guy wasn't on disability leave maybe he could
persuade her to commit suicide, too." Becca glared at her mother.

"Becca!" Harry, buried in the financial pages, didn't look up. "I've
asked you not to talk to your mother like that."

"Well, what would you do if it was me?" Becca muttered. "Make
me live in some moldy SRO?"

"Sweetie, please—not first thing in the morning, okay?" Karen said.
"It's going to be a scorcher today. If you go to the beach with Kim make
sure you put on plenty of sunscreen. You, too, Harry: last week you
looked like a very unkosher lobster when you got back from the club."

The phone rang before Becca could decide whether to make peace
or not.

Karen stretched out an arm to answer it. "Mr. Benedetti! . . . No,
no, we've been up for hours."

Becca sat up straight when she heard the Met director's name:
maybe they wanted to give Luisa her chance at a comeback.

"She did what?" Her mother's voice rose in horror, dispelling
Becca's fantasy. "I'm sorry, but we absolutely cannot— No. Mr. Minsky
has already covered over forty-five thousand dollars in other bills she ran
up. . . . You can tell the Lyric that they'll have to find the money
themselves. . . . No, we filed a formal statement: we cannot be held
liable for any of her debts, and we won't accept any part of this one. . . .
Tell Lyric to arrest her if she shows up again: maybe a few months in jail
would jolt Janice into confronting her problems, since losing her career
hasn't done so."

Karen snapped the receiver down. "It's just one thing after another
with Janice. She was holed up in a practice room at the opera house with
another woman, until one of the guards found them and evicted them.
They created a horrible amount of noise and mess and even somehow
wrecked a seventy-thousand-dollar concert grand. The opera called

Benedetti, who thought *we'd* be willing to take care of the problem. I can't imagine what Janice thinks she's doing."

Becca's eyes grew round. "A lesbian affair? I didn't know that! And you think she should be in jail for it? Didn't you ever hear of Stone-wall—"

Harry put down the paper. "Becca, enough of that. This isn't about civil rights, it's about destruction of opera house property. Please remember that before you turn your aunt into a martyr."

Becca stomped off to the beach, where she gave her friends a dramatic version of Luisa's latest escapade, highlighting her own role in bringing the Triple-F into the situation. The more her friends talked it over, the more Becca thought she should join the crowd at the hotel garage. By the end of the day, when they were sharing a pizza in the suburb's little shopping strip, Kim implied that Becca didn't have the guts to take part in a demonstration, while Corie said only crazy women or dykey feminists did stuff like that. Becca, out of a confused anger—for her aunt (was Luisa crazy? a dyke?), for herself (was she not as tough as Mara Stonds?), announced that she was going into the city tomorrow morning, and they should watch for her on the afternoon news.

Kim gasped: you wouldn't dare. Corie snorted: she won't, she's only showing off.

Am not, Becca fired back. Watch the news, you'll see who's a show-off then.

On Monday, letting Karen think she was spending the day with her friends, Becca once more rode her bike to the train station and joined the late-morning shoppers heading into Chicago. This time she moved through the crowds easily. She was exhilarated: she was part of the city, she knew how to find her way around. Street smarts, Karen talked about them as something too remote for a suburban girl to attain, but she, Becca, already had them. True, a cop she stopped for directions growled at her to go back home. True, she went down the wrong staircase first and found herself behind a loading dock, where a group of men were smoking: they greeted her sudden appearance as starving tigers might hail an ibex that had strayed from the herd. Eventually, as she was secretly wishing she had never strayed from her secure suburb, she found the right stairwell and landed amidst the demonstrators.

The atmosphere was a cross between an amusement park and a traffic accident. Street vendors were selling everything from T-shirts depicting the crack in the wall to rosaries guaranteed one hundred percent bathed in the Virgin's blood. Mothers with small children waited in line to get at the crack in the wall; other people were kneeling and praying outside the small grotto in the midst of the scaffolding.

A small battalion of Chicago cops forced people to line up right against the scaffolding: the sidewalk and entrance to the garage must be kept free for pedestrians and drivers, patrolmen snarled at anyone who escaped from their tightly defined boundaries. And if you weren't in line to kiss the wall, or kneeling to pray, a cop would tap you on the shoulder and tell you to keep moving.

Becca felt shy and out of place. When a cop asked her if her mother knew where she was, and told her no loitering, she quickly got in the line of miracle seekers. One woman invited her to pray the rosary with her Blue Aura of Mary circle. When Becca said she was a Jew the woman told her that the Mother of God loved her just the same. Someone else tried to hand her a picket sign, but for the most part no one but the cop paid any attention to her.

As the day wore on and she shuffled forward in line, she began to get hungry and tired. She wished she hadn't come, but she wanted some kind of proof for Kim and Corie that she'd been there. If she wasn't at the wall when the television cameras showed up, which the woman with the rosary said happened around two-thirty, her friends would never believe she'd gone there at all.

Around one, Becca went aboveground again for a hamburger and a Coke. As she descended the iron stairs—slowly, to make sure she was heading for the right place this time—she saw her aunt at the far end of the scaffolding. Next to her was Mara—Becca recognized her from her bald head—and a woman who looked a little like Aunt Luisa. Like Aunt

Luisa would look if she were six inches taller, and not drinking herself to—Becca bit off the word *death* before it could pop into her mind.

That must be Starr, who the paper said was either an idiot or the head of some mysterious cult. Starr's hair was kind of bizarre, enormous amounts of it piled wildly on her head. On anyone else it would have looked like a pretty lame wig, but somehow it didn't seem out of place on this woman. She was wearing a Bulls T-shirt that strained across her front and a funny kind of layered skirt that hung to her ankles. Becca couldn't take her eyes off the woman, until she suddenly realized she was staring, which you should never do, only ignorant people were so bad-mannered.

As Becca climbed the rest of the way down the stairs and tried to get to her aunt the crowd grew thicker. The police pushed people into a tight mass, but couldn't really clear the sidewalk.

Becca was short, barely five foot one, and in the press of bodies she couldn't make out anything. At one point she thought she was going to be choked to death, just by the people pushing against her. She used her soccer training, stuck her elbows out, shoved back, created a lane for herself, and made it to the scaffolding. Here her shortness was an asset: she slithered between the spiked beams until she got to the far end where Luisa was standing.

Her aunt was thrilled to see her and kissed her, European style, on both cheeks. Luisa's breath smelled faintly of beer, but she wasn't as drunk as she'd been the last time Becca saw her.

"Darling! How did you ever persuade Harry and Karen to let you come down here?" She turned to Starr. "This is my niece, Becca Minsky. This is Starr, darling."

Becca said hello, shyly. Starr ignored her outstretched hand, and Becca flushed, thinking perhaps the woman was angry with her for staring a few minutes ago. Close up she was gross, no bra, Karen would never let Becca go around like that. Starr smelled, too, of garlic and beer and something hard to identify, like the wet clay at Daddy's plant on a rainy day. Becca turned from Starr and muttered to Mara how brave she thought the older girl was, but Mara didn't respond to her, either. Becca had spoken so softly that Mara couldn't hear her over the crowd, but Becca didn't know that. Her eyes stung with humiliated tears.

Becca started to back away, into the press of people, when she felt a hand on her head. She looked up to see Starr scrutinizing her. In the shadows under the scaffolding it was hard to make out Starr's face, but Becca thought the big woman was laughing at her. That was the last straw, after a day spent in heat and discomfort, when she was trying to stand up for her ideas, for this gross woman to laugh at her misery, when Becca suddenly realized she wasn't miserable, she was in the middle of an adventure, she was young, she was excited, and her feet in their high-heeled lace-up sneakers no longer hurt, but wanted to dance.

It was at that moment that the cameras arrived. The picture Karen saw in Highland Park an hour later was of her daughter arm in arm with Mara Stonds, swaying in the confined space as if they were in a crowded ballroom. Nearby Luisa seemed to be singing, but the TV mikes couldn't pick that up over the crowd noise.

Karen watched numbly. Mrs. Nagel, and every other member of the Temple, would be whispering about her: sister-in-law a drunk, destroying an international career to live in squalor with a woman so obscene Karen's mind shied from thinking about her. Daughter allowed to run wild in Chicago with perverts and the homeless. Everyone would be repeating what Mrs. Nagel had said on the phone to her, that they would never let their children go into the city unsupervised the way Karen let Becca.

Karen watched until the news shifted, to Saddam Hussein and the Kurds, and then called Harry at the scrap iron plant. Janice is a menace. She's corrupted Becca, drawn her down to that dreadful underground place with homeless women and God knows what all. Call the cops, call Hanaper, call someone and get your sister locked up.

And when Becca came home, dirty, radiant: you're grounded for the rest of the summer, young lady. I can't trust you. From now on, you go out only if your father or I are with you. To Karen's astonishment, instead of going into a teenage huff, Becca laughed. You should go down there yourself. You don't know how cool she is, how totally awesome.

•

No, not Mara Stonds, the strange woman who doesn't talk. Starr. You can't tell on TV, you have to see her in person. When she touches you it's like she's totally reorganized your brain. You really should check her out.

39

Miracles

"DAY TWENTY-THREE on Lower Wacker Drive," Channel 13's Don Sandstrom intoned.

The television screen showed the scaffolding, with a calendar superimposed. "Since the Orleans Street shelter began barring any women who come to the wall, most of the homeless have left this site at the Hotel Pleiades garage. However, the church's action has not halted the steady stream of miracle seekers. Channel 13 talked with Mathilde Ledoq from Belgium, whose five-year-old daughter Bette suffers from leukemia."

Don's thick blond hair and square jaw were replaced by a still shot of a gaunt, anxious woman of about forty. "Madame Ledoq, speaking through an interpreter, says that after bathing her child in water from the wall for three days, Bette is already stronger. . . . Dr. Clyde Hanaper, head of psychiatry at Midwest Hospital where the little girl has been sent for examination, says it is not unusual for parents to delude themselves about the health of a child with a life-threatening illness."

A brief clip with Hanaper, looking sad but understanding in his richly furnished office, explaining the power of self-delusion that allowed people to believe in miracles. Sandstrom turned next to the archdiocesan miracle expert, Monsignor Mulvaney, who looked authoritative but caring as he explained that prayer can achieve many miracles, but if women

are relying on pagan substitutes for the Christian faith, then God is unlikely . . .

Day twenty-five on Underground Wacker. "Hector Tammuz, the
doctor who treated Madeleine Carter while she was alive, continues to
haunt the place where she died. On this Wednesday evening we caught
up with him at the wall around seven p.m. He was on his way to his post
at Midwest Hospital's psychiatry department, where all the residents are
working extra shifts because of the influx of tourists visiting the wall: a
number end up needing emergency psychiatric care. . . .

Hector haunted the wall at dusk because that was when Starr and
Luisa often came. Some miracle seekers claimed it was Starr's presence,
not the wall, that healed them. They brought her flowers or money, or
the strong beer she seemed to favor. Others believed in the wall's powers,
and hung wreaths from the scaffolding, or burned candles underneath the
bleeding crack. They pasted prayers on the concrete around the crack:
Blessed Mother, help Leon find a job . . . heal my arthritis . . . cure
Melanie's cancer . . . make me pregnant . . . end my pregnancy
. . . stop Mark's drinking . . . his infidelities . . . his beatings. Messages in Polish and Spanish and English, petitions in Korean, Russian,
Arabic, in all the languages of the city.

Don Sandstrom, knowing he was working the story of his career,
attacked it from every angle. Did Starr speak some language of her own?
Did the diva really interpret those grunts, or were the two involved in
some elaborate con? Sandstrom dug up philologists and ventriloquists to
debate the matter on the air. Starr and Luisa would not come to the
studio, so Sandstrom had to use footage of the two at the wall, where it
was difficult to make out what either woman was saying, or how the
crowd reacted to them.

Verna Lontano, from the University of Chicago's Oriental Institute,
agreed to be one of the panelists, along with three men from other area
institutions. Ordinarily Lontano regarded that kind of program with a
mocking contempt, but her connection to the Stonds family made her
interested in what young Mara was doing.

Before their on-air appearance, the four philologists gathered in a

Channel 13 sound studio to go over tapes of Starr and Luisa. Starr was hard to hear amidst the noise from cops and miracle seekers, of traffic and road construction, but studio engineers pulled as many of her grunts as possible out of the mélange and made a ten-minute master that focused on her and Luisa.

Lontano and the other scholars played it over and over. They couldn't decide, privately among themselves or on the air, whether the sounds broke down into groups that might be a language. The only thing they did agree on was that despite Starr's vaguely Middle Eastern appearance, with her bronze skin and beaked nose, whatever she was saying wasn't in a modern Semitic language.

The philologists lingered in the studio after their forty-five seconds on air, reviewing footage of Starr. The three men made no secret of their interest in Starr's bosom, and kept stopping the tape on some of the more revealing shots. Lontano, impatient with her colleagues' raucous jokes, studied Starr's hair, with its elaborately coiled and braided loops on the side. If she squinted, they looked like the horns of figurines on old Sumerian cylinder seals.

When she suggested this, her colleagues were scornful. No resemblance at all, Verna. Are you trying to suggest this creature might be a Sumerian, some science fiction figure who's been in suspended animation for four thousand years and suddenly had her DNA reactivated?

No, Lontano didn't think that. She wondered, though, whether Mara had pushed her chants to the goddess Gula one step further. Perhaps the unhappy adolescent had persuaded some homeless woman to let Mara dress her hair to resemble a figure from an old cylinder seal.

Lontano hesitated to suggest that to Dr. Stonds: he was already so incensed with Mara for parading his name around town in such raffish company, that Lontano didn't want to fuel the flames by accusing Mara either of delusions or malevolence. The professor did, however, go to Lower Wacker Drive several times after her TV debut to try to see Starr in person. The crowds were always heavy, and the professor, never tolerant of group hysteria, was unwilling to wait in the lines that formed whenever Starr and her entourage appeared.

The police kept anyone from sleeping around the wall, or from simply standing and watching. If people wanted to pray, fine, otherwise they had to keep moving. So after a short stint at the wall Starr, Luisa, and Mara would disappear through the underground streets, occasionally appearing at one of the shelters, but more often dossing down with other homeless men and women in the warm sand beside Lake Michigan.

After videotaping for a week, Jared Lowrie got tired of hanging out to see whether anyone from Hagar's House was violating the shelter's edict, and no one else felt like wasting their summer afternoons down there with a camera. A few women from Hagar's House began to return to the wall, or to wander with Starr and Luisa. Jacqui and Nanette came most often, along with LaBelle, the woman who had been eager to test the wall's healing powers to begin with.

If the miracle seekers gave them money, Mara would buy food and hand it out to any other homeless people they encountered. A rumor even spread about an evening when Mara had fed a large crowd at the beach from one bag of day-old bread.

When the TV crews heard about the story they were ecstatic: the fantasy of everyone in broadcast, to be live at Galilee. Channel 13's Don Sandstrom joined the hunt for a reliable witness. He couldn't find Luisa or Mara Stonds. He tracked down LaBelle at Hagar's House, where she wouldn't answer questions, fearful that Patsy Wanachs would bar her from the shelter if she saw LaBelle on television.

The best that Sandstrom could come up with was a drunk man who rocked back and forth on his heels, laughing. "That Starr, she somethin', man. Whew, she touch that bread and it turn into ham sandwiches, fried chicken, whatever you most got a taste for. Everybody got some, must have been two hundred people lined up for dinner. She suck out of that beer bottle and hand it around, and, boy howdy, it turn into enough Colt 45 to drown everybody's thirst."

The station didn't think the footage with the drunk made an attractive impression, so they only ran a report of the rumor, and an interview about it with Monsignor Mulvaney and the Orleans Street Church's

Pastor Emerson. Both clergymen were outraged by the blasphemy that Starr and Luisa—and Mara Stonds—were stirring up.

"It's one thing for women to believe that the Virgin is hearing their prayers," Mulvaney said, "but quite another for this creature Starr to pretend to re-create the miracles Our Lord performed at Galilee. This is blasphemy, bordering on witchcraft. I strongly urge you to stop publicizing this woman's activities—it only encourages her."

Naturally Channel 13 wasn't about to stop its broadcasts—its ratings had never been higher. Unfortunately for Don Sandstrom, he and his camera weren't on Lower Wacker Drive the day Pastor Emerson and Monsignor Mulvaney decided to take matters into their own hands and confront the women in person. They were joined by Dr. Hanaper from Midwest Hospital, who had met the two clerics on numerous television shows that discussed the women at the wall.

Midwest's psychiatric wing was doing land-office business with the people who were flocking to the wall. The summer heat, the expectations tourists brought with them, the strangeness of the city for foreigners or country dwellers, all exacted a toll from miracle seekers. A family from upstate New York, overwhelmed by the vastness of the city and the cavernous reaches of Lower Wacker Drive, jumped into the Chicago River together, all nine holding hands. Other visitors developed amnesia, or fancied themselves as incarnations of the Messiah, or the Virgin Mary. At least once a day, sometimes more often, police on Lower Wacker had to summon a Fire Department ambulance to escort a frenzied tourist to the hospital.

Hanaper, conducting rounds, listening to tales of the wall, to tales of Starr—her electric energy, her eyes that saw into the bottom of your soul, her miraculous cures—listening to vivid fantasies about Starr, wanted to see her for himself. He went to the wall several times, stopping on his way to work or drifting over during lunch, but Starr was never there when Hanaper arrived, and he had to rely on television footage, or the garish snapshots tourists on the ward managed to take.

Starr was a clear example of feminism run amok, Hanaper told his residents and medical students. Her extreme sexuality, bordering on nymphomania, made her expose herself to men in the hopes of personal validation through sexual fulfillment. "You've seen her a number of times yourself, haven't you, Dr. Tammuz? You're the expert on Freud. Wouldn't you agree? She rouses the latent appetites that the women who seek her out have repressed."

Hector, seeing the glitter in his chief's eyes, realized that Hanaper's own latent appetites were close to the surface. I'll protect you from him, Starr, he whispered to himself, and when Hanaper asked Hector for the most likely time to encounter Starr and her entourage, that ragtag troop of Luisa, Mara, Jacqui, and Nanette, Hector sent him at noon or dawn, never at sundown.

It was just a fluke, then, that brought Starr to the wall one day at noon when Hanaper, Monsignor Mulvaney, and Pastor Emerson were there as well. The monsignor explained to the police who he was, that he had come with a doctor and a Protestant minister to try to talk some sense into these deluded creatures. The police promptly escorted the men through the crowd so that they stood in front of Starr and her friends. There was a ripple of indignation from women who had been waiting since dawn for a sight of Starr, but none of the men paid any attention to it.

Hanaper whistled appreciatively under his breath. Just as he thought: her body, a handicap for the poor creature, probably had been made to feel self-conscious in adolescence and had adopted a provocative posture as a defense mechanism, the attitude of "if you can't lick your tormentors, join them," then the adage set off a vision of himself licking those breasts, cream flowing into his mouth. . . . Hanaper's glance flickered upward to the woman's face. He had a momentary illusion that she could read his mind, as if his fantasy were written on his face.

"These women belong in a hospital," Hanaper said to Monsignor Mulvaney.

Mara, hearing him, was frightened: they'll lock me up, they'll lock up Starr. She pulled on Starr's arm, then besought Luisa to explain the danger they were in, but Starr only laughed and Luisa said, Oh, don't worry, they're just here to show how important they are.

The three men lectured Starr about her pernicious influence on impressionable women. Faced with those unwinking black eyes, Pastor Emerson faltered in the midst of a plea to let the miracle seekers return to their homes and families.

I'm sure you don't mean to, Emerson said, but you're inspiring unreachable fantasies in all these people.

Dr. Hanaper said, no, she can't help it, this is the kind of condition modern medication is designed to control.

Oh, nonsense, the monsignor snapped. We use medical conditions as a shield, to avoid taking responsibility for our actions. She knows exactly what she's doing—look at her expression.

And while the men argued among themselves, and lectured Starr, none of the three could take their eyes from her body, the full red lips with their promise of fuller lips below, the arms like bronze cradles that could rock you close. Faces shining, trouser fronts bulging, all three men talking louder, harder, to overcome their treacherous bodies. And then Dr. Hanaper, furious at Starr's laugh—a raucous blast that echoed from the steel girders like an elephant's trumpet—announced he would have the police bring her by force to the hospital. But when the doctor ran over to summon one of the patrolmen he suddenly collapsed, gasping for air. By the time the police found someone to give Hanaper first aid, Starr, Luisa, and Mara had melted through the underground alleys into the dark stretch of land along the river.

Pastor Emerson blamed Mara Stonds for exacerbating the situation. He summoned an emergency session of his parish council. The church felt a personal responsibility for the situation, since the initial uproar about the wall was caused by women at their shelter. And Mara Stonds, who was really the group's ringleader, had been baptized in this very building.

Everyone on the parish council had some memory of Mara's shocking conduct over the years or the extravagant stories she made up. The time she'd spread news of Harriet's wedding, and Mrs. Thirkell bought Harriet a silver chafing dish; the time she told them her grandfather was getting the Medal of Honor for his work as a cold war spy; that her mother was imprisoned in a Russian labor camp because of Dr. Stonds; the time that . . . the time that . . . Rafe Lowrie, more in sorrow than anger, recounted numerous occasions Mara had led his own precious Cynthia astray (Cynthia's eye healing from her last beating, she was back in church, more breathless and nervous than ever).

The parish council should be able to stop Mara Stonds from embarrassing the Stonds family, the church, and the city. A few members thought the tale of Starr feeding the multitude might be true—Starr might actually be a witch, performing perverse parodies of biblical miracles. (Jesus fed people with loaves and fishes—whoever heard of fried chicken and malt liquor in connection with a divine wonder!) Remember, Rafe Lowrie said ominously, in Leviticus it says you shall not suffer a witch to live.

Nonsense, Mrs. Ephers said—there's no witchcraft here, only Mara Stonds, showing off as per usual, trying to make mischief. I'll talk to the doctor about this. He needs to get her shut up in the hospital where she belongs: that will put a stop to this nonsense.

In the meantime, the council agreed on two things: the Friday psychotherapy clinic must be stopped for the time being. Hector Tammuz only encouraged the homeless women in their support of Starr. If the church really wanted to end this blasphemous activity in Chicago, they needed to root it out from their own parish. They couldn't on the one hand tell Dr. Stonds to get his daughter off the streets if at the same time they were providing a forum for the homeless to plan further perversions.

The council's second decision was to hold a special parish service of penitence and communion a week from Saturday. Rafe Lowrie was conducting his Family Matters seminar then, his meeting of businessmen who wanted to reclaim their God-given authority over their families; Pastor Emerson should hold a family service beforehand.

Pastor Emerson had not previously been a supporter of Rafe or his Family Matters group. He resented Rafe's efforts to show Emerson how to run the church, and didn't like the books and pamphlets Rafe show-

ered him with on a better interpretation of Scripture than Emerson used
in his sermons.

But the pastor was angry with the homeless women, with Mara
Stonds, and especially Starr, for the humiliations he'd suffered at the wall.
It was time the parish exerted its authority. On Sunday he announced the
special service from the pulpit, and preached ferociously on a text from
First Timothy: "If a man does not know how to manage his own household well, keeping his children submissive and respectful in every way,
how can he care for God's church?"

Emerson told the congregation that he would open Rafe's meeting
with a community service of penance and communion, to show God
they were truly sorry for their role in encouraging the breakdown of
public morality: after all, it was the women at Hagar's House who had
first started the hysteria about the wall and Starr. It was their own Mara
Stonds who had become a ringleader down there. The whole debacle
showed that they had not done their job as a parish in guiding their
young people, because wasn't Mara a product of twelve years in Orleans
Street Sunday schools? And yet they had failed to provide her with the
bulwark of faith to withstand a dangerous cult leader like Starr. The
parish had become too focused on material wealth—looking pointedly at
Rafe—and on substituting trendy social causes for faith—here talking
directly to Sylvia Lenore—and forgotten the Lord: It was He who made
us and not we ourselves.

After the service, men began signing up for the retreat. All the
following week the phone in the church office rang with men eager to
assert their God-given authority. None of this idiotic Ironman stuff,
going off into the woods, sitting around naked pounding drums, but the
kind of sober Christian seminar a businessman could understand.

Dr. Stonds knew, from Mrs. Ephers, how upset the parish council
was with Mara as one of the ringleaders of the women at the wall. When
he heard Emerson's sermon, his own fury with Mara swelled. Every
grievance he'd ever felt against his granddaughter bounced through his
head. How dare she expose him like this to public censure?

After Hector's useless attempt to bring Mara into the hospital last month, Dr. Stonds had washed his hands of Mara: she refused help, then let her rot, as her mother and grandmother had before her. But the public gossip was intolerable. He finally agreed with Hilda Ephers, it was time to do something. And if she emulated Beatrix further, well, so be it.

But it was not that easy to unearth Mara. Starr never went to the same park two nights running. Dr. Stonds was not about to lower his dignity by hiking along beaches and rocky inlets looking for his grand-daughter, even with police in tow. He did consent to send two men from the hospital's private security force to the wall in the evenings when Mara was most likely to be there, but by the time they had forced their way through the crowd of women who gathered in front of Starr and Luisa, Mara had fled into the alleys behind the hotel garage.

Day thirty on Underground Wacker, day thirty-one . . .

40

Show Us Some Cleavage, Honey

GIAN PALMETTO, president of the Pleiades, is beside himself. The Pleiades' cancellations stand at over fifty percent: clients seeking quiet and anonymity don't want to fight their way past women praying the rosary, women douching themselves in rusty water from the wall, women nursing their howling infants, not to mention the build-up of garbage as all the miracle seekers drop their McDonald's wrappers and Starbucks cups in the road. True, these out-of-town visitors need a place to sleep, but they go to cheap motor lodges by the expressway, not luxury hotels where rates start at a hundred eighty a night and float skyward.

Palmetto's corporate masters have phoned, faxed, and now arrived in person. At the law firm of Scandon and Atter, meetings take place between Mervin Clinator, head of the Olympus Group, and Leigh Wilton, the senior partner. On Thursday afternoon Harriet, in disgrace for not somehow controlling events, sits at a remote end of the table, relegated essentially to paralegal status. Taking notes, doing research, not venturing an opinion or suggestion. Gian Palmetto is at the other end, equally disgraced for letting homeless women ruin the Pleiades' bookings.

A senior lawyer from the city—with entourage—is also present. The Olympus president fretfully wonders why the police can't keep people away—they're trespassing, not to mention littering and loitering.

The corporation counsel is sympathetic. The city knows how much the Pleiades has invested in arts in Chicago, not to mention gifts to the mayor's election funds. The city is detailing extra Streets and Sanitation crews to keep the public areas free of litter. And they'll certainly station police down there twenty-four hours a day to keep crowds from blocking access to the Pleiades garage.

Not good enough, Olympus president Clinator snaps. We want that area cleared.

Look, says the corporation counsel, if it were only homeless women down there we'd urge the cops to move them on. Of course that statement stays inside this room. All the men nod, sure.

But now there are three problems—the television cameras, the tourists, and the suit filed by the First Freedoms Forum. The hotel can't be sued for violating the miracle seekers' First Amendment rights, but the city can. Olympus president Clinator and senior partner Leigh Wilton have to understand, given the high visibility the situation has right now, the city must observe the public forum doctrine and keep the street and sidewalk open to the miracle seekers' expressive activity.

What about just tearing down the damned wall, putting in new plumbing, and ending the story? the Olympus president asks.

The corporation counsel draws a circle on the table with his finger. An excellent idea, if the hotel can wait out the current frenzy. It will just look so bad for them to be callous about the faith of very religious women, one of whom is the sister of an important bishop, another married to the head of a construction firm that gives a lot of money to the mayor's campaign chest.

And what if the frenzy never dies down? Olympus demands.

Leigh Wilton pulls out his trump card. He says he's spoken to Clyde Hanaper over at Midwest Hospital. There's a drunk, used to be a great singer, who hangs around the wall, seems to be a lesbian, having an affair with that big woman—what's her name, Harriet?—Starr, that's right, gal who's kind of a ringleader for the group. Anyway, the drunk's brother is fed up, thinks she's corrupting his teenage daughter, wants to get her off the streets into a clinic someplace. If the brother will pay for the drunk,

Scandon and Atter could kick in something for Starr, send her off for a psychiatric exam, maybe put her in a locked ward over at Midwest.

The problem is, this Starr seems to have a mesmerizing effect on the women at the wall. So they can't pick her up during the day, when the crowds are most intense, or when the camera crews are likely to be there. Also, she isn't always at the wall and they don't know where she sleeps at night. But the hospital thinks they can track her down, through a resident who's been working with the homeless women. They'll try tonight, maybe catch the women while they're asleep. If this Starr's out of the way . . .

The head of the Olympus chain laughs. I'd like to catch that broad while she was asleep. From the photos, those knockers of hers could give you a TKO with one blow.

Gian Palmetto and Leigh Wilton neigh with laughter: the head of the hotel chain is making a joke, the tension is suddenly lessened. The meeting breaks down into general ribaldry as the men try to top one another's jokes. Harriet feels herself disappearing. Not a person, not a lawyer, a note-taking thing for the first three hours, now a body thing as the Olympus president rakes her own bosom with greedy eyes, looking past her pale green suit jacket, her silk shirt, to her small breasts, even though as always they're shielded by a bra. Hers is the only female presence, besides the corporation counsel's paralegal, and as the discussion becomes more graphic, they all watch her, wanting to know if they are shocking her, scaring her. She rises without moving her hips and heads for the door.

Ah, honey, can't you take a joke? Olympus president asks.

Harriet turns in the entryway. Was that a joke? Forgive me—I never had the advantage of a schoolboy's locker room to learn humor.

She leaves, and is cornered later by Leigh Wilton. These are important clients who are undergoing a major shock. They need our support, and that includes letting them vent steam through jokes which you or I might not personally find funny.

"Don't I get any support from the firm, Leigh?" Harriet asks. "You're making me the whipping girl for a situation that no one could have managed. And when the client starts demeaning me by making comments about women's genitals, I'm supposed to laugh. Suppose I had shared a female joke—a belly laugh over how all you men measure your penises, terrified that one is shorter than the other, and the amusement women feel over your anxiety. Would that have been the same?"

"What's gotten into you, Harriet? You used to be a reliable team player. The partnership vote will be taken after Labor Day. You've been on a fast track for six years. Don't make me start to wonder whether you really have a permanent home at Scandon and Atter." Leigh Wilton stares at her, his eyes so wide they seem about to pop from his head. "Now I'm going to forget about your behavior this morning. Just let me have the meeting minutes before six. And get me cases and precedents under Section 1983 to see if we have any maneuvering room. Meanwhile I'm going to talk to that guy Hanaper over at Midwest Hospital. I think it's worth our while to cover this Starr creature's medical bills for a few days if that will defuse the situation."

He stops to see if she's going to react in any way. Her calmness reassures him—she's still a good girl, a team player.

"Clinator and I are having dinner over at the Casino Club to see where we stand. When you get the minutes ready, go home and put on a nice sexy dress, show some cleavage, and come join us—that'll let the Olympus guys know you're apologizing for being a hard-ass this afternoon. Eight o'clock. You know where it is, right?"

He slaps her on the fanny and moves on to his own office. Harriet stands in the hall. Show cleavage to mollify the client. If she displays her crotch as well, will Leigh Wilton make her a partner?

In her office she lines up a stack of legal pads, squares them against the end of the desk. She feels as though she's in an invisible box, which makes it hard to move her arms. Is this what drove Mara from the Hotel Pleiades Special Events office, these crude jokes and insults? Should she have been learning something from Beebie, instead of judging her? If this happened to Mara, she'd shave her head and show up at the Casino Club buff naked. Harriet smiles faintly, but assures herself she is nothing like

Mara—she would never do such a thing, or camp out behind Professor Lontano's office, or picket with homeless women at the Hotel Pleiades.

She wants to write out a letter of resignation and leave, but all her training is against such impulsive behavior. She needs to talk to someone who can help her decide what to do.

Grandfather. His thick white brows contracting. Don't tell me you're suddenly turning as temperamental as your mother or your sister, Harriet. You've always shown such good judgment—I thought I could count on you. Now be a good girl. I'll put in a call to Leigh Wilton, we sit on that foundation board together.

Mephers. Mara is ruining your life. If she hadn't run away to that hotel garage, stirred up all that trouble over the crazy homeless woman, none of this would have happened.

Pastor Emerson. Maybe things were said in the heat of the moment that everybody's ashamed of now. Jesus tells us to turn the other cheek— you pray on it, but this seems to be one of those situations where Jesus had the right advice.

Harriet thinks of the women she went to college with, the suitors who used to flock to the Graham Street apartment. How can she be thirty-two and have no real friends? What world has she been inhabiting, where she could be so isolated from the human race and think she was happy?

She pulls the notes of the meeting toward her and starts to dictate them into a coherent report, then erases the tape. It's five o'clock now: Leigh has only asked for the minutes by six as an extra humiliation—she would have to type them up, and research the precedents under Section 1983 herself, since it's too late in the day to get paralegal or clerical support for the job. A year ago—six weeks ago—Grandfather's good girl would have done it, but today she doesn't have the energy.

She picks up her briefcase: habit. Looks at it, drops it on an armchair. Leaves the building. She smiles autonomically at other associates, at partners, the clerical staff, who watch her departure with jaw-dropping gaze: Harriet Stonds, leaving the building without her briefcase, and before six, let alone before nine? Is the sky falling?

41

Gathering the Posse

"Dr. Tammuz. I saw you on the news this morning." Melissa Demetrios faced Hector across the desk in the tiny cubicle the hospital allotted its senior psychiatry resident. "What were you doing down at that wall? Is it true that you're there every day?"

Hector couldn't speak. He spread his hands, as if gestures might convey his meaning. Anyway, the question shouldn't be—was he at the wall every day—but—was he here at the hospital every day? Was it true that he tore himself from Starr, or the hopes of seeing Starr, or whatever it was he did with Starr, to put on his blue resident's gown and wander among the patients? For even when he was reading a chart, or talking to Mrs. Herstein in clinic, or injecting someone with Haldol, he felt Starr's lips, his own flesh clinging to her, himself buried in her wild cornucopia.

What is wrong with you these days? he heard Melissa asking. You look as though you haven't eaten or shaved in weeks. I don't even know if I should let you in the clinics or wards.

I can't tell the difference between waking and dreaming. Have I ever suckled those breasts, drunk from that sweet vulva, or has that happened only in my dreams? How can I tell? But if he said that aloud, then he'd be in one of those sixth-floor beds himself, shot full of Ativan, strapped down, kept forever from Starr's side.

". . . Because of the amount of public hysteria that seems to surround her, the hotel's lawyers have hired Dr. Hanaper to examine her.

They're trying to pick her up, along with the diva who was in here a few months ago. In addition, Dr. Stonds wants his granddaughter to come in for treatment: she's been living on the streets for over a month and he's quite worried about her. The police couldn't find any of them yesterday, although Dr. Hanaper doesn't think they looked very hard."

"Mara Stonds?" Hector tried to grasp hold of Melissa's remarks and respond to them in a doctorly fashion. "Maybe it's unconventional, her life on the streets, but whenever I see her she seems happy. She doesn't show any signs of mental distress."

"Well, you are not really in a position to make that evaluation. And in any event, it's more the woman Starr that Dr. Stonds and Dr. Hanaper are concerned about, since she seems to be behind—"

"No!" Hector shouted. "Hanaper only wants to—to—I can see it in his eyes, when they interview him about the miracles. He keeps coming to the wall, hoping to see her, and he looks—looks like—" He buried his head in his hands. Hanaper, his jowls dripping, a jackal in the veldt, slavering over a wild cow.

"And what do you think you look like, Dr. Tammuz? This isn't about some adolescent boy's fantasy life. We're an overworked urban hospital. We're now getting almost double our patient load because suburban and foreign visitors are coming to the city, looking for miracles, and collapsing from the stress of not having their fantasies met. You are not pulling your share of the load, so your fellow residents and I have to work harder than ever. If you can't be a team player here, I'm going to have to discuss your performance with Dr. Hanaper. I've avoided doing that until I had a chance to meet with you myself."

Melissa's face was white: it was hard to confront anyone about doing a poor job, but Hector couldn't imagine that. Couldn't imagine, either, that when he first arrived at the hospital, Melissa treated herself to fantasies about him, his sensitive mouth and long lean hands on hers, and was repelled by his obsession with Starr.

All Hector's detachment, his patience, carefully harvested in order to survive his mother's scorn, had disappeared. He could scarcely listen to Melissa, saw only her mouth moving like a shark's jaw, as it sucked in fishes . . . the potential to be a good doctor . . . side-railed by your involvement with homeless . . . spoke to Dr. Boten at Lenore Foundation.

Hector's head jerked up at that: Dr. Boten shared Melissa's concern for the way in which Hector had overidentified with the homeless women he was treating at the Orleans Street Church. Until the women calmed down, the church was suspending the clinic, anyway; whether it would reopen, and whether Hector would be allowed to take part, would depend very much on his conduct over the next several weeks.

Hector felt himself crumbling. His Friday afternoons at the clinic used to be important to him for the good he thought he did for the homeless. Now he yearned for time among them, for any word he could glean of Starr. If Melissa was forbidding him to go . . . No, it was Dr. Boten, Dr. Boten whose approach to psychotherapy had drawn Hector to Chicago and Midwest Hospital, was now betraying him, closing the clinic, probably jealous of Hector's special relationship with Starr.

". . . loss of dignity makes an unprofessional appearance . . ." Melissa was saying.

Longing for Starr drove any idea about dignity from Hector's mind. He would stumble along the shore in the middle of the night, but often couldn't find her. The parkland stretched over six miles, the beaches interspersed with rocky promontories, harbors, uncultivated bits of prairie. He couldn't possibly search them all. He would return to the hospital then, shivering with disappointment in the warm summer air, forgetting to eat or shave, until he looked like one of the men who huddled on Fridays outside the Orleans Street clinic, waiting for Hector himself to appear with his bag of magic tricks.

Hector resented Mara's closeness to Starr. Those times when he did happen on Starr, Mara would be at her side. Typical of a Stonds, to horn in where no one wanted her and take over. He didn't mind Luisa, who continued to be the only one able to interpret Starr's grunts—or who claimed to be doing so—maybe because the disintegrated diva didn't seem really human to him. But Mara, despite her shaved head and broken tooth, or maybe because of them, seemed vulnerable, even desirable, and he feared that Starr loved her best.

Once, just as the sun was spilling pink and gold light across the water onto the sand, he'd come on the three of them, Luisa, Starr, and Mara, lying in the shelter of a rock on a spit of land at the Montrose Avenue beach. They were naked, and Mara was lying with her head nestled on Starr's side. Hector cried out. Mara and Luisa didn't stir, but Starr awoke and looked at him.

She said nothing, but Hector thought his jealousy and desire were mirrored back at him in those unwinking black eyes. He stumbled away and collapsed on the sand. When he came to, he found himself in bed in the on-call room at the hospital. He wasn't ever sure whether Starr had followed him up the beach, folded him to herself, allowed him to enter her, drink from her, or if that satiation had happened in a dream only.

"Dr. Tammuz!" Melissa's sharp voice recalled him to her presence, but not until she'd repeated his name three times. "Are you listening to me? We want to know the best place to try to hunt for Luisa Montcrief and Starr so that Dr. Stonds can get his granddaughter off the streets and into some much needed treatment. And for their own good we need to treat Luisa and Starr. If you know where to find them, you will be doing everyone—the hospital, the homeless women, the churches, even the city—a great favor by telling me. It will also help us know that you are really committed to your career here at the hospital."

Committed to his career as a dispenser of drugs and minimalist therapies? If he went out of his way to prove that, he might be destroyed forever.

"They would prefer not to pick the women up at the wall," Melissa said, trying to get a response, "for fear of causing a riot. Do you think they're right?"

This was important, this could affect Starr, pay attention, he adjured himself. "Right about—oh, about a riot? The Blue Aura of Mary circle doesn't seem like they would try—the ones who care are the homeless women, but the church, you know, they've tried to keep them away. That bully Rafe Lowrie, his son, taking names, taking pictures . . .

Although they stopped that, but still a lot of the homeless women never came back."

"So you think it would be okay if we asked the police to bring the women in when they next show up at the wall?" Melissa persisted.

He sat back listlessly. "I don't know. It'll be on camera; even if the TV crews aren't there some tourist is usually videotaping. If Hanaper gets hold of her—they mustn't lock her up. I did it once, it was dreadful, I don't know if she's ever forgiven me for that, must ask Luisa." His voice drifted off as he knotted his fingers together: he mustn't ask Luisa—he couldn't bear to find out that Starr hated him for what he did to her all those weeks ago, shooting her full of drugs, gloating as he did it.

"Dr. Tammuz, we're all overworked here, we all make decisions that we hope are in the best interests of the patient—and sometimes, unfortunately, they're not. In this case, we've got one woman who seems delusional stirring up a large population into an unhealthy state of agitation. Whether we can help Starr, or Luisa, or even Mara Stonds, I don't know. But we can help a lot of other people by removing these three women from the streets for a while."

Hector fumbled for an argument that would matter to his superiors. "And the utilization management committee? Are they happy to take on three uninsured patients? Maybe it's only two—Mara Stonds must have some kind of coverage through her grandfather."

"Don't worry about that aspect of it. Just tell me the likeliest place where we might look for those three."

"Don't worry about the money?" His dark eyes blazed, anger pulling the fragments of his personality momentarily together. "Madeleine Carter might still be alive if this place weren't worried first last and foremost about the money. When I took this residency it was because I thought the clinics would be a place to practice psychotherapy. Instead, in between March and last fall you went to a twenty-twenty program, where all you give people is twenty sessions of twenty minutes, although really I get cut off after fifteen, and screw the patients if that doesn't make them well. You switched from therapy to pharmaceuticals because they're cheaper. You forced Angus Boten off the staff. Now a homeless woman who can't even speak has got the Great White Chief and his ass-licking sidekick Hanaper so rattled that they'll even jettison their precious cost containment policies."

Melissa became angry in turn at his lecture. "Dr. Tammuz, I'm not interested in your emotions on this matter. You are not in a position to get on a high horse about therapy, not when your own feelings are so out of control that you're neglecting your job. If you can't help me locate these women, can't help the hospital perform this part of its mission to the community, then I will have no choice but to discuss your negligence with Dr. Hanaper, who may very well put you on probation. Is that really how you wish to start your professional career?"

Self-preservation with his mother had meant a capitulation to her demands for information on all his actions. He had tried to build a little shrine in his own center where his privacy could be established, where his thoughts remained secret, but ever since he'd met Starr he'd lost the ability to hold anything in reserve.

Now, looking at Melissa, his impulse was just to capitulate once more. Here's where you can probably find Starr: usually at night she's somewhere on those six miles of lakefront, probably near Montrose Harbor where he'd twice come on her, in the prairie grasses that grew in a secluded patch of park.

Before he could fumble words into speech the phone rang on Melissa's desk. She let it go at first, hoping that the clerks, working late to service the outpatient substance abuse and group therapy clinics that were meeting tonight, might pick it up. When it went on ringing she picked it up and snapped a greeting. Her manner changed abruptly.

"Yes, sir . . . I understand, sir . . . I'll do my best." She hung up and looked at Hector. "That was Dr. Hanaper. Dr. Stonds has ordered the head of hospital security to locate these women, since the Chicago police aren't making it a priority, and bring them in. Dr. Hanaper wants you to ride along with them, since the women know you and trust you. I told him you'd do it: the head of the security department is going to be here to pick you up in a minute. Go shave, so you look more like a doctor and less like an inmate from the state mental hospital. It wouldn't hurt if you showered, either."

Hector stumbled from the room to the residents' bathroom. As he shaved, he saw himself handing Starr over to Hanaper, and then—he couldn't imagine living past that moment. He would hang himself in the morning. Or maybe he should do it now, before the moment of betrayal. He took off his tie and looked around the bathroom for something to attach it to. Before he could find a hook or knob strong enough to hold him, a man in the tan and orange of the hospital security staff stuck his head around the door:

"Dr. Tammuz? Dr. Hanaper said you'd be riding along with me to help me locate these women he wants to admit."

42

Castle Revolt

IN THE GRAHAM STREET APARTMENT Harriet hears voices in the living room. Grandfather is home already, and has brought guests. She will have to put on her public face, calm but attentive, when all she wants is to crawl into bed, to lie as still as death and let the fog that has pushed on her mind all week roll in and obliterate thought.

Mrs. Ephers, hearing the key in the door, bustles into the hall, vigilant in case Mara has taken it into her head to come home. The doorman Raymond is supposed to warn her if Mara arrives, but Mrs. Ephers doesn't trust him—he's always let Mara twist him around her finger.

"I'm glad they let you go early tonight," Mrs. Ephers tells Harriet in the dim entryway. "You've been working too hard lately, thanks to Mara. Time to settle that girl's hash once and for all. Your grandfather has brought Mr. and Mrs. Minsky home with him. They're anxious to see you, talk this situation over."

Mrs. Ephers never greets Harriet with a kiss, a welcome home, only with a dry comment, usually, thank goodness they finally let you leave, can't anyone at that firm besides you do any work? Just like your grandfather, you give everything but don't get anything back. (Except control of the hospital, a few million dollars a year, but what is that really?)

Harriet, yearning for some kind of human contact, moves forward to embrace the old woman, but Mephers becomes rigid at her touch.

Harriet removes her arms, which now feel ridiculous, flapping around pointlessly like squid tentacles.

When she came home from school as a little girl was there ever a hug at the end of the day? Or was it just, Let's see what you've done today. My, the doctor will be proud of you, what a clever little girl you are. No one in that fancy school can keep up with you: who would guess you spent six years with Beatrix. . . . Nobody at Smith as good as you. . . . Fifth in your law class, I suppose you can't always be first. . . . I'm not surprised you've made senior associate so young, nobody ever as hardworking-smart-pretty-nice, taking advantage of every opportunity the doctor gave you. . . .

"Who are Mr. and Mrs. Minsky?" Harriet asks, listless again.

"Oh, your grandfather operated on his mother, must be ten years ago now. He couldn't save the woman in the end, but of course the family was very grateful to him for everything he did. And poor Mr. Minsky, it's his sister who's been hanging out on the streets with Mara. That drunk singer, Luisa Montcrief, your grandfather used to think she had the greatest voice he ever heard, but pride goeth before destruction, I always say.

"When you meet him, you won't believe Mr. Minsky's her twin brother. Even stranger than thinking you and Mara are related—she's only your half sister, after all, but twins! It seems as though there's never enough character to spare for two children."

Harriet stands in the entryway, not moving, so Mephers prods her toward the living room. "Miss Harriet's home, Doctor," she says, performing as a servant whenever there are strangers in the place, and Harriet moves dully after her: it's one thing to flee Leigh Wilton's demands, but Harriet isn't strong enough to evade Grandfather or Mephers. Grandfather is in his usual armchair, talking to a couple on the couch who look to be in their early forties.

Harriet plants chaste lips on Grandfather's smooth cheek, always shaved a second time on coming home, accepts introductions. Like Mephers, she's startled that the man is Luisa Montcrief's twin: in her photos the diva appears lean, slim, with aquiline features, while Minsky is short, with the face of a kindly but harassed toad. His wife is an unlikely partner to such homeliness, attractive in the subdued style of a suburban matron, sandy hair cropped short to display suntanned cheeks and wide blue eyes.

"I'm glad you're home, my dear: you can advise us here." Grandfather hands her a glass of dry sherry. "As I told you, Harriet's a lawyer. She'll make sure we do this thing properly."

The Minskys launch into nervous explanation. Janice always a problem, but in the last three years totally out of hand.

"Who is Janice?" Harriet tries to be interested.

"Oh, that's her real name. Luisa Montcrief is only her stage name," Karen says, and proceeds to do most of the speaking for the couple.

The Minsky name good enough to pay bills but not good enough for the stage—Harry interrupts to say maybe Janice had a point, anti-Semitism, hard to have a public career—

Karen cuts him off: that's neither here nor there. Janice always had a problem with alcohol, not usually seen in Jews, so it took them a long time to recognize it for what it was. The director of the Metropolitan Opera liked her, protected her career.

Harry interrupts again: Karen, don't cloak the facts, Ms. Stonds isn't a baby. They were lovers, that's why Piero Benedetti covered up for her. Then three years ago she passed out onstage at the Met in the last act of *Otello*. She's kneeling in prayer in front of the Madonna, and is supposed to climb into bed while the bass viols announce Otello's arrival. Instead, my sister passed out. A huge uproar, Benedetti refused to rescue her again, no one would sign her to sing—agent put out word she was ill. Since then, one thing after another. Spent all her money, resents me for selling her assets to pay her bills.

Karen joins in again. She lived with us for a while, but after she charged forty thousand in hotel bills to Harry's MasterCard we consulted your grandfather's Dr. Hanaper. His advice on tough love.

Karen recounts the disasters of the summer, her daughter Becca, impressionable teenager, infatuated with—not with her aunt so much, as with the romance of aunt's life.

"Now Luisa—Janice—is encouraging Becca to join her on the streets with this strange woman Starr she's picked up. Becca thinks it's exciting, she thinks Janice is a martyr in the cause of free speech. She—Becca—she's started sneaking out of the house, coming into Chicago without telling us, to talk to lawyers, to picket with Janice and Starr at that wall. We said we wouldn't pay any more bills for Luisa, that she has to face up to her problems. But now we're too worried about what she may do to Becca. We want to get Janice off the streets and into a facility where Becca will have to acknowledge that her aunt is a very sick woman, not a free speech heroine. Dr. Stonds says he's worried about his granddaughter as well. And, frankly, we think Becca is imitating Mara—Mara being close to her own age, but just enough older to look like a role model to her. So we came to talk it over with him."

Grandfather snorts. Mara as a role model to an impressionable girl, would be ludicrous if his granddaughter weren't so destructive. Time to pick her up, put her under a psychiatrist's care where she belongs. Promise to the parish council . . . as her guardian an obligation to look after her own well-being . . .

Harriet sits up so abruptly, sherry spills onto the nubbed fabric of her skirt. "You're hospitalizing Mara? When did you decide that?"

Grandfather's bushy brows flip up in surprise. "We've been discussing this since last week's parish council meeting. I know you're overworked these days, my dear, but surely you know I've asked a couple of men from hospital security to try to intercept her at your client's garage this week. They haven't been able to get near her: like all psychotics she's crafty."

"Psychotic? *Grand-père* . . ." Harriet's voice trails away: she doesn't want to argue over Mara in front of strangers.

The doctor, self-assured in his rectitude, doesn't have such qualms. "Like her mother before her. Bad blood, I'm afraid it came into the family with my wife, and was accentuated in our only child, who died under difficult circumstances.

"When that prize loser, Hanaper's young resident Hector Tammuz, couldn't talk Mara into coming in for treatment, I thought I'd let things run their course, but she gets worse, not better. Our local church is actually having a prayer service tomorrow on her account. If Mara finds out about that, her swollen ego will escape its boundaries altogether. No, my mind is made up. I've told the police that it's time to track Mara down, get her into a psychiatric ward where she belongs."

Track her down. Grandfather in safari jacket with a large gun and a paddy wagon full of beaters.

"Is that really necessary, *Grand-père*? Maybe Mara is uncomfortable out on the streets, but she's not doing anyone any harm."

"Not doing anyone any harm?" The doctor's thick brows contract in annoyance. "I thought we three just made clear to you that she's encouraging hysterical women, and corrupting the Minsky girl."

Harriet turns to the Minskys, asks what her sister has actually done to their daughter. Egged Becca on to run away from home, to flout their authority, is what it sounds like. In concert with Harry's twin sister.

"Surely, my dear," Grandfather adds, "you yourself would like to see an end to your sister's embarrassment of your clients at the hotel."

Harriet thinks that her clients have spent the day embarrassing her so badly that anything Mara did would be a fitting revenge, wishing her sister would find a bazooka and blow the Hotel Pleiades to atoms.

Aloud she says only, "Illinois allows the incarceration of a mentally ill person only if you can prove that she is in imminent danger of hurting herself or others, and I don't think Mara has shown any signs of that. You could probably force a hearing, I don't know, maybe your tame head doctor Hanaper could persuade a judge that she's suicidal, but I imagine really good counsel would prove she isn't."

Grandfather is incredulous. "My dear Harriet, are you implying that *you* would defend Mara's right to run wild through this city? Surely any judge would agree that a girl who abandons this apartment to live on the streets is by definition mentally imbalanced."

Harriet shakes her head. The chasm between them seems so wide that she can't think of any words that might bridge it.

She turns bleak eyes to the Minskys. "I'm sorry, Ms. Minsky. It certainly is a pity that Madame Montcrief isn't able to perform anymore, but a judge might recommend that you try to resolve this through a family intervention, rather than in the courts. Mental health law isn't my specialty, however, so it would be better if you found a lawyer who knows the history of how courts have interpreted statutes on involuntary admissions to psychiatric hospitals."

Harriet puts her sherry glass down on the pearwood marquetry, not bothering about a coaster, not worrying about leaving a stain on the antique wood. She gets up abruptly, without even mouthing farewell platitudes to the Minskys, and goes to her own suite of rooms. The apartment is well soundproofed; she doesn't hear the visitors leave, but a few minutes later Grandfather comes into her bedroom.

"Harriet, I know you've been under a strain lately, but I must say I'm astonished at your behavior just now. The Minskys are most concerned about their daughter; they were consulting me and wanted to consult you, and you treated them with extraordinary rudeness. By the way, shouldn't you take your shoes off before lying on that cover?"

Harriet sits up and swings her legs over the edge of the bed. "I don't want you to lock up Mara."

"Harriet! What has gotten into you? You surely don't think she's sane, do you, taking up with that woman Starr, hanging around on Underground Wacker with drunks and homeless people?"

"She's not crazy, just lonely, oh, as I am myself, lonely for someone who cares about me, about Harriet the person, I mean, not Harriet the showpiece who jumps through hoops for anyone who demands it."

"You're overtired," the doctor says coldly. "You're starting to sound as melodramatic as your sister. Would a sane person confuse a homeless woman with her dead mother? Yet isn't that what Mara did, the night that creature Starr appeared? You told me yourself that she claimed it was Beatrix, when she knows perfectly well that Beatrix has been dead and buried for seventeen years."

"I'm sure she knows it deep down," Harriet says, "but whenever she asked about our mother, you or Mephers always frowned and changed the subject, so she thinks there's a mystery attached to her death.

If you'd talked about it, instead of only saying how evil Beatrix was, and the less said about her the better—"

"It's time Harriet knew the truth about Beatrix," Mephers interrupts from the doorway, where she's been standing without Harriet noticing. "Then she'd realize that the sooner Mara is put away where she can't hurt herself the better."

Harriet stares. "The truth? I—I know the truth. Beatrix died when she fell in her bath, you told me that at the funeral."

Grandfather says, what good can it do to rake up all that ancient history now, but Mephers is angry at the idea of Harriet ranging herself with Mara. A dose of the truth, like a dose of salts, would clean her out, cure her.

Grandfather and Mephers argue and Harriet listens, feeling ice build up around her, burying her in the heart of a glacier. Beatrix dealing drugs at the corner of Sixty-third and Cottage, arrested in a cheap motel along with the man—black man—she'd been having sex with that night. Grandfather furious, getting a court to declare her mentally incompetent, putting her in the psychiatric wing at Midwest. Beatrix, stealing a phonograph record from the recreation room, hiding it under her shirt, breaking it in the middle of the night and slicing her wrists open in the bathtub with the sharp plastic, dead before anyone checks on her.

The embarrassment to Grandfather—in his own hospital, the ultimate insult of an ungrateful daughter. His successful efforts to suppress any report of her death, so no one would know she was connected to him or to Harriet. Truth withheld from Harriet to protect her, from Mara because why should even Mara realize how tainted her blood is.

Harriet feels hysterical laughter rising in her that she tries to hold at bay. "An accident in her bath? You told me she fell in her tub and died in an accident. I've had nightmares all my life, her face swelling up, she's coming to get me, but it's you who came to get me, you who got her. Beatrix was your daughter. What did you do to her after Grannie Selena left? The same thing you did to poor little Beebie, telling her she was tarnished in some dreadful way?"

"How dare you?" Grandfather shouts. "Are you going to turn on

me now, like Selena or Beatrix or Mara herself? We gave Mara everything, the best education, the best neighborhood, a good religious environment, and she's repaid us just like Beatrix by hanging out with drunks
and whores. I'm calling the police right now. I want that damned brat
picked up tonight. I'm sick of the looks at church and work, the sympathy, for Christ's sake people are pitying *me*!"

As if Abraham Stonds should always be on top, never subject to the
humiliation of being seen as human. He storms into his study to set in
motion the wheels of authority.

Mephers stays behind to talk to Harriet. "I told him we should have
let you know the truth at the time. You need to know what kind of
creature Beatrix really is, I said, and Mara, too. All those stories Mara
used to make up, turning her mother into a heroine out of some adventure story, if she knew what a moral weakling Beatrix was she'd have
sobered up in a hurry. But your grandfather wanted to spare you, and
now look at the mess we've got on our hands. You need to calm down:
you're upsetting your grandfather by carrying on like this. And you've
got your job and your future to think of. This is old, old history, and
nothing to do with you."

"It's everything to do with me. Why don't the two of you rent a
billboard, a skywriter, something big, proclaim to the city: we're perfect,
we've done no wrong. Get the whole world to bow down at your feet
with wonder at your ice-cold charity."

Mephers stares at her, her mouth drawn into a tight line of disapproval, then says she'll overlook Harriet's outburst, she knows Harriet's
been working too hard lately, and stalks from the room.

Harriet flings herself onto the bed and cries so hard her whole body
bucks against the bedspread. She becomes aware of Grandfather, standing
over her once more.

"Harriet. This is most unbecoming. Pull yourself together. Hilda is
terribly hurt. I want to hear you apologize to her. She's been more a
mother to you than Beatrix ever was and you owe her more than common courtesy."

Pull herself together. When it was their careless revelation that unglued her in the first place. No, it started earlier, when Leigh Wilton patted her bottom. Or, no, when Mara ran away and Harriet felt herself split between remorse and relief. But maybe it began when her own father died, leaving her mother to spin recklessly out of control. Oh, if only Grannie Selena hadn't vanished, everything would have been different, they would have had a female protector against Grandfather's laws.

She stares up at the rigid face. "Please leave."

"Hilda is waiting in the hall for your apology. I'll tell her to come in."

She springs from the bed. "Get out of this room. Now."

When he doesn't move she deliberately unbuttons her blouse, drops it on the chair, unhooks her bra, takes off her pantyhose. He's stiff with embarrassment. As she drops her skirt and bra on the floor he backs out of the room.

She locks the door on his hissing interchange with Mephers and stares at herself in her bathroom mirror. Everything in the room is marble or glass, cold smooth surfaces that reflect her back to herself. Her blondness, her fine bones, that set her apart from coarse, tainted Mara, all these are too cold to touch. She needs someone, anyone, to hold on to. She has to find Mara. Poor little Beebie, what will it do to her, to find out this mythical mother became a drug dealer and a whore and then cut her wrists open to get away from Grandfather?

Where in this great city can she find her sister? And find her before Grandfather drops his butterfly net over her and drags her to the hospital. He'll inject Mara full of drugs, she'll know nothing, remember nothing in such a state.

Harriet dresses fast, frantic to get to her sister before the police or hospital security guards find her. Not in an evening gown with deep cleavage, as Leigh Wilton demanded, but jeans, T-shirt. She stuffs a handful of bills into her pockets with her driver's license and flees the apartment.

43

Under a Gibbous Moon

FEED ME, feed me, feed me. A constant howl for sustenance that rose wherever they went, at the wall, in the crowds of homeless who slept on the beaches at night, even among well-dressed commuters jostling past them in the coffee shops in the morning. The clamor filled her brain, drove Verdi from her mind; she couldn't believe Mara heard nothing.

Her head had always been filled with music, ever since she was five and reproduced a whole record of children's songs that Grandma Minsky played for her and Harry. (Listen to her, Morris, Grandma called to Grandpa, working on accounts in the living room; the little one heard these only once and can sing them perfectly. Grandpa grunted, while Harry, furious with her for getting special attention, threw the record to the floor and jumped on it until it broke. After that, she could hardly hear speech unless it had something to do with song or her own voice, first children's songs, then already in high school small concert pieces, Grieg or Purcell, besides always getting the lead in school musicals, Harry once more scowling as she got fitted for costumes, whisked to rehearsals, bowed to applause. The time she starred as Maria in New Trier's *West Side Story*—their very first year in Highland Park when she beat out the local girls, whom the music director had worked with for years—her jealous twin poured ketchup on her costume, but even that couldn't keep the music from flooding her.)

Now all she could hear was feed me, cherish me, heal me, save me—as if her own thirst, that bottomless craving that not even a quart of whiskey could slake, were magnified a hundred thousand times.

Mara only laughed when Luisa complained. "You've got perfect pitch, it's why you can hear everything around you. All I have to do is hand out sandwiches and watch people be happy to have something to eat."

"But they're not happy." Luisa was hung over and querulous. "Free food doesn't stop them fighting—yours is bigger than mine, I wanted turkey not ham, I hate cheese or mayonnaise. Why can't they just be grateful for what they get?"

"And you," Mara retorted. "You were happy with what you got? A diva with an international reputation, but you fought with everyone just the same."

Luisa stalked off in dudgeon, as she did once or twice a day. The first time it happened Mara started after her to apologize, to beg her to come back, but Starr seized her arm as she darted down the street and pulled Mara to her side. Even though Mara couldn't interpret her grunts and glances as Luisa claimed to, Starr's touch on her arm made her think—Luisa has to sort this out for herself; she's not Grandfather, I don't have to placate her. And then, as Starr drew Mara to herself, kissed her, licked her broken stub of a tooth so that the throbbing in it eased, Mara thought, no, I don't have to placate him, either, I can just be me, Mara. Grandfather named me Mara because I was a bitter pill to him, but I don't have to be bitter to myself. And when Luisa returned some hours later, to where Mara lay with Starr in the tall grasses, Mara rose to kiss Luisa in turn, to wipe the trail of dried beer from her mouth, to lay her tenderly in the sand next to Starr.

Despite the days and nights in the open air, the shortage of food, showers in beach houses without soap or towels, so that she woke each morning with sand in her hair, Mara felt—not just happy, but strong, as if she could run the length of the city and not be winded. On nights when they had food to hand out to people she seemed able to walk, touch, calm screaming infants, feed a whole crowd without fatigue.

By day they roamed the streets and parks with thousands of other homeless Chicagoans, and at night they slept where they landed. Their second night in the open they had wandered into the northern suburbs, to the clean beach Luisa remembered from her high school years. Police roused them around two in the morning, smacked Mara hard enough to leave her with a black eye the next day, pushed the three women into the back of a squad car, drove them to the Chicago border and warned them never to return.

Luisa had screamed curses at them: do you have any idea who I am, you oafs? I grew up in this redneck suburb and became the greatest interpreter of Verdi your generation will ever hear, and tried to launch herself into "Sempre libera," her voice coming out in a hoarse parody of music. The young cop, his fair chin still free of hair, kicked Luisa in the kidneys as he dumped the trio over the city line.

The next day Luisa was bleeding and feverish. Mara wanted to get her antibiotics, but that meant seeing a doctor, who might lock them up. She tried to explain the problem to Starr, while Luisa lay green-faced and waxen in the big woman's arms. Mara began to weep with frustration as the black eyes stared unwinking at her. Her explanations became more difficult to understand, even to an English speaker, until, to Mara's futile fury, Starr began to chew a piece of bread. Mara was about to throw away all her cautions and phone for an ambulance when Starr took the mushy bread from her mouth and forced it down Luisa's throat. Luisa choked and gagged, but within half an hour the waxy greenness had faded from her face. By afternoon she seemed very much herself again—imperious, impervious, and longing for liquor.

"What did you feel?" Mara demanded. "Did Starr heal you? What was it like when you swallowed that bread?"

But Luisa had no recollection of Starr and the bread. She thought she had been chained to the ground, that a terrifying old woman had hovered over her, wanting to keep her bound for all eternity. "And then one of my fans, one of the common people in Italy who still love music so, came along with a bottle of beer, just when I thought I might die of thirst."

Mara gave it up: Luisa had been delirious. But if Starr could cure

Luisa's kidney injury, why not her alcoholism, too? When she put it to Starr, the dark woman only stared at her until Mara felt uncomfortable, as she had all those times as a child when Mephers asked her if it was really necessary to mind other people's business. And then Starr patted her hair, a signal that she wanted Mara to comb the sides out and wind them up again in their elaborate coils.

Around nightfall Starr liked to go to the wall, but they couldn't stay long: the cops were under orders to move them off, and threatened Mara and Starr with arrest if they lingered. Their favorite camping place at night was a little spit of land at the end of Montrose Harbor which had been planted with prairie grasses, but Luisa didn't always have the stamina to trek that far. For some reason the little promontory was usually deserted after dark, so that Luisa could have some relief from the clangor that beset her whenever they were in a crowd.

They reached the promontory tonight around sundown. Families with small children were starting to pack up for the day, while dopers and bikers began joining necking couples on the rocks that lined the harbor. Mara watched Luisa stomp off to the rocks. She would cadge a bottle and come back drunk in an hour.

Mara had no way of knowing if Starr hated Luisa's absences, or her drunkenness. When the diva was gone there was no one to explain the world to Starr—or Starr to the world—but the big woman never showed any impatience with the diva.

Mara sometimes wondered if she'd only imagined the episode with Luisa's bleeding, and Starr's piece of bread. She could hear Grandfather chewing her out for making up stories in the hopes of being the center of attention. He would dismiss Starr and Luisa with a snort as well: histrionics, ignore them and they'll behave in a civilized manner fast enough.

Mara laughed to herself, trying to picture Luisa and Starr in the Graham Street apartment, Harriet prim and flustered, Mephers furious but forced into silence. And Grandfather thoroughly humiliated once and for all, as had happened to Dr. Hanaper and Pastor Emerson the day they came to the wall with some Catholic priest who claimed to be an authority on miracles.

Tonight Mara took off her clothes, hiding them with her sleeping bag behind a rock: torn and dirty though they were, someone might easily steal them while she swam. The day before, the waves had been six feet high, crashing over the breakwaters and slamming against the sand. Tonight the water was as calm and gentle as a cradle. July had slipped into August. In a few more weeks the water would turn cold, but right now it was warm, caressing her naked body like silk.

Mara swam hard around the spit of land, then turned over and floated gently back toward her cache. Out on the lake she could see the lights of dozens of sailboats. Maybe Harriet was out there with a suitor.

Mara suddenly felt a pang of longing for her sister: beautiful Harriet, did I ruin your career? Will you ever speak to me again? She couldn't stay in the park with Starr forever. If she went to Harriet, would her sister welcome her back, or at least help her find a place to live and something to live on? Or would she slam the door on Mara, her fine-boned face as rigid as Grandfather's?

The waning moon hung pendulous above her, its belly distended like a pregnant woman's. The moon's face was sallow, and looked angry and crumbly with age. Mara suddenly felt alone in the water, despite the calls of parents and lovers from further down the shore. She turned onto her stomach again and swam as fast as she could to shore, running from the water to pick up her clothes, arriving breathless at their little campsite.

Luisa had returned, bringing with her Jacqui, Nanette, and LaBelle, a tepid bottle of muscat, and a bag of cold hamburgers. The four women were hunkered down near Starr, eating. When Mara stumbled up next to them they nodded to her, and handed her a burger, but no one spoke.

The night was filled with winking lights—cookout fires, cigarettes, bicycle lamps. A flashlight stuck prying fingers around the edge of the prairie grasses. At first Mara, filling herself with the glutinous lumps of meat, paid no attention, but as the light poked through the grass, she realized it was an organized search.

She clutched Starr's arm, choking on the burger. "Someone's hunting us."

300 · SARA PARETSKY

Jacqui and Nanette stopped their murmured talk and turned to watch. Suddenly, behind the lights, a hoarse voice shouted, "Starr, it's Hector. I'm here with men from the hospital, Starr! We want to put you in restraints again, feed you on drugs. We'll take you away with us, Starr, away from the sand and the streets. Come now, Starr, come with me if you want that."

44

On the Run

HARRIET HAD BEEN RUNNING since she left the apartment, running to her car, pushing on the steering wheel so hard her shoulders ached. Let Mara be at the wall. Let me find her before Grandfather. The chant moved through her head as she idled at lights, tears of impatience pricking her—why don't they change? A narrow miss at the corner of Michigan and Upper Wacker—furious honking, swollen-faced man giving her the finger, but she so bound in her terrors she didn't notice—swinging the car into the main drive at the Pleiades, forcing a smile for the doorman, who recognized her Acura and trotted over to open her door.

"You coming to pick up the gentlemen from headquarters for dinner, Ms. Stonds?"

With a great effort she slid her mask of calmness into place and smiled at him. "No, Dimitri, I'm not able to join them. I just need to go down to the garage, check on things there. Can I leave the car here for five minutes?"

Asking about his son, a junior at MIT, smiling but not hearing the reply, automatically slipping a five into his discreet hand. Then running again, up the drive into the lobby, her shoes sighing in the great Aubusson carpet, her smile a painful grimace as bellmen and concierge greeted her with the same deference Grandfather received at the hospital. We hear you're getting things cleaned up down there, Ms. Stonds, we'll be glad when the rooms fill up again.

Dancing with impatience in front of the garage elevator while a waiting guest stared stolidly ahead, finally too nervous to wait, taking the four flights of stairs down at a reckless gallop: numerous suits filed by employees stumbling and falling on these stairs, she should know to be careful, but she couldn't slow down.

As soon as she opened the stairwell door she heard screams spilling into the garage from the street. The night attendants, Nicolo and his two colleagues, were standing at the entrance. Harriet ran to join them, but couldn't move further than the mouth of the bay, the mass of people out front was so dense.

Nicolo started to explain that it wasn't possible to get cars out tonight, very sorry, madam, but you see we having trouble. Then his voice changed, became colder: Oh, you the lawyer. You know about this trouble, right?

Harriet ignored him, climbing onto a car bumper to see over the crowd. The police had bottled up all the miracle seekers against the curb. They were demanding IDs, and shining flashlights into faces. Men in riot gear blocked the stairwells, the streets, and the alleys that backed onto the hotel. Anyone who didn't have identification was being put into one of the paddy wagons at the west end of the street. Women screamed as mounted officers pushed them against the spikes at the far end of the wall.

Up the street Harriet could see Judith Ohana from the First Freedoms Forum. Ohana was trying to argue with the sergeant in charge. Harriet couldn't hear what Ohana was saying, but guessed the Triple-F lawyer was making the mistake of assuming a policeman leading a riot was interested in the First Amendment. Harriet sucked in her breath in horror as one of the patrolmen hit the civil liberties lawyer in the skull with his club. Judith Ohana collapsed to her knees. Two officers dragged her half-conscious body to the paddy wagon.

"Who ordered this? Oh, who ordered this?" Harriet cried. "The city said this afternoon they wouldn't harass any of the people down here!

Did—did Brian Cassidy or Mr. Palmetto start this? We have to do something. I need to stop them. They weren't supposed to do this."

Nicolo grabbed her as she tried to leave the garage. "No, missus, no doing nothing now. Maybe you starting all this, but you not stopping now. They only hit you—boom—like they just do the other lady lawyer. You not going out there."

Harriet demanded Brian Cassidy: was this his doing? Cassidy had returned from his stay in the hospital, but he was still hoarse from the lesions on his lungs, and seemed smaller: his ape arms had shrunk into his suit and he spent most of his shift huddled in his office. At the sight of the paddy wagons he had disappeared into the main body of the hotel. Nicolo's English disintegrated from the effort of trying to explain this.

Harriet, too distracted to pay attention to her own question, or his stumbling answer, interrupted him. "My sister. Mara, do you know her? She—she's often with Starr, she's tall, she shaved her head . . . did they . . . was she here tonight?"

"Your sister? That girl your sister, missus, and you treating her so bad? Why you want her now?"

"I need to tell her, find her, hide her, they want to put her in the hospital, shoot her full of drugs, Oh, please, just answer me, was she here when they started this?"

He looked at her suspiciously. "You lawyer, you make these spikes, one lady, poor *ingenua,* kills herself, now this! What you do to your sister now?"

The cords in Harriet's throat stood out. "Oh, what can I say to you—I have to find my sister before my grand— before the police do. Please help me. Where does she go at night, surely you know?"

Nicolo frowned at Harriet, trying to decide whether to trust her. At last he said, "Is okay, missus. Your sister here before, but is away when these polices come. They wait, the polices, until no television, then suddenly, boom, all come on horses, like you seeing."

"Do you know where she goes when she leaves here?" Harriet was gulping on her words, poised to take flight again, to continue her search.

The attendant shook his head. "The doctor, he knows, he coming

with men, oh ten minutes from now, I think they saying, the beach, they
go to the beach."

Ten minutes from now? Harriet was too frenzied to make sense of
Nicolo's depiction of time. She pressed her hands across her face, trying
to force herself into enough calm that she could think. The doctor. That
couldn't be Grandfather—he'd been in the apartment when she left. Dr.
Hanaper, maybe? He would always do just what Grandfather said. Whoever it was, the ten minutes from now lay behind them, the doctor had
been here already. And now was out looking for Starr.

Nicolo couldn't tell Harriet what beach. "The homeless ladies, very
many sleep by the lake in summertime, but is a big lake, missus."

Harriet turned from him and began running again, through the
garage, back up the stairs. The lobby was bizarrely quiet and serene, the
few guests moving like the blessed in heaven, impervious to the howls of
the damned at their feet.

In the drive she sprinted past Leigh Wilton, come to pick up the
Olympus president and Gian Palmetto for dinner. Harriet didn't recognize them until Wilton called her name, sharply, and demanded to know
where in hell she thought she was going.

"Leigh!" She was panting. "Do you know what's happening down
at the wall? Do you know the cops just hit Judith Ohana on the head?
Your stupid clients are up to their armpits in boiling water but you are
not going to blame this fiasco on me."

He stared slack-jawed as Harriet whirled around and ran on down
the drive, past the doorman's smiling "See you soon, Ms. Stonds," into
the car, trembling so violently she could hardly turn the key in the
ignition, so distraught she had trouble steering.

The beaches started at Oak Street, at the edge of the Gold Coast.
That was where the rich kids hung out, along with white suburbanites,
who called the cops in terror if a black Chicagoan showed up in their
little towns, but had no problem using the city's beaches for free.

Harriet, not knowing where to look or how to organize her search,
decided Mara wouldn't drag homeless women into this dense pack of
tourists. She drove to North Avenue, her skin quivering with anxiety as

she tried to find a place to park her little sports car, finally squeezing it between a couple of vans, not quite a parking space, bruising her thighs as she slid out the half-opened door.

Harriet stood by her car, feeling desperate as she studied the crowded park. Even at twilight joggers, Rollerbladers, bicyclists were thick on the cement paths, while the beach itself was covered with families and necking couples, solitary drinkers and rowdy parties. Dozens of volleyball nets stretched up the lakefront here; despite the fading light some people were still playing.

How could she ever find Mara in such a mob? She snaked a hand back into her car and fished a flashlight from the glove compartment. She began to jog along the beach, feet slipping in sand, shoes filling with sand, until she finally took her shoes and socks off and made her way barefoot. In the waning light she scanned the clumps of people, looking for Starr's gigantic pompadour, Mara's bald head. As the dark deepened she zigzagged along the beaches, shining her flashlight, eliciting indignant insults from couples sharing love or drugs, too frantic to notice what she saw or heard.

For a mile the beach was a thin corridor between lake and highway, but when she got to the outdoor theater at Fullerton Avenue, the sand disappeared. The shoreline turned jagged, with rocky outcroppings surrounding inlets and harbors, while the park spread away to the west in an expanse of grassland and trees.

Harriet sat down on a rock to put her shoes back on. She was gasping for breath, clutching her side as she staggered, rather than ran, from one dark clump to another. Night was now absolute. She had to use her flash to make sure she didn't trip over some person or rock. The batteries began to fail. She stumbled over discarded whiskey bottles and beach balls, until she tripped on an exposed tree root and fell heavily to the ground.

She lay sobbing. She was alone, with no one to turn to. She could hardly remember now why she had set out. She needed Mara, which was strange: she never needed Mara.

When Mara was small Harriet used to hear her crying sometimes in the night. She would tiptoe down the hall to the baby's room, never decorated for a child, always hung with dull crimson drapes, and pick up the little sister and hold her, feeling a strange comfort from the milky smell, the wet warmth against her, the baby howls subsiding as Mara fit herself around Harriet's skinny teenage body. One night she fell asleep in the chair holding the baby.

Mephers was shocked when she came on her in the morning: look at you, Harriet, that nightgown soiled. You should be ashamed to be sitting here with that diaper leaking over you: you'd think you hadn't learned any better than Beatrix or Mara here to keep yourself clean and sweet. The doctor will be very disappointed. We'll have to throw out this nightgown: I'll never be able to wash out this stain. What were you thinking of, anyway, to let this bad baby get you up in the night? If you start giving in to them when they cry, pretty soon they'll cry just to manipulate you.

After that, Harriet let the thin howling go on unanswered in the night. She would lie rigid in her bed, willing the noise to stop, thinking what a bad baby it was to be so demanding, not realizing until now, this moment lying here on the earth on the edge of Lake Michigan, that the wailing infant had been giving voice to Harriet's own sorrow. In leaving the baby to cry uncomforted, she had lost all comfort herself.

She fell asleep. When she awoke, it was after midnight. Her right cheek was sore, bruised from a rock she'd hit when she fell. She got to her feet, stiff from her long run and her nap on the hard ground, and walked slowly across the park. The moon overhead, cold and disapproving, showed her a handful of other bodies sleeping under tarps or bits of cardboard. She felt unbearably lonely and vulnerable, a target in the emptiness for anyone who might pass her with malice in mind.

A police car slowed on its way up the lake path and shone its light on her. She froze, remembering the scene at the hotel, the patrolman hitting Judith Ohana over the head.

As the men in the car studied her, Harriet tried to remember she was a Stonds, an important citizen by definition, as well as a member of the bar, but she was acutely aware of her dirt-stained clothes and uncombed hair. She had always taken for granted that the police were there to defend her, Harriet Stonds, to safeguard her person and her possessions. Although her training had taught her in theory that no one was guilty until proven so in court, until now she'd believed deep down that the police didn't arrest anyone if they didn't deserve it, and police brutality was only a cry criminals raised to try to deflect attention from their crimes. Tonight at the wall, she'd seen that anyone could be vulnerable. Trapped in the searchlight, she tried to forget an impassioned account by Mara of a policeman raping one of the women at Hagar's House.

The men switched off their lamp and drove on. Harriet released a tight-held breath and continued to pick her way across the park to the highway. With some difficulty she flagged down a cab: to her humiliation, the driver insisted on seeing her money before he would take her back to her car at North Avenue beach.

It wasn't until she was driving out of the park that she realized she couldn't return home tonight. Grandfather's disapproving rage, Mephers's hurt sulks, were more than she could face. She pulled over to the shoulder and counted the money she'd stuffed in her pocket. Fifty-three dollars. Could she even rent a hotel room on so little money? In her haste to leave home she hadn't thought of bringing credit or bank cards. She hadn't brought her mobile phone, either—she couldn't call motels, she'd have to drive from spot to spot hoping she could locate something cheap but safe.

She made a loop under the highway and headed south, into the heart of the city. She drove randomly through the downtown streets, looking for hotels, when she passed the massive complex of the Midwest Hospital. Perhaps Hector Tammuz was on call tonight. Grandfather's prize loser. On television they said he spent a lot of time with the women at the wall. Maybe he had found Mara and had her safe. Abruptly she turned into the parking lot, found her grandfather's space, and went into the building through the staff entrance.

The hospital was ghostly after hours with nothing but empty chairs and gleaming file cabinets in the corridors. The fear she'd felt in the lonely park returned, and she was absurdly pleased when she reached the emergency room and found nurses and orderlies gossiping under bright lights. She ducked into a bathroom and cleaned her face. There was something unnerving about the calm oval in the mirror. She had been in anguish all night, but her eyes remained a clear, remote blue. Except for a bruise on her right cheek from her fall, her face gave back no record of her troubles.

She walked out to the counter, her patina of authority so smooth that no one questioned her identity as Abraham Stonds's granddaughter, nor challenged her demand that they page Dr. Tammuz.

45

Supplicant Lawyer

He was floating in an underwater grotto without fins or a mask: he was not only able to breathe, but eat and drink, for he realized he was holding a cup of coffee in his right hand, from which he sipped now and then. Sea grasses swayed in the currents of the deeps, and fishes, as gold and red as poppies, glowed in their midst.

Little drops were falling like rain outside the grotto—drifting slowly down from the surface to the ocean bed. He gave a fish-style twist with his legs, and moved to the grotto entrance. Another drop drifted past and he plucked it from the water. It was a pearl, pink and ivory, and even this far from daylight glowing as if the sun shone on it.

He looked up. A woman was weeping on the water's surface. He couldn't tell who it was—his mother, or Jacqui. She wanted to dive down to him, but couldn't—the water that he moved in so easily was like glass to her. Her tears were turning to pearls as they cut through the glassy barrier, jewels for him to harvest.

The pearl in his palm began to grow, until it was the size of an ostrich egg. It cracked open, and Starr floated out. Her black hair came uncoiled in the water and streamed around her, reaching to her ankles. With one bronze arm she pushed it from her face. With the other, she drew Hector to her and kissed him briefly, sweetly, then she somersaulted and spun away.

He was left alone with the fishes, and the pearls, but he felt for once happy, and wholly at peace. Only briefly: a giant freighter was moving overhead, the vibrations of its engines shaking the grotto. He swam toward the surface, determined to move the ship away from his sanctuary.

His pager was vibrating against his thigh. He was in the residents' bunkroom at the hospital, without any notion of how he had arrived there. He remembered being at the beach, with the head of the hospital's security department. He had grabbed the man's bullhorn, and shouted a warning to Starr, and the man had turned on Hector in anger.

"That was pretty stupid, if you don't mind me saying so, Doc," the security chief said. "Dr. Hanaper warned me you might feel divided in your loyalties and I see what he meant: that kind of message will scare off these gals, and our job is to make them want to come to us for help."

Sweat leaked down Hector's neck into his shirt collar, making him shiver in the warm night air. His warning had been the impulse of a moment; he still didn't know how he came to shout it out. He thought he'd felt Starr's presence when they came to the prairie grasses, some special fizziness in the air that made his blood race—although in his current state he couldn't tell the difference between desire and its object, and didn't know if he imagined the tingling in his blood or not. Still, at that moment he envisioned Starr flinging him from her side, her flat black eyes reflecting back to him his own weaknesses—Hector, the bravest of all the Trojans, collapses once again; Luisa would pipe up, Starr doesn't want you near her, now or ever again. He grabbed the bullhorn from one of the guards and yelled through it.

As he strained to hear Luisa or Mara, or a grunt from Starr over the other voices in the park, he barely listened to the security chief's reproof. It seemed to Hector he heard a hasty thudding of many feet running inland.

"There are some benches near the water here," he said. "When they come here that's where they set up camp."

He was pleased with himself for thinking of so clever a lie. It would move the patrol north, toward the edge of the promontory, and allow

Starr—if she indeed had been there, indeed was running—to slip into the body of the park and find a hideout elsewhere. To his dismay, after a short discussion (whose side is this guy on, anyway, do we trust him? Hanaper warned . . . maybe he doesn't want . . .) the other three men fanned out along the spit of land.

Hector held his breath, not moving seaward with the posse. He was waiting for the eruption of sound and fury that would come when someone tried to put handcuffs on Starr's massive arms. In the end, though, the men returned only with a sleeping bag and a McDonald's sack containing two uneaten burgers.

The security chief said, "Looks like someone abandoned this in a hurry. Suggest anything to you, Doc?"

Under the powerful police lamps Hector recognized the soiled blue bag as Mara's, but he shook his head "no" in answer to the question. Mara wouldn't have abandoned her bedroll unless she had fled too hastily to stop for it. He must have shouted his warning in time.

Relief flooded him: the women had escaped. Starr would love him best now, she wouldn't fling him from her. The wave of joy washed past, and exhaustion pushed on him like a boulder. After a month without rest, his days and nights alternating between frantic searches for Starr and his time at the hospital, he didn't have strength to think or move. He tried to say something that might draw the security team further away from Starr, but collapsed midsentence onto the sand.

He wasn't aware of the patrolmen carrying him back to the car. He didn't hear the security director phone the hospital, with a command that a clerk start calling women's shelters all over the city to see if anyone fitting Starr's description had shown up tonight. He didn't hear the negative messages start to trickle in as they drove south: no one in the search party combing North Avenue had found her. No one at Foster. Negative from Rachel's Rest, Lucy's Place, Angela's House. Definitely not at Hagar's House, where Patsy Wanachs would have notified Dr. Stonds at once.

Hector didn't even stir when a call came in from Dr. Stonds and one of the guards tried to shake him awake to talk to the surgeon. The man had to tell Stonds that they might have come on Starr and Mara, and that Hector, shouting to them, could have scared them off. The surgeon was understandably furious, but Hector was oblivious to the scratchy ranting crackling through the car phone.

Finally, back at the hospital, two officers half carried, half dragged Hector to the residents' bunkroom. He was on call tonight, as on every Friday night since Hanaper had assigned him to the Orleans Street clinic. The patrolmen knew about Friday nights in the hospital—they placed just as much demand on the security staff as on the doctors. Fridays brought in people whose thin veneer of stamina snapped at the thought of a long weekend alone, they brought runaway children, disoriented tourists, attempted suicides, overworked business travelers breaking down after too much work and too little sleep. Their help was in the hands of this exhausted resident. Glad that their lives didn't depend on Hector, the men dusted their hands and returned to the ward room.

In the familiar bunkroom Hector's protective sleep lightened. When the emergency staff paged him at ten—for the third time—he finally rose to the surface of consciousness. This was a mercy, the clerks agreed, since the place was filling up faster than usual, with the shattered survivors of the violence at the hotel wall.

Millie Regier, the night charge nurse, who'd been stiff with Hector ever since their night with Starr and Luisa, made a point of telling him that Dr. Stonds wanted to speak to him as soon as possible. The surgeon was very very angry with Hector for driving away Starr and Mara tonight.

Hector, still half asleep, blinked at Millie without answering and went in to deal with a man who'd heard a private message from Michael Jordan during a car commercial, telling him his wife was a dangerous criminal and should be asphyxiated. When Hector finished with the man he turned to a South Dakota woman who'd been hit on the head at the Pleiades garage. After that he was listening, soothing, and dosing for the better part of two hours.

He had just returned to bed, and was drifting back into sleep, when Harriet paged him. Hector stuck his feet into his shoes and stumbled to the wall phone outside the bunkroom to answer the call. Millie Regier, still abrupt, told him that Dr. Stonds's granddaughter was waiting to see him. Clinic Room A.

Hector felt the familiar tightening across his groin: if Mara had come to the hospital, then Starr would be nearby. And if Mara was there, some busybody would already be on the phone to her grandfather. His hair was wild, but he couldn't waste time on grooming. He trotted down the hall to Clinic Room A, his shoelaces flapping, and stopped short at the sight of Harriet.

Before he could back away in confusion, Harriet sprang to her feet. "Dr. Tammuz? I'm Harriet Stonds. I'm sorry to barge in on you, I know what it's like when you're on call, but I need to find my sister. I hoped— I thought—"

She was clasping and unclasping her hands, but he didn't note these signs of distress: she was the lawyer who had caused all his ills, by pitting the Pleiades against him and his homeless women.

"If Dr. Stonds sent you, you're wasting your time," Hector said, not bothering to come all the way into the room.

"My grandfather?" Harriet was so sure he would be empathic that she didn't at first notice his coldness. "No, no, he doesn't know I'm here. I had to use my name—his name—otherwise they wouldn't have paged you for me, but don't you see—oh, you don't know us, you don't know him—he wants to lock Mara up, my little sister. I thought—you know where they are, don't you? They said on TV you often are with them."

"And you think I'll tell *you* what I wouldn't tell the hospital security staff or your grandfather? After what you've done to me, and to the women under my care?"

Harriet stared at him as he raged at her: the hotel's determined persecution first of Madeleine Carter, then of Starr, Luisa, and Harriet's own sister . . . the spikes on the wall, her church's refusal to let homeless women into Hagar's House if they were seen at the wall . . . the attitude that the needs of the wealthy counted for everything and that the poor existed only to prove by their suffering that the rich were powerful

. . . now, tonight, the worst excesses of all as the police attacked a group of defenseless women.

"You say I don't know your grandfather, Ms. Stonds, but believe me, I do. I feel his personality every day in this hospital. When he speaks, everyone must bow down and obey. Now I've done the unthinkable: I dared to say no when he said yes, and he threatened to have me beheaded. When that didn't cow me he sent you to coax me into obeying him. Well, I don't care if I never practice medicine again in my life, I won't do it."

"Oh, don't! I can't take it!" Harriet's tears covered her face like a layer of glass that would splinter at a wrong touch. "I've never stood up to him before tonight, and it's too hard. Everything's awful, my mother's death, he lied about it just like Mara always said, he's always been cold, he never loved me for what I was, only for what he wanted out of me. He drove—we drove—poor Beebie away, but I want her back, I want to find her—before he gets to her—and shuts her up."

By now she was heaving so violently that Hector could barely understand her. "They'll listen to him—I know how—the courts are—with mental fitness—I have to take her—take her someplace—safe."

Looking at her Hector saw, finally, not his mother, Lily, not the senior resident, Melissa, who'd chewed him out that afternoon, not even the cold Harriet who had frozen his bones over the phone the afternoon her sister ran away, but a woman in misery. He filled a paper cup with water at the sink and made her drink it.

"Try to calm down, Ms. Stonds, so we can talk this through together." You mustn't touch patients, but she was so desolate that he patted her shoulder.

"I ran up and down the beach looking for her, because the man at the garage said that's where she went, but I couldn't—couldn't—find her." She was swallowing her sobs heroically. "Do you know—know where she is, Dr. Tammuz?"

He shook his head and led her to a chair. When she'd calmed down enough to listen, Hector told her about the search the hospital had mounted at her grandfather's command.

"You know your sister better than anyone, Ms. Stonds. Do you have any idea where she'd flee? What friends she might run to?"

"I don't know her very well: she's thirteen years younger than me, and I've always been judging her, not knowing her." Harriet blew her nose. "She only has one friend that I know about, Cynthia Lowrie. But Cynthia lives with her father, he's a dreadful man, he beats her horribly. If Mara showed up there he'd send straight for the police."

"Rafe Lowrie? I've met him. No, I agree, not a place for your sister, let alone Starr and Luisa."

It felt strange to discuss Starr in such a remote way, without his usual yearning seizing hold of him. It was as if in warning her he had somehow lessened his need for her. The thought made him feel bereft, and he turned his head away as he tried to rekindle his desire.

"Where should I look next? I don't want to sit here, waiting to hear that she's been brought into the hospital. I wouldn't be able to get into the—the locked ward, she'll do like Beatrix, like our mother, find something sharp and dig a hole in her veins, she'll never submit to being locked away." Harriet started to shudder again.

Hector gave up his efforts to conjure Starr's image. "You should go home and get some sleep, Ms. Stonds. There's nothing anyone can do at one in the morning."

"Home?" she whispered, as if she'd never heard the word. Was home that immaculate apartment with its pale drapes and walls, its glass and marble surfaces, Grandfather and Mephers breathing out white puffs of dry ice? If she walked past them and climbed into her own chill white bed, she would be dead of frostbite by morning.

"I'd take you to my own apartment, but I'm on call tonight and we're terribly overworked." Hector's beeper had been vibrating almost without pause for the last ten minutes. "And even though I'm worried about your sister, and about Starr, I can't abandon the fragmented people showing up in the emergency room."

He draped his jacket over her shoulders, trying to still her shivering. "Maybe you could lie down in the women residents' bunkroom. In the morning we might try to talk to Cynthia Lowrie. Would your sister call her, even if she couldn't go to her?"

Harriet, grateful for the jacket, for the personal concern behind the jacket, began to relax. She was sleepy, she realized in astonishment, so sleepy she could hardly think now, even of Mara.

"Cynthia." Her voice aloud pulled her briefly from the edge of sleep. "Yes. Mara always calls Cynthia. Even from the park when she ran away. In the morning . . . Cynthia will be at church. There's going to be a special Saturday service because of Starr and Luisa and Mara. . . . Talk to her there."

Hector steered her down the hall, cracked open the door to the women's bunkroom, spotted a bed that hadn't been used tonight. He guided Harriet up the ladder, pulled a blanket over her, and returned to the emergency room, to Millie Regier's brusque efficiency, and a crowd of distressed women.

46

Heretics in Church

Aт тне Orleans Street Church, Cynthia Lowrie was helping prepare sandwiches for three hundred people. The parish was holding its special service of penitence and communion at the start of Rafe's Family Matters meeting and expected to be hungry and thirsty by its end. Cynthia, with Mrs. Ephers, Mrs. Thirkell, and a handful of other women, had been at work since six.

Rafe had awakened her at five and told her to get her lazy butt over to the church to help him get things ready. In fact, he spent the morning rehearsing his lecture for the hundredth time while Cynthia photocopied songs and inspirational sayings from Saint Paul (Adam was first formed, then Eve. . . . A man is the image and glory of God; but woman is the glory of man. . . . Women shall be saved in childbearing. . . . If a man does not provide for his relatives, and especially for his own family, he has disowned the faith and is worse than an unbeliever. . . .) and then went into the kitchen to work on the food.

Pastor Emerson had not been very supportive of Family Matters until his fateful outing at the wall with Dr. Hanaper and Monsignor Mulvaney. Rafe said it was typical: guys thought they could coexist with feminists like Sylvia Lenore until they were threatened personally, and then suddenly wanted not just to jump on the bandwagon, but lead the parade.

When one of the deacons repeated Rafe's remark, the pastor

laughed it off in public. A church was like a family, with children always telling on each other to Mom; he couldn't be seen responding to such third-party reports.

Privately he was angry. It was exhausting to run a church as big as Orleans Street, with its warring factions. Parish leaders like Sylvia and Rafe made his job harder by always attacking him instead of trying to help their followers accept compromise.

For instance, Sylvia was furious that the parish had voted to close the Friday mental health clinic for the homeless. She accused Emerson of being afraid of both women and the poor. But it wasn't that simple. When Sylvia persuaded the parish to provide sanctuary for Salvadoran refugees in the eighties, Emerson had backed her fully, despite negative pressure both within the church and from the State Department.

Sylvia refused to understand that the situation was totally different now. The parish was so badly divided over the issue of the homeless women that it might well split. Sylvia wouldn't acknowledge that, or give Emerson credit for keeping Hagar's House open over the virulent objections of Rafe and his camp.

Sylvia and her supporters also failed to see how dangerous the creature Starr was. Unlike the doctor and Mrs. Ephers, the pastor didn't blame Mara Stonds for the problems in the parish and the city. He had baptized Mara, and presided over her confirmation; she had always been a turbulent, passionate girl, not easy to work with like her beautiful older sister, but needing more outlet for her energies than he suspected she found in the Graham Street apartment. It didn't surprise Emerson that Mara attached herself to Starr; Mara was the kind of intense person who would be an easy target for a charismatic charlatan.

And the public should be fully aware that Starr was a dangerous cult leader. Whether Starr was a kind of genuine medium, speaking in grunts that only Luisa Montcrief could interpret, or whether she was a charlatan cynically playing with the emotions of women like Mara, Emerson didn't care. The point was that Starr threatened the stability of his parish, of the city—really, of all human relationships.

Emerson realized this the day he encountered Starr at the wall. Her mocking smile, her voluptuary's body, didn't arouse him the way they did both Dr. Hanaper and the monsignor. Starr's wantonness seemed to Emerson more dangerous than mere sexuality: in her face he read a delight in overthrowing—everything. Emerson thought she took a malicious pleasure in Hanaper's and Monsignor Mulvaney's discomfort, that she laughed as they lost self-control. Emerson had a sudden vision, through her eyes, of people all over the world casting off authority. The anarchy she invited would destroy property, families, churches, all the deepest structures of civilization.

He came back to his church determined to restore the faith once delivered to the saints, with a strong home, a strong family as a bastion of stability. He couldn't get Sylvia Lenore to see that didn't mean he shared Rafe's vision of the historically sanctioned patriarchy. Sometimes authority is necessary for stability, but Sylvia wouldn't agree.

On the other side of the aisle, Rafe's faction was almost crowing in public: Before last Sunday's sermon, fewer than twenty men—including Rafe's own son Jared, under duress—had signed up for Rafe's seminar. By the end of the week, with the promise of sex and sin from the pulpit, with the chance to exchange titillating stories over sandwiches, almost two hundred people had decided to attend. Even Dr. Stonds had decided to attend, at least the communion part of the service, with his housekeeper and granddaughter, Harriet. His chin thrust out, he told Emerson he was not going to have the community think they could embarrass him into skulking at home.

Now Cynthia, her back aching, spread mayonnaise on the six-hundredth piece of bread while Mrs. Ephers laid on ham or turkey in alternating slices, Mrs. Thirkell added a piece of lettuce, and Patsy Wanachs cut it in half before putting it on one of the trays.

Of course, the church's janitorial staff was doing the actual setup for Rafe's meeting in the big assembly hall—moving chairs into the concentric quarter-circles Rafe specified, the podium in the middle, testing the PA system, organizing refreshment tables in the rear—but the women's work for such a large gathering was not physically easy.

Once the sandwiches were finished, the women set out hundreds of plates, clean forks, thirty dozen pottery cups, and filled the great coffee urns with water. Then they brought out silver trays of communion glasses, and carried them into the chancel with several gallon jugs of grape juice. A couple of the homeless women, Nicole and Caroline, drifted along to help. The shelter was closed during the day, but no one could turn them away from a worship service.

Cynthia thought she heard voices in the organ loft as they started filling the glasses. She squinted down the length of the nave, wondering if someone from the choir was there early, but couldn't see anyone.

Back in the kitchen fragments of Rafe's talk wafted in from the big assembly room. He had been reciting it to Cynthia all week at home, enraptured at the thought of a whole church listening to him; now he was doing it again with Jared an unwilling audience, ostensibly to test the sound system: The millennium is at hand, but what have we really accomplished in two thousand years? . . . The loss of respect for the family, and the father as its real head. . . . Women in the New Testament were devout, and respectful of male authority. . . . When the Puritans came to America . . . apostolic form of government . . . the city on a hill . . . abomination upon abomination. . . . Now, women gathering around a broken-down wall . . . symptomatic of end to . . . men could learn something from the feminists: assertiveness training . . . doormats were made to be walked on . . . Christ will judge us on how we look after our families . . . abrogated responsibility to the feminists . . .

Cynthia's head was pounding from the racket—Rafe, the snorts and glugs of the coffeemakers, Mrs. Ephers whispering in her ear. Every now and then the housekeeper would dig a bony hand into Cynthia's shoulder and breathe new imprecations against Mara as the root of all the evils the Stonds family was undergoing—perhaps of all the evils Rafe was claiming had befallen America since the New England theocracies were overturned for good in the 1820s.

"You thought Mara was so special," Mrs. Ephers hissed, "but you see different now, don't you?"

Muttering that she'd forgotten something, Cynthia went back through the vestry into the apse. Inside the doorway she stopped in terror: burglars had broken in and were looting the chancel. No, not burglars, women from Hagar's House. Where they shouldn't be. Her knees still shaking from her foolish fright, Cynthia tried to march in on them authoritatively. Her squeaky reprimand died in her throat. Mara Stonds. That horrible woman Starr, her breasts swaying as she bent over one of the grape juice jugs.

"Cynthia!" Mara caught sight of her. "We're just drinking some of the leftover grape juice. We watched you filling the glasses and saw you didn't use it all up. Everyone's thirsty. Don't worry, we won't get stuff dirty. What's going on?"

"Mara." Cynthia couldn't get her voice to rise above a dreamlike squawk. "Mara, you can't stay here. There's going to be a church service in an hour. Communion and everything."

"We'll be quiet," Mara said, looking at Luisa, who didn't stay quiet anywhere for long, and was querulous now because she'd been hoping the jugs contained wine. "We're seeking sanctuary here, like those Salvadoran refugees. I don't think the cops can haul us right out of the church, can they? Anyway, just to be on the safe side, I called the television stations. They'll probably be here in time to cover the service. What's it about?"

"You, you dummy," Cynthia squeaked. "We're being penitential because we produced a loser like you. And Daddy's Family Matters seminar will start right after, so get out of here before you get me in trouble one more time. And take *her* with you."

Starr stopped her exploration of the chancel: fingering the embroidered crosses on the covering to the stone communion table, rubbing the four-foot-high gold candlesticks, which she lifted as though they were cardboard, inspecting the great Bible on its massive lectern.

Starr walked over to Cynthia and tilted her chin up. When Cynthia turned red and backed away, Starr laughed, a low, mocking hoot. An echoing laugh behind her made Cynthia whirl around: that black homeless woman, whatever her name was, was sitting in the front pew with her white sidekick, drinking from another one of the half-empty jugs. The two of them seemed to think Cynthia was some kind of joke.

"Get out right now, or I'll go call Daddy!" Cynthia screamed.

Mara tried to put an arm around her friend, but Cynthia wrenched herself free. "I mean it, Mara Stonds."

"Okay, okay, calm down. We'll get out of the chancel before the service starts. If Rafe sees us, we'll tell him you tried everything to get rid of us, even bleach, but the stain was too big. No, no, just teasing, sorry. We won't let on you laid eyes on us."

As Cynthia watched, Mara conferred with Luisa, who was sulky but finally seemed to agree with her. Luisa pulled Starr's head down near her own, while Mara went down the shallow steps to Jacqui and Nanette and talked to them. In a moment all five women got up and trooped toward the back of the church. A sixth figure, LaBelle, who'd hovered in the shadows around the middle of the pews, joined them.

"What are you doing?" Cynthia cried as they made their way not to the exit, but to the north side of the narthex, where stairs led to the choir loft.

Mara's voice, muffled by the stairwell, bounced around the empty nave. "Don't worry about us. We'll be in the galleries and no one will know we're there. If Don Sandstrom shows up from Channel 13, tell him where we are, okay?"

Mrs. Ephers found Cynthia a few minutes later, standing at the top of the chancel steps, her fingers in her mouth. If it was true that Rafe Lowrie beat her, he had provocation, the housekeeper thought: the stupid girl looked like a sheep. Typical of Mara to take up with her.

"Cynthia! What are you doing mooning around like this when there are a million things to do? Your father wants to see you—he doesn't like the way you've pinned up his slogans. And what are these grape juice jugs doing on the front pews? Have you been sitting here drinking out of the communion bottles while Patsy Wanachs and I were slaving out back?"

"No, ma'am," Cynthia muttered. She looked up to the right, to the north gallery, where Starr's horns of hair were faintly visible, then followed the housekeeper back into the refectory.

47

Grapes into Wine

"GOD ORDERED EZEKIEL to put a mark on those few who were horrified by the abominations they were witnessing: the righteous who hated the women wailing at the north gate of the temple for their pagan god Dumuzi and his consort Ishtar, those who abhorred the harlot and her filthy acts. Ezekiel searched out that handful who despised the pornography and blasphemy around them, and he put on them the mark of salvation. Only those who bore that mark were spared. The angel of the Lord went through Jerusalem, that great city, and smote all who were without the sign of salvation, from the oldest grandfather to the newest born daughter."

Pastor Emerson paused to survey the congregation. They were listening intently: good, not like earlier, during the long dull litany Rafe had insisted on writing and leading. While Rafe's hoarse bullying voice recited his neighbors' sins, Emerson had noticed people leafing through their hymnals, fiddling with things in their purses, and welcoming the stir caused by Harriet Stonds's late arrival with the young Jewish doctor.

Everyone had seen that Harriet wasn't with Mrs. Ephers and Dr. Stonds at the start of the service. The doctor came in, alone, during the prelude. He looked more forbidding than usual when he joined Mrs. Ephers in the pew at the front of the church, so much so that no one felt like approaching him to ask about Harriet.

Perhaps she had to work on Saturday, neighbor whispered to neighbor. After all, the riot at the wall last night had been front-page news; she was the hotel's lawyer, who knew what fresh trouble those monstrous women had caused.

No, no, Mrs. Thirkell said: I asked Hilda Ephers while we were making sandwiches if Harriet was coming, and she said Harriet was behaving abominably, had started to turn on the doctor just like her mother and her sister. You should have heard what she said to Hilda last night . . . yes and then slammed out of the apartment, leaving Hilda to hang up her clothes, as if she wasn't eighty years old and recovering from a heart attack.

A louder murmur went up when Harriet actually arrived, halfway through Rafe's litany. She was pale but tidy in a blue cotton dress—she'd watched Grandfather leave the apartment before going up to bathe and change, spending as little time as possible in her cold marble bathroom.

A thin dark man was at her side. The young doctor, Patsy Wanachs spread the news along the opposite aisle, that Jewish doctor who encouraged the homeless women to riot at the wall. The ensuing whisper rose to such a buzz that people at the front of the church turned to stare at Harriet and her escort. Even Mrs. Ephers heard the comments and turned to look. Mrs. Thirkell was close enough to see the veins in the old woman's cheeks burn red at the sight of Harriet. The housekeeper looked away quickly and began to read loudly in unison with Rafe: We have forgotten the Fifth Commandment. Our children no longer honor us as parents because we have not been strong enough to make them respect us.

Cynthia, squashed between Jared and Mrs. Thirkell, only dared look when her brother did. If Rafe, moving from the Fifth to the Sixth Commandment, saw she wasn't listening to him . . .

Harriet spotted Cynthia Lowrie and pointed her out to Hector, which made Cynthia quickly face front again. Others noticed that Harriet was not taking part in the service at all: a typical Stonds, too snotty for peons like them. If she wasn't going to read the prayers, why had she even bothered to show up?

Rafe, annoyed at the loss of attention, called the congregation to order in his loud hoarse voice. "We're committing fresh sins while we're asking God to forgive old ones."

Pastor Emerson noticed with satisfaction that this was too unctuous even for Mrs. Thirkell, while Sylvia Lenore, in the front pew the Lenore family had occupied since her great-grandfather endowed the church in 1893, gave pantomimed nausea. The two women sitting with her snickered.

Waiting now to be sure he had everyone's attention, Emerson moved to the peroration of his sermon. "Who among you here, my brothers and sisters, can step forward to receive Ezekiel's mark of salvation? Who here has not been tempted by rumors of miracles into praying at that wall? The women who tempt the weak into worshiping there are the same harlots, practicing the same abominations that Ezekiel saw a thousand years before the birth of Christ. They are committing the same evils that John foresaw in his Revelation in the first century. Harlots and mothers of harlots. Daughters of harlots. Like the poor, they are always with us. Turn your back on them. More than that, eradicate them from our midst, so that we may be found worthy of that holy city, the New Jerusalem, adorned in purity as a bride for her bridegroom. Amen."

A buzz of approval drifted up to Emerson as the choir began an anthem. He was a good, really an inspired preacher, but his sermons often didn't wholly please the more fundamentalist members of the congregation. Today, though, he had given them exactly the kind of message they preferred: strongly grounded in the Bible, condemnatory of outside sinners, congratulatory to their own righteousness. As the preparatory words for the communion part of the service began, they pulled out billfolds with more alacrity than usual.

Mrs. Ephers, Rafe, and the other deacons went to the chancel. After Pastor Emerson pronounced the words of commemoration over the bread, the deacons carried it to the congregation. When they had offered bread to everyone, they returned to the chancel to serve each other, and finally, last of all—for the last shall be first—the pastor. Emerson next spoke the commemorative words over the grape juice. The deacons took the trays of little glasses and again began serving the congregation.

Dr. Stonds drank, made a startled face and sniffed the empty glass. A ripple moved through the rows as each person swallowed. It was wine. Not juice, but wine. Whose idea was this, and on such a day, to insult them by substituting wine for the pure unfermented juice of the grape? Sylvia Lenore? Was that why she'd come to a service she disapproved of? The Jewish doctor? Had he put Harriet under his thrall and persuaded her to sacrilege?

By the time the pastor and the deacons drank, the noise in the congregation had become the titillated hum of hornets. Emerson was aware of the uproar, but not until he drank—last of anyone in the church—did he understand the cause.

"Who did this?" the pastor angrily demanded of his deacons.

"Cynthia Lowrie was up here with the jugs when I came out to look for her right before the service," Mrs. Ephers announced.

No one in the congregation could hear what was said in the chancel, but they all saw Rafe's face turn red. He seemed to swell like a balloon, Hector thought, wondering why the congregation was so upset. Don't Christians use wine at their communion services? he whispered to Harriet. She tried to explain that some Protestant denominations, like this one, were governed by teetotalers, but Hector couldn't hear her over the noise.

Rafe went to the microphone in the middle of the chancel. "Cynthia Jane Lowrie, come forward."

The angry buzz died down as people craned their necks to watch. Cynthia didn't move.

"Cynthia Jane Lowrie, come forward to explain yourself," Rafe repeated.

Jared stood and yanked his sister out of the pew. He trampled on the feet of Mrs. Thirkell and Mr. Stith, who were sitting by the aisle. Some in the church, like Sylvia Lenore and her friends, stirred uneasily, but no one moved to help Cynthia. Jared shoved her up the walkway; when she tried to hold on to a pew back for support, the brother dragged her bodily up the shallow steps to the chancel.

"Cynthia Lowrie," Rafe said into the microphone when she reached his side. "What did you do to the communion juice?"

Those close to the front could see the pleasure shining below the fierceness of Rafe's voice. The noise in the pews died away as people leaned forward to watch.

"Nothing," Cynthia whispered, her answer inaudible to the rest of the congregation.

"Don't lie to me, not in this house of worship under the eyes of Almighty God, Cynthia Jane. Mrs. Ephers said just now that she found you alone in church with the communion jugs. What did you put into them? Tell us the truth."

"I didn't," she wailed as Rafe stuck the microphone under her nose. "I came in here and found Mara Stonds with that woman. They were drinking out of the jugs and I made them leave, I never thought they were doing something to the grape juice."

"Mara!" Mrs. Ephers hissed behind Cynthia. "You made her leave? I was standing right next to you and you didn't tell me she was in the church? What was going through your mind, or does nothing ever go through that tapioca pudding you have between your ears?"

Cynthia started to cry. Her gulping sobs were magnified by the PA system. Mr. Stith and Mrs. Thirkell watched greedily.

Harriet had heard Mrs. Ephers say those words a hundred times, no, more like a thousand—every time Mara did something that was too impulsive for the tomblike calm at Graham Street. For the first time Harriet seemed to feel them, the blow to the heart that lay in the scornful words, as harsh as the blow to the face that would follow. She was on her feet, pushing past Hector into the aisle, knowing the second before the microphone amplified the smack of palm on flesh that Mrs. Ephers would slap Cynthia.

"Don't start sniveling to me, young lady." *Thwack.* "Where did she go?"

"You heard her, girl," Rafe put in. "What were they doing, trying to put on a black mass? Where are they?"

Harriet, with Hector on her heels, reached the chancel steps as

Rafe's fist was swinging reflexively toward his daughter's face. Harriet tried to grab his arm, and ended up taking the blow herself. Hector caught her as she staggered under the impact.

"They're up there, they're up there," Cynthia wailed, pointing at the gallery. "Don't hit me, Daddy."

Harriet and Hector, Rafe and Mrs. Ephers, the pastor, the whole congregation, twisted their necks, but could see nothing in the upper reaches of the nave. There was a brief silence—the electric quiet between the fork of lightning and the roaring sheet metal of thunder—and then Jared led a surge of men down the aisle to the rear. Their feet pounded up the stairs, along the stone floor of the gallery, a pack of elephant-sized hounds: the cries, the yelps of gladness as they found their prey and dragged it with them into the body of the church.

Harriet gripped Hector's hand so tightly that she left bruises on his palm. From the top of the chancel stairs she could see Mara wrapped tight in Jared's arms, Starr and Luisa behind them with three other homeless women whom she recognized from her visits to the wall.

Harriet longed to go to her sister, but the crowd between them was as impenetrable as a sea of boulders. "Oh, Mara, oh, Beebie."

The mike picked up the whispered words and carried them beneath the mob's roar to Mara. She saw Harriet's white strained face at the top of the stairs, heard her involuntary cry, smiled: Harriet didn't hate her, after all.

As soon as Rafe called Cynthia to him Mara knew they would be betrayed: Cynthia was too cowed, not so much by her nineteen years with him, as by her return to him after her brief night of freedom.

Mara whispered to Jacqui that they should leave: there was only one way out of the gallery, down the stairs past the choir loft, but they could escape now, before Cynthia pointed them out; they'd have a head start, they might be able to run somewhere. But where? Jacqui whispered back: they were rabbits in an open field surrounded by hunters. And then the hounds were on them, they were seized, shamefully without landing as much as a kick on men who grabbed them, hit them, pinched their breasts as they wrapped thick arms about them. Even Starr seemed powerless against that pack.

The men surged up the chancel steps with their bundles and stood panting in front of the pastor. In the congregation people climbed up on the pews to have a better view. So this was that creature. Mrs. Thirkell turned to comment to Mr. Stith, sitting on her left, and withdrew from him in disgust: his face glowed with avidity. He was leaning forward to stare more closely at Starr; a thin thread of drool bubbled from the corner of his mouth.

Patsy Wanachs, sitting behind Mrs. Thirkell, tapped her on the shoulder: Look—those are some of the women we put up in the shelter. Mrs. Thirkell, turning around, glad to escape the sight of Mr. Stith: It just goes to show. Sylvia Lenore will be eating her words now. Give them an inch and they take total advantage. I never thought that shelter was a good idea.

Sylvia was conferring worriedly with her own friends: This is looking really bad; we should try to stop this, but—stupid to call the cops to come to a church service—go to the front, try to reason with people? Shut off the sound system?

Rafe tried to make the congregation attend to him. "We just heard a condemnation of the harlots and daughters of harlots who've defiled our city. Here they stand in front of us. What shall we do with them?" His hoarse voice made no impression on the uproar in the pews.

Pastor Emerson grabbed the mike. "You women have desecrated the House of God. What do you have to say for yourselves?"

His voice thundered through the congregation. As his parishioners grew quiet he repeated the question. Luisa Montcrief slipped from her captor's slackened clasp and moved to the microphone. To the fury of everyone in the chancel she began to sing.

48

Diva in Peril

Luisa wondered why they were in a church. Had Mara engaged her to sing at communion without telling her? Was that what she and Jacqui were whispering about up in the gallery? Then the audience came to fetch her, wondering where she was, but no need to hold her so roughly.

Well, if it was a church service, they no doubt wanted a religious aria. They were an ignorant rude bunch, probably only able to recognize Schubert's cloying, overperformed "Ave Maria." She listened for a pitch in her head, and began to sing.

To her dismay, instead of the sweet B-flat of the Schubert, she produced Verdi's somber E-flat. In her mind she heard the urgent violins produce the minor chord. Against her will, against all her efforts to banish the aria from her mind, she was singing Desdemona's "Ave Maria" from the last act of *Otello*.

And then the angry tenor was standing over her, his face swollen, as it had been in her dreams since that dreadful night at the Met. You bitch, shut up. This is a church, not a carnival.

She shut her eyes and let her voice rise to the high A. Yes, she had come down on the note, they were wrong, those fools who said she was a spent force.

Now that red-faced cretin was shouting over the music, not trying to sing, not even saying the lines right, speaking English, not Italian.

"*Prostituta,*" yes, he was calling her a whore, telling her to be quiet. Idiot, didn't he know that came in previous scene? And then his hands were around her throat again and he was lifting her by her neck, her voice, her voice, he would destroy it forever. A babble from the chorus, they were trying to stop him. Her maid was screaming for help, but Luisa was falling down a hole that had no end. She was cold, colder even than Desdemona's chastity: perhaps she, too, would be gathered into heaven.

49

Mother of Harlots

RAFE'S RAGE WAS EXTREME. He was sick and tired of god-damn women totally out of control, snotty libbers like that frozen bitch Harriet Stonds taking jobs that men ought to be doing, his wife walking out on him, humiliating him, his daughter sneaking around behind his back, and now this—this field-bitch, preening herself in front of the congregation, smirking when he told her to shut up in church, closing her eyes on him, singing louder, until he had no choice, she forced him to act to preserve the sanctity of the sanctuary.

He wasn't trying to hurt her, just to make her behave. It was Harriet Stonds and that Jewish doctor grabbing his arm who did the damage. Rafe shoved them aside and flung Luisa' away from the microphone.

Her head struck the corner of the stone communion table and she fell backward, sprawling across the chancel steps. Her neck flopped to one side, like a sparrow that has broken itself against a plate glass window.

Mara was screaming. "You killed her, you killed her."

Rafe wanted to take a swipe at Mara, too: couldn't Abraham Stonds control his damned granddaughter, not let her howl like a fucking ban-shee in front of God and everyone?

From his front-row pew, Dr. Stonds observed Mara with distaste. He had forgotten how ugly she was, and now, with her head shaved, her clothes filthy—the contrast between her and Harriet, so cool and clean nearby, had never been greater, only now Harriet was turning on him, too, flaunting herself in front of the congregation with that useless resident of Hanaper's.

And now the young man was kneeling over Luisa Montcrief. Clumsy oaf, shouldn't be allowed to touch someone with a broken neck, although Stonds thought she probably was dead, judging from the strange angle at which she lay. Harry Minsky was lucky, really, his sister off his hands, even if it was a tragedy, well, a scandal, Luisa dying in church. Rafe Lowrie, no sympathy to waste there, Stonds would have to call it murder if the police asked him. Still, he was the best neurosurgeon in the city, perhaps in North America, maybe young Vitibsky at Stanford could give him a run for his money; he'd better stop young Tammuz from touching Luisa, see if the famous hands of Abraham Stonds could do anything for her.

The congregation surged forward with him as Dr. Stonds made his way up the chancel steps. No one noticed the Channel 13 crew come in through the great entrance doors at the back. So intent was everyone on the drama in the chancel that the hot lights, the cameras, and Don Sandstrom with his ubiquitous mike climbing up to the gallery to get a good angle on a great story (mayhem in a rich city church unfolding live for you on your television screen) didn't exist behind them.

Jacqui and Nanette broke free from their captors and ran to Luisa's side, chafing her hands, trying to feel her pulse. Harriet tried to go to Mara, but found herself unable to move or even think of what to do next.

Rafe hovered over Luisa, wondering if he should help her to her feet. There wasn't anything wrong with her, there couldn't be, she was just playacting, as women liked to do, all those times his wife or Cynthia had howled the rafters down pretending they were hurt when there wasn't anything the matter. He leaned down to pat her on the back and tell her what he always said to his daughter: sit up, stop making yourself important—I'll get you some water; you go to bed for a while.

"Don't touch her again," Hector snapped, shoving Rafe away. "You have hurt her very badly. Harriet! Find a phone and call the police, call an ambulance."

His voice, sharp, authoritative, doctor to staff, jolted Harriet into motion. Phone. Leave the church through the vestry, no way to fight through the crowded nave. She'd find a phone in the offices back there.

"And you," Hector said to the youth who'd been Luisa's captor, "see that Lowrie doesn't leave the church before the police get here."

Emerson was sputtering at Hector, demanding to know what right he had to give orders in such a place. Hector ignored him, and knelt next to Luisa on the chancel steps.

In a gentler voice Hector also told Jacqui and Nanette not to touch Luisa. "If her neck is broken we don't want to move her: let's wait for an ambulance crew."

Dr. Stonds joined Hector on the stairs. "Young man, I doubt you know anything more about head and neck injuries than you do about mental disorders. Move to one side."

To his chagrin Hector found himself instinctively giving way to the neurosurgeon. Stonds took Hector's place next to Luisa and laid two fingers on her throat. As he'd thought: no pulse.

The accident was still so new that everyone around Stonds was jabbering, demanding information. Even his younger granddaughter had edged closer to him—to Luisa—and inquired, not of her grandfather, an authority on the brain and spinal cord, but of the insolent young doctor: Is she dead? Mara asked timidly.

The question echoed by Sylvia Lenore, by Patsy Wanachs and Mrs. Thirkell, by a dozen others who were pushing in on Stonds and Luisa. Dr. Stonds angrily ordered them back: he was not having disorder in his operating sphere. Mrs. Ephers tried to enforce his command, but no one heeded her.

Sex and death, Starr's body, Luisa's broken neck, a heady combination. Tom Caynard is going to be sorry he decided not to come, Jared said to his buddies, forgetting that he himself had tried to avoid the meeting.

Above them Don Sandstrom greedily put it on tape, irritated with his cameraman for not being able to get a clear shot of Luisa through the crowd. But now what—oh, this was good, very good, Starr was coming into the foreground of the picture. Tight on her, he told his cameraman: she's the center of the story.

Starr grabbed Dr. Stonds's shoulders and shoved him out of the way. "Dr. Tammuz, kindly remember—" he started to say, and then saw her face and fell silent.

Starr's expression was so fierce that Jared and his friends stopped their excited jokes. The cameraman flinched at the sight and moved the lens away. The Bulls T-shirt, torn by the men as they dragged her from the gallery, opened to show her breasts as she bent over Luisa. There was nothing erotic about them, Hector realized. They seemed instead to be boulders that might grind him to dust; he felt himself choking under their weight.

Starr scooped up the diva as easily as if she were a kitten and laid her on the communion table. Hector tried to stop her: you mustn't move someone with a broken neck. Pastor Emerson blurted out a rebuke for using the Lord's table.

Starr elbowed both men out of her way. She ran long fingers around Luisa's neck and head, grunting softly. Starr leaned over Luisa and kissed her, deeply, on the mouth, and then the forehead. The diva stretched like a baby waking from a nap and opened her eyes.

Those nearest heard Luisa laugh and say, "Starr. You didn't forget me after all."

Jacqui clutched Nanette. "Praise Jesus, oh, praise Him, she's speaking."

Rafe turned scornfully to Hector. "See: she's not dead after all, you damned busybody.".

Starr turned to stare at him. Rafe tried to stare back, but the reflection in those flat black eyes was too appalling. He saw himself, not very big, trying always to make himself bigger by forcing everyone else to be small. He tried to blink and look away and found himself gasping for air. He wanted to cry for help, but his voice, his instrument of power in the cattle futures pit, had disappeared. Cynthia! Jared! Why didn't they come to help him? Or that Jewish doctor, so sympathetic over the stupid homeless women . . . Dr. Stonds, couldn't the high-and-mighty Dr.

Stonds notice a man in genuine need? He'd come fast enough when that stupid cunt, mocking Rafe's service, pretended to be hurt. Damned arrogant bastard.

But Luisa's recovery had unsettled Dr. Stonds. He'd been sure she was dead, no pulse, that angle of the head. He couldn't be losing his judgment, not on something so basic. He looked at his hands. They could not have lied to him. It must have been Mara; the brat had staged the whole performance just to make a fool of him in public.

Anger swelled within him, amplified by the mounting roar from the congregation. They were watching him, mocking him. It was Mara, and that creature she'd picked up, that Starr. She'd even turned his sweet Harriet on him, the things Harriet had said to him last night, she never would turn on him or her own, only under the influence of that damned goblin, that changeling. He'd show Mara who was boss, march her out of the church, into a straitjacket.

Everyone in church was on their feet now, trying to see what was happening. Those in front saw Abraham Stonds reach for his granddaughter, pin her arms behind her. One man called to his neighbors to help out the doctor: A bunch of old women and preachers can't handle that Starr by themselves—feeling her body in his own hands, blood pounding in his temples, around him faces glowing with the same desire, pushing into the aisles: yes, let's help out the doctor.

Those in the back of the nave could only see the shadows that the altar candles cast on the back wall. In the shadow play Starr seemed to be a great horned beast, a wild cow. A witch. Kissing a woman in church . . . Mother of harlots . . . Pastor Emerson said eradicate . . . In the Bible . . . suffer a witch . . .

They poured into the side aisles. A few timid hands tried to hold them back, but were knocked away. If you side with witches you are a witch, one youth shouted.

The tide roared up the chancel stairs. Pastor Emerson tried to restrain them but was brushed aside, a piece of driftwood in a raging sea. A dozen hands grabbed the great gold candlesticks and heaved them at Starr. Mara broke away from Grandfather. She took Starr's arm and tried to drag her to safety, but frenzied fingers tore her from Starr's side, threw her and Jacqui and Luisa to the floor. Manic fists punched Hector in the eyes and mouth, shoving him away from Starr.

The cameraman caught what he could, but bad light, bad angle, could see the backs of the mob on top of Starr but not what they were doing.

Oh, yes, again, smash again, the bone turns to pulp beneath the skin, yes, she's a slug, a reptile. Crush, smash, destroy her. On the wall the shadows danced. The candlesticks were giant maces rising and falling until the cow's head collapsed and disappeared onto the floor.

50

Murder in the Cathedral

Mara lay in Harriet's bed, her head on her sister's lap. After weeks of sleeping on the ground it felt strange to be in a bed again, especially her sister's, in the room where she had often sneaked uninvited. With her eyes shut Mara tried to believe she was still on the beach and that it was Starr's head, with hair wilder than her own had ever been, above her. Her lips twisted in a painful smile at herself: for nineteen years she had tried to become Harriet. Now she wanted Harriet to become Starr. No, not that. What she wanted was the vile slaughter at the church never to have happened. She wanted to be home as she was, with Harriet tenderly holding her, and for Starr to be wandering the city someplace where Mara might come upon her.

She clutched Starr's red T-shirt closer to herself. Everything in the room was pale, from her sister's white-gold hair, to the ivory walls and drapes needing a spectroscope to find out they had lavender or pink in them. As Starr was the most urgently alive person Mara had ever met, it was perhaps right that the only color in the room be the Bulls shirt Starr had on when she died.

Harriet stroked the shaved head in her lap. It was sprouting little black curls now, like sea moss. Mara wasn't quite asleep, but Harriet had nothing to do but stroke her head, and let her sister sleep or not as she would. For the first time in the twenty-six years since she'd moved into this room she was on no schedule, awaiting no event.

340 · SARA PARETSKY

When Harriet brought her sister back to Graham Street, Mara was still sobbing out her grief and horror at Starr's murder. Harriet herself was moving in a marble trance, not crying or thinking. Like an automaton she took off her bloodstained dress, put on a robe, ran water in the tub. As Mara needed to hold on to Starr's shirt, Harriet needed to hold on to Mara. While she was undressing her sister, bathing her, running shampoo through the tiny new curls, Harriet wouldn't collapse.

By the time Mara climbed from the tub she was quieter. She looked at the large wet patch down the front of Harriet's ivory dressing gown and said she would dry herself, she was ruining Harriet's robe.

"It doesn't matter," Harriet said, thinking first of the blast from Mephers for being so careless: good silk, didn't you pay three hundred dollars for that, telling me it would last forever? and then how ridiculous it was, to care about a dressing gown after seeing—her body shook at the memory of what she'd seen, and she gathered Mara more tightly to herself.

After she had gone into Pastor Emerson's office to call an ambulance for Luisa, she ran outside to wait. She was rattled, but alert enough to prop the vestry door open with a book so she wouldn't be locked out. While she waited, immobile in anxiety, she could hear the rising roar from the mob inside. Mara, what are you doing? Reckless little sister taking on Rafe, his bullying son and all those engorged men? Why isn't the ambulance here, why don't they come, looking at her watch, only three minutes? Two days was what it felt like, starting back inside the building to call again when the paramedics pulled up.

"Over here," she cried as they trotted toward the main entrance with their stretcher. "You'll never get to her through the front of the church."

They didn't hear her. She had to run across the grass to intercept them, to tell them a jerky confused story of Luisa—a bad accident, maybe broken neck, angry crowd.

The medics were used to panicked people: rich white woman, probably seeing her first crisis—if someone had fallen in church probably all the old ladies were fainting and thought they needed an ambulance.

The medics patted Harriet soothingly and followed her into the building. Through the vestry they could make out the clangor: screams, shouts, maniacal laughter. Their indulgent contempt of Harriet's alarm died; they moved cautiously to the chancel entrance.

They couldn't at first make sense of what they were confronting. A ritual of some kind—backs and arms lunging up and down in a massive parody of a dance. But there was a smell, of blood, of singed hair, and an unholy noise, like the baying of a thousand hounds. This was a mob, worse than any they'd ever seen on the streets. The paramedics backed hastily out of the church and dashed to their ambulance to summon police in riot gear.

They ran past the minister, not seeing him slumped in one of the carved stalls behind the altar. His lips were moving soundlessly in his waxy-green face. Harriet spotted him as she looked about in terror, hoping for a sight of Mara or Hector.

"Pastor Emerson." She flung herself at the minister. "What's happening? My sister—"

He didn't respond. She shook him, and he stared at her uncomprehendingly. Harriet gave a despairing cry and launched herself into the pack. When the police arrived with bullhorns and billy clubs, she was still at the edge of the mob, unable to push through to her sister.

The paramedics had let the vestry door slam behind them when they ran off to call for help; they had to bring the police in through the great doors at the front. The cops felt silly, walking down the aisles of a cathedral-sized church with riot gear on, but when they saw the ferocity of the mob they were glad for their helmets and face screens. They called for order through their bullhorns but no one paid any heed.

The police started wrestling people on the fringes of the melee to the ground, snapping on plastic riot cuffs at random, moving deeper into the fray. Patsy Wanachs and Mrs. Thirkell stared at each other on the floor in their cuffs before looking away in shame.

As police thinned out the crowd and the noise died down, those at the heart of the riot grew quieter. Men and women looked at each other, saw glistening eyes and slobbering mouths, and backed away in disgust.

The paramedics, who'd been hovering in the rear of the nave, made their way unhindered to the top of the chancel steps. Starr lay in front of the communion table, her face a bloody mass. The great black horns of hair were gone, pulled out in clumps, leaving her scalp patchy with blood.

Jared Lowrie stood near the body, holding a black tuft in his left hand. When a cop went to put cuffs on him, Jared was smirking. He jerked his body away in indignation.

"What did I do? Why don't you go after the real ringleader, that Mara Stonds down there?"

The officer, wrestling the cuffs over Jared's wrists, came away with a handful of wet hair. He stared from it to Starr's lacerated scalp and threw up on Jared's arm.

Hector and Mara were cradling Starr. Hector's own face was covered with blood from the blows he'd taken at the start of the riot. His right eye was swollen shut, but he didn't seem to realize it.

Behind him Jacqui, Nanette, and Luisa crawled out from beneath the stone communion table where they'd ridden out the fury of the storm. Near them, not with them but safe also, were Dr. Stonds and Mrs. Ephers, Rafe and Cynthia.

"Jesus, have mercy," Jacqui whispered, kneeling next to Hector.

Harriet pushed through the remnants of the horde to reach her sister. "Oh, Mara, oh, Beebie, my precious baby, I'm so sorry."

She sat next to her sister and embraced her, trying not to flinch from the torn flesh in Mara's lap. Mara wouldn't let go of Starr's head, but she leaned against Harriet and began to weep.

A police sergeant came up with the paramedics. He tried to question the group around Starr, but no one was able to respond. Dr. Stonds muttered something about Mara, girl a troublemaker from the day she was born, while Mrs. Ephers nodded in savage approval; Harriet raised her head to protest, then realized Grandfather was speaking so incoherently the police weren't paying attention to him.

Don Sandstrom suddenly loomed behind the paramedics, his mike in hand. He thrust it in Mara's face, and saw to his delight that the

woman holding her was the lawyer for the hotel, the mediagenic Harriet
Stonds. Usually so calm you felt you needed an icebreaker to talk to her,
today looking like the tail end of a tornado.

"Ms. Stonds. Were you present at this horrendous event as a repre-
sentative of your law firm?"

Harriet looked up involuntarily, her eyes almost black with anguish.
"Were you here? You filmed all this and did nothing to stop it? Did you
think you were a spectator at a game that you couldn't put down your
camera to call for help?"

Her lips were so thick she could barely frame words. She leaned
forward to hold her sister more closely. Don backed away from the chancel. Tight-ass broad, always on her high horse about something. He had
footage of her covered in blood, see how she liked having that all over the
five o'clock news. He gathered his crew together—no point in staying for
the rest of the cleanup. They'd get statements from the cops back at the
station.

The paramedics gently removed Starr from Mara's and Hector's
arms. The crimson Bulls shirt, now wet with blood, came away in Mara's
hands.

"What will you do with her?" Mara whispered to the medics.

"We'll take her to Midwest Hospital," one of them said. "And,
buddy"—to Hector—"you'd better come along, get someone to patch
up your face. Your cheekbone's broken, by the looks of it."

"Does that mean she's not dead?" Jacqui asked. "If you're taking her
to the hospital and all?"

The medics paused in embarrassment.

"No." Hector winced as he became aware of the pain in his face.
"She's quite dead. They have to get a death certificate from the hospital
before they take her to the morgue."

"Is one of you next of kin?" the medics asked him.

Harriet braced herself for Mara's claim that Starr was her mother,
but it was Luisa who spoke. "I'm her sister."

One of the medics turned to Luisa for details, and the diva, as fluent
as though she were reciting from a score, provided them with a last name

and an address for Starr. No autopsy, Jacqui said, we don't want them cutting on her. Nonetheless, she has to go to the morgue, the medics explained: the law. You can claim the body for burial next week. The police can give you a case number for her.

As the medics started to load Hector onto a stretcher Dr. Stonds stood, dusting his knees. "I'm Abraham Stonds, head of neurosurgery at Midwest. There's an old woman here with a bad heart who ought to be looked at before this young man. He's perfectly able to walk. She needs the stretcher." Dr. Stonds's voice was once more firm, authoritative.

The medics turned to Mrs. Ephers: heart attacks were something they were used to, adept at treating. They'd take her out, hook her up to an EKG, oxygen, phone for another stretcher unit for Hector. Dr. Stonds was annoyed at their coddling of Dr. Tammuz, ought to know better than to try to hog medical care when an old woman was in need, did he understand the oath he'd sworn?

Harriet turned her head aside. How like Grandfather. He'd seen acquaintances of sixty years slavering like jackals at a kill, but he was blotting that out, trying to pretend that if anything serious had happened it was Hector or Mara's fault.

She drew Mara tighter to her, walked with her behind Starr's stretcher. Jacqui and Nanette were in attendance, as well as a weeping LaBelle, who'd hidden under the side stalls near the altar and emerged only when her friends started to leave. Luisa climbed into the back of the ambulance and waited for Starr.

Harriet held Mara's hand while her sister knelt to kiss Starr's bloody lips, held on to Mara while she herself bent to embrace Hector, pressing a piece of paper with her home number scribbled on it into his hand. "Call me when they finish with you, I'll drive over to get you."

"And Hilda?" Grandfather demanded from the rear of Mephers's ambulance. "You are going to let the woman who was more to you than a mother take off for the hospital without so much as a glance, while you lavish attention on the very people who caused her so much distress?"

Mephers more to her than a mother? Perhaps. At least, within her lights. Harriet gave her sister to Jacqui for a moment and went to climb into the ambulance, where Mephers lay attached to monitors, her heart as steady as a clock pendulum.

Mephers kept her eyes shut, turned her head to avoid Harriet's lips. "You're making your bed, Harriet Stonds. Be sure it's the one you want to lie on."

Harriet climbed back out of the ambulance and took Mara with her to the mausoleum on Graham Street. By and by little sister slept.

51

And the Wall Came Tumbling Down

"No ONE KNOWS exactly what happened at the Orleans Street Church this morning," Don Sandstrom said. "There's no doubt that the grape juice the church uses for communion had turned into wine, but whether this was the prank of an alcoholic singer and a disturbed teenager who were hiding out in the church, or the demonic intervention of the homeless woman Starr, as some church members believe, we will probably never know."

Becca Minsky, with her dog Dusty and a nest of stuffed animals around her, was watching the six o'clock news in her bedroom. Ever since the police beat up Judith Ohana at the wall last night, Becca had been frantic to get into Chicago. What did she propose to do in the city, Harry demanded: get herself beaten up as well?

Becca couldn't say what she wanted—to be a hero, to rescue Luisa, to be part of the excitement of the city. Karen and Harry decided they'd better not leave their daughter alone for a minute. In the middle of the night, when Becca tiptoed out of her room an hour after her parents went to bed, she stumbled into one of the security guards from her father's scrap metal yard. She'd known the man her whole life, but neither her cajoling nor her tears brought her anything but a visit from her father, and the news that she was not to leave the house.

If her father couldn't trust her, Becca snapped, if he had to spy on her, hire guards to look after her, then Becca wasn't going to come out of her room until school started.

If you think I'm bringing you your meals on a tray, young lady, think again, Karen said, appearing behind Harry in the hall, so Becca turned up her nose and announced grandly she was on a hunger strike. After skipping breakfast and lunch, she was wondering if fasting was really necessary, but she forgot her hunger when she turned on the news. Footage of Luisa flung against the side of the communion table, a close-up to show the thickness of the stone; Becca was tumbling out of bed to scream for Karen, Luisa's been killed, when her aunt sat up and smiled, embraced Starr. Becca stopped in her doorway, her fingers in her mouth. While she watched, all hell broke loose on the screen.

"After the bodies were pulled apart, there was one death, that of the aphasiac woman Starr, and numerous injuries, the most serious to Hector Tammuz, the idealistic young doctor who's been dedicating himself to these homeless women." The screen briefly showed Hector swathed in bandages in his hospital bed.

"An important question remains: what happened moments before the mob converged on Starr? Was Luisa Montcrief's neck broken, as Dr. Tammuz believes? Or had she merely collapsed, as neurosurgery chief Dr. Abraham Stonds claims? We were unable to talk to Dr. Tammuz: he is recovering from surgery to rebuild his broken left cheek, but Dr. Stonds assures Channel 13 that Luisa Montcrief was faking her injuries, as part of the same scam that led her to pretend to interpret the dead woman Starr's various grunts."

Sandstrom had gone to the hospital to get Hector and Stonds on tape, and been disappointed that the young man was too groggy from anesthesia to speak. He'd been lucky in one respect: Monsignor Mulvaney was in Dr. Stonds's office. The archdiocese had sent the priest over to find out if the creature Starr had really raised a woman from the dead. It would place the church in an intolerable quandary if they had to assign miraculous powers to an aphasiac nymphomaniac; Mulvaney was counting on Stonds's assurance that Luisa had either been acting, or collapsed in a drunken stupor.

Stonds and Mulvaney actually went with Dr. Hanaper to Hector's bedside to order him not to make irresponsible statements to the media. Stonds in particular was furious at the idea of that damned young resident making it look as though he, Abraham Stonds, couldn't tell if a woman was alive or dead.

Sandstrom, paddling happily in their wake, secured footage of Hector's swaddled face, and a promise from Monsignor Mulvaney to participate in a panel discussion, "The Woman Starr: Saint or Psychopath?"

When Sandstrom's unctuous pronouncements were replaced by a trio of children singing in a wheat field, Becca ran down to the kitchen. Karen was frying chicken in the hopes of tempting her daughter out of bed.

"It was awful, Mom. They didn't say whether Aunt Luisa got hurt in the riot. Why were they doing it? Because they thought Mara put wine in their grape juice?"

She looked and sounded young and scared. Not the tragedy queen of the last few weeks, but the child she still partly was.

Karen pulled her close. "I don't know, sweetie. I don't know what makes people act like that. It's very scary, isn't it?"

Becca clung to her mother. "Was Aunt Luisa—they didn't show her, didn't say . . ."

"She's in the hospital. Someone called from there—she listed you as her next of kin. The doctors want to check her head and neck, to make sure she doesn't have any fractures from her fall in that church." Karen hesitated. "After dinner we'll go down and visit her. But that doesn't mean she's coming home with us, right?"

Becca hesitated, then nodded agreement into her mother's breast. She had tried to look after Luisa and look what happened. The lawyer from First Freedoms, that nice Ms. Ohana, got beaten up by the cops. Then the mob in that church, Luisa hurled to the ground, Starr killed— at the moment the adult world seemed too frightening to take on. In the future, oh, in the future she would be strong, a valiant fighter, living up to the promise of her combat boots. But for now she was content to subside into childhood again, and let Karen soothe her with murmured phrases and fried chicken.

Upstairs Don Sandstrom spoke to Becca's empty bedroom. "In a related story, the wall outside the garage of the Hotel Pleiades on Lower Wacker Drive collapsed this afternoon. Structural engineers believe that the weight of the steel scaffolding, which the hotel put up to try to keep the wall from crumbling, actually hastened its destruction.

"This wall has been the focus of much of the activity surrounding the dead woman Starr. Miracle seekers from as far away as the Philippines flocked here looking for cures. It was here that police rounded people up last night in a sometimes violent confrontation. Despite the excessive zeal displayed in moving visitors away, police action undoubtedly saved many lives, as large chunks of concrete fell in the area where miracle seekers had congregated. Pleiades Hotel president Gian Palmetto, who was inspecting the garage at the time, was struck on the head by a pipe from the scaffolding; he is in Midwest Hospital with serious injuries."

The screen showed footage of the entrance to the garage. The facing had broken away from the wall; tile and masonry lay in jagged hills along the sidewalk and spilled into the street. Work lights, set up so that crews could begin clearing the rubble, cast grotesque shadows: the spikes from the scaffolding poked out like writhing limbs, so that anxious viewers thought hundreds of bodies were buried in the debris. Calls came into the station all night long from distressed relatives in Perth and Peoria, Perth Amboy and Pretoria, wanting to make sure their own mothers or friends hadn't been injured in the wall's collapse.

Don Sandstrom had never been happier: every overseas call meant so many more viewers he could point to in his résumé. His agent assured him that NBC was days away from an offer in their New York bureau. He briefly dipped his head to thank whatever providence had brought Starr to Chicago: she'd made his career.

52

Bravest of All the Trojans

Troy had fallen, in flames and anguish, while the body of Hector, breaker of horses, bravest of the Trojans, lay on a funeral pyre ready to be consumed by the fire that was eating the city.

His mother had given him a child's version of the *Iliad* for his eighth birthday; he read for himself how the bravest of all the Trojans was killed, his body dragged around the city. We named you for him, Hector, his mother said, so that he grew up expecting to meet a bloody end. The dream recurred at any failure, whether small—a loss at a cross-country meet, failure to get into Johns Hopkins—or great, as when Madeleine Carter killed herself.

His mother loomed over his bier, an enormous figure, so huge that he and the dying city might be toy figures and she alone human-sized. Before she could mock him, Starr appeared next to her. Starr's hair was restored to its magnificent horns and curls. She picked Lily up and held her in the palm of her bronze hand until the mocking mother was small, smaller than Hector on his bier, and unable to laugh at him, or even see him. Starr leaned over him, her black eyes gleaming with compassion. "You are the bravest of all the Trojans, Hector; I am well pleased in you. The scar along your cheekbone will be your permanent reminder of your courage."

The bonds that tied him to the bier dissolved and he sat up. He stretched his arms out toward Starr, but she vanished.

He woke sobbing, his face throbbing. He tried to wipe his eyes but found a cocoon of bandages encasing his left cheek and eye. Oh, yes, he was in his familiar place, the hospital, but in an unfamiliar posture, patient instead of doctor. He'd undergone surgery to repair his shattered cheekbone and now was lying in bed, the resident's dream come true, bed for several days, rest for some weeks after, at a point in his life when he didn't care if he lived or died or ever slept again.

His pain was so intense that he found it difficult to concentrate his ideas. Bandages and anesthesia made it hard to see the pages of his journal: his writing looped around like a drunkard—like Luisa—stumbling in circles on the beach. He was attached to a morphine pump but he refused to use it, cherishing the pain as a last connection to Starr.

A passing nurse scolded him: he mustn't cry, not following surgery on the face, or his scars would seize. Against his wishes she pushed on the morphine pump and sent him down the well of sleep once more.

The morphine made him doze and wake without any sense of time. He would blink up at a nurse or a surgical resident and then drift off again. At one point he woke to Dr. Hanaper's fingers on his wrist. He thought Dr. Stonds stood behind Hanaper, barking out orders about Luisa Montcrief. She's not my patient, Hector said, his lips swollen from surgery not shaping the words clearly. Another time he thought he saw a priest, which frightened him: I'm dying, and they think I'm a Catholic. No last rites, he whispered, I'm a Jew, and then he tumbled back into sleep, hoping he would find Starr there once more.

He was on a high-speed train that was moving away from Starr. If he could only get off, get on a train going back, back to Saturday morning, to Starr, everything would be all right. He kept trying to stop it, the way they did in movies, pulling on a magic cord, but the train whizzed past stations. Dr. Boten, dressed as a conductor, told him it was not possible. The trains on this track went in one direction only.

Sunday morning the pain had subsided. He knew where he was again: in a room at Midwest Hospital, with Starr many stations behind him on the journey.

53

Hospital Sideshow

H ARRIET LEARNED about the garage wall's collapse when Leigh Wilton phoned on Sunday afternoon. The senior partner interrupted Grandfather in the middle of a tirade against Mara.

Grandfather hadn't realized his younger granddaughter was in the apartment until he was getting ready to leave for the hospital Sunday morning. When he returned from seeing Mephers the day before, the sisters were asleep in Harriet's bed. He looked at Harriet's shut door, thought about checking to see if she'd come home, but was too angry with her: let her make the first gesture.

When he went into the kitchen for breakfast the next morning, Dr. Stonds was stunned to find Mara perched at the counter with a cup of coffee. Shock and disgust chased through his mind. How dare she come back here, how dare Harriet let her! Typical of Mara, absolutely typical, after mocking him in church yesterday to flaunt herself at him in his own kitchen. And uglier than ever. Forgetting all the times he'd criticized her weight, he looked in distaste at her gaunt frame, the flesh leached away during her six weeks on the streets.

At her tentative "Good morning, Grandfather," his cheeks turned an alarming shade of magenta.

Don't "Grandfather" me, he bellowed. He wanted nothing more to do with her: yesterday's performance in church topped anything she'd come up with to date. Not even Beatrix or Selena displayed such wantonness. To create a vile public display with that drunken slut Luisa just so that everyone in Chicago could make fun of him, say that Dr. Stonds had lost his grip, and then to saunter back to Graham Street as bold as a streetwalker—he was on his way to the hospital to collect Mrs. Ephers; Mara had better be gone by the time they got back or she'd suffer the consequences.

He stormed out without waiting for her response. But the hospital, his private preserve and refuge, provided no solace. From excited gossip at the nurses' station he learned that television crews were in the hospital to shoot Luisa Montcrief. He didn't even know the miserable drunk had been admitted. In fury he called the neurology department and learned that the woman had received—at hospital expense—a CAT scan, an NMR scan, and a bed. Thanks to that officious young resident of Hanaper's. Who was also in a hospital bed, whining about an injury to his cheek. In Stonds's day residents accepted a few aches and pains as part of their training, didn't bellyache about a black eye.

And not enough that Tammuz was saddling the hospital with a good fifteen thousand dollars in unfunded care for the wretched woman—the resident was preening in front of the television cameras when Stonds went down to the ward to order Luisa's release. The neurosurgeon couldn't see into Luisa's room because of the crowd of reporters and cameras that spilled from her bedside into the hall, but he could hear Hector's stammering remarks.

Actually, the barrage of cameras had taken Hector by surprise. When he woke on Sunday, he wished he could be with Jacqui or Mara, who would share his grief and therefore magnify it. He had never liked Luisa: her elaborate postures, her pretense to herself that she was not a drunk but a great singer in temporary exile, had grated on him from their first meeting in Hanaper's office. Only his obsession with Starr enabled him to tolerate the diva's cackling jokes and theatrical woundedness during the weeks she and Starr wandered the streets together. But Luisa was in the hospital; she might be able to speak with him of Starr and grief.

The diva was sitting up in bed. Bathed and in a clean robe—emerald silk, chosen by her niece—she looked more organized than Hector had ever seen her. Of course, she hadn't had a drink for two days—this might be the first time he'd seen her sober.

"Luisa? It's Hector Tammuz."

She was concentrating on her breathing, one hand on her diaphragm, the other in front of her mouth, and she refused to acknowledge him until she felt air flowing out to her satisfaction. Pain flooded through Hector's face as he ground his teeth—was the diva putting on a show for him or for herself? He walked to the window so she would realize she didn't have an audience.

Behind him she panted like a child imitating a steam engine, then said, her voice richer than he'd heard it before, "How kind of you to stop in, dear boy. But your face! What on earth happened to you?"

"I got beaten on by some of the thugs in church yesterday when I was trying to—to help Starr." He pulled a chair up next to Luisa's bed. "How are you feeling?"

She gave a throaty trill of laughter. "Never better, thank you. So well that I'm eager to get back to work. But I know I have to move slowly to keep from damaging my instrument."

"You know that Starr is dead, don't you? Doesn't that bother you?"

She stared at him in astonishment. "Of course I know she's dead. Are you going to preach at me for not weeping all my nights and days? She gave me back my voice. If I don't go back to work—that will be a real tragedy. I've already spoken with Dr. Glosov in Philadelphia. He's a rehabilitation specialist who works exclusively with the voice, and he'll meet with me first thing Tuesday."

It was at that point that the camera crews swarmed in—not just Don Sandstrom, but the four networks, Julia Nordstrom from Channel 8, print reporters, all crammed into the tiny hospital room and overflowing into the hall.

Madame Montcrief, what did you feel when your head hit the altar? Madame Montcrief, what was your relationship with the dead woman Starr? What did she do to you up on that altar? Did she bring you back to life, raise you from the dead?

Luisa never shrank from publicity, but she fumbled these questions.

She couldn't say what Starr had done, because her memory of it was so confused. She'd been in some cold and lonely place. She had an image, like a dream fragment, of an old woman pushing her head into a vat of clay. Starr had appeared and somehow hauled her out of the cauldron, maybe there'd even been a fight with the old woman, Luisa didn't know, all she remembered was Starr's strong fingers digging mud out of her throat. When her lungs opened and she could breathe, she felt a joy that nothing could equal, not the applause that had never sated her, nor the roles, the honors, certainly not the liquor.

For the first time in twenty years she didn't want a drink. The liberation from that thirst was so exhilarating that nothing could overset it, not even the loss of Starr. But she couldn't tell that to the reporters: it was one thing to acknowledge privately that she had been killing herself with alcohol, quite another to confirm on tape the ugly slanders of the opera world. Cesarini and Donatelli would split their costumes laughing at her.

"This young man can tell you," she finally said, pointing at Hector. "He's a doctor, and he was with me in the church."

The buzzards swarmed over Hector. What had happened to his face? In the effort to save Starr's life? He was the psychiatrist who'd attended the women at the wall, wasn't he? What had happened in the church yesterday morning?

"I only examined Luisa—Ms.—Madame—Montcrief—very briefly. I—I thought her neck was broken, and I couldn't detect a pulse, but she clearly is healthy today. Maybe—" He broke off. Maybe what? If she had died, then Starr had raised her from the dead, a thought so unnerving he shied from it.

Behind one of the cameramen blocking the doorway Hector heard Dr. Stonds bray: "The woman obviously wasn't dead, because she's here in the hospital, taking up a bed that someone who's really sick could use. She's a drunk. She probably passed out and then came to, and the gullible want to believe they witnessed a miracle."

No one paid the least attention to the world's greatest neurosurgeon when he tried to shove his way into the room. "Will you get out of my way, you oaf," he demanded of the Channel 5 cameraman who was blocking the door. "This is a hospital, not some rock star's dressing room."

"Wait a minute, buddy, we're just about finished." The cameraman wanted a tight shot of Luisa's face in bed.

The reporters turned away from Hector and back to the diva: And Starr, who was Starr, anyway, was it true that Madame Montcrief had been able to understand her? What language did Starr speak? What nationality was she? She looked Arabic or Jewish, maybe, with that copper skin and those huge black eyes.

She never spoke of her past, Luisa said. Oh, spoke, she didn't use a verbal language that a linguist could dissect, she just made it clear what she thought, what she wanted, and she always understood exactly what was on the minds of people around her. It's not important how she communicated, is it? Just that she did.

Luisa was impatient with the quest for detail, and then angry when Julia Nordstrom from Channel 8 suggested she was making it all up.

Others burst in wanting to know if Starr had really performed miracles: didn't she feed a crowd of homeless people on the beach? Heal the sick? Was she a saint, a demon, a psychopath? What did Hector think?

"That she was more alive than anyone I ever met," he said. "I will never recover from her death."

"I'm Dr. Stonds," the surgeon announced, beside himself with rage at being ignored in his own hospital. "I insist that you let me into this room at once, or—"

"Dr. Stonds?" Julia Nordstrom whipped around, microphone in hand. "Dr. Stonds, you were present at the Orleans Street Church yesterday. Dr. Tammuz, who was also there, says that he was convinced Luisa Montcrief was dead after she hit the altar. Was that your impression also?"

"Dr. Tammuz is the most undertrained, irresponsible physician we have ever taken on at Midwest. He has no judgment, no judgment whatsoever, and no business discussing a patient's condition with the media. And now, if you don't leave, I'm going to call hospital security and have you forcibly removed. Dr. Tammuz, you may consider yesterday your last day of employment at this hospital."

Stonds stormed off to his office to dictate a letter to Hanaper, ordering Hector's dismissal. When he finished that he dictated a letter to his attorney to disinherit Mara. Neither letter stilled the rage that burned within him. Indeed, it only burned more fiercely. He went to the surgery wards and upbraided nurses and residents for mistakes real or perceived before storming off to the cardiology floor to check on Mrs. Ephers.

Her cardiologist told Stonds that Hilda was fine, no irregularities in rhythm or expulsion rate; she was a remarkably strong specimen. She could go home today.

In the cab home, Stonds warned his housekeeper that he had found Mara in the apartment that morning.

"I ordered her to leave, but she's grown so brazen she may still be there. Just so you know, my dear Hilda: I don't want you subjected to the kind of shock I felt when I encountered her this morning, stuffing her face at my expense with not so much as a by-your-leave."

Sure enough, when they got to Graham Street, Mara was in the living room. She was using his phone to make funeral arrangements for that wretched nymphomaniac. Dr. Stonds snatched the receiver from her hand and slammed it into the cradle. Instead of weeping or yelling back at him, Mara looked at him with what seemed to be pity. Pity! It was the last straw.

His fury with Luisa, Hector, and the media boiled over first onto Mara, then Harriet, who came running to the living room at his bellowing rage. "How dare you try to hide Mara from me, how dare you succor this monstrous changeling, this serpent!" He announced he was calling the police to come pick up Mara: she was going to the psychiatric ward where she belonged.

Harriet followed him to his study. "I am Mara's lawyer, and I will fight you through every court in this state to keep Mara out of the hospital. Serpent? She was a poor little orphan baby whom you hated on sight and hounded relentlessly for nineteen years. It is my job now to see that you never do so again."

His face swelled. She was frightened for a moment, not of what he might do, but that he might have a stroke, the rush of blood to his head was so extreme. He spoke with studied quiet.

"I'm very disappointed in you, Harriet. At the moment I most need to be able to count you, you're showing yourself to be childish and unreliable."

"Please, *Grand-père*—" Harriet held out her hands, beseeching.

Mrs. Ephers appeared in the doorway. "Didn't either of you hear the phone? It rang almost twenty times. It's your boss, Harriet, and he's got something more important to discuss than Mara and her infantile behavior."

Force of habit sent Harriet to the phone, although she was not interested in anything Leigh Wilton might have to say. Like Grandfather, his voice puffed outrage at her as he told her about the collapse of the Pleiades wall, and the injury to Gian Palmetto.

"The Olympus people are meeting here right now, Harriet, on Sunday. We need you, badly: no one else in the firm is up to speed on their problems. Things are very serious. The Ohana woman from First Freedoms is going to make things difficult for us: she's apparently claiming that since we were the Pleiades legal counsel we were a party to the decision to use violence Friday night. The head of the Olympus group is implying that our advice caused their problems, from the suicide of that crackpot in July to Palmetto's injury last night. We need to stroke him, big time, and fast. I gave up a sailing weekend with my family. You have to put your personal feelings aside and think of the good of the firm."

"Does that mean you want me to display my cleavage for him? Anyway, I'm not interested in the good of the firm: I'm resigning. You'll get a formal letter from me tomorrow."

Mustn't feel that way . . . Bright future . . . Partnership vote in three weeks; Harriet a shoo-in . . . not like her to be childish and petty over an imagined slight from an important client . . .

It was all gibberish. She hung up on Leigh Wilton, but she couldn't hang up on Grandfather. He was pacing up and down in front of her, not shouting, but biting off words as if they were cigar ends to spit out.

"What," he demanded. "You're turning your back on a golden job because of your wretched sister and her miserable companions? Are you bearing a grudge for my not telling you the truth about your mother's death? I can't believe you can be so petty, Harriet."

No. She wasn't bearing a grudge. The news had seemed shattering when she heard it—was it only two days ago?—but not important now. It didn't matter how Beatrix died. All that mattered was that she separate herself from this house of coldness and find a place to start living. Tomorrow she would find an apartment, with Mara if her sister wanted.

"This house of coldness?" Grandfather was outraged. "This house where I rescued you from filth and chaos and gave you every opportunity?"

"Yes, yes, every opportunity. You did much for me. You gave me a shell that can move me from one end of life to the other. Now I need to put some life into it."

"No mother ever loved a child as much as Hilda loves you, or I for that matter. She's been through a great deal this past month, thanks to Mara. I don't want her to have to face the shock of your ungrateful—your really ugly—attitude."

Harriet nodded. "You loved that child Harriet as much as you could. Both of you. But you only loved the facade, and the child Harriet polished and polished that exterior to make it shine for you. I'm truly sorry, *Grand-père,* but I can't do that anymore. Maybe after I've been away for a while, in my own home, you'll see—we'll see—"

"I'm ready to make allowances for the shock you sustained yesterday," Grandfather interrupted. "I'm even ready to give Mara one more chance to behave like a civilized, sane person instead of the histrionic hyena she's chosen to emulate. What you need is a vacation, a chance to recover. I'll call Air France. You can go to Paris tomorrow—that always does you good."

"You don't understand," she said sadly. "I have recovered. Or at least I've started on the road to getting well."

When she left his study she found Mephers hovering in the hall, wearing a smile that was shocking for its gloating edge.

"So you're turning on him, too?" the housekeeper said. "That makes four of you I've seen. Selena, a whore dressed up like a lady. Beatrix, at least she didn't make any effort to dress herself up. Mara—too ugly to dress up. I thought with you he had someone he could count on, but you're all alike, you Vatick women."

"Mephers!" Harriet, trembling from her confrontation with Grandfather, felt herself dissolving into tears at the housekeeper's venom. She put an arm around the old woman but Mephers slapped it away.

"I've been trying to protect him from Vatick women since old Mrs. Stonds brought me here in 1942. Oh, that Selena, butter wouldn't melt in her mouth, you can be sure of that. She was like a cat, creeping around the apartment on her patty-paws, smiling, then slinking off into the night. *He* was away fighting for his country for two years, and what was she doing? Not volunteer work for the Red Cross, I can guarantee you that. And then she up and leaves us with a baby, while she gallivants off to the Middle East. The day I learned she'd died I was a happy woman. Until it turned out Beatrix was just a blowsy frowsy replica of her mother—only without the outer charm, if you think that counts for anything.

"When the doctor wanted to take you in I begged him to think hard about it, about how difficult Selena and Beatrix had made our lives, but he always sacrificed himself. He never put himself first, it's always been his patients, his family, never his own needs.

"I thought you for one would never disappoint him. But now I find you're as bad as the rest of them. I never said a word as long as you made us proud of you. But that was just a hollow shell, you say? Well, miss, you need to know you have no claim on him. None at all. I kept it to myself for eleven years, so he wouldn't be hurt, so he wouldn't lose his faith in you, but now—you deserve to know. You've earned the right to know, threatening to take him to court, standing up for Mara—I might have known, mongrel to mongrel. I thought you had class, but he's right, blood shows in the end."

Harriet stared at her, slack-jawed. The housekeeper thrust an envelope into her hand.

"Read that. It's what your drunk spying sister found snooping around my room. And if you think it's a lie, I suggest you check with that precious Professor Lontano. *She* knew from the outset and never said a word to stop him from taking you in."

54

The Face in the Mirror

Chère Mademoiselle,

Maintenant que je suis une femme âgée et seule, il est trop tard pour continuer à nourrir de vieilles rancunes. J'ai rencontré votre mère, Mme Selena Vatick Stonds, en Irak, il y a de nombreuses années mais je ne la connaissais pas bien. Elle était venue sur un chantier près de Nippur où son père et mon mari travaillaient au sein d'une équipe d'archéologues envoyée par l'Institut d'études orientales de l'Université de Chicago. . . .

Harriet, her brain numb, read the difficult French script many times before it meant anything to her.

My dear Miss Stonds,

Now that I am an old and lonely woman, the time for continuing to hold a grudge is long past. I knew your mother, Madame Selena Vatick Stonds, in Iraq many years ago, but did not know her well. She came to the site near Nippur where her father and my husband were part of a team of archeologists sent by the Oriental Institute at the University of Chicago. I must confess I disliked Madame Stonds intensely, but that was perhaps a by-product of our circumstances. We had only one interest in common: my husband, whom Mme. Stonds knew during the Second World War.

The war found him at the Oriental Institute in Chicago, where he was a student of Professor Vatick's. It was inevitable that he should meet your mother, and even more inevitable, knowing my husband's character as alas I do, that he and your mother—who possessed an extraordinary charm—should establish a liaison. The war ended, we returned to Nippur, my husband found other interests—there was a young Italian girl, an Assyriologist also—not the beauty your mother was, but of great spirit.

I ask myself now why I stayed with him. At the time it seemed a matter of pride as much as one of duty. . . . I longed for children, and it was not possible, so when Madame Stonds arrived, claiming that the baby daughter she had given birth to eight months before was Emil's child—I was furious, and wounded in a manner that beggars description. But Emil was not going to leave me, or the fortune of my family which helped fund his passion for archeology. And the prospect of being a father would be the last thing to change his mind. At any rate, you must surely know your mother died, pursuing Emil into the mountains on the ill-fated expedition that also claimed Professor and Mme. Vatick's lives.

Emil survived that avalanche, and many other large catastrophes. He died a decade ago—ignominiously—struck by a taxi on a Lyons street, and I have lived alone in my family's great house in the Auvergne ever since. Now the angers and jealousies I felt all those years have been replaced by a desire for some token of his life, no, perhaps not of his life, but of a hostage to the future. I am wondering if there is any truth to Selena Vatick's story. I have no way of knowing how to find it out, but I enclose a photograph of Emil, taken when he was about forty. If you see a resemblance to yourself, well, perhaps you would be good enough to write me back.

Zoe Farrenc

"Well?" Mephers was watching Harriet read, fury and triumph mixed in her face. "What do you have to say now, Miss Holier-than-thou?"

"You've known this for eleven years? And never said anything? How did you even get this letter?" Harriet was shaking so hard that it was difficult for her to speak.

"She sent it to Beatrix, but Beatrix was already long dead. I don't read French: no one ever spent a fortune on my education, only to have me stab them in the back! I took it to the French department at Northwestern University, and even then I refused to believe it. Of Beatrix and Mara, but not of you. But the photograph, it was too clear. Only you were bringing him so much pride—first in your class at the Latin school, earning honors at Smith—I wasn't going to take that away from him by letting him know you weren't his to be proud of. But now—you've chosen to ally yourself with weakness. You chose Mara. I never wanted her in this apartment. I argued with the doctor then: find someone to adopt her. But he insisted. Look what pleasure Harriet brings us, he said. Well, never a day's joy did we get from this Mara. He named her rightly, Mara, for the Lord has dealt very bitterly with me."

Harriet hadn't noticed the photograph, so intent had she been on the letter. When Mephers pulled it from the envelope and thrust it under her nose, she was startled, as Mara had been before her, by the likeness to her own face.

"So Mara didn't imagine this. You—you subjected her to life on the streets, accused her of lying, got her in trouble for the thousandth time—"

Before Harriet could say anything—before she knew what she wanted to say, Mephers slapped her across the cheek and swept from the room.

Harriet sat on the bed, rubbing her face, unable to think. At last she turned again to the letter. It must be a lie. But if it was a lie, what motive would Mme. Farrenc have to send it after all those years? Perhaps she had grown senile in old age? But, then, why else would Selena have abandoned her baby daughter, if not to go in search of its real father?

Harriet uselessly churned these questions. Finally she turned back to the photograph. It showed a man looking directly at the camera, blond, with fine features and sensuous lips beneath a cropped moustache. It might be she herself, Harriet, dressed up in a moustache for a costume party.

She scrabbled frantically in a drawer for a handful of photos of her own father and studied them next to her face. It was no help. She still looked like Emil Farrenc.

55

The Lady Vanishes

"THE DRAMA THAT HAS BEEN UNFOLDING in this city since early July took a new and bizarre turn today, when Cook County Medical Examiner Dr. Clarence Ciliga confessed that his office lost the body of the woman known as Starr."

The television showed a solemn-faced Don Sandstrom outside the county morgue. Internally he was jubilant: Channel 13 had reaped an incredible ratings coup from his footage in the church, but the story—and national network interest in him—had started to fade. The missing body brought it back to life. He hoped to be in New York by Labor Day.

"Starr was brought here Saturday afternoon from Midwest Hospital, where a pathologist issued a death certificate. It is standard procedure to bring the body of anyone who has died violently to this building."

The producer inserted some footage of the mayhem at the Orleans Street Church to remind viewers that Starr had died violently.

"The medical examiner provides the police with forensic data which are essential for use in legal proceedings, from arrest through trial for murder or assault. Although those close to Starr asked that there be no autopsy, Dr. Ciliga did make a detailed examination of her wounds. Despite what some of Starr's supporters may have hoped, there is no doubt that the woman was dead."

Hector gripped Harriet's hand. They were watching the news to-gether in his hospital room, with Mara. Hector realized he was one of the supporters who secretly hoped—wished, against the evidence of his own hands, clasping her bloody head in church—that Starr had survived the attack and left the morgue on her own.

Harriet was too numbed from the shocks of the last several days to feel much response to the report. Anyway, she already knew that Starr was missing: she learned that early in the afternoon at the funeral parlor, where she was waiting with Mara and Jacqui to receive the body.

Mara, insisting on a chapel that had never handled a funeral for an Orleans Street parishioner, got Jacqui to recommend a place on the South Side. When the sisters arrived, Jacqui and Nanette were already in the chapel with LaBelle, Caroline and a handful of other women from Hagar's House.

Luisa wasn't there—she had left for Philadelphia the night before, eager to begin her rehabilitation program. She sent a massive wreath (paid for by Harry, although he didn't know that yet). Mara picked out the message: *"Cessarono gli spasimi del dolore; in me rinasce, m'agita insolito vigor."* It was Violetta's last line in *La Traviata:* "My pain has ended; I am reborn, stirred by an unusual vigor," Harriet translated for the other women.

How like Luisa, Jacqui said, to think only of herself at such a moment—couldn't she have waited one more day before trundling off to see that voice doctor? And couldn't she have left a message of mourning for Starr, instead of a celebration of her own recovery?

Word of the funeral location whipped around the news community, so that even before the chief mourners arrived, television crews were outside the funeral parlor, along with a phalanx of print photographers. An hour after the body was supposed to arrive, everyone was getting restive. That was when Harriet called the medical examiner's office and heard the news.

"What do you mean, you've lost the body? Aren't there sheriff's deputies at the morgue? No one could just come in and help themselves, I presume?"

Dr. Ciliga said *lost* was too strong a word: the toe tag had probably fallen off, or been switched somehow. They were inspecting all the cadavers. Ms. Stonds needed to realize there were several hundred in the morgue at any one time; they had released eleven today and were contacting all the funeral homes involved to make sure everyone had the right body. It was very unfortunate, he understood how difficult this was for the family, but if she would only be patient . . .

By the time the six o'clock news came on it was clear that Starr had disappeared. As Don Sandstrom explained, it wouldn't be impossible for someone to get access to a body unlawfully: they'd only have to fill out the right information on a standard request form from an authorized funeral home (the camera zoomed onto such a form). Who would have wanted to take Starr's body was, of course, a mystery, but viewers could count on Channel 13 to pursue the story zealously.

"What do you think?" Hector asked through his mask of bandages, when the commercial came on and they switched off the sound. "Could Mrs. Ephers have taken Starr away in her rage against you and Mara?"

Harriet made a gesture of helplessness. "I'm beyond thinking, about her or anyone. My whole body aches, as though I'd been tied up and beaten with sticks. Up in intensive care this morning she was wild, screaming that I was no grandchild of his, that I wasn't to go near him—I always thought she loved me but couldn't express it—now I—I don't know what to think, about her or him or anything."

Grandfather—and Harriet could think of him by no other name—had suffered a stroke in the night. Harriet learned about it only when she arrived at the hospital to visit Hector. She ran up to the intensive care unit.

Mephers, patrolling the hall, launched herself on Harriet, raking the younger woman's cheek with her fingernails. You killed him, Mephers screeched, turning on him like that, taking Mara's side against him. After all he did for you, you turned into the worst viper in the nest!

Harriet backed away from her, into the arms of a nurse, who cleaned her face and told her it was not uncommon for family members to crack under the strain of an illness like her grandfather's, that Harriet must not take Mephers's outbreak personally.

Harriet managed to calm herself enough to sit by Grandfather for an hour, holding his hand and talking softly to him, but the actions seemed to be performed by an empty body. Her own mind, her own feelings no longer existed.

It seemed as if when she left the apartment to find Mara Friday night, Harriet had stepped into a canoe at the head of a rapid, where she'd been tossed willy-nilly ever since. The shock of learning that Grandfather was (probably) not related to her was extreme. She had received so many shocks in the last few days, though—the news of her mother's forced hospitalization and ultimate suicide, the dawning realization of Grandfather's coldness, no, not just coldness but cruelty, to Mara, to Beatrix, really to Harriet herself, everything culminating in the horrible events in church on Saturday—that she could barely bring herself to think about Grandfather, or Grannie Selena, or Emil Farrenc. .

These blows didn't matter as much to Mara. It wasn't just that Harriet was the adored, Mara the abhorred, child, but Mara's life had been so changed by her time with Starr and Luisa on the streets that nothing else seemed important to her. Yes, Mara remembered the picture she found in Mephers's desk, the face that looked like Harriet's, but Harriet should stop worrying about all that old history. What happened now was what mattered, what they made of their lives now.

Sunday afternoon Harriet sat in her ivory-colored bed, knees to her chin, thinking, he gave me a home, education, love—and then she tried to remind herself of occasions of his love, and found herself remembering only his self-congratulatory praise when she pleased him: we were right to take you in, he would often repeat.

Her past with Grandfather was like a spiral nebula, with chunks of rock flying from it as it wound further and further into itself, until she saw that the end of their relationship had been there from the beginning, from that first day she tiptoed around the apartment in her new patent Mary Janes, afraid to touch or speak lest the doctor and his formidable shadow Mrs. Ephers send her back to Beatrix. Grandfather angry, with Mara, or a hospital committee, she saw it many times over the years, until she forgot how hard she worked as a small child to keep him from ever being angry with her.

When his rage spilled over onto her on Sunday she flinched from it, and almost started to placate him. All afternoon, as she and Mara packed and talked, she could feel his fury pulsing through the apartment, pounding into her like a bruising fist. Was this what you felt all these years, she asked Mara. How did you ever survive?

Sunday night, before she and Mara went out to a restaurant for dinner, she told Grandfather she'd be gone by Tuesday, that she and Mara would move into their own apartment and leave him in peace. His face crumpled briefly, like a child whose mother is leaving it. But on Monday evening, when he returned from his normal rounds at the hospital, he had shellacked his shell of anger over the hurt. He announced to Harriet that he wanted Mara kept out of Hilda's sight: Hilda was old, she'd had a dangerous heart episode, she didn't need any more shocks from this monstrous thing he'd nurtured.

When Harriet tried to defend Mara, Mrs. Ephers bounced from her chair and began pouring out her own vitriol, directed equally against Harriet and Mara. Harriet was appalled, as much by the housekeeper's contorted face as her words, and tried to still her furies, but Mephers had moved beyond reason into a fantastic zone where Harriet became the cause of all the doctor's misfortunes. If not for Harriet the doctor would never have taken in Mara. Even more, if not for Harriet, the doctor would have married her, Hilda Ephers, who had given her whole life to his care.

"You think Mara is a changeling," she screamed at the doctor. "They both are."

Stonds, confused by the outburst, thinking Hilda beside herself with fatigue, bustled her down the hall to her bedroom, where he hoped to induce her to take a pill, calm herself: Remember your heart, he counseled. In the privacy of that room, where Mrs. Ephers thought to consummate her love, she pulled out the damning letter from Zoe Farrenc, the photograph of Emil, thrust them and her own iron bosom on the doctor.

Harriet heard Mephers's thin voice rise to a squeal of rage and felt ill with disgust. She was exhausted by the day's passions—by the week's passions—and left Graham Street while the doctor was still closeted with his housekeeper. Mara had found a furnished apartment they could rent by the month. When Harriet got there, in a reversal of roles Mara rubbed her sister's hands, made her tea and coaxed her into bed.

In the morning, after Mephers's assault on her at the hospital, Harriet spoke to the senior neurologist about her grandfather. The neurologist knew Harriet from those dinners at Graham Street and spoke to her gravely but frankly: They were doing their best for Dr. Stonds, but even if he regained consciousness he would be very ill. People did make amazing recoveries: Dr. Stonds himself had presided over many, but the neurologist did not want Harriet to feel an unwarranted optimism.

Harriet sat with Grandfather until it was time to go to the funeral home to receive Starr. By that point, the news that Starr's body was gone seemed like a minor disturbance, a small swell at sea after a ferocious storm.

56

Funeral Games

D R . S T O N D S D I E D two weeks before Thanksgiving. During the months of his illness, Harriet went to the hospital every morning to see him. She sat next to the stertorous figure, talking softly, dredging up what memories she had of joyous times with him and recounting them.

In the afternoons she returned to the house she had bought with Mara at the northeast tip of city. While the weather held, the sisters swam and walked and tried to construct the past for each other: What was their mother like? Why did she take to drugs and drink? How much did it matter that Mara would never know who her father was? And what difference did it make if Emil Farrenc was their blood grandfather?

They talked about it with Hector, and with Professor Lontano. The professor was a frequent visitor during that period. Lontano came in part because she'd been one of Abraham Stonds's few real friends, but she also welcomed the chance to talk to Harriet and Mara about their grandmother Selena, and about Emil Farrenc.

At first when Lontano came around, Mara treated the professor with her old rudeness. She was incredulous of the professor's claims that she never noticed Harriet's resemblance to Emil Farrenc in all the years she'd visited them at Graham Street.

It was Hector who made Mara see things differently. People have an amazing capacity for denial, he said, and for putting things into boxes. Surely Mara had noticed that with Dr. Stonds and Mrs. Ephers—even in her own life? For the professor, if she was ashamed of herself for falling in love with a man who didn't care for her, she might easily have blocked the memory of his face: And, after all, by the time Grandfather Stonds adopted Harriet, Lontano's affair with Farrenc had been over for more than a quarter century. It was surely the last thing the professor would have expected, to see her old lover's features in the face of the doctor's granddaughter.

Mara grudgingly accepted Hector's interpretation but didn't greet the professor with any warmth until the day Lontano said that Grandfather's ideas about blood were outdated rubbish. The sisters had been arguing about whether to try to dig up information about Emil Farrenc's family. Harriet had discovered that Zoe Farrenc had died two years earlier, leaving no heirs. Now Harriet wanted to find out what she could about Emil, perhaps because she looked so much like him, while Mara argued against the idea: Emil Farrenc didn't sound like much of a prize, based on the letter from Zoe to their mother—why get involved with one more beastly grandfather?

Over dinner that night, Harriet taxed Lontano. "Surely you must know something of his family. All I need is the name of the town where he was born—with that I could find out the rest."

The professor raised thin brows. "And why do you want to know, my dear Harriet?"

Harriet flushed at the ironic tone. "His blood is in our veins, after all, and if I ever have a child—"

"This obsession with blood." Lontano threw up her hands. "I never could talk Abraham out of it, but don't you girls start on it. It's at the root of every horrific act of the twentieth century. I sometimes think you Americans are as bad as the Nazis ever were, worrying about mixed races, or degenerate races, and the effect of Asian or African peoples on your Nordic blood. It's a social construction, nothing else. For you, Abraham was your grandfather. I see no reason to stop calling him that, or to dig into that long-dead past."

After that Mara started looking forward to meals with Lontano. The professor, rummaging through old papers at the Oriental Institute, even found a diary that Grannie Selena's mother had kept. It had been shipped to Chicago with all of August Vatick's papers after his death, but no one had ever looked at it—what light could the scribblings of a mere wife shed on ancient Sumer, after all?

In those brown and curling pages, Mara and Harriet read about their grandmother's decision to pursue Emil Farrenc first in Iraq, and then on the ill-fated expedition in the Taurus Mountains. The diary recorded Selena's death in a blizzard, when she wandered astray trying to find Farrenc's tent in the storm. After the blizzard ended, Farrenc, as the strongest survivor in their party, hiked out to summon help. It took him two weeks to reach the nearest village. By the time the rescue party returned, the Vaticks and the rest of their team had died.

Harriet and Mara read the faint scrawl of Helen Vatick's final entry:

I see this journal is full of petty whining about August and Selena. If I could start over—try to find joy. Life is so short, don't waste it on re-proaches. I wish I could get that message to Abraham Stonds, and to my little granddaughter, whom I'll never see.

That last sentence pleased Mara: Someone had wished her mother joy, even if it was only a grandmother whose good wishes she never heard. At the same time, Mara threw up her hands in amazement over Selena: How could you be so foolish, and so passionate, that you'd go out in a blizzard after a man who wasn't interested in you?

Lontano looked quizzically at Mara: You fled this same house with that same kind of foolish passion. It was Mara's turn to flush and grow silent.

One night, Professor Lontano asked the question she'd wondered about since the day she saw Starr at the wall: Had Mara found Starr on the streets and dressed her hair to look like the horns of the gods on old Sumerian cylinder seals? The question popped out at a dinner where Jacqui and Nanette were explaining why they'd sat in on a television debate on Starr: Was she a saint or a demon, a homeless psycho or a supernatural creature ("That Don Sandstrom, he offered us a hundred dollars each," Jacqui told Hector apologetically. "That's a lot of money for a couple of homeless women").

"I remembered your researches at the museum last spring, Mara, and the question has been troubling me," Lontano said.

Mara was puffing out her cheeks in belligerence, but Hector and Harriet asked what a cylinder seal was.

The professor pulled a small blue tube from her handbag. "I shouldn't have this with me: It belongs to the museum. It's a lapis lazuli seal from ancient Sumer, almost five thousand years old. The figure with the horns is the goddess Inanna, the most important female deity to the Sumerians."

The young people bent over her hand. Lontano held a magnifying glass over the stone so they could make out the carvings.

"So you think Mara really brought the goddess Gula to life with her chants," Hector teased the professor.

Lontano didn't know what she thought. She couldn't help wondering about Mara, and her penchant for fabricating drama. Had the girl examined the old seals and then persuaded a homeless woman to dress her hair like Inanna's? Lontano could imagine Mara, in her unhappy loneliness, rocking the city to its foundations by creating a cult around Madeleine Carter's visions of the Virgin Mary's blood.

"She wasn't like that, Starr, I mean," Mara stammered. "You couldn't make her do anything—she pretty much did whatever she felt like. She liked me to comb her hair, though. Every night she'd unbraid it, and in the morning I would comb it and wind it up again. So I know it was real hair, not like these on the seal, these are cow's horns."

Lontano didn't know whether to believe Mara or not: She had heard the girl tell so many stories over the years. But Hector had been there, and he didn't seem to think Starr was some creation of Mara's.

"You don't really think she was a goddess, do you, Professor?" Harriet asked. "I know people got hysterical about her for a while—had she performed miracles, did she raise Luisa Montcrief from the dead in church that day. But you know there's a rational explanation for everything that happened. Even *Grand-père* thought at first that Luisa was dead, but he said someone as drunk as—well, as she used to be—she seems to be recovering now—but anyway, someone that drunk could have passed out so thoroughly that she didn't seem to be alive."

"Oh, why does it matter?" Mara said. "Why do you have to label her? It's enough that she was here. She healed me, she healed Hector and dozens of other people. She saved my life, and Luisa's too. Does it matter whether she did something supernatural or not? You looked into her eyes, and you saw yourself, just as you were. For some people that reflection was too horrible to endure, like Rafe Lowrie—he couldn't bear to see himself as he really was. But if you could stand your own reflection, you discovered you could like yourself."

Inevitably, the fervid interest in Starr—both her life and her death—grew less intense. Hector stopped trying to find her missing body. In the first months after her death, people were constantly reporting that they'd seen her: in a garage, a football field, a shopping mall. Hector would drop everything and run to the site, only to suffer a horrible letdown. Finally he would merely shrug on hearing of a sighting: Mara was right, the image they carried of Starr in their minds was the only sighting they would be given. Perhaps it was the only one they needed.

Harriet for her part stopped trying to force the state's attorney to make an arrest in Starr's murder. No one could—or would—testify to who had actually struck the blows that killed Starr, his office kept telling her. The television footage wasn't helpful; it showed the mob in action but not the faces of those around Starr. And to make mass arrests in a congregation so filled with wealthy Chicagoans as the Orleans Street church—the state's attorney blanched at the thought of such deliberate political suicide. Harriet finally put the matter to rest.

With the coming of autumn, Jacqui and Nanette stopped visiting Mara in Rogers Park and retreated to their old haunts on the streets. Professor Lontano returned to Padua, as she did every winter. Talk shows stopped mentioning Starr, and Don Sandstrom found himself stuck in Chicago still.

Grandfather Stonds's death seemed to Mara to bring an end to the first stage of her own life. She wanted to move on, but she didn't know to what. Her new closeness to Harriet was losing its first intensity as well. She would always cherish Harriet, but the two didn't need to cling to each other now as they had for the past three months.

The growing intimacy between Harriet and Hector also made Mara—oh, face it: jealous. Okay, Hector was Harriet's new suitor, just as Mara had foretold the day she first saw Hector in the clinic. It wasn't that Mara wanted Hector to be her own lover—rather, she was jealous of him for taking Harriet's attention just when she and her sister were coming together for the first time.

Midwest Hospital hadn't fired Hector despite Dr. Stonds's last dictated order to that effect. The residency committee, reviewing Hector's record with Dr. Hanaper, said perhaps young Tammuz had gone overboard in his support of the homeless women downtown, but that situation had resolved itself, and they really couldn't afford to run the psychiatry department short a resident so late in the year.

Even though he still had his job, Hector didn't think he could bear to spend another eighteen months doling out drugs and little scraps of therapy. It became natural for him to talk over his plans with Harriet: She was his own age, after all, and, like him, was trying to decide whether she still wanted the profession she'd begun training for at twenty.

Harriet started meeting Hector for dinner before he had to go on call. When Sylvia Lenore asked Harriet to be the general counsel for a new foundation that would focus only on the homeless, Harriet talked it over more with Hector than with Mara. Harriet saw a role for Hector in Sylvia's plan, to provide consistent mental health care for those on the streets. Hector began to feel excitement for his discipline again. He talked to Dr. Boten, the man he'd hoped to work under when he first came to Chicago, about getting supervision as a therapist while he finished his residency at Midwest. Hector and Harriet stayed up late at night, not to discuss Starr, but to laugh and talk over the brave new world they planned to create—and, naturally enough, Mara thought, those discussions ended in Harriet's bed.

It was natural, too, then, for Hector to join them at Grandfather's funeral, and Mara tried to be glad that Harriet was comforted by his presence as much as by her own.

The overflow crowd at the service included generations of Dr. Stonds's students and colleagues, along with most of the members of the Orleans Street Church. The congregation thought the man filling in after Pastor Emerson's abrupt retirement did a beautiful job on the eulogy. Still, as Wilma Thirkell whispered to Patsy Wanachs, it was shocking to see Mara Stonds sit there so boldly, as if she hadn't brought on the doctor's stroke by her outrageous behavior in this very building. And that Jewish doctor, Patsy whispered back, what's he doing here—and didn't he grab Harriet's hand when they sat down?

Linda Bystour leaned over the back of their pew to join in. I hear she's living with him.

Of course, Mrs. Thirkell muttered under cover of the voluntary, I never thought Harriet was as good as she made herself out to be: too perfect to be true, that cat-in-the-cream-pitcher smile, those polished manners—all window dressing, I always said.

Mrs. Ephers was beside herself when Harriet and Mara took their seats with Hector in the Stonds family pew. Not noticing, or not minding the avid interest of her neighbors, she called angrily to one of the ushers to escort the sisters elsewhere.

Harriet tried to talk to her. "Please, Mephers, I know you're upset, but can't we sit in harmony for *Grand-père's* sake—"

Mrs. Ephers cut her off. "Don't call me by that name, and don't you dare refer to the doctor as your '*Grand-père!*' You turned against him in life, you and that—that Mara—you brought on his stroke—" She went on and on, her voice rising to a shriek, until the sisters and Hector moved across the aisle.

The doctor's illness had affected Hilda Ephers sadly, Patsy Wanachs noticed. The housekeeper's rigid grooming was a thing of the past; she often appeared at Sunday worship with dribbles of food down her unironed dresses. At meetings of the parish council she kept interrupting discussions with incoherent rants against Harriet, who now loomed as a larger villain in her eyes even than Mara.

On Graham Street, while the doctor lay between life and death in a nursing home, Mrs. Ephers moved herself into his king-size bed. She ate all her meals there, and seldom stirred from the building, except to attend church. Today, as Mrs. Thirkell pointed out, she was wearing one of the doctor's old T-shirts beneath her ill-buttoned dress.

Linda Bystour hissed back, Look at Mara! What right does she have to appear so triumphant?

Similar comments rippled around the nave, in a sigh like wind through spring wheat: Mara was gloating at the doctor's death. That was the only way people like Patsy Wanachs or Linda Bystour could label the change in Abraham Stonds's younger granddaughter. Mara had slouched scowling in the Stonds pew for so many years that to see her sitting upright, looking—well, not pretty—she would never be pretty—but striking, anyway, with those strong cheekbones and green eyes—such a transformation could have come only at the doctor's expense.

As the service wore on, Mara's feelings for Grandfather surprised her. She didn't mourn him, but she realized she felt sorry for him. Hector claimed Grandfather couldn't possibly be an object of pity, both because of the power he'd wielded, and his international renown—far more recognition than most people ever achieved. But to a nineteen-year-old, professional success couldn't make up for the anger that made Grandfather push his own wife and child away from him. Not that Beatrix was his own child, but he hadn't known that when he was raising her. As the interim pastor extolled Abraham Stonds's virtues, Mara shook her head in pity for a life wasted on grudges.

After the interment, she and Harriet hosted a reception at the church. Cynthia Lowrie pushed her way through the crush of people to Mara. It was the first time the two had met since that Saturday in church three months earlier. Mara hadn't felt like talking to Cynthia since. She didn't exactly blame Cynthia for pointing Starr and the others out to the mob to save herself another beating by Rafe. But when she imagined a conversation, Mara pictured Cynthia waving her arms wildly as she thought up one excuse after another, while Mara said, sure, sure, and patted her on the shoulder. Mara felt she'd changed too much to want to join in Cynthia's tearful complaints.

Cynthia had changed as well, at least on the surface: She had cut her lanky hair and was wearing makeup, a fierce application of color like a warrior's battle paint. Mara's eyes widened at her old friend's startling face. The two greeted each other awkwardly.

"So, the old doctor died. You sorry?" Cynthia asked.

A shrug—Mara didn't want to explain her feelings about Grandfather. "New hairdo, huh? What's Rafe say about the makeup?"

"Rafe isn't talking. He lost his voice when—that day, you know. He's been to all kinds of specialists, I guess. No one can figure out what the problem is. I can't say I care much. I'm leaving, anyway."

Life had changed in the Lowrie apartment. With the loss of his voice Rafe seemed shrunken and fearful. He stopped going to the exchange, since he couldn't scream out his orders, and he wandered around home in angry bewilderment. Cynthia forced him to add her signature to his bank accounts so that she could buy herself clothes and a car. She told him she wasn't cooking for him anymore. If he wasn't working, he could hire a housekeeper or get his own meals, she didn't care. She was moving out, anyway, to go to college, which he would also pay for, and he and Jared could do as they damned well pleased.

It didn't seem to please Jared to do much. He spent his nights wandering from one whore to another, hoping to recover from the impotence that had afflicted him ever since that Saturday in church. He didn't bother to open the letters from his college asking whether he planned to return for his senior year, letting them stack up on the floor of his bedroom with his empty bourbon bottles. Like Rafe, he seemed to fear his sister now, moving out of any room she entered, talking to her only when he wanted to beg a fresh bottle of whiskey.

Cynthia didn't feel like telling Mara about the changes at home, or her gloating in her new power, and said only that she was off to the University of Illinois in January. "I hear Harriet's going to dedicate her life to the homeless with that dreary do-gooder Sylvia Lenore. You going to team up with her?"

The jeer in Cynthia's voice made her sound uncomfortably like her brother and father used to. Mara backed away. She marveled at a time when she and Cynthia had spoken every day: She couldn't imagine sharing her most personal feelings with this truculent person. After a few more awkward half-sentences the two young women parted, never to speak in the future except at public events.

Everywhere Mara turned at the reception she was aware of a sense of strain, of people staring at her but not wanting to talk to her. When they looked at Mara they had to remember their own madness the last time they saw her, and no one wanted to think of that. In fact, the parish had voted to close Hagar's House, so they wouldn't have the homeless women around to remind them of the day their passions boiled into murderous frenzy. It was hard to find anyone who would admit even being in the church when Starr was killed, although Sylvia Lenore was only too happy to remind Wilma Thirkell and Patsy Wanachs that she'd seen them led off in handcuffs. Members of the parish preferred to think of "that dreadful Saturday when the homeless women invaded the church and caused so much damage." The sight of Mara Stonds brought the memory of what really happened too close to the surface.

Mara was finding it hard to remember she had promised Harriet not to snarl at anyone. When she saw the interim pastor bear down on Hector with an enthusiastic description of the church's adult inquiry classes, Mara decided she'd had enough.

"Dr. Tammuz would love to hear more about this, but we have to take my sister home. She's worn out from the strain of Grandfather's death and from organizing today's revelries."

The sisters' exit with Hector allowed the condolers to speak without restraint on the arrogance of Abraham Stonds's granddaughters.

57

The Swan

THE SECOND WEEK IN DECEMBER Luisa Montcrief gave a recital at the Northwestern University campus in suburban Chicago. She had wanted to burst forth in full splendor in Berlin or London, but the big opera houses and concert halls of the world weren't ready to take a chance on her recovery. The rehabilitation experts in Philadelphia and Luisa's agent, Leo, both advised her to start with recitals in small venues.

Her glory would return as soon as people heard her, Leo said: Luisa's voice had never sounded so rich as it did now. Leo hadn't wanted to waste his time on the train ride to Philadelphia to hear her sing at the rehabilitation institute, but when she finished he could hardly contain himself. What miracle had transpired, that her years of alcohol poisoning had left her with a voice so rare you might go a lifetime without hearing its equal? She had been a lustrous soprano in the past, but in comparison to her sound today, her voice of ten years ago was thin and amateurish.

She also quelled his doubts about her drinking: she was the same self-absorbed, temperamental diva she'd always been, but in a rare burst of honesty told him she knew she'd almost destroyed herself with drink. She even apologized for anything unpleasant she might have said to him while drunk.

Leo returned to New York and bullied Northwestern into adding her to their winter concert schedule. He called not only the New York critics but those in Hamburg and London and told them they would regret it forever if they were late in climbing onto Luisa Montcrief's comeback wagon.

On a day when the wind was whipping waves over the boulders onto Lake Shore Drive, Luisa arrived at the Ritz. In addition to Leo, her entourage included her old accompanist, a new dresser, and her personal trainer. The diva kept her throat tightly wrapped against the cold. She refused to leave her suite until it was time to climb into her limousine the next afternoon. She did, however, ask Leo to dispatch tickets to her niece, to Mara, and to Jacqui and Nanette.

Luisa and Leo had chosen the program carefully: the centerpiece was to be Mozart's "L'amerò, sarò costante." Around it they added a series of shorter lieder and arias that all had as their theme the idea of song itself. The concert ended with Grieg's brief "Ein Schwan," in which a dying swan bursts into such extraordinary song that the singer wonders if she was hearing a phantom, not a living bird. Leo thought the Grieg too somber for the concert's conclusion, but Luisa insisted on it.

Sitting in the front of the recital hall with Jacqui and Nanette, Mara was amazed by the change in the diva. In their months on the streets, Luisa had been so emaciated that she walked with difficulty. Since leaving Chicago she had gained weight. Skin and hair both shone with health; when she entered the stage in her flame-colored gown, she walked with impressive assurance.

By the end of the concert, Mara had forgotten all she knew of last summer's querulous drunk. The audience was on its feet roaring acknowledgment, but Mara sat weeping, unable to move. The beauty of that voice, taking her to heaven, what could she ever do with her life that could compare with Mozart's music, or Luisa's singing of it?

Luisa had invited Mara to join her at a small post-concert party in the recital hall. Mara stayed briefly to congratulate Luisa, but the diva, sipping herbal tea, was so besieged by critics that she had time for only the most perfunctory greeting. Becca Minsky, her eyes glowing, could hover near her aunt, soaking up the plaudits, but Mara didn't want to be on the fringe of Luisa's triumph, as she was on the fringe now of Hector and Harriet's life together.

The next morning Mara walked south along the lakefront to the little spit of land where she had sometimes camped with Starr. The wind biting her face during the four-mile trek matched the bleakness of her mood.

As she wandered through the prairie grass, she came on the remains of her old sleeping bag. She had abandoned it that August night she fled from Grandfather's security patrol and had forgotten about it. The blue fabric was faded and torn and most of the lining had spilled out; no one would get any warmth from it again. She tossed the remnant into the wind and watched it cartwheel down the shore.

The tall grasses, brown in the winter, rustled in a comforting way. Mara knelt within them, scattering the small birds who nested there, and stared unseeing at the water.

Starr had changed her life by allowing her to stop hating herself. Mara thought at first that meant all decisions would flow easily to her, that she would know what to do next, or even more, that she would be given some wondrous gift like Luisa's that would move her hearers to tears.

She saw now that the journey was not to be so easy. She could not will the world around her into one where the homeless had shelter, or grandfathers spoke only words of loving praise to their wards. She would still have days of despondency. She still sometimes wanted to be cruel to Harriet. Her own healing was not a completed thing, but something she would have to struggle every day to maintain.

Perhaps she needed to return to school, as Grandfather had always insisted. That would be funny, to be doing in the end what he had demanded of her. She still yearned for a great gift, like Luisa's, or a strong vocation, like Hector's or Harriet's, but she would not find that by lingering in the house in Rogers Park with her sister. Tomorrow morning, no, this very afternoon, she would go to the library and choose a college that might help her on her way.

She sat awhile longer among the grasses, letting the winter wind blow through her hair, enjoying the peace that came from reaching a decision. She sat still for so long that the sparrows gathered again, cheeping loudly as they pecked among the plants for food. Their cries grew so shrill that Mara looked around, to see who was approaching.

A swan that had strayed from the lagoons into the open lake swam to shore and moved toward her through the brown grass. When it came on her it stopped, and cocked its head to examine her. Mara stared into the flat black eye and thought she saw herself reflected back, sweet, not bitter, with strong wings of her own poised for flight.

The swan fluffed out its feathers and took to the air, scattering the sparrows. The sands were empty. Mara got to her feet and slowly started home.